HOPE'S END

HOPE'S END

stephen chambers

TOR®

A TOM DOHERTY ASSOCIATES BOOK
NEW YORK

HOPE'S END

Copyright © 2001 by Stephen Chambers

This book is printed on acid-free paper.

Design by Jane Adele Regina

A Tor Book
Published by Tom Doherty Associates, LLC
175 Fifth Avenue
New York, NY 10010

www.tor.com

Tor® is a registered trademark of Tom Doherty Associates, LLC.

Library of Congress Cataloging-in-Publication Data

Chambers, Stephen.
    Hope's end / Stephen Chambers.—1st ed.
        p. cm.
    "A Tom Doherty Associates book."
    ISBN 0-312-87349-2
        1. Young men—Fiction. 2. Life on other planets—Fiction. I. Title.

PS3603.H355 H6 2001
813'.6—dc21

                                                        2001027195

First Edition: August 2001

Printed in the United States of America

0 9 8 7 6 5 4 3 2 1

To Ceceley,
and to my Mom and Dad

Acknowledgments

I want to begin by thanking my agent, Peter Rubie, without whose help none of this would have happened. Years ago when I questioned whether or not to keep writing, he helped keep the words coming. I also want to thank my editor at Tor, Jonathan Schmidt, whose advice made this a much better book than it might have been.

The collected writings of William Blake, that eighteenth-century prophet who just won't go away, were instrumental in the evolution of this book.

For their help, whether conscious or not, I also want to thank my brother Daniel, Ceceley, Ben Reno-Weber, Mike Pellegrino, Victoria Cameron, Jacob Cottingham, Brother James Kelly, Rebecca Reisert, Leslie Kazanjian, Jeanne Cavelos, Harlan Ellison, the Odyssey Class of 1998, my parents and grandparents, my uncle, Widdle, Mamasan, and various Mexican restaurants across the Midwest.

O Rose thou art sick.
The invisible worm
That flies in the night,
In the howling storm:

Has found out thy bed
Of crimson joy:
And his dark secret love
Does thy life destroy.

—William Blake (1757–1827),
    "The Sick Rose"

HOPE'S END

Swords drawn, a company of ten soldiers advanced down a stone tunnel. Two at the front of their formation held torches, one at the rear; the tunnel walls were also lit with a faint blue light that seemed to generate from the smooth rock. Still, they held their torches, the fires casting long shadows in the narrow passage.

"Should have found him already," one man said under his breath, and they all heard, although the commanding officer pretended not to notice. They had been told it would take a half hour's travel through the underground passage to the chambers where they would find their prize. How long had it been now—two hours? Three?

The soldiers' blue and gray coats and pants swished in unison in the silence. The passage continued ahead—still no sign of the Frill or the baby they had been sent to retrieve for Justice Hillor.

"Halt," the lead officer said, and they froze, weapons ready. The torches hissed and sputtered, and the officer squinted in the regular light. Something cluttered the center of the floor ahead: dark mounds, like clothing.

The officer held up one hand and ordered two soldiers to accompany him as he moved closer. They followed, one with a torch, to inspect the piles. Bodies. The officer remained several feet from them, his sword held defensively across his torso, as if the dead men might stand. Without speaking, he tried to count.

All soldiers, their swords scattered uselessly on the floor, unused. Some of the dead still cradled the hilts with limp fingers. An arm lay severed at one wall, palm up, and another shape that might have been a head had rolled into the center of the tunnel farther on. Twenty-three, the officer thought. Twenty-three men, all armed, now lay dismembered. All soldiers. And they had not been dead long.

He frowned at his group of nine. By now they had all seen the bodies, and they remained silent.

"We're here for the kid," the officer said, still looking at his men. But he wasn't speaking to them. "We want the kid, then we'll leave." No response from the bloodied hallway. "Justice Hillor sent us."

A pair of red slits flashed in the blackness ahead, gone as quickly as it had come. One of the soldiers shook his head and began to speak quietly, praying.

"We are not here for violence," the officer shouted, and he backed away from the bodies. "In exchange for the boy, no one else will trespass again."

Nothing. The soldiers looked at their officer for a sign that they should fall into defensive formation. The officer didn't give the command—the twenty-three corpses had died in a perfect defensive formation.

"Please," the officer shouted again, facing the dark tunnel ahead, and now two red slits flashed behind them, unnoticed.

"All right," the officer said to his soldiers. "We go forward. They—"

The blue light vanished, and red slits appeared on both sides of them—gone—shadows blurred in the torchlight.

"Formation! Turn—"

The men fell in a frantic screaming, cut down by the red-eyed shapes, their torches dropping, extinguishing. It was over in one moment, one instant of screaming chaos, and then darkness.

"The frill?"

"Yes, Justice, but they don't know the details. It's better that way. The Lord's miracles must sometimes be enacted through the works of man. What is it they believe? 'Shadow and Sky'? They gave him to his father."

"Casually hand the kid over to his father—after they butcher my men."

"It is a different culture, Justice."

"I don't know that it's a culture at all. We made the deal, not

his father. The boy belongs to us, not that idiot, Sulter, or the Frill. I don't think the artifacts are important anymore. The Frill are too dangerous."

"You're losing your faith, Hillor."

"My faith doesn't involve sacrificing myself—I'm not prepared to die for this, Denon. I trust the Church understands the importance of secular interests. The spiritual only gets you so far."

"The Church understands."

"Good. Then you understand why it's over. It must be ended. Blakes cannot be trusted. Things are—"

"That's irrelevant. People have an almost infinite capacity for taking things for granted. You've known this might happen from the beginning. It's too late to stop, and the line must be kept. Once he's in place, the Frill will die along with the rest of them. A burning man shouldn't carry his books into the fire with him."

"And the quickest way to end a war is to lose it. You're wrong. It has to be ended, or we won't live long enough to burn."

carefully avoiding the irregular candlelight in the surrounding windows of houses, a figure slipped past the police, his heart racing. He turned, then crept down another alley, eventually stopping before a closed door. Red clothing hung loosely on his lean body, and with both hands he cradled a crying package. Stars glimmered overhead as the man knocked twice on the sealed door before him, holding the bundle in the crook of his arm.

"Open the door," he said.

No response. He glanced warily down the alley, as if afraid the shadows were watching. Wooden houses, each ten to twenty feet high, stood on both sides.

"Open it."

Finally, from within, a latch clicked, and light flickered out into the alley. A young couple stood just inside the entrance: a large, stern man with a tense, dark-haired woman at his side.

"Sulter," the large man said, and he looked at the bundle in the other man's hands, "you're not supposed to—"

"Quiet. Petrok, there's no time." Sulter stepped into the room, kicking the door shut behind him. "I can't stay. Take him."

Sulter extended the child, and the baby flexed chubby fingers, motioning to the couple. Petrok hesitated, touching the woman's shoulder. The baby giggled.

"Just like this?" Petrok said.

"It's what we talked about. Now, no second thoughts. Here."

The woman moved forward. "This is too soon, Sulter." But she accepted the child, gently cradling it in her arms. It made a startled noise, and the woman rocked the baby, her eyes on Sulter.

"Just as we discussed. This is the last time I can come here."

"It's really happened?" Petrok asked as Sulter moved back to the door, opening it.

"I'm afraid so. Yes. It has. The most important thing is that he"—Sulter's finger paused in the air, indicating the child—"never comes back. He's not mine anymore."

"What are you going to do?" the woman said.

"I'm not sure." Sulter backed out. "Anyway, it's not your problem. You'll never hear from me again."

Petrok extended a hand. "Be careful."

"You be careful." Sulter forced a smile and shook Petrok's hand. "He's the one that needs protecting."

Sulter stepped into the alley, slipping away from the candlelight, into darkness. The couple hesitated in their open doorway, candles dancing wildly behind them. Sulter's boots sank into the dirt and, after a dozen steps, he turned a final time. The air was cool.

"Go back in!" he hissed. "Do you want someone to see this?"

The door closed.

sulter walked quickly through the main entrance hall of the Palace. Police soldiers stiffened as he passed. The hall was spacious, the ceiling thirty feet above his head. Golden trim laced the wood-paneled walls, adorned with splash paintings and mirrors. Side rooms appeared at regular intervals through broad, open doorways, and at the far end of the hall, a red carpet filled the center of a staircase.

Sulter's feet hit rapidly, echoing in the silence, and as he passed, the mirrors created an unending mirage of identical men.

"Sulter," a voice rang out.

His footsteps slowed, but he did not stop. Behind Sulter, a grave-looking man in a stiff officer's uniform stepped into the hall through a side doorway. Short, slicked-back hair made his thin face bulge against the muscles of his neck. No longer a part of the police, this man had been an officer once, and he still wore their uniform.

The gray and blue coat and pants looked as if they had been cut for a man with smaller shoulders and a weaker torso, and they had been. After being appointed Chief Justice—a position of military and judicial power, second only to the King—Hillor had retired from his old post with the police, trading official command of a single unit of soldiers for unofficial command of the entire military police force of Hope.

Sulter paused. "What is it, Hillor?"

"What are you doing?"

Sulter balled his fists, then relaxed, but he did not turn. A long space of empty hall separated the two men. "Is the King in his chambers?"

"We're in recess," Hillor said. "I saw His Majesty at the table of the Executive Council ten minutes ago."

Sulter turned reluctantly. "Where's my brother, Hillor?"

Hillor's eyes narrowed, as if he were trying to remember. "We can talk about this somewhere else. . . ."

Nearby, the police seemed to ignore the conversation, standing rigidly at their posts. Their arms hung stiffly by the swords at their waists. Sulter glanced at them, at Hillor, and he backed away.

"I'm not in the mood for this," he said. "Where is the King— in his room?"

"Your brother, the King, is waiting for you, I'm sure," Hillor said, and his expression hardened, a cynical smile forming on his pale lips. "Now think about something besides your own interests for once. Men gave their lives for that boy. Think about the bigger picture."

Sulter stared at him. "He doesn't belong to you."

"He belongs to the state." Hillor began to walk forward. "Where is he?"

Sulter's voice rose, "My son, not yours, you arrogant bastard." Sulter waited for a response, but Hillor remained unchanged, as if he hadn't heard the insult. *"Where is the King?"*

Hillor stepped closer, bringing them within three feet of one another, and Sulter's pulse quickened.

"Why do you want to see him?" Hillor asked.

"You can't intimidate me like this, Justice—I'm not my brother."

"That's right," Hillor said, "you aren't your brother—you aren't King. Your brother is smart enough to understand the concept of sacrifice for the greater good."

"My brother is drugged," Sulter said, and he started up the staircase.

"You're making a mistake."

"You made the mistake, Hillor. I won't roll over like the rest of them." Sulter continued—more loudly, so all the soldiers in the hall could hear. "My brother appointed you, and he can take that position away."

Hillor said softly, "You don't want to do this. Now, what did you do with *him?*"

"Go to hell."

Hillor watched as Sulter continued at a rapid jog to the second floor. A pair of police soldiers stood rigidly at the summit, and Sulter hurried down a hallway of red carpet and elegant doors.

"Brother!" Sulter called. "Your Majesty!"

He glanced back—no one behind him. Throwing one of the last doors wide, Sulter stepped into the King's quarters. A lavish bed, dressed in gold and furnished with soft red tassels stared at him. Mirrors blinked back a worn, unshaven face. Sulter staggered into the room and turned from one wall to the next. Not here— the King wasn't here. His throat tightened, and the door shut behind him.

A metal click.

Sulter began to turn, and a cold blade caught one side of his throat, tugging at the skin. He froze, refusing to tear open his own flesh. Large fingers held his shoulder, and Sulter felt the warm breath on his cheek.

Sulter whispered, "Wait . . . don't. I—"

There was a sickening rip as his throat opened, and blood spurted onto the carpet. It ran through the fabric like water, oozing across the wooden places where the carpet did not reach. Before he dropped, the flash of an engraving on the blade's handle passed close to Sulter's face.

B. Mussolini

Sulter fell. Color drained from his cheeks, and he rolled, murmuring something unintelligible. His knuckles pounded against the carpet—once, and then three times, twice, and then his hand laxed, striking a final time. And he was still.

c h a p t e r 1

YEARS LATER.

"And you're not going to see another one like it, I can assure you."

Midday in a crowded street full of merchants, their rickety wooden stalls lining both sides of the road. Broad Street on Solday—the only day in the seven-day week free of work for most of the city of Hope. During the harvest season, the grass farmers still worked, but most of the artisans and factory workers were free to spend the money they had earned the past week. And the merchants were happy to take it from them.

A boy in his early teens sat across from two women at a small table he had set up at one corner. The women were in their mid-twenties, both workers in a clothing factory in Old Town. They kept small bags on their laps, and the boy, Vel, knew that the sacks might be empty. Or they might contain all the money the two women and their husbands had in the world. In an old can behind Vel's legs, there was a concealed mound of similar bags, all full of weighted sacks of dirt.

A group of young children ran past, and one grabbed a piece of green fruit from a nearby stall—a man in the crowd snatched it back, but the kid got away. Perfectly common for the merchants to plant security in the traffic of the dusty street.

Vel was showing the women one of two elaborate black and white paintings that sat on the table between them.

"And you're sure this is an original?" the older of the two women asked. Vel thought of them by their hair color: the older was Red, the younger, Blonde.

Vel nodded. "Yes." He rubbed dust from his eyes, and said with restrained emotion, "My family has had them for generations.

We've never even hung them—they've been perfectly preserved for all that time in these." And Vel indicated the black cloth beneath the paintings. "Selling them now to help pay for a new house."

Blonde looked at Red, smiling. "You don't think Jason would like that one? I think he would."

"I don't know," Red said, and to Vel, "How much are you asking?"

Vel drew in a breath, pretending to admire the lines of black and gray that might have been old paint—or smears of dirt—on canvas.

"You know they're originals by Mitanis," Vel said, and he shielded the most expensive of the two from the dirt clouds of the street with the black cloth. "Probably a century or two old."

"They *are* nice," Red said, and Blonde brightened, looking happily at Vel.

"I think my husband would love one of these," she said. "Our anniversary is in two days. And we want to celebrate." She patted her stomach, and Vel realized that both women were slightly pregnant. Good for them, he thought. They each probably had a household of children already. Vel could imagine the pretentious brats, all helping to increase their parents' wealth. They were free on Solday because they worked in a factory and not in the fields or with Hope's garbage. Good for them.

"Three hundred crowns for the first one, two-fifty for the other." The second painting was slightly smaller than the first. Still, two hundred crowns was easily one week's wages for these women, possibly more.

Blonde started to say something, but Red shook her head. "Three hundred? That sounds high."

"That's less than what my father told me I should sell them for," Vel said. "I promise, I'm only trying to get what they're worth. I had an offer earlier today of two hundred for each, and I said I'd take it if I couldn't get anything higher."

"You've already had an offer?" Blonde asked.

"Yes," Vel said.

"And you want five-fifty for both of them?" Red said.

"Yes."

She shook her head. "That's too much. Come on, let's—"

"I *like* this," Blonde said, indicating the three-hundred-crown dirt smears. "What about two-fifty for this one?"

Red sighed, but Vel saw the way she was eyeing the cheaper one.

"I'll sell you both of them for five hundred," he said.

They didn't answer immediately, and Blonde looked at Red for a sign that she would agree, Blonde's fingers tugging at her bag, as if she was desperate to spend her money.

"All right, four seventy-five," Vel said at last.

"Four-fifty," Red said, and Vel pretended to consider it. He started to shake his head, frowned, and then Blonde said, "Oh, come on, his family needs the money. Here." She handed Vel a pouch of coins. "That's three hundred. We'll give you five hundred."

Red said, "Five hundred is—"

"It's less than what he's *asking*," Blonde said, flashing a smile at Vel, and he returned the gesture. "Come on, we don't want to cheat him."

Red frowned, undid her bag, and counted out twenty ten-crown coins, putting them with the rest of the money in the bag Blonde had given Vel. Vel spotted more inside Red's bag—at least another five hundred crowns, probably more. Vel wrapped the paintings in matching segments of black cloth, waved at the women as they thanked him and started away, dirt-paintings under their arms. Then he turned, and with one hand selected a bag that was very similar to Red's purse, at the same time catching the eye of a boy leaning against a nearby building. The boy was his own age, taller than Vel and thinner, his hair cropped slightly shorter.

Vel nodded, and a moment later, the boy casually approached; as he passed, Vel slipped the matching bag into the other boy's hand and said, "The red one, Ponce."

Ponce nodded, not looking at Vel, and disappeared into the crowd after the women. Vel hid the can of bags under a mound of rotting fruit in an adjacent alley, and found Ponce again, still trailing the women. They wound through the street, past stalls selling weapons and others with candles and food. A man carried a satchel of expensive black market books, but the police soldiers in the crowd did not seem to notice.

Finally, Vel was ahead of the women, and he readied himself at a busy intersection. It was crowded even for Solday, he thought, and wondered how long this new money would last at the summer festival next week. People were buying new weapons and clothes for the approaching holiday, and, Vel thought, my parents are still working. With Vel, their one child, not even officially registered as was required, his parents would pay for their lack of children and money by laboring in the grassfields with the rest of the lower-middle class.

Vel watched the women draw nearer, both still holding their prized paintings, Blonde talking animatedly. Vel spotted Ponce, and they made eye contact—Ponce scratched his hair—and Vel sprinted through the street. Closer to the women, they still hadn't seen him, and Vel clipped Red hard, an elbow in her side, and she fell, losing her bag—Ponce caught it, letting the counterfeit fall in its place—and they ran.

Shouting behind Vel, "Hey, isn't that—"

"—all right?"

Vel and Ponce turned into a smaller street, then another, running too hard to talk, until finally they reached another, less crowded district, closer to the river. When they slowed, Vel put his hands on his knees and laughed. The two boys propped themselves against the outer wall of a long building, noisy inside. It was one of the factories, and through long, open windows, Vel could see rows of tables where dozens of people sat weaving, their shoulders hunched. They talked as they worked, hands moving almost unconsciously over piles of fabric on their tables, making clothes from fur moss, dyed from crushed berries and daylight. The goods would go to the government first, of course; the remainder would be sold to the merchants, then to the general public.

Vel tried to ignore the drone of conversations from inside, the excited voices that meant their work week was nearly ended. Most factories—where the government licensed private owners to hire artisans to mass produce everything needed by the city—were off work on Solday. This, apparently, was one that was not.

Some factories made clothing, others crafted swords and arrow-heads, and minted coinage.

"Vel," Ponce said, panting hard. He began to sort through Red's purse. "How much did you get?"

The factory building was built of strong, faded wood, like the majority of the city of Hope, although there were larger, older structures constructed of black stone—the Palace, the Church Cathedral, and the Garrs.

"Five hundred." Vel grinned. "I don't believe I've ever seen women quite that willing to part with their money. How much is in there? I saw at least another—"

"Seven hundred!" Ponce said, and he accidentally dropped a handful of coins into the dirt. "Can you believe it? What were they going out to buy?"

"Dirt on canvas. Come on."

Ponce recovered the coins, and they passed merchant stands similar to the ones on Broad Street. After putting all of the money in the same small pouch, Vel fastened it in a pocket on the inside of his pants. Ponce drop-kicked Red's purse into the center of the road, attracting some attention, but neither of them cared.

A woman at one of the stalls waved. "New sword? Either of you gentlemen? I have candles too."

They both stopped. The woman ran her fingers across the assortment of blades on the stand in front of her.

Vel looked at his companion. "Ponce?"

"You know I don't use swords."

"I think we'll pass," Vel said to the woman. "Maybe some other time."

She winked at him. "Maybe."

The two boys continued in the dirt street, kicking up more dust, and the street gradually became more crowded with merchants and shoppers. Vel wondered again what it would take for his parents to get jobs in the factories, rather than the grassfields. Factory workers made more money, got more days off from work, and were generally considered of a higher class than the farmers and cleaners.

The government and the Church encouraged children, outlawing all forms of birth control. Those without kids rarely rose above

the rank of farmer or city cleaner. It usually took five or six registered children over their "fragile fours" to advance a family. Most
factory workers had at least that many kids. Because children
could not be registered until they officially counted—having survived the first three dangerous years of disease and child-death—
it was difficult for families with little money to raise many children to that age.

Ahead, a team of men were repairing a broken support beam
on the front of a medicine shop called Pure Blood. A crowd of
children had gathered in the street to watch the operation, as the
men hoisted with ropes, some perched on the roof, slowly raising
the wooden column onto one of the shop's front corners.

Vel glanced at the children as he passed, and when the repairmen lost the ropes—plank slamming to the dirt street in a cloud
of brown dust—the children laughed loudly, backing away from
the repairmen. The workers tried to ignore the noise, one cursing
under his breath as they prepared to try again. The rich stay rich,
Vel thought, because they can afford to have plenty of kids and
mistresses. And the rest are locked in place because they *can't*
pay for more children; they can't keep them alive to the age of
four and have a chance to advance socially. Children sold on the
black market were executed by the government, as were their
sellers, and the couples who paid for them.

Ahead, on the left side of the road, between merchant stalls,
hung a row of three men and two women, black bags over their
heads. The people in the street ignored the gently swaying bodies
that had been hung from the roof beams of a local tavern, feet
dangling ten feet overhead. Their shirts had been cut away, to
expose pale stomachs with the words *Life over Lies* carved crudely
into the skin. Their hands were tied behind their backs.

Vel had never actually seen a public hanging, but these five had
probably not been dead long, as most criminals were left on display for only a day or two before being cut down by the police
and burned. And the "dead-on-display" was perfectly common.
The principle of Church doctrine—*Life over Lies*—was usually
scratched into the flesh of book printers and makers, owners,
writers and dealers in black market children.

The executions were something that happened, a part of life

that Vel had grown up with, only occasionally remembering that his parents technically defied the laws. Vel's parents *did* own books. It wasn't illegal to be able to read Enish—Hope's language—but it *was* against the law to own or manufacture any kind of writing, unless you worked for the Church or ranked high in the government, and then it was illegal to distribute it to the general public.

Writing and book production carried a death sentence, and book possession might bring ten or fifteen years in one of the Garrs; in prison. Criminals connected with black market books were often called Laumians, after a man named Laum who was killed twenty years before Vel was born. Vel knew little about the specifics, but from what he had gathered, Laum had believed in transcribing and distributing the holy scriptures of Blakes to the general public, rather than allowing the Church to maintain complete control over the gospel.

This, of course, went against the Church and government teaching that books in the wrong hands were damning lies, both in this world and the next. Proper upbringing and guidance was needed for the proper interpretation of all texts, which was why books were only legal for some members of the Church and government. And so Laum had been executed, and he was still cited as a heretic who was largely responsible for the book crimes in the present. Vel had never seen anything to indicate that his parents were Laumians, they simply liked reading books.

It was part of the reason Vel believed he had never been registered with the district clerk. Officially, every child on his or her fourth birthday had to be registered with the government. Then the child would be assigned a job—usually to be fulfilled starting at the age of fourteen. Most children were given jobs that their parents could teach them, and the clerks would then periodically check on their development. This continued throughout a person's entire life, meaning that every change in job had to be cleared with the government.

Technically, all "gifted" children were specially recruited for high positions in the Church or government, and they were taken to officer training or the Church, where they were taught. In reality, however, Vel knew that the kids chosen for these positions were usually chosen because they came from the Indenan or Balm or any number of other large, well-known families rather than for being any more "gifted" than anyone else. These families were the aristocrats—the owners of the factories, who usually had seats on the Executive Council and had many ties with the government and Church already.

Kids could also voluntarily apply for recruitment into the police or Church, in which case the parents no longer mattered and the kid became a member of the state, not the family. In these cases, the children were trained to fight, not think, and they became police soldiers or members of the Religious Guard. Though Vel had heard that oftentimes the Religious Guard *were* educated along with those higher in the Church hierarchy. It was an opportunity for the young to advance, leaving their parents behind. If children were orphaned under the age of twenty, they would automatically be drafted into the police force.

Twenty thousand people in Hope, Vel thought, and how many live like I do? I don't exist because my parents like to read. Because if they registered me with the district, they would be visited more often by the local clerk who might discover a dozen illegal books. Vel had yet to see anything that had convinced him it was worth risking fifteen years in prison or death to *read.* Most of his parents' books were boring treatises or made-up fantasies. Anyone can make anything up, Vel had thought; it isn't worth facing prison or making less money for *that.* And so what if it's illegal?

Ponce was thirteen, not yet old enough for a position in the fields with his parents—the spot he had been given and would most likely work for the rest of his life. Naturally, if Vel and Ponce were caught sometime in their routine, that spot would be traded for prison or something worse. But no, Vel thought, that won't happen, we won't get caught.

"You know what I think?" Vel said.

They had been moving in silence for some time, and Ponce smiled. "Yes."

"I think Darden's going to have to start helping us with these jobs." He rubbed his elbow. "He drinks just as much as we do."

"Just as much as the two of us combined, you mean."

They turned a corner, the houses growing bigger, more elaborate. Several restaurants and a bar lined the road. A beggar was shouting from the gutter, waving a small black stick in the air with a piece of white cloth attached to the end of it. The small cloth had what Vel thought of as a "spiraling cross" in the center of it, a tilted black cross that looked like an open, square wheel moving to the right. It was the Church insignia—called a swa— the symbol that meant *Life over Lies*, the general rule behind every law. Vel gathered from his rantings that the beggar had lost his children to the Church—they had joined without his permission, leaving him with nothing.

Most people in the street dressed similarly—coats and shirts, pants, occasional dresses—in a range of colors from black to red, all made in the factories and later sold by the merchants.

A priest in white pressed his way through the crowded avenue, armed men also in white flanking him, swords at their sides. They wore black armbands with swas on their left arms just below the shoulder, as a sign of their honor. They were the Religious Guard, the Church's private military, and the crowd let them pass. It was illegal for anyone to hire a private group of more than two body-guards—except for the Church. Vel knew little about the Church, mainly because he simply didn't care.

The priest-soldiers learned prayer and swordsmanship. Whereas the police numbered in the thousands, the Religious Guard only contained a few hundred of God's soldiers. The Church proved the government laws through scripture, and the police enforced general obedience. The Religious Guard did very little, as far as Vel knew. They lived with the higher priests at the Cathedral, theoretically guarding their sacred interests—whatever that meant. *Darden knows about them,* Vel thought, *because Darden attends services.* Vel's friend Darden was somewhat religious. Vel's parents had always been too busy to take Vel to Church regularly, and he had never been curious enough to go on his own.

At the far end of the street, the dirt turned to a ditch of brown grass. The ditch dropped into a shimmering, flowing river, flanked by rows of some of the most expensive properties in Hope. The houses were surrounded by wooden fences, and Vel spotted a table of laughing, well-dressed men through several beams. They were drinking wine in their front yard. The aristocracy. With too many kids to name, they ran the factories for the government, controlled the merchants—and they took orders only from the Executive Council and the King.

Ahead, at the river, people descended to the banks with buckets, and a woman called out at her children to wait with their small pails, overflowing with water. She shook one of the kids and tilted his bucket, dumping some of the excess water into the river again. At this, the boy's face contorted, and he started crying.

A group of children had gathered near a trio of heads mounted on wooden poles. More criminals. Vel heard the kids laughing and poking the rotting faces with sticks, insects buzzing around them. A police soldier approached, shouting at them to stop, and the children scattered.

Vel and Ponce continued on their way. As they drew closer to the river, Vel's feet passed across a rectangle of smooth metal, imbedded in the dirt. Worn letters stared at them. Sections of the metal had long since crusted over, rusting into obscurity.

Hope—Founde
When I have
The rich pro

Vel's footsteps wavered, and Ponce squinted at him, following his companion's gaze to the ground. Vel had seen the plaque several times, but he had never directly walked over it before. It felt too smooth—slippery—under his boots.

"You ever wonder about this?" Vel said.

"I don't usually walk this way."

"Everybody's seen the plaque. You ever wonder about it?"

Ponce shook his head. "What's there to wonder about? It's illegal to mess with it, and the thing's too old to read. It's like the ruins."

Life, not lies, Vel thought. *I shouldn't even be able to understand it.* Vel couldn't remember how he had actually learned to read, but he *could* read, without a memory of having been taught. More than once, Vel had wondered if his parents had taught him—but then *why wouldn't I remember the lessons?* he thought.

"Wish we could get out there," Ponce said.

Vel followed Ponce's stare to the horizon—and there, above the wooden buildings of the immediate city, skeletal points of darkness rose in the distance. Miles of distance made their outlines vague, and Vel crossed his arms across his chest.

"Yes, so do I. So what?"

Ponce shrugged. It was illegal to break the city boundaries, illegal to go beyond the stone wall that encircled Hope and the plots of farmland. That wall was always manned, Vel knew, one soldier every twenty or thirty feet. The wall was about five feet high and without a pass issued by the Executive Council, the guards wouldn't let anyone go over.

Of course, there were reasons for common passes: when the government commissioned wood collections for buildings, fur collections for clothing, or the collection of metal deposits for weapons, they gave temporary passes for the teams who ventured out to the leafless southern forests. Wood from the trees, fur from the thick tree moss, and metal buried just beneath the forest floor that could be melted into weapons.

But often, only part of a team returned. The survivors supposedly told stories that reminded Vel of the made-up legends of the Nara and the demons of the wild. Vel paid them little attention, and Darden had once said that they were a handy way to keep people from trying to break the city boundaries. Still, despite the precaution of the barrier wall, people left. It didn't happen often, and Vel wasn't sure that it had ever happened in his lifetime— but people *had* fought past the soldiers, into the fields of high grass. And the ruins.

"I need to get home," Vel said.

"Nah," Ponce said. "We need to meet Darden, remember?"

Vel shook his head. "What are you talking about?" He smiled mockingly. "Darden can create his own illegal cash flow. He needs to start helping us with these jobs."

Somehow, Darden had avoided working in the fields, despite the fact that he was a full year older than Vel *and* registered. Darden's parents were farmers, just like Vel's and Ponce's—but Darden had shrugged off a life of tending grassfruit. Exactly how he had done it, Vel wasn't sure. And when Vel's parents brought up employment, Vel thought of Darden, and his delinquency; Darden was an inspiration.

They continued toward the river, nearing one of the bridges. There were four in all, widely spanning the river from east to west, from one side of the city to the other. It was still early afternoon, but already it was beginning to grow colder.

"Come on, Vel. You do want to spend some of that money, right?" Ponce's face brightened with the words.

Vel looked at him, and his lips creased.

"You're just using me so that you can liquor Darden into giving one of his 'life's-a-mistake' speeches, aren't you?"

Ponce kicked dirt onto Vel, and then broke into a run toward the opposite end of the bridge. "Last one's buying!"

"Wait a second," Vel said, but he was already hurrying to catch up, crashing into the crowd around him. A mother cursed, quickly pulling her children out of their path, and Ponce gave a cry, jumping onto the narrow railing of the bridge.

"I'll beat you from up here!" he shouted.

"You're not carrying the money," Vel said, and he closed on Ponce's early lead. They were nearing the bridge's end, and Vel slowed, hopping onto the opposite railing. A large cart of grain and produce sat at the far end of the bridge, blocking the road.

"Don't fall!" Ponce said.

Vel slipped on the wooden beam, but he caught himself, glancing briefly at the river twenty feet below.

"You go ahead," Vel said. "You don't have to wait for me if you want to drown."

"No, I meant the money. I was talking to the money," Ponce called, and he reached the opposite end.

Vel arrived a moment later, and Ponce laughed, pointing at an angry-looking elderly couple on the bridge behind them.

"You made a scene," Ponce said.

"No," Vel said. "When I make a scene, you'll know it. Let's hurry up, I'm feeling much too sober for this time of the day."

They passed a cemetery on the right, full of neatly arranged wooden grave markers, surrounded by a large wooden fence. Through the gaps in the fence beams, Vel saw black stones among the regular wooden graves. The stones marked the graves of former government representatives or high-ranking officers. Some of the oldest objects in the city of Hope were these unreadable stone monuments, long since smoothed by the elements.

Bright flowers rested over the newly dead—those few who had not been cremated. Still, the anonymous "city fathers" often garnered the most attention from the general public, and the ancient graves were littered with debris, more so than the recently deceased. Why do they care? Vel thought, as he passed. Why not pay tribute to tombs that might still contain a body resembling a human being? Tradition, he thought. It is a tradition to neglect the living for the dead.

The cemetery was large, spanning a dozen blocks in every direction, and beyond, Vel saw the outline of the stone Palace. The Palace rose three stories, occupying an entire block of its own, encircled by a regular, protective wall.

Vel hesitated, spotting something through the cemetery fence. "Ponce . . ."

"What?" And then he saw it too. A hole in the dirt—it looked as if the workers had been digging a new grave, with a mound of fresh sod beside it. Except that the hole was too small and too deep for a coffin, even a child-size one. And it glowed a dim blue.

Something about it was very familiar, as if Vel had seen this hole a moment before he actually had—as if he had been intended to turn at just the correct instant to spot the light. Vel gripped the cemetery fence and strained, pulling himself to the top, palms sliding on the strong wooden beams.

"Vel, there are cops stationed all around here; you can't—"

"Look at this," Vel said, and he dropped to the opposite side, approaching the fresh hole. Ponce held onto the fence but didn't climb over.

"Vel, stop it!"

The blue light had stopped, and now Vel stood over the small, deep hole. What is this? he thought. It looked as if it had begun as a grave and then fallen through, deeper than graves were intended. Vel saw only darkness at the bottom, impossible to tell how deep—it dropped at least twenty feet, probably much farther.

"You saw the light?" Vel shouted, without turning.

"Get back here or throw me the money!"

Vel glanced back, and saw Ponce, looking very uncomfortable in the street. A group of men passed behind him. They might have been police soldiers, but probably not; if they were soldiers, Vel would have already been arrested. The Palace was several blocks away, and the main police school was at the end of the street, meaning there were numerous garrisons of soldiers stationed nearby.

"You saw it?" Vel said.

"Yes, now stop it."

Vel looked at the hole a final time, and then he returned, climbing back over after three tries. Ponce punched Vel's shoulder, frustrated at being left alone in the street.

"Have you lost your sense of self-preservation? Why the hell did you do that?"

It was a tunnel, Vel thought. Something very deep underground—but what had the light been?

"What was that light?" Vel said. They started walking again.

The streets were emptier here, lined with barrooms and restaurants. As they moved farther from the river, more soldiers could be seen, some moving in rigid formations, others lounging outside the brothels with darkly dressed women.

"I don't know that there was a light."

"But, you saw it—you said you did."

"I don't know what that was, Vel."

Vel shook his head. "No, Ponce, either you saw it or you didn't."

"All right, I saw it. Let's forget about it—it was a goddamn graveyard, all right?"

"You're right," Vel said. "It must have been a demon or a ghost—there's no other explanation."

Ponce sighed, his cheeks reddening slightly. "Knock it off, you know what I mean. Not safe to be in there."

One building at the corner was boarded shut, a red X painted onto its door. The Pox, Vel thought, and he deliberately kept his distance as they passed. What had that light been?

An attractive girl with short brown hair watched them pass from her cross-legged position in front of a brothel. She smiled at

Vel. "Got a friend who's sick, you want to help me out?"

"Is your friend as nice-looking as you are?" Vel asked, and Ponce made a let's-get-going groan.

"Serious," the girl said. "She's sick—in here." The girl pointed to the boarded building.

"Does she believe in ghosts?" Vel asked, glancing at Ponce.

"What?"

"Nothing. Is it the Pox?" Vel said.

She nodded and stood, making no attempt to brush the dirt from her pants. "Help me, please?"

"What's your friend's name?" Vel said.

"Come on," Ponce said, and to the girl, "We don't get conned, it works the other way around."

"Not a lie," the girl said, and she pressed open the X'd door, glancing back to see if Vel was following. "Please."

Vel knew enough about the Pox to know that if what the girl was saying was true, her friend had probably spread the disease to *her* as well. It happened by association, Darden had explained to him two days ago. One sinner is struck by the Pox as a punishment and like a fire it leaps to the other contaminated souls; all of it, everything about the Pox, was explained by the Church. If only Vel would go once in a while. Darden had drunkenly explained that Church services were a nice insurance against whatever kind of depraved life one chose to lead.

Vel's kind included. Vel had yet to see money as depraved, so long as it continued to pay for alcohol.

"Her name's Jak," the girl said, and through the opened door, Vel saw the outline of someone—very pale, skin and hair faded, as if their color was being sucked away—lying motionless in bed. "Please, you got any money?"

"You've got to love it," Ponce said, and he motioned Vel on.

"Money," Vel said. She *is* sick, he thought, and he turned away, following Ponce down the street. "Money's going to cure her, right?" Vel said, trying to flush the memory of the dying girl, Jak, from his mind.

"Maybe we should pray," Ponce said, and they both chuckled.

"Maybe."

Police laughed with more women at a corner ahead.

"You can almost taste the sin, can't you?" Ponce said.

"So long as it stays on this side of the river," Vel said.

"That's right," Ponce said, chuckling. "Where we go drinking, right?"

They were ignored as they turned onto another road, away from the Palace.

"So, you want to rob a cop?" Vel asked. It was a routine they had developed over the past few years. The first line referred to the impossibility of attacking a police soldier. The lines had developed late one night, with alcohol, of course—and the next morning none of them had really remembered why they said it. But, they still did. An obscure inside joke for three boys who had been very drunk, and Vel always began it.

"Yes," Ponce said, as he always did, "but I'm still seeing straight."

"As long as the executioner's drunk, the crime is not a crime," Vel said, and he spat. Usually it was Darden who finished the routine.

Vel and Ponce entered a small barroom, acknowledging the waitresses and owner before heading directly to a staircase that led to the second-floor balcony. Darden was waiting for them at their usual table. Darden wore a light beard, and had already finished two drinks when they arrived.

"Gentlemen," Darden said, sloshing his third glass in the air toward them.

"Vel hit them good," Ponce said, punching Vel in the shoulder. "A thousand two hundred."

Vel set the closed pouch of money on the table in front of them. He waved the nearest waitress to them. She was in her early twenties and dressed in the same white smock the serving staff always wore.

"We need drinks," Vel said.

"How many?"

Vel shrugged. "I'll take ten. No, twenty."

"The boy intends to vomit," Darden said.

"How about I bring you each one now?" the woman asked, and Vel opened the pouch, showing her the money.

"How about you bring me twenty," Vel said, still grinning, and the woman left without another word.

"What would we do if we didn't waste money this way?" Ponce said as Darden took a swallow of his alcohol, pursing his lips.

"We would probably live into old age," he said.

"And then what?" Vel said. "You want to become a *safer*? Act respectable? Vote? Pay the government taxes?"

"I didn't say we'd cut our hair," Darden said, and he sat back. "We aren't safer as short-hairs, but there's something to be said for survival. You know, I sometimes think these peasants should

be sent to the ruins. And then, anyone who comes back alive—
simply by virtue of being alive—wouldn't be dumb enough to fall
for *your* little cons, Vel."

"We're all peasants," Ponce said, and the waitress brought a
tray of drinks, setting them in the center of the table. The boys
cheered, and all three finished one glass in a great splashing and
gulping of alcohol. When they began to slow, Ponce said, "So,
you're not a peasant then, Darden? Everyone who pays taxes is a
peasant, and that means everyone. Regardless."

"Peasant, peasant, peasant," Darden said. "All right, it's irrelevant. It's implausible that we send anyone to the ruins—so then
we lock them up in a house with the Pox instead? Those left won't
get suckered."

"Yes, but they'll be cremated by the police," Ponce said. "So
what good does that accomplish?"

Darden shrugged. "It isn't my fault the government wants to
contain the epidemic. It's still a good plan."

Vel pushed away from the table.

Ponce said, "Where are you going?"

"I have to pee, is that all right with you?"

Darden smiled. "Don't fall in."

"No," Ponce said, "by all means, fall in. Just leave the money."

Vel left the pouch of coins on the table and went back down
to the first floor, through a full bar and restaurant. More than half
of the tables were full of off-duty police and women. Two men
and one woman waited at the rear wall at a closed door marked
Chamber Pot, and Vel fell into the end of the line, waiting for his
turn. One of the soldiers in the line was speaking to the woman,
obviously trying to impress her, and when his turn came, he asked
if the woman cared to join him inside. The tiny room smelled of
piss and feces through the open door.

"I can wait," she said.

The soldier shrugged, slightly drunken, and closed himself in.
Vel's turn came and he held his breath, pissing into a large metal
pot that had been fitted into the wooden floor. Someone had
scratched out a long block of graffiti from the wall behind the
chamber pot, leaving only the words *Piss on This.* And Vel finished, returning to the main room, heading for the stairs. He

passed several men in white—Religious Guard—at the bar, flirt-
ing with the waitresses.

As Vel returned to the table, Darden was ranting.

"—and so what if they can't handle that?" Darden said, nodding
to Vel, before he continued speaking to Ponce. "The goddamn
rainy season is over, because summer's over, and we never even
had a rainy season."

"All right, Darden. Made your point," Ponce said, downing
more of his liquor. To Vel: "You fall in?"

Vel leaned toward the edge of the balcony and the railing over-
looking the first floor below. He swallowed more alcohol and said,
"You see this? Police are in here all the time, but now even the
Religious Guard go whoring, it would appear."

Vel pointed out the group of men in white with swa armbands
at the bar. Ponce looked down and laughed, drawing attention up
to them. One of the guards shook his head, pointing up to the
boys, and Vel sighed, moving away from the railing again.

"I have no problem with you exploiting the working and mer-
cantile class," Darden said. "After all, the majority of the wealth
is in several well-placed districts—in the hands of the aristocracy.
What difference does it make if you readjust some of it? But don't
go against the Church, Vel."

"Wouldn't want to piss off God," Ponce said.

Darden frowned at them and finished his fourth, reaching for
a fifth.

"The Church of Hope is our only connection to the real world,"
he said.

Vel and Ponce exchanged a sarcastic glance, and Ponce leaned
closer, pressing Darden. "Oh, how's that?"

"We're agreed that Hope was founded by people from the stars,"
Darden said. "God's prophet created and brought life to Hera from
the stars. Without the Church we would have all forgotten that,
wouldn't we? They are the only ones who keep our past alive."

"Superstitions and brainwashing," Ponce said.

Darden shook his head slowly, studying his glass, not Ponce.
" 'God will torment Man in Eternity for following his Energies.' "

Ponce said, "How drunk are you? That was from scripture—
the *Rebirth*, wasn't it?"

Darden continued, ignoring his comment, "This is the ghost of what we once were. Why do you think they believe that they have sacred artifacts? Those artifacts no longer work because they're too old, but they're—"

"They're fake," Ponce said, looking at Vel for support. Vel merely nodded and finished his second drink. "Have you ever seen any of them? No, I didn't think so, and why do you think that is?"

Darden smiled. "Because I'm not in the Church hierarchy."

"Come on, Vel," Ponce said. "You've been to Church, haven't you? What do you think?"

"I don't know," Vel said. "So what if we were founded by people from some comet?" He looked pointedly at Darden. "Hmm? What relevance does that have to say . . . beating a cop out of his money?"

All three grinned.

"None," Ponce said. "But, I can still see straight." And he held up both hands to demonstrate his ability to discern one from the other.

Darden said, "So long as the executioner's drunk, crime is not crime. So long as God is drunk, we'll remain on this little rock of a planet called Hera, in this sick little hole called Hope." He raised his glass, and they each met the gesture with glasses of their own. "Amen."

"I love it when you talk dirty," Ponce said, when he had finished drinking.

A group of uniformed police approached their table from the staircase, each armed with a sword. Vel glanced at the soldiers and continued drinking as if he had not seen them. There were four of them, and they spoke in low tones as they drew closer. Vel nodded to the group when they had reached their table.

"Is something wrong?" he asked. Ponce visibly tensed, one hand sliding unnoticeably to the bola he kept in a strap on the inside of his pant's leg.

The lead soldier indicated the bag of coins on the table.

"Mind if I have a look?"

"Why?" Vel said.

The soldiers stepped around them, hands resting easily on their sword hilts. All were in their mid-thirties, with neatly cut hair.

"How much money is in there?" the lead soldier asked.

"Is it illegal to have money?" Vel said, and Darden laughed loudly. The soldier stiffened, and he stepped closer, reaching for the bag.

Vel touched the bag protectively, and the soldier stopped. He sighed irritably.

"It isn't wise to flash that much money around."

Vel looked at the bag, at the soldier, and then at the bag again. It was almost entirely closed.

"I'm sorry," he said. "I didn't realize I was 'flashing' anything."

Vel heard the metal sliding of a sword behind him, and Ponce started to his feet. The lead officer held up one hand, shaking his head, still glaring at Vel.

"You boys have your permits?"

Every registered citizen received an official permit from their district clerk at the age of four, a means of keeping track of the populace. People seldom carried their permits, but the police could technically ask to see them at any time. Vel wasn't sure what the punishment was for failure to produce a permit.

"You want to show me some papers?" the officer said. "Now hand me the bag or I'll have you all arrested."

"Arrested!" Darden said loudly. "Just because we don't have them with—"

"Extortion," the officer said. "Theft. Robbery. And that has nothing to do with your papers. I can make you guilty, don't worry." The officer extended one hand. "Don't make this more difficult than it has to be, boy. You don't have your permits—any of you born on the black market? You bastards know what that brings? Give me the bag."

Ponce said, "Vel—"

"I've never done anything wrong," Vel said, keeping the bag where it was, and he felt the point of a sword between his shoulder blades.

The officer reached for the money, and Darden snorted, as if he could not believe that Vel was allowing the soldier to take it. Vel did not struggle, staring back at the officer as he took the bag, backed away and opened it. The officer chuckled artificially.

"You want to explain this?" he said. "Or should I take it, let you leave, and we'll call it even?"

Again Ponce tried to stand, and another soldier drew his sword, leveling it at Ponce's throat.

Ponce said, "You can't—"

"We'll go," Vel said. He raised his last glass and took a last swig.

Darden shook his head. "No, this isn't right. There's procedure that has to be followed. Vel, what's wrong with you?"

"Come on," Vel said, and the other two followed him past the small company of police. The officer nodded to him.

"That's a smart thing to do," he said.

Vel did not turn, already descending the staircase to the main room. "I know."

When they were outside, Darden stumbled, catching himself on the building wall.

"Talk to him, Ponce," Darden said, and he tried to walk, thought better of it, and decided instead to lean.

"Why did you do that, Vel?" Ponce asked. "What are we supposed to do now?"

Vel studied the surrounding street. It was narrow and almost two blocks from the nearest main road. The buildings were all several stories high, with dark alleys between them. The sky had begun to darken.

Vel shivered. "Is it supposed to be this cold? It's still the long summer season, right?"

"Vel," Ponce said, "why did you do that? We needed that money. With the new ration system, none of us are going to get enough to eat without it."

"You think I don't know that?" Vel said.

Darden groaned, rubbing his stomach. "How many was that in there?"

"Four," Ponce said. "There were only four of them. We could have called the owner up. He knows us; he would've—"

"He would've told us to get out." Vel shook his head and pointed at a small alley on the side of the building. "My guess is they're from the Palace garrison, which means they'll have to go in this direction, toward the cemetery." Vel began to pace, examining the smaller alley. Bits of garbage and ash filled the corridor, and it smelled of old urine.

"What are you doing?" Ponce said.

"I meant how many drinks," Darden said softly.

"We'll wait here," Vel said, nodding to the filth in the alley, and when they pass, you'll take one down with the bola, I'll hit another with my dagger, and Darden . . ." He hesitated. "Darden will try not to be seen."

Ponce took Vel by the arm, leading him back, but Vel shook him off.

"You're joking," Ponce said.

"I'm not joking," Vel said. "You're right, we need that money. Without that money, I'm not only going to stay sober, but I'm going to slowly starve on one meal a day. My parents don't make enough to qualify for extra rations."

"It isn't your parents' fault," Darden said. "It's the crop. The crop's not yielding what they expected, and the weather's changing when it shouldn't be."

"We know that," Ponce said quickly, and then to Vel, "You're serious? You want to try and fight them?"

"They'll be drunk. Chances are not all four of them will come out at once, right? I think we can take two inebriated cops."

"How do we know which one will have the money?"

"The lead one," Vel said. "You don't think he'd let the others hold it, do you? No, he's probably their officer."

Ponce considered it, and he recoiled at the stench in the alley.

"This is crazy," he said at last. "You realize that."

"Come on," Vel said. "We're doing it." He drew his dagger and slipped into the alley. "Darden, get over here."

"It could be hours," Ponce said.

"What?" Darden said.

"No," Vel said. "If they're from the Palace garrison, they're expected to check in every three hours, remember? Even when they're off duty. They've probably been gone at least an hour already. They're not supposed to get drunk, but they will."

"I know," Ponce said, and Darden came to join them.

"What are we doing?" he asked.

"We're going to wait and attack the cops that stole our money."

Darden smiled. "No, seriously, what are we doing?"

"You can leave if you don't think you can handle it," Ponce said, and Darden groaned.

"You're not kidding." He sighed. "Someday you're going to wish we hadn't done this."

"I already do," Ponce said, and Vel made room for the other two in the alley.

Vel said, "When they come, we'll hit them fast, knock them down, take the money, and split up. We'll meet back tomorrow. Darden, are you sure you can do this?"

Darden snapped his fingers and spat into the filth around them. "I guess the important thing is not to get killed."

"That's crucial," Ponce said. "I'd say that's in the top three most important things about this, right behind remembering to take the money."

"So now we wait?" Darden asked.

Vel nodded, his hand tightening on the small dagger. Why hadn't he brought his sword? Two years ago, his father had given him a full-size sword and sheath. Of all the days not to bring it, he thought. There might not be time to go home and return.

Vel said, "So now we wait."

Time passed, and in the main streets, soldiers lit the posted torches at each intersection. Faint, rhythmic music was audible from several blocks away.

Darden said, "The summer festival's—"

"Shh," Vel said, and they were silent again.

Vel's legs cramped, and he shifted uncomfortably in the garbage. Ponce held his bola in both hands—a long strand of wire with two stones connected at either end. Darden had begun to sober, and he readied a piece of heavy stone from the alley, gripping it in both hands. Still, they waited. People passed, and with each shadow, the boys tensed.

Vel began to wonder if he had been wrong. What if the soldiers had been from a different garrison, or what if the Palace had changed policy for some reason and were allowing the soldiers to remain out without checking in? They might conceivably wait in this trash all night . . . Then the soldiers appeared. Three of the four soldiers stumbled in the center of the road, laughing and singing.

"Now?" Ponce said softly, his arms tensing.

Vel squinted, and the group began to pass. "I can't see if the officer's with them."

"Now?"

"Do it," Darden whispered. "Come on."

Vel nodded, and he lowered his dagger. "All right," he said. "Now."

Ponce twisted his arm violently, and the bola whistled out, catching the lead soldier's legs, and he shouted, falling helplessly. Vel sprinted toward them, but the remaining two had already drawn their swords, staggering as they turned to face the boys. Ponce drew a dagger of his own, circling behind them, and Vel sliced at the nearest one, knocking him off balance, and the man fell. The officer was not with them.

"Wait," Vel said, and Darden hurled his stone onto the head of the policeman who had just fallen—a cracking—and Ponce tried to trip the remaining soldier. The soldier spun, knocking away Ponce's dagger easily and clipping Ponce across the chest, knocking him to the dirt. Vel threw his dagger, and it hit the soldier in the center of his back. The man cursed and stumbled, turning on Vel wildly.

"Wait," Vel said again, beginning to back away. "They don't have it."

Darden was already running, and Ponce stood, heading in the opposite direction. The soldier charged Vel, and Vel ran, narrowly dodging a blow that would have severed his head. He heard the man behind him, shouting, and again the sword, past his ear, brushing against Vel's hair. Vel shouted, imitating Ponce's earlier call on the bridge, and in the distance there was a similar cry, and another. Vel turned a corner, into an alley, over a fence, and another turn, and he was at the bridge—the soldier was gone.

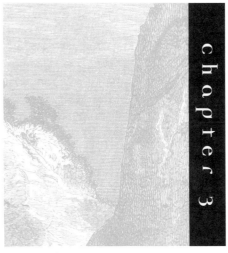

chapter 3

Vel pushed open the front door and stepped into a small house that resembled every other single story building along the street. Flickering torchlight misted the inner room; a simple living room, doubling also as a dining room. Wooden chairs, several black and white paintings, and a table. The outside door closed behind him, and Vel stepped deeper into the house.

"Mom?"

A moment's pause, and then, through one of the two side doors he heard a feminine voice singing. It was a song Vel remembered from his childhood, a lullaby.

"Trip, trip, tripping . . . tripping out into the world. Trip, trip, trip out, my darling."

"Mother?" Vel called again, and he stepped into the nearby doorway. His mother sat in a chair near her bed, knitting a collection of white fabric into what might eventually become a shirt. She was working by the light of a small candle, her long black hair framing her beautiful, full face.

"Vel, I didn't hear you," she said, setting down the fabric. Her dark eyes glittered beneath a curving brow, and her figure was slight, her movements graceful. "How was your day?"

Vel shrugged. "Not bad." He remembered the cemetery. "Mom, is there anything under Hope?"

"What?" She looked for any sign that he was kidding. "What do you mean *under?*"

"Any tunnels or anything?" Like something that would glow blue, Vel thought, and suddenly realized how ridiculous it sounded. He grinned. "Never mind."

"What were you talking about, Vel?"

"Just a joke, but I forgot the punch line. Sorry."

She nodded, stood, and stared at the room behind Vel, as if distracted. She kissed Vel's forehead as she passed, walking to the dining table. White candles and several hardbound books lay on its surface. His parents might serve twenty years if the police ever found their book collection. The Church helped to condemn reading; books are a path to sin, it said. And it's probably right, Vel thought. He smiled to himself.

"Did you talk to the team master today?" she asked.

Vel hesitated. "No."

"You know, Vel, we talked about that, and you agreed that you would try to get a position yourself."

"I know."

"I'm sure if you asked, your father would agree to teach you to work the fields himself. If I wasn't working the night shift, I would, but I don't want you working at night."

"I'll talk to the team leader tomorrow. I just don't want to work the fields."

She held up her hand and looked at him sharply. "Vel, your father and I both work harvesting the grassfruit. Farming is a respected trade."

"Chopping down grass isn't a trade," he muttered.

"What did you say?"

"Nothing."

She watched him, debating whether to press further. "Vel, it isn't a matter of what you *want* to do, that's why it's called *work*. When I was your age, I didn't want to make clothing, but I made it—because that's what was needed. My dream isn't to mend clothing during the day and work at night." She forced a smile. "We would have more opportunities if you were bringing in money on a regular basis."

Vel picked a small brown nut from one of the drawers, and he rubbed it on his sleeve, closing the drawers again. "I could enlist."

His mother's face tightened.

"Yes, Vel, you could join the police force. Or you could be recruited into the Church. But those require a lifetime commitment. Some time from now, if you still don't want to work the fields, maybe you can do something else." She pointed at the nut. "You haven't eaten today, have you?"

Vel frowned, cracking it between his palms. "No, I didn't have time."

"What were you doing all day that you didn't have time to eat? The summer festival doesn't begin until next Archday."

Vel pretended not to hear the question. "Have you been outside? Why is it so cold already?"

"I don't know, Vel. Ask your father when he gets home, he might have heard something." She flipped open one of the books, as if looking for something, and then went to one of the windows, staring at the darkness beyond the glass.

"Are you all right?" Vel asked.

His mother rubbed her arms, shivering. "Yes."

Vel went into his room, still eating the nut. The bedroom was tiny and cluttered with old clothes and papers. A chalk sketch of black spires hung from the wall over his bed. Vel slipped under his bed and began to sort through the mess.

"I'm going out, all right?" he called.

"Why don't you stay until after your father gets home?"

Vel found what he was looking for—a small sack of four coins. They were worn and silver. Enough that I won't go to bed hungry, he thought.

"Dad won't be home for a while," Vel said, pocketing the coins and returning to the main room.

Vel's mother was twisting the sleeves of her shirt nervously and humming. She glanced out the window again and said, "Vel, your father's tired when he gets off of work, and he hasn't seen you in a while."

"He saw me this morning."

"Don't argue with me." His mother held up her hand as a signal that the discussion had reached its end. "Just stay here until he gets home."

Vel sat at the dining table, tilting the front legs of the chair off the floor. He watched one of the candles waver and finished his nut.

"Here he is," his mother said, brightening, and the front door opened. "Don't lean back in your chair like that."

Vel's chair came down. A large man stepped through the front door and shut it behind him. He kissed Vel's mother and loosened a black scarf around his throat, coughing roughly.

"Hello, darling," Vel's mother said. "I didn't think you would be home for a while. How was work?"

She kissed his cheek, and his father wrapped a set of massive arms around her, pulling her thin body to him. Dropping a sack of heavy tools to the floor beside the front door, he covered his mouth and coughed again.

"Long day, and too cold." He grunted. Then he let her go and walked further into the room, stopping to watch Vel. "I wasn't expecting to see you here. Why aren't you out with your friends?"

"I decided to wait until you got home," Vel said, making no attempt to hide the resentment in his voice.

The man's form was a mass of shadows, and he stepped closer to the table. He swallowed and winced, as if the act was terribly painful. Vel saw beads of sweat on his forehead.

"That was nice of you," his father said sarcastically. "Did your mother tell you what we decided?"

Vel said nothing.

Vel's father looked at his mother, and then turned back to Vel.

"It's time to begin earning your keep, Vel. I'm tired of feeding us all. You're no better than anyone else, and you're going to start earning some money too." He coughed again, his eyes watering, and Vel's mother touched his father's shoulder gently. "Got that?"

"Your father has a cold," she said.

Vel looked at the door behind them. "I don't want to be a farmer."

"Don't want to get dirt under your fingernails?" Vel stared at the floor, unanswering, and his father began to redden. "Look at me when I'm talking to you." Vel obeyed, and his father said, "Are you above working?"

Vel looked him in the eyes, his legs trembling. "Yes."

"You're not going anywhere tonight," his father said, suddenly shouting, and he coughed. He dabbed the scarf to his mouth, hiding spots of blood from Vel's mother.

But Vel saw.

"Just because you and Mom have to work, doesn't mean I do," Vel said.

His father flared, one hand raised to strike Vel—but he forced it back. "You've turned into a selfish little brat, haven't you? We should have sent you to work years ago."

"I have money."

"Where is it?" his father said, and he nodded, as if he had just defeated Vel's argument. "You're not leaving tonight. And you're going to the fields tomorrow morning, either with me or with the team master."

"No—"

Vel's mother cut him off, stepping between them. "Vel, don't talk back to your father." To his father: "Do you want me to fix you something to eat?" She went to the bookcase, opened a small panel and took out one of their good goblets, a tin cup that had been in the family for generations, and a small pitcher of water. Vel's mother wiped off the cup, polishing the faded words *Campbell's So* on the side.

Vel's father shook his head, still staring at Vel. "I've already eaten."

She said, "Vel? What do you want to eat?"

Vel stood, not looking at them. "I'm not hungry."

"Sit down," his father said.

"Your father's had a long day, Vel."

Vel went to the door, and as he passed his father, he smelled a faint, sweet smell. The smell of sickness. Vel rubbed his eyes, and opened the front door.

His father said, "You're not going anywhere—*sit down.*"

"I'll be back later," Vel said.

His mother said, "Vel, please . . ."

Vel didn't look back. I don't belong to them, he thought. I'm not a piece of property—a candle or a shirt they can do whatever they want with. To hell with them.

He left.

chapter 4

Justice Hillor sat at the end of an empty rectangular conference table. He wore a heavy black military coat, and his skin seemed to have grown too tight over the muscles and bones of his face. His dark hair was streaked with premature gray on both sides, and he waited patiently as a police soldier entered the long stone room, walking past white tapestries with the Church swa in their center. The wall hangings were arranged Church, Royal, Church, Royal, so that the King's insignia of a red star with five points in the center of a black square contrasted perfectly with the Church's black swa on white. It had been Lord Denon's idea.

The soldier saluted Hillor, but Hillor did not return the gesture, scratching at his nose as he looked up.

"Yes?"

"Sir," the soldier said, "I have received confirmation that the Western Garr district will not vote in favor."

Hillor knew the answer, but he asked anyway, "How many does that leave?"

"There are only twenty-two, perhaps twenty-three in favor, sir."

Twenty-two, he thought, not twenty-three. And he needed twenty-five to overrule the King's veto. Not nearly enough, and the remaining districts would never easily alter their votes—they were home to the poor, and their representatives were also poor.

Hillor said, "I trust it will be properly handled."

"Yes, sir. We're doing what we can."

"Good." Hillor sat straighter in his chair. "Is the girl here?"

"Yes, sir." The soldier swallowed uncomfortably, as if he didn't want to say something that had to be said. "Sir, the King's condition has worsened."

Yes, but he's still well enough to veto, Hillor thought tiredly. Still well enough to attend the Executive Council meetings, even if the police have to carry him down on their shoulders.

"Thank you," Hillor said at last, and he waved the soldier away. "Send in the girl."

"Yes, sir."

The soldier left, and a moment later a fragile-looking girl in her early twenties entered the room. Hillor had not expected her to look this bad—perhaps it wasn't even worth the effort. He told himself that he had the time to talk to her, and he stood, pulling a chair out for her on his left.

She had deep circles under both eyes and her long blond hair looked matted, as if she had been sweating. The girl shivered, as she sat near Hillor. He remained standing.

"How are you feeling?" Hillor asked.

"Worse," she said.

"Jak, I know it's hard, but I think you'll want to take this seriously."

Jak rubbed her arms, too weak to even laugh at him. "Look at me."

"I know," Hillor said. "But I think you're strong enough to do what I'm asking. You got my dispatch?"

"Yes. It didn't say—"

"It's a cure."

Jak's eyes widened, and Hillor thought, Yes, this *is* worth the time it's costing me to be in this room with her.

"You're sure?" she said.

"Yes."

"I'll do it."

"Good." He removed a large handful of coins from one pocket of his coat, setting them on the table in front of her. "And there's something else." She stared at the money, unmoving. "Once you're well, of course, I have another job for you."

"What?"

"I want you to find an unregistered boy for me—can you do that?"

"What's his name?"

Hillor put more money on the table. "Vel."

vel's outline cut a dark shape against the bleached backdrop of the city, Hope. He stood on a hill near the center of the
city that was used as a dump for most of the factory trash. Rusted
debris and filthy, discarded clothing were piled to allow small
walkways for the workers. There were few houses here, and as
he walked around the summit of the trash-hill, all of Hope was
visible below, surrounding the dump.

Stretching its blocky limbs out below, the city of Hope swept
briefly down the hillside and across the dirt plain. The buildings
were closest, of course, giving way to the outer fields, arranged
in careful blocks of cleared farmland, then the black stone wall
that encompassed the entire perimeter—and beyond that a rolling, shifting expanse of high grass went on for miles in every
direction. To the south, it led to the dark spires of the ruins, and
just past the ruins, almost too far to see, the southern forest
stretched from east to west.

A long strip of water curled like a serpent through the heart of
the city, striking out north and south. Its banks were narrow, but
the crush of buildings were erected away from the edge of the
rushing water, giving it room. In the south, the river's course led
it to the ruins, and in the north it vanished into grassland.

Within the past few days, some of the farmers' fields had been
abandoned, entire crops lost to the unseasonably cold tempera-
tures. Still, most of the fields were in use, and Vel could see the
forms of several farmers moving between long rows of grass, cutting it down with scythes, then working on their hands and knees
to pull out the roots and the fruit that grew underground. The
farmers worked in unison, and Vel knew that they sang songs as
they labored, chopping grass, pulling up fruit, chopping more, and
on and on. My parents do that, Vel thought, wondering which,
if any, of the small forms he could see from the trash-hill was his
father—his mother worked at night, sewing during the day.

The towerlike buildings at the northern edge of the fields, near
the perimeter wall, were granaries. No one spoke about how much
food had been stored, but it was only a fraction of what was
supposed to be harvested. The grassfruit were growing smaller,

the fields dying in the cold air. Not nearly enough food had been
stored for an approaching winter of even normal length.

The normal seasonal cycle lasted thirty years: twenty years of
ordinary weather; summer, autumn, winter, spring; followed by
five years of bountiful harvests in a five-year summer, followed
by another five years of cruel winter. Now, for the first time,
winter had come early, after only six months, not sixty. It should
be the long summer season, Vel thought. And the granaries were
almost entirely empty. No one had known the crop yields would
be cut short, and so they had stocked in the traditional method.
Something new is happening, Vel thought, and no one knows
what it is. The summer festival begins today, and it isn't summer
anymore, and it should be.

Vel breathed purposefully, watching the cloud of his breath
dissolve.

"—worker?" Vel turned and saw a policeman approaching. The
cop said, "What business do you have up here?"

At his waist, the cop wore a longsword in a scabbard that was
worn with overuse.

"I'm waiting for someone," Vel said.

The man drew closer, squinting at Vel as he ascended the hillside.

"Waiting. Don't look like a garbage worker. Why are you meeting someone here?"

Vel brushed his hair from his eyes with one hand.

"We're going to start our own festival up here. Is that all right?"

The cop drew closer. "What's your name?"

"Vel."

"Is that supposed to mean something to me? You have a last
name?"

"It's also Vel. I'm Vel Vel."

"Look." The man was now within a few feet of Vel. "Don't go
giving me trouble."

"Is that name illegal? My middle name's Vel too."

Vel tensed at the sound of metal against sheath as the police
soldier drew his sword slowly, to emphasize the movement.

"All right," Vel said. "Go ahead and empty your pockets."

The soldier paused, sword in both hands, as if he didn't understand.

"What?"

"Empty your pockets," Vel said again.

The soldier stood for a moment, and then a smile spread across his face, revealing a set of crooked teeth.

He chuckled. "You're robbing me?"

"That's right," Vel said. "Empty your pockets. Now."

"I don't think so."

Vel tried to swat a nearby insect, as if it was more important than the cop. The smell of distant smoke rose in the air.

"Drop your sword and empty your pockets," Vel said again. "I'm not in a good mood right now."

"You're under arrest, kid."

"No, I don't think so."

There was a fast whistling, and the policeman turned in time to bring up his sword. Wire caught against his head, and there were a series of successive poundings as something hit and wrapped around his face and upper torso. He let out an unconscious grunt, and his body twirled, the sword falling away. A second later, the policeman hit the ground, rolling in the garbage.

And he was still.

"Not a bad throw." Ponce stepped out from behind one of the nearby garbage piles. "If I do say so myself."

Darden approached behind Ponce.

Vel knelt over the policeman.

"Vel Vel Vel," he said.

Ponce unraveled the bola from where it wrapped around the soldier's head.

"Think we might be overdoing it?" Ponce asked.

Vel shrugged. "You said we mug the first person along here."

"That's true . . ."

Ponce pulled viciously on the bola and stomped into the cop's side. The soldier rolled slightly and let out a groan. Thick, brown dirt clung to the sides of his wet face, where Ponce's weapon had drawn blood.

"Yes," Darden said. "Let's add murder to the list of charges in our profile, shall we?"

"All right, all right," Vel said. "Darden's right. You already hit him with your little string."

Vel fished into the man's pockets, taking out a handful of metal objects and a small, clanky pouch.

Ponce methodically rolled his bola over one arm. "Don't want him to wake up before we've spent his money."

"I know," Vel said, not looking up. "So how long does that give us?"

"I'd say . . ." Darden looked at the end of the street, past the dump. "Five minutes, maybe ten if Ponce nurses his drink like an old woman."

"I'll have it spent in three," Ponce said, grinning.

With a smile, Vel picked up the policeman's sword. "Either of you need a new sword?"

Ponce studied the weapon and scoffed, "My little string's better than that."

"Thank you, but no," Darden said.

Vel left the motionless policeman, starting a steady pace down the street. With an offhand gesture, he tossed the sword into the gutter. Ponce and Darden fell into step on either side, and the three descended into Hope.

Ponce asked, "How much did we make out of that deal?"

"Looks like forty-six crowns, and a few trinkets. They'll bring in another ten."

Ponce sighed. "Would have thought he would have more than that on him. That will hardly be enough to get blasted out of my mind."

"Obviously the police force is underpaid," Darden said. "I was always under the impression that extortion and physical brutality were where the money is."

"The money's right here," Vel said. "How long were we up there? Has the festival started?"

Darden said, "Vel, it doesn't officially start until we arrive."

People began to speckle the street, most wearing heavy coats, pants and hats. A group of three girls sat huddled around a nearby doorstep. Their eyes rose as the three boys approached. Two of the girls were much younger than the third, who was in her late teens or early twenties. She had red hair and wore a short green dress that did little to keep her warm.

Ponce smiled as they drew nearer. "Hello, ladies."

The red-haired girl grinned, sizing up the boys. "Hi there."

Darden stood directly over them, pointing at one of the younger girls. "I know you. Your name is . . . ?"

"Nuvia," she said, blushing.

"That's right," Darden said, and as he continued, Ponce led Vel closer.

"You going to the festival?" the other young girl asked Ponce.

"My friend here *is* the festival." Ponce chuckled, pausing several feet from where the girls sat.

Vel bowed briefly. "You ladies want me to tell your fortunes?"

"Will you tell me mine?" the red-haired girl said. She uncrossed her legs deliberately and stood, looking Vel over. He took her arm carefully, opening her palm.

"I foresee that you will consume great amounts of alcohol," Vel said, looking at her face rather than her hand. "And then that you will enjoy a passionate, colorful evening in the arms of a stranger."

She laughed. "Are you always this adorable?"

"It's what I do," he said, tapping her palm. "I only read what the lines tell me."

Her eyebrows raised. "Oh, you do? It's hard for a girl to find a decent meal. Do your lines tell you to buy us all dinner at the festival tonight?"

Ponce whistled, and Vel patted the sack of coins they had just stolen.

"They do indeed," he said, taking her arm. She ran her hand across his back and over his shoulders. Ponce, Darden and the other two trailed behind them.

"What did you say my hand says?" the girl asked, smiling.

"Which part did you want repeated?" Vel said.

"I heard something about passion," she said quietly.

Vel winked. "You heard right."

AT THE main courtyard, the music of old stringed and wind instruments, carved from the tough wood of the southern forests, created a dreamlike atmosphere. Notes scuttled through the air, soaring up and into the blackened night sky. The melody was light and uplifting. Some people stopped to take in the scene around them, before moving on. Others found themselves drawn into the crowd that had gathered—spotting friends, relatives, or simply recognizing the songs—and they stayed. Several hundred people scattered about the area and more—thousands—moved in and out, from one street to the next.

Vel, Ponce, Darden and the three girls sat at an outdoor table at a restaurant, their table covered with used plates and empty glasses. A small collection of stones separated the dining area from the main area of musicians, performers and dancers. A woman was juggling knives, while at the opposite end of the courtyard a small group had gathered around an elderly man, listening intently as he told them a story in a slow, growling voice.

The music became lively. A group of musicians sat in the center of the open area. A lone figure stood in front of them, moving his arms fluidly, creating forms in the air with the pulse of the tune. A mumbling conversation persisted throughout the courtyard, and, periodically, there were good-natured shouts and groups erupted into laughter.

Some of the crowd sat in simple wooden chairs, while most stood, gathered together in larger groups. An impressive, cleanly shaven man, dressed in an extensive white robe with an elaborate black swa, made his way easily through the crowd. The Religious Guard moved noiselessly in a loose perimeter around him, all wearing swa armbands. Even Vel, who had never been to Church in his life, knew who this man was: Lord Denon—head of the Church of Hope. Denon passed near Vel's table, people bowing as he continued on, and Denon smiled, greeting them all briefly.

Hairy men, dressed in long clothing, and slender women in loose-fitting, flashy colors. Clusters of younger people. Families and relatives. The larger the family, the greater its wealth, and Vel saw the aristocracy in their elegant black coats and colorful dresses, some with personal bodyguards of their own. The handful of *known* families, whom the crowd recognized and whispered about as they walked through the courtyard, held the best seats, closest to the music.

Elderly couples spoke quietly to one another of when they had been young. An obese woman wore a bulging cloth outfit of brown, and children ran in noisy circles through the yard. Vel had not been alive during the last summer festival, and he knew only what his parents had told him about it: the festival was a time when Hope momentarily forgot its districts and divisions. But not entirely.

Around the exterior of it all were men in gray and blue uniforms: police soldiers. They observed without comment, swords at their sides, and several held crossbows. Pouches hung from their backs, long arrow shafts of black, striped with lines of blue, protruding from within.

Someone was shouting from the crowd in the center of the courtyard, trying to be heard above the music and noise.

"A few words," the man shouted, "a few words about the summer festival!" The noise continued, oblivious to his cries. "The summer festival is made up of three things." There was a pause in the conversation at Vel's table, and they all listened. "Three things," the man shouted. "Viewing art and tradition. That's number one. Getting laid, number two. And then getting so drunk that you forget all about the first two by the next morning."

There was a surge of laughter in the courtyard, and Vel saw a large group tossing clothing in the air—a shirt, a pair of pants. Darden banged his glass on the table, his arm around the young girl at his side.

"Right. Jolly right," Darden said. "Those are exactly the kinds of things I believe in."

All six of them had been drinking for some time, and the red-haired girl rubbed Vel's leg, sipping at her fifth drink.

"You know, Darden," Ponce said. "Why don't you tell us what you think of authority?"

"All right," he said loudly, and he kissed the young girl with a wet sound that made them all laugh. "All right, it begins with the first man and his family."

"Oh, God," Vel said. "What have you done, Ponce?"

"No blasphemy," Darden said, frowning at Vel, and then he thought a moment before continuing. "First man and his first family, and there you have the beginnings of the state. Are we agreed on that?"

Vel felt the red-haired girl tracing up and down his leg with her hand. He smiled, and she leaned onto him, staring with a contented look as Darden continued.

"Agreed," Ponce said. "I'm agreed that you're full of it, but by all means, proceed."

"And now authority has led us to *this*," Darden said with disgust, waving his arms at the courtyard. "We have the state, the rich and the poor, and if you're not in with the rich when the time is up, then you're with the dead, because the rich have the muscle."

"What is he talking about?" the girl beside Ponce asked.

Ponce stroked her hair. "I don't know. What are you talking about, Darden?"

Vel stopped listening to the conversation for a moment, focusing instead on the shouts and conversation in the courtyard.

"—you know my place is empty tonight, and . . ."

"—Jak, at the Watchman, and she survived the Pox. Swear to God, she lived. Jak survived the Pox."

Vel turned in his chair, back from the table, pulling away from the red-headed girl. The courtyard tilted, and Vel rubbed his eyes, forcing it to remain in focus. He squinted, trying to catch the voice again, to connect a face with what he had heard. Couples passed, soldiers, and a group dressed in intricate, bright clothing . . .

"What's wrong?" the red-headed girl asked, touching Vel's chest to bring him back.

"Nothing," he said, still watching the courtyard.

"Vel," Ponce said. "You all right?" Ponce stood abruptly, grabbing Darden's shoulder. "Oh, no."

"What?" Darden said, refusing to stand, and the girls started asking questions at the same time. And now Vel saw them too. The officer and two of the police soldiers from yesterday—the men who had stolen his money, all one thousand two hundred crowns of it. There are only three, Vel thought. We can get away, but already the officer was pointing at their table, pushing his way through the crowd, drawing closer.

"No," Ponce said, and he tried to force Darden up again. "Come on, we've got to go."

"We're not going," Darden said, and Vel staggered to his feet, heading for the nearest side alley.

"Get up, Darden," Vel said, and the girl shouted something at him. He was not listening. Vel glanced at Ponce, and Ponce waved once, in the signal to meet back at the third bridge. Darden looked around in confusion.

"My analysis is not that boring," he said. "Sometimes the truth is difficult to face, but—"

"Get up, Darden!" Vel shouted, but he was too drunk to do anything more. "Police!"

The police soldiers had almost reached their table, and Vel ran. One soldier broke away from the main group to catch him, and Vel slipped into a shop just inside the alley, immediately searching past rows of candles and stone figures for another exit. He found one and emerged onto another street. Vel was running again, toward the river. But the soldier was still behind him, sword drawn, and Vel heard shouts as he ran.

"Stop him!" the soldier cried. "Don't let him pass!"

Vel turned a corner, into the partially opened door of a large, vacant factory. Charging past rows of wooden tables and benches, all empty and dark, Vel neared another exit. Wood and metal were piled along the room's walls—probably a crossbow or furniture factory, he thought, spotting several metal anvils with chimneys and hearths, where rows of blacksmiths presumably worked—and he reached the opposite door. Footsteps behind him, and Vel pulled at the door. Locked.

No, he thought. This can't be locked, I have to get away. Vel fingered his sword, and he heard the soldier closer behind him. No time to break it down.

"Drop your sword and put your hands in the air," the soldier said, quickly advancing on Vel. The skin around the soldier's left eye was still swollen and black from the stone Darden had smashed against his face.

There has to be a way out of this, Vel thought, and he drew his sword. The soldier tensed, readying his own weapon.

"I don't want to hurt you, kid."

"Then don't," Vel said. "I'll give you all of my money." He focused on the first door, at the far end of the giant room, behind the police soldier.

The soldier glared. "No, it doesn't work that way."

"It did the other night," Vel said. "I'll turn all of you in. That was my parents' savings that your officer stole from us. You arrest me and I'll tell. What kind of discipline will you get for that?"

The soldier circled, preparing to strike. "You're under arrest."

Vel paused, then casually slipped off one shoe.

"All right," he said and dropped his sword.

The soldier nodded. "Smart." He took a length of rope from his waist and quickly wound it around Vel's wrists. "Let's go."

Vel started forward, and then he slipped, his shoe rolling onto the dirt floor behind him.

"Sorry," Vel said, and the soldier nodded.

"It's all right." The cop started to retrieve the shoe, leaving Vel an opening—and Vel grabbed his sword and ran. Back outside, and Vel returned to a main street and spotted a column of approaching soldiers.

Vel yelled, "There's a criminal dressed as a soldier! Broke into a government factory!"

The soldiers hurried closer, and Vel hobbled away; the soldier emerged from the factory, his path quickly blocked by the new column. Vel ran.

His side burned when he finally reached the third bridge, and he was sweating, despite the cold air. Ponce sat on the bridge railing, waiting.

"So?" Ponce said.

Vel nodded to his wrists. "Will you cut these please?" Ponce chuckled, and he accepted Vel's sword, carefully sawing away the rope bindings. It frayed and finally split.

"Do I want to know about the ropes?" Ponce asked. "You didn't stop for a quickie with Ms. Redhead, did you? Forget your shoe in the confusion?"

Vel smiled. "Where's Darden?"

"I thought he was with you."

Vel felt a chill, and he stared at the nearby buildings and alleys. People laughed and drank, stumbling in large masses through the street. A woman was dancing for money at a far street corner.

"You haven't seen him?" Vel said.

"No," Ponce said slowly. "He was just sitting there."

"I know." Vel motioned to the bridge. "We can't go back to the other side. They'll be watching."

"But Darden—"

"Darden's fine," Vel said, and he looked across the bridge. He didn't see soldiers at the far end, but that meant nothing. It was the most obvious escape from the summer festival, and the police knew it. Anyone on one side of the river would logically want to get to the other side before the police could spread his or her description to the garrisons on the other end of the city.

To stop an escape, to trap suspects on one side of the city, the police immediately planted sentries on the *opposite* end of all four bridges. Vel had heard of numerous criminals being caught in just that way: racing across one of the bridges, thinking that they had been faster than the police, only to be caught at the opposite end. Vel had also heard from Darden that the sentries were usually removed a day later.

Vel said, "I can't go home tonight, can I?"

Ponce glared at the bridge, as if it was inconveniencing them. "Not worth risking it. You can stay with me tonight; we'll go back and find those girls—but what about Darden?"

"Darden knows where you live."

"Yes," Ponce said, sounding unsure. He looked at the streets behind them quickly. "Darden's not stupid."

Vel didn't answer, and they started walking along the river bank. The only other option would be to swim across, and that would draw even more attention.

"My mom and dad gave the get-a-job speech again last night," Vel said softly.

Ponce was obviously not listening, looking uncomfortably at the nearby alleys and streets for any sign of Darden. "Again?"

"Yes," Vel said. "They'll think I didn't want to come back tonight."

"Do you?"

Vel snorted a laugh. "Of course not."

---

vel stood alone in a room of blue stone. Overhead, the ceiling was a faintly glowing dome of rock, and the air around him shifted and whispered as he breathed. The room was a large square, and Vel turned in a slow circle, noticing a doorway in the far wall. The corners of the room were dark with bluish shadows, drawn by the dim light that flowed from nowhere and everywhere. Something was hunting him.

He walked toward the doorway, and someone stepped into it, concealed entirely in shadows. The figure was small, gripping the sides of the doorway with both arms. Red slits where eyes should have been, steadied on Vel, and he heard thick, wet breathing. The sound was muffled and strained, like the sound of a child slowly choking to death. Vel stepped back, unable to look away from the figure. It didn't move.

"Who are you?" Vel said.

The figure stared at him, the red spots disappearing for a heartbeat, and then flashing back into existence. The sick gasping noise continued, and the back of Vel's head began to burn.

"Who are you?" Vel said again, and his feet slipped on the stone. He steadied himself, watching the motionless figure. "What's wrong?"

Everything you will ever love, everything you will ever be, everything you will ever have, will die.

The words rolled through Vel, finding places under his skin to send cold flashes. He shuddered and reached for his sword. The handle was warm and slippery to the touch. He let go of the weapon, it hit the floor, and he drew his hand back, staggering away from the object. That wasn't his sword. Vel's fingers and palm were wet with blood that streamed down his forearm. That wasn't his sword. And it was lying in a pool across the floor. No. The red slits still watched him.

We are the same, boy. We are the same . . .

vel jerked awake, trembling with cold sweat that drenched his hair and rolled down his forehead. He sat on the side of

Ponce's bed, moonlight from the window creating a world of gray shapes around him. The door to Ponce's small bedroom was shut, and against the wall on another bed, Ponce was curled into a ball, his chest moving regularly in sleep. A dream. He had gone out with Ponce, and they'd come back here with the girls—Vel couldn't remember what had happened after that.

Vel went to the door of Ponce's room, into another room, entirely dark, the sound of Ponce's parents snoring from a hallway to his right, and Vel found the exit. Outside, the air was sharp and cold in his lungs, and Vel huddled by the doorway. Across the street, a group of city cleaners were planting a wooden pole in the dirt, testing it to be certain it would stand.

One produced something round, the size of a large grassfruit, from a satchel and stuck it on the top of the pole. Vel looked away, trying to remember the dream. The girls must have left, he thought, and Vel tried to remember the details. The workers finished, leaving the pole and fruit. But that isn't fruit, Vel thought, and he went back inside, instinctively shutting off the nervous ache in his stomach that sometimes came when he glimpsed the city's justice. It's a part of life, Vel reminded himself. It happens.

Back inside Ponce's room, Vel lowered himself to the bed on the wall opposite Ponce's bed. His heart slowed, and he stared at the veined wood of the ceiling. Something in the dream had been very important. This is not new, he thought. I have had these dreams all my life. And now they are more frequent—when was the last time? Yesterday night? Was it that recent? Dark shapes slid into the recesses of Vel's mind, and he closed his eyes. After another moment, the vague outlines of the dream were gone, and Vel rolled onto his side, already on his way back to sleep. It was just a dream, after all.

chapter 5

"This shoe was issued to a merchant on Falding Street who said that he sold it to you. Do you recognize it? Take your time."

Vel's father coughed dryly, his hands shaking involuntarily as he stared up at the trio of police soldiers near the front door. He sat beside Vel's mother at their kitchen table, unable to respond to the sudden intrusion. All three were armed, and one had drawn his longsword, pacing near Vel's parents' empty bookshelf. They had hidden their books under their bed when the knocks had identified themselves as police. It was early in the morning, still dark and quiet outside. Vel's mother had just gotten off work, and now sat bleary-eyed at the kitchen table.

"I don't understand," Vel's mother said, looking from the soldiers to her husband, and then back at them again. "Why did you come here—where did you find that?"

"It was taken off the body of a young con man, ma'am," the officer said. "We know only that he called himself Vel."

Vel's parents visibly stiffened, and Vel's mother rubbed at her tired eyes, making no attempt to hide the flood of emotion.

"The boy seriously wounded several soldiers and cheated—"

"What happened to him?" Vel's father asked, the veins in his throat bulging.

The officer frowned. "Did you know him? You recognize this shoe, then?"

"Where is he?" Vel's mother said. "I want to see him."

"He was a criminal, and he was killed while trying to escape capture. Disemboweled." The officer paused, and Vel's mother paled, slumping in her chair. Vel's father coughed again, looking very weak as he put a hand on his wife's back. She did not respond.

"Very strange," the officer said. "You see he was *unregistered.* That's illegal, you understand. Might be black market. You two don't have any children, do you?"

"What do you want?" Vel's mother asked, and her eyes teared as she tried to say something else.

"It's all right," Vel's father said, and then to the officer, "What do you want us to say?"

The officer seemed to consider it, then he dropped one hand to his sword, glancing at the bookshelf. "Noticed you have a display case."

"It's been in the family," Vel's father said, and his voice rose. "Please, leave us alone."

"I think the kid was yours, and I think you bought him off the black market."

"We didn't buy him," Vel's mother said, her lip trembling. She covered her face. "Go away. Please, just go away."

"Ma'am, you know the penalty for an unregistered child?" When she didn't respond, the officer stepped closer, and shouted, "Encouraging the black market—you know what goes with that?"

"Don't talk to her like that," Vel's father said, and he stood.

"Sit down, sir." The other two cops moved in on either side, swords ready, but Vel's father remained standing. "Illegal texts? You understand that?"

Vel's father: "Get out of our house."

The officer turned on him, Vel's mother shuddering, face buried in her hands. "Sir, I see a motive for not registering your child."

"I told you to get out." Vel's father started to cough, and the officer drew his sword.

"Possession of illegal texts. It's not unheard of—it's a reason to keep your kids a secret, so the district officers won't stop by."

"Get out."

"You're under arrest," the officer said.

"No," Vel's mother said. "No—"

The cops advanced, and Vel's father backed away from the table, toward the wall. "I'm not going anywhere. Listen to me—"

The officer sidestepped the table, sword up. The other cops closed on Vel's father from both sides.

Vel's mother shouted, "No, please!" And tried to grab the officer's sleeve, but he shook her away.

Vel's father faced the officer, fists at his side. "I have rights—"

The officer stabbed him in the chest, the point protruding from Vel's father's back—and then again in the chest—and Vel's father stumbled, but he didn't fall. Blood on the wall behind him. Blood soaking his shirt, dripping onto the wooden planks of the floor.

And now Vel's mother was crying hysterically. "God, oh, God."

The officer chopped Vel's father across the throat, and Vel's father collapsed against the wall, red spray spouting onto the soldiers' uniforms. Vel's father started to say something, and then slackened, motionless, blood pooling around him. Vel's mother charged the officer, who kicked her hard in the stomach, and she fell, sobbing and wheezing. The officer sheathed his sword, and the two other police did the same.

They ignored Vel's mother as they headed for the door, and then outside, the officer said, "Let him see that." They chuckled. "Little bastard thinks he can rob a cop."

Inside, after the door had closed, the room returned to normal. For a moment. The sinking, dead feeling that nothing had happened settled into the house.

And Vel's mother was all right. Her husband's throat was not leaking blood across the floor, and if it were, she would clean it up, until it returned to normal. Until her husband was alive again. And Vel would come home—and they would not argue—and she would explain to him again why it was important that he learned to work. He would be alive too.

But then voices—insane, wild voices—yelled at her inside her mind. Voices that she recognized, and that might have been her own, told her to wake up.

The moment passed.

And the world was dying around her. Again.

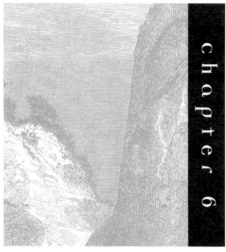

Chapter 6

"I dreamed I saw death. High upon his pedestal. Staring down at me with empty sockets of indifference. I dreamed he beckoned me. And I approached. He spoke of a time and place that I knew well. He spoke of living in darkness and of bleeding from the inside. He spoke of wasting away. And that's what I'm doing now. I'm wasting away. And death doesn't care."

"Enough."

"Do you know who I am?"

"Yes, of course, Your Highness. Why did you call me here? You should rest."

"You know who I am. You know where I came from, and those who will follow after me. You've been setting this up for a long time, haven't you, Hillor? Been plotting it all out. Been working on it, so that you're ready. I think I understand what you're trying to do. You're afraid of the Frill, and he keeps them in check, doesn't he? I know you're using that mercenary girl again. He's the leverage you need, because you can't force me to give you anything I don't want to—I'm already dead."

"You're ill. This is not a good time. Perhaps it would be better if I—"

"Perhaps you should listen. You must know it won't work. You're losing control, Justice. And what you've set into motion can't be stopped. God is reaching down. They believe, in the Church, that we may someday return to our past. The city has lost its past. You, and every man like you, has taken it from them."

"Are you now taking Lord Denon's side?"

"Are you now wearing your heavy coat?"

"Your Majesty, I have nothing more to say to you. Rest."

"Die, you mean."
"Goodbye."

vel dropped to the floor. It hurt, and he was slipping. Falling down, faster. Faster. Fire. Fire burning up inside his chest. Vel stumbled and crashed against the wall. Breaking his hands against the hard surface. Against the walls. Tearing his skin. Breaking his skin. No, not this. Not this. Not now. She was still there. Still talking. Still making him believe that there was a way to deal with things. Making him see that life didn't end in the gutter. And that there was a purpose, even if you died sooner or later. But she didn't have to die. She didn't have to die like that.

In her room. In her bed. Cutting up the insides of her arms. Taking out pieces of the flesh and letting the blood soak into her sheets. Letting it soak into Vel's mind. Lying there, smiling at whoever walked in the door. Smiling with those drained eyes. Still wide open. He'd jumped back when he entered, and she'd been sitting up in the crimson bed. But the bed wasn't supposed to be red. It was white.

The bed was white. It wasn't red. And she cut her arms, letting them drain out into the sheets. Leaving that note on the table. Vel couldn't read that note. He couldn't. He hated her. Hated the whole thing. Hated the way the house was dark and quiet when he got home. Hated the way she wasn't breathing. Hated the way that sucked him and tore him down so that now he was lying, shaking against the wall. Just shaking. And he was the strong one. Vel was the strong one.

This would never happen again. Vel would never lose control again, not like this.

Even as the tears traced down the sides of his cheeks, he knew that it was because of him. His fault this had happened. Slash across Vel's father's throat. Holes in his shirt where a sword had broken through—very deep. Into the chest first, then again, in the opposite side, then the neck. Calculated, and Vel knew that it must have been the cops. And they knew he lived here now. My fault, he thought again.

The house smelled of sickness and dried blood. No, he thought,

I'm sorry. To hell with the goddamn police. To hell with the Pox. To hell with his mother—I'm sorry. She didn't have to die like that. She didn't have to cut open her arms. God, he thought, it didn't have to end that way.

And the walls around him began to shake with his breathing, and he heard her singing from the next room. But she couldn't be singing. She was just sitting there smiling, watching for him to come into the room with those sunken, wet eyes of hers. She just sat there grinning, the knife still resting in the palm of her hand. And she was singing.

Trip, trip, tripping out into the world. Trip, trip, trip out, my darling.

He heard her slicing her flesh.

But she was dead. She wasn't singing. She wasn't in the other room singing. His mother was dead, and so was his father. They couldn't be, but their bodies lay, quiet and cold, in the other room. Side by side. And now what am I supposed to do? he thought. Where am I? She even left me a note. God knows what it says.

Won't you trip, trip, trip with me? Trip with me, my darling.

God, shut up.

Trip, trip, trip with me. Trip and we'll be merry.

He opened his eyes and saw her standing over him, smiling. Her forearms were torn. Carved into with the bloody knife, the liquid running between her fingers. She was smiling at him.

Trip with me, my darling.

Vel rose and stumbled forward. His mother resumed her place in the next room. Silent in the bed. He crashed into the table. It flipped onto its side, and Vel dropped beside it. He groaned at the sudden flare of pain in his forehead. Why was he here? Why the hell? Where was he supposed to go? Why was he the one still alive? I should not be doing this, he thought. I have to take control of this situation. I have to handle this. It's my fault.

Vel trembled again with the strained sobs that shook his lungs and made it hard to breathe. His parents sat in the next room. She must have set his father's body up to rest beside her. Except for that grin. That smile on her face. Wide and easy. And she wasn't moving. Neither one of them was moving.

Enough, Vel thought, but the image would not leave his mind.

Vel swallowed, and he took a slow breath, filling his lungs. They hurt. His hands shook as he grabbed the nearby table and closed his eyes. He was trembling. His fingers tapped violently. Like a twitch. He thought, I have to reason this through. I can't just leave them here. The police will know she's dead too soon—they might already—and they'll know that I'm still alive. They'll come in here any moment now, checking to see if I found them.

And Vel knew that his father had been sick before all of this. Maybe the Pox, Vel thought. Maybe a goddamn cold. I'm not registered officially, Vel thought, but some of my parents' friends know I exist. The police required that all deaths be cleared, especially those related to the Pox. And then the police *contained* the Pox. Vel had heard rumors about what happened to those people who reported such deaths. The police made sure the Pox died there.

Vel sat in the nearest chair, pulling it from the table with a dull scraping—the floor and wall behind him stained very dark. Probably happened here, he thought, but he stayed in the chair. Where should I go? he thought. Is it worth finding Jak now? A chill slid down his spine. What if I'm sick? he thought. My parents' sin to me. God, I probably gave it to them: because I'm sick, Vel thought. Yes, Jak is still important.

Silence. This was my life, he told himself, this was my life, and I've destroyed it. And he tried to ignore the way his pulse quickened at the thought of his mother waiting on the other side of the wall, animated. Still dead, but animated. It would be so easy to give up now. Now, before anything else fell apart. First Darden—Vel knew that Ponce would not find him—and now his parents. Vel would never see them again after tonight. Happening so fast. He rose, went to his room and collected a simple bag of clothing and a few coins, securing his sword and a dagger, and he returned, taking the note his mother had left him.

His mother's voice. *Vel . . . ?*

He left the house without answering.

"vel, you look terrible. What's going on?"

Ponce stood in his front doorway, the house dark inside. The street was empty, and Vel waved him out.

Ponce said, "I didn't find Darden. He's not home."

"I need your help," Vel said.

"Now? With what?"

"I'll understand if it's asking too much."

"Don't piss on my head—what are we doing?"

At one of the factories, they climbed a rear fence, awkwardly stealing a heavy wheelbarrow. Vel passed it over the fence to Ponce, and they transported the bodies under a blanket out of the city, into the farmland. Once Ponce stopped, waving at the shadows in the street behind them. The night was frozen, and their breaths misted white in the darkness.

"We're being followed. Did you hear that?"

"No," Vel said, and they resumed their pace.

The farmland circled the city for several hundred yards in every direction, and beyond these plots rose the black perimeter wall.

Vel and Ponce dragged the wheelbarrow through one of the open, plowed fields, roots breaking underfoot. The dirt was cracked, and they hunched, the wall an unbroken barrier in the near distance, faint wisps of light visible just over the top. Police soldiers were stationed every twenty feet on the interior of the five-foot-high wall, little more than shadows now.

"There," Vel said, indicating a mound of broken wood and debris in the center of the plot. Vel knew this field must have been abandoned when the crops failed, when the air changed suddenly. The farmers had expected four and a half years more of summer—that was the reason for the festival, the festival that would probably be cut short for the first time in recorded history.

They arrived at the debris pile, and then unloaded the heavy bodies one at a time, carrying them onto the pile itself. Vel kept his eyes fixed on the perimeter wall, ignoring the faint smell of his father's flesh. Then he took his mother's wrists, lifting uncomfortably. Neither he nor Ponce spoke as they laid her facedown beside his father, wood splintering as they jumped off the pile. Vel produced a box of wooden matches.

"We might have to leave," Ponce said, glancing at the wall.

"I know," Vel said, and he struck a match, shielding it from the wind with one hand. Carefully, he knelt and lit one of the smaller wood fragments. It caught, and the fire smoked and slowly spread, flickering and eating at the debris around it. Vel stepped beside Ponce and studied the dark outlines of his parents' bodies. Ponce blew on his hands, rubbing them together.

"I think it has to happen this way," Ponce said. "Screw the cops. Better than letting them do it."

"Yes," Vel said, and the wood broke loudly, sparks spraying the inner pieces.

Ponce said, "This is the only way to do it without the police definitely knowing. The river wouldn't carry them far enough. The graves are all officially sanctioned, and there are guards at the cemetery."

"I know," Vel said, as the fire reached his parents, blackening their clothing.

They watched in silence, looking occasionally at the dark shapes of wall-soldiers who remained at their posts, apparently oblivious to the boys' bonfire.

"We should go," Vel said at last.

The entire pile was on fire now, shooting sparks into the night sky overhead.

"You don't want to—"

"No."

Ponce followed him away from the bonfire, toward the city again.

"We have to find Jak," Vel said. "I want to go to the Watchman."

"Cops there," Ponce said, and when Vel didn't respond, he added, "Might still be looking for us, Vel."

"I have the Pox."

"You don't know that."

"My dad had it." But what if I don't have it? Vel thought. What if I'm wasting my time?

"You overheard someone at the festival—who?"

"Don't know," Vel said simply, and he did not look back.

He continued walking through the darkness. His parents hadn't been dead for long, and Vel was dealing with it. He was accepting what happened. I can handle this, he thought.

Won't you trip, trip, trip with me?

I'm doing just fine.

chapter 7

Vel heard shouting from the street outside. He and Ponce sat in a back room of the Watchman, across a table from the fat owner. On the wall behind their table hung an old wooden sign that read *Men Willingly Believe What They Wish.* The Watchman was a squat building that attracted other residences to creep close and lean against its scraped sides for support.

Built in the genesis of Hope, it remained one of the original structures—with the Church, Palace, and Garrs—close to the river. The Church taught that two hundred years ago, in roughly the year 300, Hope had been torn by a civil war that cost many lives. Little was known of the actual war, except that the leader of the rebel faction had been a madman, intent on leaving Hope to found another city on Hera.

The government had stopped him, but the madman had followers. When open warfare broke out, fires started and spread, destroying all of the original wooden buildings in the city, except the Watchman. For whatever reason, the Watchman survived, along with the stone structures: the Palace, the Garrs, and the Cathedral. Supposedly, the thick black rock of those old buildings had come directly from the ruins.

Repaired and renovated more than two hundred years after the civil war, the Watchman still appeared sturdier, more elaborate than most of the other buildings in the city. Its foundations were more complex, and heavy wooden pillars supported a three-story roof. The Watchman was the most famous bar in the city, and the oldest. The upper floors contained expensive apartments and a handful of rooms that could be rented by the hour.

Vel and Ponce sat at a small round table in a room that smelled of sweat and alcohol. There was only one door, leading into the main tavern. Vel had not spoken of his parents since leaving the bonfire less than an hour ago. Across from them, a very fat man with bushy sideburns sat talking. Each time the owner's glass began to run dry, Ponce filled it from a large, half-empty pitcher in the center of the table. There were two other pitchers, both entirely empty.

Ponce and Vel had finished one drink each, and their seconds remained untouched. They had not seen Jak in the main room of the Watchman, but the owner claimed to know her. In one over-sized hand he cradled his tall glass protectively, and he nodded to Ponce for the most recent refill. The owner resumed his story; Vel nodded, and Ponce grunted when appropriate.

The owner was saying, ". . . and I heard that they were consid-ering him for the force—my brother—but that was back before Justice Hillor took over. That was twenty years ago."

Vel said, "And when did he come down with the Pox?"

The owner thought for a moment.

"I don't know. Hell, it must have been a year ago. That was about when the disease was just starting up, right? Nobody really knew about it then. Well, 'course a few people knew 'cause they were getting sick, but there are enough ways to die that they didn't really associate it with anything. Pox symptoms, well, hell, they aren't too obvious. Could just be a cold—and then you're dead."

And then you're dead, Vel thought. The owner set his glass on the table, and Ponce poured him more alcohol.

"Bad timing to catch the Pox when a flu is going around," Ponce said.

The owner nodded distractedly, and he took another drink, considering something.

"That's about it," he said quietly. "That's all there is. He's dead now."

"What about Jak?" Vel asked.

"Jak?"

Ponce said, "Yes. Jak. As in the reason you were talking about your brother. You said he knew Jak."

The owner shrugged, spilling alcohol onto the table. "Well, he did."

Vel waited, and he exchanged a brief look with Ponce. Perhaps it hadn't been such a good idea to get the owner drunk, he thought. They might hear more literal truth, but the trade-off was that they might not hear anything of substance at all. Ponce sighed. "So who is Jak?"

"Oh." The fat man breathed, annoyed with the return to that subject. "I pretty much told you all there is to know."

"Except you haven't told us who Jak is," Vel said. He was losing his patience.

Something clicked inside the fat man's head. "Jak's in here regularly, and she was sick. My brother knew her better than I do."

Vel said, "And you said she doesn't have it anymore, the Pox?"

"Right."

"Did you ever meet her?"

"Once or twice."

"Did she strike you as being sick?" And Vel thought, I saw her—she *was* sick. If that had been the same girl.

The owner took another drink to jog his memory, shook his head, and Ponce refilled his glass.

"No, don't know, but it's hard to tell. You know how many people have died of it since it began?"

Vel said, "No."

"Around five hundred or so, sound right?"

"I'd say more," Ponce said.

"Of all those people," the owner said, ignoring Ponce, "how many you think knew they had the Pox? Only the ones who knew others who had it. How many you think have died of the Pox who didn't know they had it until they were about gone? Probably twice that many. Maybe a thousand."

"Maybe," Vel said.

"So I think Jak had it—but could be she just had a cold."

The way the owner's eyes darted convinced Vel that he was lying. Something about this was wrong. Or am I imagining this? Vel wondered. Why would the owner lie about Jak—and *how* if he's drunk? Assuming he's actually drunk.

"When was the last time she was here?" Vel asked.

"A few days ago."

"Do you know where she lives?"

"Yes." The owner's face paled. He tried to mask the change with another drink. "She's living in a small community."

"What kind of community?"

"Don't know." The man shrugged nervously. "Just a community. My brother had the address. I can give it to you if you want it."

Too convenient, Vel thought. Something's happening here that I don't understand—and the owner headed for the door. Vel didn't move. Ponce motioned to Vel that they should follow.

"All right," Vel said, "give me the address."

The owner led Vel and Ponce into the main room. Long, square tables were arranged in rough X's, and a black stone swa had been fitted into the wooden floor, probably when the Watchman was built. Torches hung from the walls, providing full, warm illumination. A soiled bar ran the entire length of one wall, and several staircases rose to the second floor through open doorways.

Large, drunken men from one of the nearby tables had begun to shout at a group at another table. "—paying for our round of drinks. You hear me?"

Vel paused as the owner continued toward the staircases, spotting the back of someone's head with long blond hair. The owner paused and followed Vel's gaze, and now Ponce saw her too.

"Wait," the owner said. "Over there . . ." He pointed to the girl Vel had been watching. "That's her. That's Jak."

Vel squinted, his eyes watering from the smoke of the torches, and Ponce caught his shoulder before he could move any closer.

"Not yet," Ponce said, and before Vel could respond he realized why. Jak sat in the midst of a company of police, all uniformed and armed. And she looked nothing like the way Vel remembered her. But it's still her, Vel thought.

A man from the drunk table was advancing on the other group, still screaming, his words slurring unintelligibly.

"Just the usual lot," the owner said dryly, shaking his head at the noise. "Always a few people in here can't handle themselves. Never amounts to anything."

"That's her," Vel whispered to Ponce, and Ponce nodded.

"Think you're right."

She was sick, Vel thought, and now she's not. Jak's cheeks were a healthy pink, and as far as Vel could see, she looked in perfect health, laughing with the cops around her. But what if it wasn't the Pox? He thought of that girl on the street, begging him for money. And the building had been marked with a red cross, the way all Pox houses were. Whoever marked it might not have known, he thought. Jak might have moved there after a family was wiped out.

Still, he stared at her.

From across the room, Jak looked up, and she met Vel's stare with full blue eyes. Her cheeks flushed, and one of the soldiers slipped his arm around her, fingers playing with her hair. For a moment, Jak ignored the policeman, and then she glanced away from Vel, joining in the conversation around her again.

"I saw that," Ponce said softly, and the owner started toward Jak's table. "Vel, you hound."

"Just going to stand here?" the owner said. "I'll introduce you."

"We'd rather have the address," Vel said quickly. "If it isn't too much trouble."

The room was growing louder—someone dumped alcohol onto a policeman's head—and the owner pressed one hand to his ear as a sign that he had not heard.

"The address," Ponce said. "We'll take the address."

They followed the owner toward the stairs, and then he stopped with an obese smile, producing a slip of paper.

"Here it is," the owner said.

Vel took the paper, pocketing it uncomfortably. He backed away from the owner. The owner said something and started up the stairs.

"I don't get it," Ponce said, shouting over the noise of the barroom. "Thought it was upstairs."

More than a coincidence, Vel thought. Just what the hell is going on? Vel nodded—something heavy crashed into his side, and Vel was thrown backward. He stumbled and grabbed at the wall, maintaining his footing. The police, he thought. But it was not. One of the men, a lumbering creature with a gray beard— the loud drunk—sprawled on the ground nearby.

A large man with a prominent overbite and long hair stood in the center of the room. His shirt had been ripped and his lower lip was slightly swollen. Vel watched, unsure of what to do, Ponce beside him. The room was packed with people.

A group of police approached, some drunkenly, from the far table, and the recently downed man groped back to his feet. Someone from the drunk table laughed and threw a bottle at the police. It smashed a cop in the stomach, and as he staggered, alcohol and glass spraying his group, the police reacted. They shoved the crowd aside, heading into the center of the room. Vel didn't see Jak anymore.

"I'm not finished with you!" the wounded man shouted, oblivious to the police, and he charged the group he had been harassing earlier.

A back door opened.

"We have to get out of here," Ponce said.

"I know." What if one of the policemen recognize us? Vel thought. "Ponce, we'll—"

"Vel."

Vel turned. A slight girl dressed entirely in black. Her eyes glittered, and her skin was flawless.

"How did you—"

"All right!" a policeman in the middle of the room yelled, "You people are under arrest!"

Someone was thrown against Vel's right shoulder. As he dropped, Vel saw Ponce duck a piece of what had been a chair, and then someone took Ponce from behind, one arm around his throat. Vel's skull slammed against the wall, the room flashing. A table flipped onto its side, bottles smashed, and blades met in a violent, metallic scraping. A fire started on the far wall, and someone shrieked like a dying animal. Police crossbows discharged into their attackers, and people fell. Some retreated from the building, and more lashed back at the police with swords, bottles and chairs. Bodies broke.

Vel sat up, bracing himself against the wall. The bar had become a confusion of smoke, noise and wounded bodies. A mob of drunken citizens collided with the cops, and the police soldiers struck in formation, struggling to knock them back. The cops effectively created a human wall against the mob, still giving orders, demanding that the attackers drop their weapons. No matter how drunk the police might be, their technique was effective.

Already bodies began to fill the floors, some screaming, some not moving at all, and the room was quickly filling with smoke, the rear wall burning in yellow light.

"Come on."

That girl stood over Vel again. She grabbed his wrist, and as she pulled him to his feet, a bottle whistled through the air, smashed across Vel's forehead, and a flash of white sent him down again. He winced, opening his eyes in a sharp red fog. Ponce was crawling under a nearby table, fighting off a drunk twice his size. Swords crashed against swords, and the police were outnumbered and surrounded. Several of the police gave way under the onslaught of the mob—their formation began to fragment, the cops disappearing in the smoke and chaos.

A large man in a black overcoat stepped through, cutting a swath through the people with his body, tossing people out of his path as if they were nothing more than a minor annoyance. His shoulders looked exaggerated, too broad, and the greatcoat seemed to have been cut specifically to fit them. He strode forward from the rear door, his overcoat turning like a living shadow, and when he steadied himself in the direct center of the turmoil, he did not look, he glared—as if disappointed with a group of children.

The man ducked a bottle, and a shirtless attacker came at him, pushing others out of his way. As the shirtless man closed, he raised a longsword, shouted—the man in the coat dropped one hand into his greatcoat, moving fluidly to face the new opponent. No hesitation as he raised his hand directly into the attacker's face—a flash of light, a crack of noise, and the attacker fell, his body crumbling to the floor.

The room was still.

The crowd froze, watching this dark figure. He held a black device into the air, and a small trail of smoke rose from the end of it. Dark lines flickered across his high cheekbones as the man in the overcoat took a single step forward, examining the room. Glass snapped beneath his boots, and flames crackled. The high ceiling was covered in a fog of smoke.

No one moved.

The body of the shirtless man lay broken amid the debris. The man's head was smashed in a puddle of wet brains and blood— it had become an open wound. Vel trembled as he stared at the body. My God, he thought. What's happened? The man in the overcoat had not fired a crossbow, he had simply pointed something at the other man, and now that drunk lay broken on the floor. Vel felt a sick fascination, and his mouth became very dry. What had he just seen?

"My name is Justice Hillor!" the man in the black overcoat growled. His voice was sharp. It rolled out in a low bass, shaking the walls. "You all know who I am. Attacking a police officer is an offense that brings severe punishments." Hillor touched the motionless body with the tip of his boot.

"Hey!" one of the men closest to Hillor said. "This isn't your court!" The man indicated the mangled body. "He didn't get much of a trial, did he? What the hell is this?"

The crowd seemed ready to respond, to strike again. Hillor rammed his knee between the man's legs. The man groaned, and, as he dropped, the dull end of Hillor's black device caught him across the back of the neck. The man slumped, collapsing to the ground.

"Any of you attack," Hillor said, and he pointed his device into the face of a young girl nearby, "and she dies first." The girl was in her late teens. Everyone remained exactly as they were. "Anyone moves, and her head turns into a piece of meat."

Vel heard his pulse loudly in both ears, his legs beginning to tremble. Hillor was the head of the police force, second only to the King of Hope in terms of the military. He was also the chief magistrate, which meant that he approved sentencing. And those hangings Vel had glimpsed—the bodies with writing carved and burned into their pale skin—they had been Hillor's work. He was responsible for enforcing the city's laws and maintaining discipline within the police army. He also had one of the thirty seats on the Executive Council, meaning that he had been elected by the people of whichever of the thirty districts he lived in—which meant that he helped to create the laws as well.

Hillor scanned the room carefully—he saw Vel. There was a

kind of recognition, but Hillor frowned, as if unable to register what he saw, and he looked away.

"Now," Hillor said to the crowd. "This bar will be closed for the rest of the night. I want everyone here to disperse."

The group responded, silently filing outside, while the owner rushed in with a team of buckets. Vel touched his forehead gingerly where pieces of broken glass still clung to it. Ponce approached behind him.

The girl in black was gone.

"Never seen that before," Ponce said. "What the hell just happened?"

Vel glanced through the wreckage—Jak was missing as well. Several of the police were speaking with Justice Hillor near the far wall, and Ponce mixed with the others, heading out.

"Come on," Ponce said. "What's wrong with you? We've got to get out of here."

Vel looked back a final time. "Did you see that girl?"

"Who, Jak?"

"No," Vel said. "She had dark hair, dressed in black." They slipped out, returning to the cold city streets. Vel said, "What was that the Justice had? Is that what they pass down—what each Chief Justice keeps?"

"It didn't look much like a gavel, did it?"

"What was it?"

Distantly, a slow song played faintly. A woman's voice sang with it from the near-distance, barely discernible.

> "And we'll believe,
> Sometime we'll believe,
> That things are not,
> What they mean."

"I don't know what it was, Vel. Never heard of anyone doing something like that before."

"God's magic," Vel said, and he forced an uncomfortable smile as they wandered away from the Watchman, onto a side street. "You think that was magic, like what they talk about in Church?"

"Thought you didn't go to Church."

"Come on, Ponce, seriously."

"Seriously? Seriously, I don't know what the hell it was. A new kind of crossbow probably."

Vel knew something of the Church teachings, of the sin of pride and of learning and reading. The blessing of fertility. But he had also heard of God's fire striking down the wicked. Darden would know more, Vel thought. Wherever the hell he was.

Heading through the streets, they passed a different corner of the cemetery again. People danced in the streets, and a woman passed them, offering her body for forty crowns. The summer festival continued, ignoring the weather. They moved for the river.

"What's that book of scripture called?" Vel asked.

Ponce sighed. "What?"

"It's by Blakes, right?"

"Called *Rebirth*, Vel. Blakes's *Rebirth*. Even I know that."

"So what's it say in there about the relics—the artifacts the Church has?"

"I don't know," Ponce said. "You're going to convert now, right? After you saw Hillor use his magic crossbow."

That wasn't a crossbow, Vel thought. There were no arrows. Small and black and it had spouted fire and opened that poor drunk's face. What if it *had* been God's power in the bar? Because Justice Hillor was appointed by the King, and the King was blessed by the Church. That meant Hillor was doing God's will, even though his job was independent of the Church's swa. Church law and civil law were the same, except that the Church relied on Hillor and the police to enforce its teachings.

Lord Denon—the head of the Church of Hope—was on the Executive Council as well. Whatever passed in the Executive Council had already been proven in Blakes's teachings or—logically—it would never have passed in the first place, as God would not have allowed sinful rules to come into being.

"Did Justice Hillor get that thing from the Church?" Vel said.

Ponce stopped walking. "Knock it off. What's wrong with you?"

"You don't wonder what we just saw?"

"I wonder, but so what? What are you going to do, ask the Justice where he got his magic crossbow? You going to ask the Church what they've got locked in their vaults? I'll tell you what

they'll say—they'll say they got them from God, Vel. And the
Justice got his from the Chief Justice before him, and that Justice
got it from the one before him, back to when the good Lord—
forgive me if he exists—dropped our great-great-grandfathers on
this rock."

Vel said, "You're right."

"Damn straight. And I sure as shit hope God doesn't exist,
because then we've got bigger problems than the Pox."

Vel grinned. "At least you know what the inside of the Cathedral looks like."

"Ah, but you forget what else I've seen the *inside* of." Ponce
loosened his belt and then paused, pretending to suddenly realize
something. "Gosh, Vel, you're right. This really is important, isn't
it?"

Vel chuckled and tapped his scabbard. "You want my sword to
see the inside of your face, keep it up."

"Save it for the ladies—I think it's time we converted. Right
now. Let's go to the Church and ask them to take us in." Ponce
pretended to walk toward the river again, in the direction of the
Cathedral. "Maybe we can still be saved. Do they do two-for-one
specials? Maybe they have a bargain day, like at the market, when
there's—"

"All right," Vel said, and he punched Ponce lightly on the shoulder. "I won't ask anymore questions about anything. You satisfied?"

"So, what's the address?" Ponce asked.

That girl in black knew my name, Vel thought, and wondered
why he hadn't thought of that before.

"You can go home, Ponce."

"You want me to throw you in the river? Come on. I'm not
going to get any sleep knowing you're on the verge of heading to
the Cathedral. It's my job to keep you honest. Where's Jak?"

Vel reached blindly into his pocket and took out a wrinkled
paper.

Vel was my son—
No.
It was the wrong note.

He wadded that paper up, putting it away again. Why haven't I gotten rid of it? Vel thought. Why haven't I read the damn thing? It was the last thing his mother wanted to say. What if it was important?

"What was that?" Ponce asked.

"A suicide note," Vel said. "My mom's."

A part of him, something Vel didn't understand, told him to forget his mother's note. It told him to still his curiosity. To shut off the urge to read the note. He silenced it.

Vel felt the emotion pushing . . . and he was again inside his house, and his parents . . . Ponce was waiting. Again, frustration raged inside his chest, aching. I can control this, he thought. Thinking about it won't help me. I won't think about it. Vel's hands became fists, and deliberately he looked away, shielding his face from Ponce.

"Here's the right one," Vel said softly.

He would never see his mother again. Flashes of her. Sunken, pale limbs. Blood flowing onto her hands and forearms.

No.

He felt the other paper, smaller than his mother's note and took it out, unfolding the material. Ponce leaned over his shoulder to read.

Turn Tables: A Place to Call Home
63 West End Street

" 'A place to call home,' " Ponce said, and he continued talking, but Vel wasn't listening.

They headed for the end of the street. Someone watched them from an alleyway, and they continued.

Ponce said, "You ever get the feeling that you're not awake? That this isn't real, and sometime we'll just wake up and be someone else?"

Vel thought, I am the reason my parents are dead. The cops found them because of me. If I had come back earlier, I could have been there, I could have done something. Don't think about it.

"No," Vel said. "I don't."

chapter 8

Lord Denon sat alone on a wooden pew in a cathedral of black stone. Candles burned from their ornate metal stands around the exterior of the huge room, their light flickering up to the high ceiling. The candlestands were tall, with metal swas embedded in their stalks midway to the top. On each candlestick, just below the summit, a strange creature was built into the metal: an animal with a point where its mouth should have been, and broad arms outstretched very wide, grooved with regular curves, ending in smoother lines, rather than hands. Its feet were curled talons, gripping two bundles—the first held what might have been a kind of grass strand or branch, while the second gripped a parcel of arrows. This was a symbol of Hope's harmony: work tempered with divinely sanctioned law.

Two rows of pews, with a central aisle, led to the front of the church, where a blue circle was inscribed on the floor in front of an altar set with an elaborate white cloth and more candles. A black swa filled the center of the cloth, and all of the walls were hung with white tapestries—more swas.

A thick hardbound copy of the scripture of Blakes's *Rebirth* sat in the center of the altar, opened to a section near the front. Beyond the altar, three closed doors were set into the solid stone wall, and overlooking the scene was a balcony—carved out of that wall, thirty feet above the floor—where three empty chairs had been set.

This main room of worship, where Denon now sat, head bowed in silent prayer, filled the center of the Cathedral. A set of rear double doors, at the far end of the aisle, led into Reich Hall and some of the living quarters.

The doors opened, and a young man in white dress with a swa armband and sword hurried down the aisle, bowing at Lord Denon's side.

Denon did not move. "Yes?"

"Dispatches, Lord."

Denon held out one hand, palm up, and the young priest-soldier dropped a sealed white paper into it. When he was alone again, Denon sat up, broke the five-pointed star seal—that meant it was from within the Palace—and he read the brief note. Finished, Denon methodically tore the paper into strips. He took the fragments to the altar, where he burned the small fragments in the candle flames.

Distracted, Denon read a line from the opened page of the *Rebirth*:

> Thus I seize the Spiritual Prey:
> Ye smiters with disease, make way!
> I come Your King and God to seize,
> Is God a Smiter with disease?

"In public," Denon said softly, as if he couldn't believe what he was saying, and he glared at the altar. "He used his office in a *bar*."

Denon stepped onto the blue circle in the center of the floor. Desperate, Denon thought quietly, he's desperate now. And vulnerable. But, no action yet—no, he will still find the boy. And *then* the Frill may become a factor. And Blakes. And Hillor believes that the boy is all of the insurance he needs; leverage against *me*, to seize the sacred relics.

Frowning, Denon moved to the altar again to be certain none of the pieces of the note remained. He read again from the book:

> He bound Old Satan in his Chain,
> And bursting forth, his furious ire
> Became a Chariot of fire:
> Throughout the land he took his course,
> And traced diseases to their Source . . .

Blakes, Denon thought. You're the cause of this. I see that now.
God has given us this chance so that we might correct the errors
of our youth, years ago; when men died in tunnels underground
and somehow the boy escaped; when we betrayed the Frill; when
I trusted you.

Denon turned the book to another page, near the end, and he
read.

> But now, alone, over rocks, mountains,
> Cast out from the lovely bosom,
> Cruel jealousy, selfish fear,
> Self-destroying: how can delight
> Renew in these chains of darkness
> Where bones of beasts are strewn
> On the bleak and snowy mountains
> Where bones from the birth are buried
> Before they see the light?

He closed the book.

Lord Denon walked down the central aisle—past the swas that
meant Life over Lies—out the doors, into Reich Hall.

vel knocked on a wooden door, waited and glanced
around, shivering in the cool air. Ponce shrugged, leaning against
the long building, searching the streets around them.

"Swear to God somebody was following us," Ponce said to himself.

"Maybe," Vel said, and he forced a smile. "Maybe it was Darden."

Ponce glared at him for a moment. "Maybe the police, smart-
ass."

Vel knocked again. "I hope so."

Muffled voices behind the door frame. Vel swallowed, taking
a step away from the entrance.

"Remember," Ponce said. "Be on your best behavior."

Vel offered him the position on the doorstep. "You want to do
this?"

A voice from inside asked, "Who is it?"

Vel said, "We're looking for Jak."

A brief silence. The door was unhooked and opened to allow a sliver of flickering brightness into the night. A round woman with a face that might have been attractive thirty years ago, stood in the doorway. She wasn't fat, just unusually large.

"Who are you?" the woman said, obviously unimpressed with what she saw.

"My name is Vel, and this is Ponce." Ponce bowed slightly. "We're looking for someone named Jak. Heard she was living here."

The woman squinted, her face contorting. "This is a support house. We don't give out the names of those in residence here."

Vel stepped closer, but the woman stood her ground.

"Who did you say you were?" she asked.

"We're not selling anything," Ponce said.

"If we could just speak with Jak," Vel said. "This won't take long."

The woman hesitated, and then she allowed them inside. It was a small, uninviting room. Several doors stood shut along the far wall, and a table had been set for five people. How many other rooms were there? The building took up almost half a block, just as some of the bars did.

"How many people do you have here?" Vel asked.

The front door closed, and the large woman glanced at Vel uncomfortably. He began a slow pace around the room, and Ponce remained by the door.

"I can't give out that information," she said.

Vel stopped. "Why? What kind of a place is this?"

"I told you. It's a support house."

"Support house," Vel repeated, advancing on her. Ponce tried to stop him, but he continued. "What does that mean? What do you do?"

She shook her head. "Who are you?"

"My name is Vel. He's Ponce. I told you that."

"I didn't ask your names. I asked who you are."

"I heard what you asked." Vel came closer to her. "I don't have to explain myself to you."

Ponce smiled artificially, stepping between them. "We don't mean to inconvenience—"

One of the doors opened, and a bulging man with a red beard entered.

"I found . . ."

He stopped, rapping his fingers against the surface of a hardbound book. The man's hands were powerful. Thick fingers capable of crushing, trained into subtlety. He looked educated, and a white scar marked his cheek below his left eye. The woman retreated from Vel, to stand beside the man.

"What's going on?" he said. He turned from Vel, to Ponce, to the woman, then back to Vel again.

The woman said, "I don't know. They're here asking about Jak."

Something passed across the man's face too fast for Vel to follow. When it was gone, the man took a broad step forward.

"What do you want with Jak?"

"A conversation."

"What's your name?"

"Vel."

Ponce extended his hand. "My name's Ponce. We don't mean to trouble you at this time of night. It is rather late."

The man ignored Ponce for the moment, still watching Vel. "How do you know Jak?"

Vel ran a hand through his hair. "Listen, I just want to talk to her, ask her a few questions."

"Oh? What kind of questions?"

Vel's jaw tightened, and he sneered darkly. "Look, I know what you think. We're not here to do anything but speak with Jak."

"Why do you want to speak with her?"

Ponce said, "We need—"

And Vel nodded, heading for the doorway behind the couple. "Then she's here."

The woman's face grew tense. "We can't give out—"

"Yes, she's here," the man snapped, stopping Vel's advance. Shadows shifted across the lines in his skin.

"Can we see her?" Vel said.

"Why?"

Ponce said, "There's a chance she might be able to help us."

"With what?"

Ponce said, "It's complicated, sir . . ." He glanced at Vel for any indication that they should explain. Vel stared at the man for a long moment.

"It won't work," Vel said at length, and to Ponce, "Jak isn't going to help us." Vel walked back to the front door.

"Before you just leave," the man said, "if you *do* need to see Jak, then there might be a chance."

The woman cleared her throat.

"Just not tonight," the man said deliberately.

The woman glided to the table, shaking her head, and the man set his book down.

"Have either of you eaten?"

Vel said, "No." And Ponce's face brightened.

"You can join us."

Vel moved closer, and Ponce sat at the table. Several wooden plates had been set with peeled fruit, speckled with black seeds.

"Grassfruit," Ponce said. "You've got to love grassfruit."

Vel sat, watching his plate.

"That's right," the man said, pulling out his own chair.

"Yes." Vel stared at his food. "My father used to harvest grass-fruit during the season."

Ponce raised a piece to his mouth and stopped, noticing that no one else was touching theirs.

"Oh?" The man straightened, folding his massive hands. "I sometimes work the fields. What's your father's name?"

Vel smiled grimly. "He's not named anything anymore. He's dead."

The man swallowed and sat slowly back in his chair. "I'm sorry."

"Yes, so am I."

The woman leaned forward and tried to meet Vel's gaze. She stared at his face, mouth creased. Vel did not look up.

"Let's pray, shall we?" the man said. He folded his hands care-fully, as if he'd practiced the act many times. Ponce set his piece down.

"Lord, we thank you for this food, and for delivering us from the hardships of those who have gone before us. We give you thanks and praise for your glory and wait in joyful hope for the return to our past."

My parents are dead, Vel thought.

"Amen."

The man's hands dropped lightly to the table.

"Amen," the woman echoed. She tore at her food with one hand, and Ponce began to eat quickly.

I should be hungry, Vel thought. When was the last time I ate a full meal? Did we eat at the festival? Vel watched the door, then turned to Ponce.

"We shouldn't have come here," Vel said, pulling himself up from the table. "I'm sorry. We'll leave."

The man stopped eating and watched him, while Ponce swallowed another bite. The woman's eyes rose as well, her mouth continuing to chew.

"Wait a second," Ponce said, and Vel nodded to him.

"You can stay, Ponce. But, there's no reason for me to be here. I don't think I'm sick, and they're both gone now."

"Vel," the man said, "when did your father die?"

And you deserve to know, Vel thought, because we know each other so well. He glared at the man.

"Today," Vel said. "He died today, along with my mom."

The couple exchanged a quick glance, and Ponce stiffened.

He said quickly, "We've cleared it—"

"I'm sorry," the woman said. "We didn't know. You should have told us."

Vel shrugged weakly. "Why? Why should I have told you?"

"Because that's what we do. We look after people who have lost their parents. We take care of you, so the police don't. If you're under twenty you can be forced into enlistment if your parents die, and if they die of the Pox—"

"I know. I don't need to be taken care of." Vel stepped to the doorway. "If you take care of all these people, where are they?"

The woman said, "Asleep."

Vel went for the door again. "I can take care of myself."

"Are the police looking for you?" the man said quietly.

Vel said, "Look. If the police found me they wouldn't just draft me into the force." A moment of silence, and Vel continued, shaking his head. "I've been doing this for long enough to know how to avoid the police."

Ponce coughed, nodding at Vel's shoeless foot. Vel followed his gaze.

"Listen for a moment," Ponce said. "Maybe we should, Vel."

"Then go ahead," Vel said. "Stay here if you want, Ponce."

"We can give you a place to rest," the woman said.

"Weren't you listening?" Vel said. "I can take care of myself."

The man took another bite of his fruit, grinning. "We can give you new shoes."

Vel frowned and folded his arms across his chest. "Two minutes ago you were ready to throw me out."

The man leaned closer, his voice dropping. "You know this isn't legal. We could be in prison for the rest of our lives for what we do."

"Then why do you do it?" Vel said.

"Can you read, Vel?"

"Yes."

"So can I," the man said. "And that isn't technically illegal, is it? It's frowned upon, unless you work for the government—but what about this?" He patted the book that he had brought earlier. "Owning books *is* against the law."

"What's your point?"

"My point is I think I have a pretty good idea of what's right and wrong. I used to be a district clerk." He scratched at his scar. "They're using the police soldiers to keep the city in check. Already, there are food rations. You both must know that. Even without that experience, it's not hard to see what will happen. What's happening now."

Ponce sighed. "Tell me about it."

"I'm not with the government anymore," the man said, looking directly at Vel, "*because* I understand it. You realize the King has the Pox, and he doesn't have an heir. When he dies, his line ends. The Executive Council needs a King to balance them, to keep any one person from having too much control over the police."

"And?" Vel said. "You're telling me I should stay here because the government is falling apart?"

"I'm explaining to you why we do what we do."

Ponce said, "I thought you gave kids a place to stay."

"We break the law."

"Congratulations," Vel said. "So do we."

The man said, "People aren't expendable. If the King dies, the Council may split. Do you know what that means?"

"No," Vel said. "But you're going to tell me aren't you?"

"It means they'll sell the food that's stored," the man said patiently. "Who do you think's going to come out with the most? It won't be you or me—it will be the government executives and the aristocracy, the people with money. And if anyone tries to stop that, what will happen? The Chief Justice, Justice Hillor, may well decide to use his authority with the police, and there will be military rule."

"And you think that by protecting kids from the police, you're fighting some kind of revolution?" Vel said.

The man shook his head. "Every child we keep from the police force is one less soldier working for the government. And someday, when they may need to choose sides, we want them to choose ours. Do you understand, Vel?"

"I understand."

"If you stay here, you can spend time with Jak."

"I don't want to spend time with *Jak* anymore." Vel took a deep breath. "I didn't come here for help."

He turned away from them, and Ponce rose.

"I guess we're leaving," Ponce said. "Thank you for the grassfruit."

"The police patrol this section of the city quite a bit," the woman said.

"I'll take my chances," Vel said.

His hand went out, and, as he touched the doorknob, there was a knock from the other side.

"Mr. Till?"

Vel froze, slowly forcing himself to back away from the door. Behind him, the large man got up. Ponce started to speak, and Mr. Till silenced him.

"Yes?" Till asked.

"This is Sergeant Kir from the garrison at the Western Garr. May I come in?"

Vel waved uselessly at the door. "Perfect."

The woman was on her feet in a swift movement, grabbing the book.

"Into the back room," she said, ushering them to one of the rear doors. As she went, she quickly collected the plates, clearing the table faster than Vel had thought possible.

"One minute, Sergeant." Till turned to Vel and forced a smile. "You don't have much of a choice now, do you?"

"When he's gone, we're gone too."

The woman finished, and she led them down a darkened corridor. It was a tight space, extending back for thirty feet, ending in a doorway. Along the cracked walls were rows of closed doors, across from one another, like hotel rooms.

The woman said, "Hurry, you can hide in an empty room."

Muffled voices behind them. Vel pulled away from the woman.

"I want to hear this," he said.

She said, "They might come back here. You shouldn't—"

"I want to hear this."

She looked at Ponce. "You can't stay in here. You have to get into one of these rooms. Doesn't he understand?"

Ponce shrugged. "Yes, I think he understands."

Vel pressed his ear to the door they'd just come through. A gruff tone. The sergeant. Till answered the policeman's questions calmly.

"Have we disturbed you, sir? I'm sorry."

"No, no trouble at all, Sergeant. What can I do for you?"

"Just you tonight? Have you already eaten?"

A pause, and the woman tugged at Vel's arm. He shrugged away from her. She slipped the book into an uneven hole in the wall.

"Vel," she hissed.

Ponce whispered, "I don't think he's moving. Vel's known to get pretty stubborn at times."

Vel glared briefly at him, and Ponce smiled for a moment, and the voices continued.

"Yes, I've just eaten," Till said. "What can I do for you, Sergeant?"

A chair being pulled away from the table. Creaking as weight tested its strength.

"Well, it's like this. We've been following a thief, name of Vel. Recently, he crippled one of my men. Moving with another kid, tall. You know this is my district, and I was wondering if maybe you'd seen them. The one named Vel also steals money from people through con acts. Cheated a few honest people last week."

"No," Till's voice was quick to answer. "I haven't seen him."

There was a pause.

"Sir," the Sergeant said, and Vel winced, "I haven't told you what he looks like yet."

The woman grabbed at Vel's arm again.

"Come on," she said.

Vel shook his head, holding his ear against the wood.

"See?" Ponce said. "Pretty stubborn."

"Well, I haven't been out tonight or today," came the prompt reply, "so I haven't seen much of anybody."

A nervous chuckle.

In his mind, Vel could see the sergeant, leaning back in his chair, and he heard the wood adjusting to the man's body. More footsteps. There were probably four of them in there.

Three police, Vel thought, along with the man, Mr. Till.

"Where's your wife, sir?"

The woman near Vel straightened. She glanced around the hall, unsure of what to do, and Ponce urged her toward the door.

"She's here. She was eating with me when you came in."

"Well, where did she run off to? Did I scare her away?"

Vel looked at her.

"There's a rear door," she said.

Vel shook his head. "They're outside too."

He could imagine the archers, posted around the street, on the rooftops, just watching the exits. Watching for a target. They would shout a few standard orders, and when he didn't stop, they'd shoot him down. They might not be there, but chances were, if a sergeant had come, they would be prepared for someone to slip out a rear entrance.

"Mr. Till, can I speak with your wife?"

Ponce lightly pushed her again, and she went to the door. Vel
grabbed her arm.

"You can't just go running out there as soon as he mentions
your name." He looked pointedly at Ponce. "Can you?"

Ponce started to answer, and then from behind the door, Mr.
Till said, "I'll have to go get her."

"Please do."

Vel heard the heavy footsteps approaching. He pushed himself
between the door and the wall, flattening his body. Ponce backed
into the nearby corner.

The door swung open. Vel turned his head, tightening muscles
as the wood pressed against his chest and stomach. He couldn't
see Mr. Till, but from the other side of the door, Vel heard his
voice.

"Oh, there you are Orula. Done with everything?"

She nodded briskly, moving into the doorway.

"Yes."

The door shut, and Vel's muscles relaxed as he resumed his
position against it. Ponce stepped beside him, breathing fast.

He whispered, "You know, Vel, this isn't the smartest thing
we've ever done."

"And what is the smartest thing we've ever done?"

From behind the door, "Good day to you, ma'am."

"Good day, Sergeant. But, it's hardly day, is it?"

"True enough. Sorry to disturb you at this time of night, but
we're looking for someone in the area, and we're wondering if
you or your husband can help us."

"I'll do what I can."

Vel heard her sit and several even footsteps stalked across the
floorboards toward him. Those legs were trained to pull tightly
and fall in exact precision. They came closer.

"I don't know," Ponce said quietly. "Maybe the con with those
women that raked in twelve hundred."

"Maybe this will be smarter than that when we look back on
it," Vel said. "We don't have the perspective yet, do we?"

"Perspective is overrated," Ponce said. "It's dumb to stand here."

The sergeant said, "The boy's name is Vel. We don't know his
last name, or anything more about him than that. He was un-

registered. He's about average height, has black hair—long, like you've probably seen kids wearing it—and he's skinny. I have a report that he was seen around this area very recently."

A pause.

"I might add," the sergeant went on, "that something of a reward has now been put on this boy."

Vel's heart stopped, and they both were quiet. He edged away from the door.

The shallow reply, "How much of a reward?" It was the man's voice, Mr. Till.

"Twenty-five crowns."

"I'm disappointed," Ponce said softly. "Should be two hundred thousand."

Vel looked at him seriously. "Don't be stupid, Ponce. That's a day's wages. Why wouldn't they turn us in? That description was about right. We are thieves."

Another pause, and Vel heard his own heartbeat. Oh, no, he thought. Is it worth running? There might not be archers, but their chances were not good.

"We're screwed," Ponce said.

Vel nodded. "Out the back."

"Archers—"

"I know," Vel said. "You have a better suggestion?"

"I wish I could help you, Sergeant," Orula said at last. "If I see the boy, I'll let you know."

Feet paced uncomfortably on the floor.

"Both of you are certain you haven't seen him, then."

"Sorry, Sergeant. We'll let you know if we run into him."

Silence, and then the rough sound of the sergeant clearing his throat. Feet approached the door, and Vel tensed.

"We'll be leaving then. If there's nothing else."

The wood creaked—the sergeant was leaning against the door. Vel's eyes grew wide, and he staggered back, down the hall.

Ponce went for one of the doors, quietly opening it, and Vel was about to follow him, but there wasn't enough time.

"Nice seeing you tonight, Sergeant."

Vel grabbed one of the doorknobs closer to him, and Ponce nodded, shutting himself in across the hall.

"If you don't mind—" The sergeant was opening the door, and Vel opened the side passage, shutting it behind him. "—I'll use the rear door."

Vel stood panting in a sea of blackness.

"Wait, Sergeant!" Mr. Till shouted.

The policeman paused.

"Yes?"

A small room, and gray shapes moved in the darkness. Behind Vel—behind the door—the sergeant and the others were talking again. Movement to Vel's left. He spun and felt the swirl as something crashed against the side of his head. Distantly, he heard the soldiers leaving, laughing as they exited through the rear entrance. Vel's arms reacted too slowly, and the darkness spun. With a single grunt, Vel staggered to the side, falling to his hands on the floor.

He blinked away the sharp pain in his head, and the same blunt object came down again. This time, Vel's hand was there to catch it. He pulled, turning his weight with the movement. His assailant spun over Vel in the blackness, crashing to the floor beside him.

Vel tossed the weapon away. Small fists struck his stomach, knocking the air from his lungs. Vel coughed and threw out his elbow, connecting with the bony flesh of someone's cheek. A quick, female cry, and a figure stumbled back, falling to the ground.

Light swept into the bedroom, and Vel stood over a young woman, Jak. She was older than him, although probably only by a handful of years, and he caught a glimpse of Mr. Till in the doorway. Jak's hair was the same, curling blond he remembered from the Watchman. Her eyes glowed blue in the light from the hall, and she wore a white robe that had slid to expose one of her legs, tanned evenly up her thigh.

"Oh," Till said simply. "You've met."

Jak straightened her robe and struggled to her bare feet. Lip swollen, left cheek bright crimson, she pulled her robe tight and frowned at Vel as if she knew that she should recognize him, but didn't. Jak dabbed at her lip, much more attractive than Vel had realized at the bar.

She said, "You want to tell me what's going on?"

Vel took a painful breath of air and propped himself against the wall. On a table by her bed was a folded, black paper with red lettering. A pass, Vel thought. It was one of the official passes issued to allow someone past the perimeter wall—Jak must have been on one of the salvaging teams.

"I take it they're gone?" Vel said.

Mr. Till nodded, glancing at Jak. "Yes. What were you doing, Vel?"

He shook his head, shuddering at the hot pain inside his skull. "Just getting beaten up a bit."

Jak brushed off her white robe, sat on the edge of her bed and picked up a club from the floor.

"Who are you?" she said, nodding to Vel. "I've seen you some-where before."

"This is Vel," Till said. "He's going to be staying with us for a while."

"I'm not staying here," Vel said, and he looked at Jak. "At the Watchman. You saw me at the Watchman."

"That's right," she said, her expression changing slightly, as if she had just deciphered something. "My name is Jak." She frowned. "I'm sorry, by the way." She grunted. "I thought you were with the police."

"You always hit policemen like that?"

"When they sneak into my room at night." She tilted her head and touched her lip.

She isn't sick, Vel thought. Just like at the Watchman—if she had the Pox, it's gone now.

"Police sneak into your room at night?"

Jak grinned, licking her lip. "No. But, if they did, that's what I would hit them with."

"So you're Jak," Vel said.

She looked at him. "And you're Vel. Congratulations. What can I do for you, Vel?"

"I've been trying to find you."

Mr. Till went down the hall, leaving them alone.

Jak crossed one leg, and her brow wrinkled. "Why?"

"You survived the Pox."

Jak paused, and then she asked, "Why didn't you say anything at the Watchman?"

"I didn't like your company."

She stared at him, and a bitter smile spread across her lips. With slender fingers, she tucked hair behind her ears. "Who told you that I survived the Pox?"

"The owner of the Watchman mentioned it."

She put her hands in her lap and looked away. "Winds told you that? Why do you think I'm here, Vel?"

Vel shook his head. "I don't know."

"My family was killed by the Pox, Vel. That's why I'm here. That's what these people do. They give us a place to stay. Homeless 'kids.' You know what happens if you report deaths of close relatives to the police?"

Vel's jaw tightened. "I know what happens."

"No, I didn't survive the Pox." She looked at him tiredly. "I never had the Pox. That was a lie."

Something inside Vel turned as she stared at him, and he stepped back into the hall. This doesn't make sense, Vel thought.

"But, you *were* sick recently—you had something, didn't you?"

She shook her head. "What are you talking about?"

I saw you, Vel thought. If it was you—it had to have been Jak. The name had been the same, and he had *seen* her. Why would she lie about this?

"You weren't sick?" Vel said.

"No. What's wrong?"

I'm going out of my mind, Vel thought, and he said, "I need to get out of here."

"Why?" Jak got up.

Vel closed his eyes and touched the door frame, pulling himself through.

"Thank you for the truth," he said.

"Is someone you know sick?"

Vel walked away, down the silent corridor. "No. Not anymore."

Ponce appeared through his own door. "Are they gone?"

"Yes," Vel said.

Behind him, Jak called. "Vel, wait."

He hesitated. She stood near the open doorway, watching him.

And she was beautiful. She was as he remembered her from the Watchman. What if I'm wrong? Vel thought. People had been trying to find a cure for the Pox—a prayer or a place to let blood that would wash the disease away—but nothing could make it go away.

"You're just going to leave?" Jak said.

"Hey," Ponce said. "You're Jak, right?"

Vel nodded. "That's right, we're leaving. Is there anything wrong with that?"

"What?" Ponce said. "I thought she—"

"She didn't survive, Ponce." Vel looked at her irritably. "She was never sick. She had something else."

Jak watched him silently. Vel lingered, then turned and walked further down the corridor. Ponce trailed behind him, waving at Jak as they left.

"It was nice meeting you."

Jak did not reply.

She is just a face, standing there in the hall, Vel thought. Just a pretty face. He opened the door and returned to the first room. The table had not changed. Ponce followed.

"This is getting more and more irrational," he said. "You realize that, Vel."

"I can't help it," Vel said. "It was a lie." He went to the door. "I should have known."

I'm not supposed to get better, Vel thought. If I have the Pox—and I do, because my father had it before he was murdered—I deserve to have it. But, I don't feel sick yet, Vel thought. I don't feel sick, but somehow I *know* it's inside me. Maybe I've earned that.

Vel stepped to the front door and touched the latch.

Ponce looked at the empty table, and they heard Orula and Mr. Till speaking from the far end of the corridor.

"What are we going to do?" Ponce asked.

"We're going to leave."

Vel walked out.

chapter 9

A cold thrill ran the length of Vel's spine, and he froze, still holding onto the doorknob with one hand. Three policemen stood talking on the other side of the street, all armed with the usual longsword. And yes, a rooftop nearby was marked by an archer. As quickly as he could, Vel ducked back into the building and shut the door. His chest rose and fell, sweat forming in his hair and along his forehead.

He leaned against the door, shutting it completely, and drew the latch. How were they going to get out of here? There were too many soldiers out there.

"They're still there," Ponce said softly. "They haven't left, have they? They didn't see you?"

Vel shook his head. "No."

"Vel?"

He shook a loose strand of hair from his eyes. Orula stood behind the table, pulling out one of the chairs. She looked down Vel's arm to the doorknob.

"There are a lot of them out there."

"I know," he said.

Vel glanced bitterly at the walls, and Ponce went to the table again.

"Why don't you eat something?" Orula said. "As long as you're here."

"I don't want to eat something," Vel said. "I want to get out of here."

Without answering, Ponce accepted another piece of grassfruit.

Mr. Till came into the room, and he nodded to Vel. "Thought

you were going to do something stupid and make a liar out of me."

Vel swallowed. "I can't stay here."

Mr. Till walked around the table, sat down, and nodded to the seat opposite him.

"Why don't you take a seat?"

Ponce said, "We're here for now."

He's right, Vel thought and reluctantly lowered himself into the chair.

"Why did you do that?" he said.

Mr. Till picked up the grassfruit from his plate and began to chew it casually.

"Do what?"

"Why did you lie to the police? Why didn't you turn me in? You don't know me."

"Exactly. We don't know you. Why don't you fill us in?"

Vel stared at him in the candlelight and pressed his fingers to the tabletop. A moment passed, and Vel's gaze did not waver.

"We're businessmen," Ponce said.

"Thieves," Vel said at last. "We're thieves."

Ponce resigned himself to silent eating. "Businessmen sounds better. Same thing."

Vel continued, "We're thieves and con men. We cheat people and take their money. The police were right. You should have turned us in for the reward."

Till glanced at his wife, then back to Vel. He chewed his food and shrugged.

"What else can you tell us?"

Vel grimaced. "You have many thieves staying here?"

"Enough."

"Maybe some people we know," Ponce said.

"You aren't worried that I'm going to steal from you?" Vel asked.

Orula leaned forward in her chair. "Vel, my husband just lied to the police and saved you from being arrested."

"I know," he said. "I don't understand why."

Till frowned, and for a moment he didn't answer.

"Vel," Till said, "why don't you eat something, and then my wife will show you to a room you can use tonight."

"I'm not going to stay here."

"Oh, I know you're not going to stay here. But you can sleep here tonight and then, after the police leave, you can go out again. The police may be out there all night."

"He's got a point," Ponce said.

Vel asked, "Why are you doing this?"

Mr. Till considered the question, then said, "I told you earlier. If you aren't among us, you're against us. You know enough to have us both thrown into prison if you were a part of the police force. It's in all of our best interests that you stay here tonight. If for no other reason than to keep us both out of prison. Fair enough?"

Vel considered the words, and he touched his forehead without thinking. Pain seared through his skull, and Vel winced, closing his eyes. White spots lingered under his eyelids.

He shook his head and the pain dropped from one side to the other, then back to the first, growing more intense. The world lurched, and the table swayed back from him. The chair he was sitting in tilted. People were shouting, and someone grabbed his arm as the floor rushed to greet him. It struck Vel roughly across his cheek. He never did anything about the wound. The beer bottle.

Orula stood over him. He couldn't hear what she was saying, and her lips moved slowly.

Vel.

Ponce beside her, reaching for water.

Blackness crept around his vision. The pain receded to the base of his neck.

And then darkness.

The world smelled of dust and candle wax. Vel's eyes fluttered open. Alone in a square room. Covers were drawn up to his chest; across the bedroom a single candle flickered, the flame bending to an invisible wind. Vel sat up, and a dull ringing echoed in the back of his skull. This room was no different than the bedroom he had been in earlier, Jak's bedroom. The bed, table and dresser were in different places—but the room itself was identical.

A mug of liquid sat on a scratched nightstand. Vel touched it weakly with one hand, raising the container to his lips. The water was room temperature—warm—but it felt good in his throat.

Voices behind the doorway. There were no windows in the room. How long had he been here? The clothes he wore were not his clothes, and, as he ran a finger along one cheek, he found hair that shouldn't have been there. Nearby, a small pile of clothing littered the floor, his scabbard and sword beside it.

"I don't really care whether he is or not; he needs to get up. We need that room. If he keeps sleeping—"

The voice was rough and male: Mr. Till.

"*If* he keeps sleeping. Listen to yourself. Not two days ago you were telling me we should adopt the boy and now all you can think of is getting rid of him."

Orula.

Vel took another drink of water.

"Keep your voice down. You want to wake everyone up?"

"I'm not going to wake that boy up until he's good and ready. He needs rest. He was wounded pretty badly."

"Don't tell me how bad his wounds were; I dressed them, remember? He had blood on his clothing that . . ."

Vel moved one hand to his forehead. A mass of tight bandages wrapped around his scalp.

"He stays here, and he sleeps here until he's fully recovered."

"We agreed that he wasn't going to stay that long. *He* doesn't want to stay that long."

Orula's voice dropped to a barely audible hiss. Vel heard the sound of her whispering, but nothing more. Till retorted with a whisper of his own; then his footsteps moved heavily away down the hall. The floor creaked with each movement.

A doorknob turned, and Vel set his mug on the table. He eased back in the bed, watching as the door opened. The hallway beyond was dimly lit, dropping a faint square of light across the floor. Orula's large form hesitated, and she shut the door behind her, stepping closer.

Vel coughed, and she jumped and looked around, startled.

"You're awake," she said.

"Yes. How long was I out?"

"Two days."

Vel sat up, his arms complaining at the work.

"Two days," he repeated.

"That's right. How do you feel?"

"Like I was beaten over the head with a beer bottle and a hunk of wood."

Orula smiled, walking to the night table. She picked up the mug and sloshed it from side to side.

"Are the police still watching?"

"No," she said. "They aren't."

"Where's Ponce?"

"Ponce is staying with us until you're recovered. He's several rooms down, but you aren't ready to leave yet."

"Why not?"

"You're still weak. You haven't eaten much in the past two days, and the wounds haven't fully healed."

His stomach growled, and Vel winced. "I'm hungry."

"I'll have someone bring you food." Orula walked casually back to the door. She turned. "And more water if you want it."

"Thanks."

Opening the door, Orula stepped out, disappearing into the corridor, and Vel was alone again. Vel wasn't wearing a shirt, just a pair of short, tight pants that belonged to someone smaller. Through the open door, a slender figure appeared, carrying a tray of food and a large mug of water. Vel opened his mouth, but couldn't think of anything to say. She approached, shutting the door behind her with one leg.

Black curls dropped onto her shoulders. The girl was watching him with the eyes he remembered from the Watchman—eyes that made the rest of her slight, attractive face a background. She was small, and as she approached, Vel wondered if somehow she had learned to control her arms and legs fully because of their size—the girl made no noise. She was dressed entirely in black, with a short wooden stick fastened at her waist.

"You," Vel said.

She smiled, setting the tray on the night table. The girl stood for a moment, examining Vel. Her gaze flicked from his face to his chest, to the bed, then back up to his face again; like a predator searching for a weakness or a blind spot.

"That mark." She pointed to a discoloration on the right side of Vel's stomach. It was a splotch, in roughly the shape of a crescent moon.

Vel followed her finger, and his eyes narrowed. "What about it?"

"Have you always had that?"

Vel pulled the covers up. "Yes. Who are you? I saw you at the Watchman."

"I know." She sat on the floor nearby. Again, when she moved, her body made no noise, as if she had rehearsed each gesture beforehand.

"What are you doing here?"

"I'm here to protect you, Vel."

"How do you know my name?"

She smiled. "I know a good deal more than your name."

"That's great—you want to tell me who you are?"

"My name is Lydia."

Vel reached for the mug of water—drank—and eyed the plate. Grassfruit. More grassfruit.

"All right, Lydia. Did you follow me here?"

"It doesn't matter how I found you."

"Yes," Vel said, "it does."

"I need you to trust me," Lydia said.

"Well, that's a real trick these days, isn't it? Tell me why I should trust you again. I think I missed that part." She watched him drink more water, then Vel asked, "Are you here alone?"

"What do you mean?"

"You don't look like you're with the police, and if you *were* I don't know why I'd still be in bed."

"I don't work for the police. My people are much older than the police."

"Historically," Vel said, smiling, and Lydia nodded. She looked about his age.

"That's right," she said. "We were established—"

"I'm not really interested in history right now, all right?"

Lydia said, "My order was founded around the time that the Frill helped to build Hope."

"And the punch line is . . . ?"

"It's not a joke, Vel. There's a lot you don't know."

"There's no such thing as the Frill," Vel said, laughing, and pain thudded in the side of his head. When Lydia didn't find it funny, he sighed. "I'm not in the mood for this, sorry. The Frill aren't real."

"You're half right."

"What—I'm only partly in the mood for this?"

Lydia said, "The Frill aren't real *anymore.* They're extinct now, but when Hope was founded five hundred years ago, they were very much alive."

"Just like unicorns and the Nara, right?"

"Why did you mention the Nara?"

"Because they don't exist."

"The Nara aren't just a story to scare children," she said. "The Nara *did* exist at one time, just as the Frill did. They were very different, but that didn't make them any less real."

"Except that they're not."

"The Nara may still be real, Vel."

"Listen, I'm having a hard time believing you're real." Vel waved one hand at her. "When I wake up, this is all going to go away, right?"

"Vel, my order is outside the law because we were not established by the law. That's why I don't work for the police."

"So you're a terrorist."

"I didn't say that," Lydia said calmly. "We work against the police when it is in our interests to work against them."

"Like now?"

"Yes," she said, "like now."

"Like the Frill told you to."

"The Frill did more for the stability of Hope than most people alive today," Lydia said.

"The Frill are demons that appear in stories to grant wishes," Vel said, and he ignored the sudden tension in his chest. "They're like genies, they're not real. And if they were, they wouldn't be good." He paused. "I can't believe I'm having this conversation."

"I know the stories," Lydia said. "But the Frill were very real at one time. The ruins are theirs." She said seriously, "You're in a lot of danger now, Vel. There are powerful people who would like to see you thrown into prison. Or worse."

"Yes." Vel sat back in his bed. "I'm well aware of that."

"You're more important than you realize," she said. "It isn't what you think. What do you know about your parents?"

Something flared in the back of Vel's mind, and he pushed the emotion away. "What do *you* know about my parents?"

"I know that they weren't your parents."

Vel tensed. "Get out of here."

She watched him. "Vel, you don't understand. You're in the middle of something you can't even see yet. We need time to talk."

"I'm very tired." Vel picked up his mug again and took another drink. "I don't want to do this now."

"I'll be back later, then," she said, standing. "But this cannot wait long. You're involved whether you want to be or not."

"Involved in what?" he asked.

"We'll talk later, Vel."

Lydia hesitated before leaving. Vel picked up the grassfruit and began to chew on it. Yes, Vel thought, I know as much about the Frill as anyone does. They're just waiting to kill anyone who doesn't stay within the city boundaries—to harass kids who won't go to bed when they're supposed to, although Vel's parents had never spoken of them.

Vel had seen a children's book once on the black market, while working a con. And there had been a crude illustration of a creature with a metal face and candle-eyes; that was what came to mind when Vel thought of the Frill. In the book, the demon-Frill had protected the ruins. Vel thought, the Frill and the government, and I'm in the middle of something—what?

He ate more, letting the bitter fruit linger on his tongue. The government consisted of the Executive Council, the Council's bureaucracy, and the police soldiers. Thirty members on the Council, one from each of Hope's thirty districts. And the King, who was there for life and couldn't vote. The elections happened every six or eight years—Vel wasn't sure which—and that Council voted and debated legislation. Most of which no one outside the government ever heard about until it became law. They needed a majority of sixteen to pass a measure, but the King could always veto—that was his power. To overrule that veto, they needed a vote of twenty-five.

Vel closed his eyes and started to sleep.

A knock on the door.

For God's sake, Vel thought.

"Who's there?"

"Jak."

Vel's heart quickened. An image of that girl flashed through his mind.

"Come in."

She entered, closing the door behind her. Jak looked more rested than she had when he'd seen her last. She was still wearing the same white robe she had before—and she looked even more beautiful. I wasn't paying attention earlier, Vel told himself, and he smiled.

"I wanted to see how you were doing," Jak said.

"I've been better."

She walked forward. "You mind if I sit down?"

"Go ahead."

She lowered herself onto the foot of his bed, and Vel finished a bite of the fruit. Definitely not as alert as I should have been the last time, Vel thought, as he noticed the way the robe formed over her body.

A moment passed, and Vel felt one of her hands tracing the outline of his calf through the sheet.

"So," Vel said, setting the mug down again.

"So. I just wanted to say that I'm sorry for hitting you like that. If I'd known . . ."

"It's all right."

She watched him, her face growing more sincere. "It's hard being here alone, without really knowing anyone."

"You know me."

"Yes," she said, and her embarrassed grin sent blood into Vel's cheeks. "It's just . . ."

"What?"

"Do you know how lonely I get?"

She edged closer to him, her hand still tracing his calf.

"I'm sorry," Vel said again.

"It just hurts sometimes. You know?"

He nodded. His mother stood in the corner, watching him quietly with sunken eyes.

"Yes."

Only shadows.

His mother was never there.

Jak leaned down to him, and he felt her lips against his bare skin. Against his chest. She was kissing his chest. Vel couldn't move, and he stared at her.

"No." He pulled away. "No."

Vel closed his eyes, running one shaking palm across his cheek.

"What's wrong?"

"It's not right. I don't know you. I'm sorry, I can't."

"Vel, sometimes you need to forget all of that."

He felt her hand against his shoulder. Soft fingers rubbing his skin. Vel's jaw tightened, and he thought of the bonfire, of carrying his parents' bodies—I'm responsible, he thought.

"No," he said again. "It isn't your fault, it's me."

Jak eased away, standing beside the bed.

"It's all right," she said. "Will you eat breakfast with me tomorrow?"

Vel took a full breath of air. The room wheezed with him.

"Sure."

Vel closed his eyes, listening to her go, and then the click as the door shut again, leaving him alone.

He rolled over, swallowing roughly. Who did she think she was, walking in on him like that? God, what was he doing here? Alone in a bed with people all around him who barely knew his name. To hell with all of them. A distant song.

The room faded.

And Vel was alone inside his head.

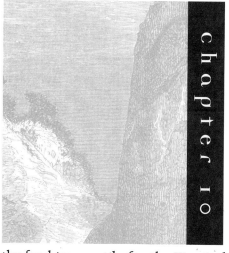

chapter 10

"Has the King spoken to Blakes?"

"The King doesn't speak, except to damn me to hell. And that should be your department, shouldn't it, Denon?"

"Justice, you're moving too quickly. You can't control this without the King. If any of the Executive Council die, you'll be blamed, and we're not ready yet. Stop pushing the food issue until *after* the King is dead."

"No. There's a chance it may pass now—that will give us an advantage. We'll have leverage over their money. If we can start selling the food before the King dies, everyone with any money will become an ally when he's dead."

"That won't stop the rest from revolting, if ordinary people see what's happening—they feel it every time they walk outside and the air isn't as warm as it should be. The spirit of the heretic Laum is not dead. And they're organizing."

"I think you give them too much credit."

"You're rushing because of the King."

"And why shouldn't I? Why should the masses need to know anything before we've prepared for their response?"

"When the King dies, they'll know. You can't control that."

"Yes, but I'll have the boy before the King is dead."

"You know where he is? After all of this time, you suddenly think you can find him?"

"I know his name is Vel. Yes, that's being taken care of. It's not an issue."

"And if Munil finds him first?"

"He won't. Then with the boy—with the relics—the Executive Council will break apart. That's what's crucial. I need your support in this; I must have the Church behind me."

"Our artifacts aren't enough, you want God on your side?"

"It's what we agreed. Yes."

"If Blakes understands what you're doing—and he will—he won't let it happen. The boy, Vel, is our only link with Blakes. That's more important than I think you realize."

"I'm not a child. Blakes is the process, not the outcome. Don't you think I've considered that? He won't be destroyed."

"But if the boy is ill, we'll lose Blakes as well. Don't you understand that? There aren't any others who can speak with him. And you can't get rid of the Council, because the King is part of that."

"I just want to know that I'll have your support, Denon. I've taken care of the rest."

"Listen to me. God's will overcomes the plotting of men, unless they work *within* His plan. You're moving too quickly; you haven't even considered that the Frill might intervene, have you?"

"Will I have your support?"

"All of the city will die, and we'll die along with it, if you don't move more slowly."

"Denon . . . ?"

"Of course you have my support. Did you hear what I said?"

"I heard. You used to push me to move faster, now you're afraid we might actually succeed. I understand. You're old and tired, and you've been inside this Church too long. And you're wrong. I've already won."

vel's arms trembled at his sides with the flow of adrenaline. Blue stone walls formed a square around him, rising into a dome. There were scratches on the walls, and Vel turned instinctively to the doorway behind him—to the crimson slits. A slight, weak figure stood propped in the blackness of the doorway, red slits where eyes should have been. Vel had been here before. He had seen this blue light somewhere—he had been in this room.

Yes, boy, we remember you.

Vel backed away, his fingers trembling as he reached for his sword. People were watching him through the walls, something was readying an attack.

"What's going on?" he said.

The figure made a strangled, wet sound, as if it was suffocating. *We remember you.*

His sword handle was warm and slippery to the touch. Vel recoiled, shuddering as he let the weapon drop. It wasn't his sword. Vel could no longer move, and the room faded away behind the quivering form on the floor in front of him. That wasn't his sword. A pale, tiny body flexed chubby fingers, and one eye stared at him.

"No," he said.

In front of him was half of a baby's body, split down the center of its head, chest and torso. One leg, one arm, one eye, one nostril; the thing stared at Vel, moving its pink lips into a smile. The grooves in his palms were stained with blood—he'd grabbed its leg.

We are the same.

"No," Vel said, and the figure hobbled closer from the doorway, beyond the half-baby.

Hate us, and you hate yourself. We will destroy you.

Vel's voice was weak, and he tried to shield his eyes from the thing on the floor. It still moved and waved its fingers at him.

"Stop."

Vel staggered, his feet slipping on the stone, and he turned away from the creature. Fingers grabbed at his elbow.

"Let go of me."

We are the same, boy.

Vel spun, teeth flashing as his fists lashed out.

The same.

"Vel!" Lydia's voice. "Vel, what's wrong?"

"Get away from me," he said.

Vel's muscles trembled under his skin. His arms were shaking, and his left hand was sore, strained. He gripped the bed sheets, his knuckles whitening. He was back in the bedroom, still at Turn Tables.

Lydia stepped back. "Vel, I heard you screaming."

"It's okay," he said. "God . . ." The images began to fade, and he tried to remember what he had seen. "It's all right."

Lydia eased closer to the door. Mr. Till yelled from the hallway beyond, "Who's shouting? What's going on?"

She glanced into the hall, still dressed entirely in black, still wearing that little stick at her side. Lydia looked ready to bolt into the hall, and she frowned at Vel, as if considering whether to bring him along.

"You were dreaming?" she asked.

He nodded. "I don't know. I think so."

Vel rose from the bed. Sweat dripped into his eyes. His hair clung tightly to his forehead and cheeks.

Footsteps approaching in the hall outside, and Lydia clicked open the door. "We'll speak later."

"I'm going to leave, Lydia. I can't stay here."

"Wait until we've spoken," she said quickly, and before he could respond, she was gone. Vel stared at the empty space she'd left, and at the lines in the wood around the open doorway. I have to get out of here, he thought. I have been in this room three days now. Mr. Till stepped into view.

"Good morning, Vel."

Vel wiped sweat from his face, and his muscles began to relax. "Good morning."

"Were you shouting?"

Vel nodded. He walked back to the edge of his bed and sat. "Yes."

Till thought about it—clearly he hadn't expected Vel to admit to the noise. "I think if your wound is nearly healed, you might be able to be on your way."

Vel watched him blankly, then nodded, sorting through the pile of clothing nearby.

Vel said, "I don't want to inconvenience you any more than I already have."

Till cleared the doorway for him. "Your friend Ponce left last night. He wanted to speak with you, but you were asleep, and you wouldn't wake. Told us to tell you that when you're healthy again, he's at his house."

"Thank you," Vel said.

"They stopped posting police around our building the night Ponce left. It should be safe now."

Vel picked up his old shirt and put it on. He yawned, rolled his neck, and started for the door. Till remained motionless.

"Thank you," Vel said again.

Till touched his red beard and nodded simply at the dismissal. Vel watched until Till turned and moved away, down the corridor. How many days have I been in this room? Vel wondered.

Something caught his eye. Something he hadn't seen in the darkness. No telling what time it was now—it might have been the middle of the night—but there was enough light from the hall to see. A mirror hung nearby, a lone ornament on a bare wall.

Vel's parents hadn't owned a mirror, and now he collected his belt and sword from the floor, as his reflection frowned back at him. His father . . .

Rhythmically clicking the blade in its sheath with one hand, Vel tried not to think of his father's weapon. The sword had been his dad's. Eleventh birthday present, and Vel vaguely remembered almost chopping off one of his fingers when he had played with it the next morning. Not a fake, he thought, not like some swords I've sold, made of wood dipped in hot metal. He looked from the mirror to the sword, and the sliver of reflection there. His mother had tried to convince Vel's father to take it from him, saying Vel wasn't old enough . . .

Ignoring the tired face in the mirror, Vel checked to be certain that he wasn't leaving anything behind. The pouch of coins was still in his pocket, and Vel froze, staring at his reflection. Discolored bandages, brown—perhaps from overuse or blood—wrapped his forehead, and Vel peeled them away. A scar.

It ran along the top of his forehead, just below his hairline. Vel touched it gingerly with one finger and felt a slight thrill of pain.

"You're up."

Looking in the mirror before he turned, Vel saw Jak in the doorway, arms crossed across her chest. "You knocked earlier."

"Well, this time we know each other." She wore a brown jacket and a simple shortsword, her lips painted bright red. "You look better than you did the other day."

"Thanks."

"That's not saying much."

He smirked.

"You hungry?" Jak said.

"I guess."

"You guess? You're either hungry or you're not hungry. You promised me breakfast, remember?"

"I don't remember promising you anything," Vel said, and he gave the room a final appraisal, deciding that the sudden thought of food was more important than anything he might leave behind.

"Has anyone told you what's happening outside?"

"What's happening outside?"

"It's colder. The summer festival has been canceled."

He nodded to the doorway. "I've decided I'm hungry. What are we going to eat?"

"Something edible," she said.

Jak led Vel out of his room and into the same hallway he could remember hiding in days ago. Had it really been that long?

"How long was I in there?"

"Three nights."

Dust churned in the light as they moved down the passage.

"The eastern bank is picking up more bodies. Pox victims, and they say it's moved west."

Jak opened a door at the far end of the hall, and they were on the street. Dry scents and frigid air rushed into Vel. He shivered, following her out. Hair stood across Vel's scalp, and his sweat began to freeze. The houses huddled together, leaning haphazardly onto one another for support, red X's painted along every door of the block on their left.

A team of three men with a wooden cart were collecting trash from the street, their hands covered by thick black gloves. Still, it was obvious that the street cleaners had slackened their usual routines. Clusters of solid waste accumulated on both sides of the road. The people who hurried past were wrapped in loose, layered clothing, and they ignored the filth, entirely silent. Most passed without making eye contact.

"It's good to get out of there," Vel said, and he tried to make sense of what was happening. People were normally more friendly, smiling, even if they didn't know one another.

"I'd imagine."

"Something's wrong," Vel said.

Jak nodded, not slowing her pace, and she led him further from the orphan house. Vel found himself unconsciously probing the rooftops and back alleys for any sign of the gray and blue uniforms.

"It's the weather," she said.

"Where are we going?"

"Breakfast."

This isn't just the weather, Vel thought. These people are frightened—and a middle-aged woman ran into his shoulder hard.

Vel said, "I'm—" But she was already gone.

Jak moved even faster, and Vel started a slow jog to keep up.

"I'm not *that* hungry," Vel said.

"You look like you need the exercise." Jak nodded to a nearby alley that looked as if it had been recently cleaned. "There's a good place in there. They actually serve more than grassfruit."

Vel forced a smile. "How long has it been this cold?"

She started down the alley. "I don't know. A few days."

Patches of brown grass clung to the dirt path. A black insect scuttled away, and Vel followed Jak deeper into the alleyway, toward a single door on the right. On both sides, the houses rose two and three stories, the wood a grained version of the color his bandage had been.

Vel smelled something burning, and he hoped that the restaurant had a hearth. Chimneys were rare and almost always made of stone—but it wasn't unheard of for places like restaurants to have them specially installed with government permission. But no, Vel decided, what he smelled was too far away, and it wasn't food. He thought of his parents.

They reached the side entrance, and Jak rapped against it lightly.

Footsteps. Vel turned.

Police. Two approached from the far end of the alley. Each held a long sword, already drawn.

"Oh, no, Jak—"

Vel spun in time to see the nearby door open, and three more police emerged, shutting it behind them. Jak smiled at Vel, drawing her own sword. Two soldiers walked around her, one on either side, and the third fell back, leveling a crossbow at Vel's chest. Standard entrapment, Vel thought, two with Jak, two behind, and the crossbow for insurance. Already loaded.

Vel shivered, stepped away from Jak. "What's going on?"

"I'm sorry," she said, "but I'm going to have to ask you to drop your sword."

No way out of here, Vel thought, and he let his right hand slide closer to his sword handle. Both sides cut off, no other doors. Grass raked Vel's knees, and he took several more faltering steps away from her. The two nearest police closed on him.

Vel said, "Why did I come with you?"

She held up her sword, pointing the blade to him.

"You were hungry." She shook her head. "You were going to eat with me. Don't make me kill you, Vel. The other night I was very careful not to damage you. I can't promise that will happen again."

"No," Vel said. "You couldn't have planned this." And still he edged away. They were pushing Vel closer to the two soldiers behind him. "You *wanted* me to find you at Turn Tables? What about the Watchman—that wasn't a setup."

She shrugged. "That's not important."

The alley walls shot straight up two stories, the carefully aligned planks of wood stopping only for tiny square windows, all closed. No good. They could stop him before he made any kind of progress. An arrow in his leg, and Vel would be back down without another chance.

"Drop your sword Vel. Don't make me ask you again."

The front soldiers were ready to strike, but still Vel had not drawn his weapon. *Five* police, he thought, and Jak. Frustration began to form a knot in Vel's muscles, waiting to be released. There's no way out, he thought. What can I do? Vel tightened his fingers on his sword, the soldiers paused, and Jak started to say something—but Vel cut her off.

He said, "Why didn't you just get me while I was asleep? Why didn't you catch me then?"

"Take off the belt and drop your sword."

"You had the Pox, didn't you? I know you did."

"Vel—"

"Tell me how you got rid of it."

Jak said, "You aren't in any position to—"

There was a loud snap from somewhere overhead. The policeman with the crossbow swung his arm up as a shaft bit into him violently, piercing his scalp. The man toppled, his body shuddering under the impact.

Vel squinted in the dull light, spotting a lone silhouette on one of the overlooking rooftops. Adrenaline ran through him. The person held two instruments, one in each hand. A second snap, and another deadly shaft lanced down—another policeman near Jak dropped to the dirt, grabbing at the end of a black arrow in his chest. The two policemen behind Vel charged, and Jak trotted to the loaded crossbow on the ground.

The figure overhead stepped back from the building's edge, vanishing from view. Reloading.

Vel drew his sword as the nearest policeman attacked. The world slowed, heat pounding through Vel's veins as the soldier sliced low with his longsword. Vel parried down, hopping back. There was a clank of metal, and Vel nearly lost his grip on the sword. The policeman pressed his advantage. Vel was pushed back toward the men behind him. Twisting thrust and counterthrust, and Vel stumbled, knocked off balance.

He pulled his own blade up too slowly to stop a hit, instead deflecting it enough that the policeman slashed Vel's shirt lightly—raking away a layer of skin—rather than plunging his sword deeply between Vel's ribs. With the sudden rush of pain, Vel's eyes teared, and he remembered fighting the drunken soldiers with Ponce and Darden. This time, the cops weren't drunk— this time, Vel thought, I don't have a chance.

Vel pivoted, dodging another attack.

Behind the policeman, Jak fired up at the figure on the rooftop. The shadow ducked, narrowly missed by the incoming shaft. Once more, he leaned over the side and aimed his weapons into the alley.

Vel ducked another thrust, and the policeman kicked his kneecap hard. Throwing both arms reflexively out to keep his balance,

Vel was not ready for the policeman's sword—stabbing directly toward the center of his throat. No time to stop the attack. Vel saw the weapon—imagined he could *hear* it—but his muscles would not react in time.

The point lanced closer—and with a sound like wood splitting, an arrow struck the policeman at the base of the neck. The policeman's blade shifted, spinning uselessly into the air, inches from Vel's throat. The policeman spasmed under the sudden impact, eyes wide, as if more surprised than hurt. Vel watched him spit blood as he tossed forward, landing in the grass.

Vel's palms were slick with sweat, his eyes wide. His heart resonated violently in his ears, and he thought, I am going to die. There are too many of them. I am going to die here. One of the two soldiers behind him surged forward. Vel raised his weapon—again too slowly. The distant snap, and an arrow cracked the center of the man's forehead, the end of the shaft sinking fully into the policeman's skull, knocking him off his feet. Carried by his own momentum, the cop crashed onto his side and stopped moving.

The last policeman froze, several feet behind his downed companion. Cheeks drained of color, the cop shook his head, watching the nearby rooftop. Vel followed the man's gaze, and Jak did the same. A lone figure, dressed entirely in black, came over the top of the building, crouching for a heartbeat on the ledge of the roof.

Jak looked at Vel, noticing the bodies around him. "For God's sake . . ."

Behind Vel, the last policeman ran, bolting from the alley. The cop was running away, Vel thought. The bastard was actually retreating.

Overhead, the figure jumped, dropping in a dark blur to hit the alley floor and gracefully somersault into a stance between Vel and Jak. Black hair fluttered in the air, and it took a moment for Vel to register what had just happened.

Jak said, "Who are you supposed to be?"

"Lydia," Vel said, and a twinge of heat flushed his cheeks.

Lydia removed a small wooden stick from her waist. With a faint murmur—like the sound of someone drawing in a deep breath—it elongated and became a staff four feet long. The weapon almost looked too ridiculous for Lydia to use; she was just over five feet tall. Lydia twirled the weapon casually with both hands—the movement as fluid as if she were stretching an extension of her arms.

"Leave now, or I'll kill you," Lydia said.

Jak swallowed, moving her sword back and forth. "I don't get it. You're his guardian bitch?"

"That's right."

"You know what happens if I don't bring in that runt?"

"You're not taking him," Lydia said. "Now walk away."

Vel's chest had begun to burn where the first cop hit him, his shirt ripped cleanly from one end to the other, stained crimson around the edges. He saw patches of blood through the hole.

Lydia said, "I'm leaving, and I'm taking the kid with me. Do you understand?"

Jak shook her head. "Why should I let you go? Firing a cross-bow from the roof doesn't prove anything—anyone can do that."

"No. *Anyone* can't."

"You're enjoying this, aren't you, Vel?" Jak said, and she glared at both of them. "Us fighting over you. Must be pretty damn important."

Lydia said, "Come on, Vel."

They started to leave the alley when Lydia stopped. Jak was leaning over one of the bodies, quickly working with a crossbow. She raised the loaded weapon, and Lydia planted her legs, her staff leveled horizontally across her chest.

"Get back," she said to Vel.

Vel went to one of the walls, and Jak smiled, carefully aiming the crossbow at Lydia's torso.

"You think you can dodge arrows?" Jak said.

Lydia waited, strangely calm. "Yes."

The snap sounded mechanically.

A quick flash of movement as Lydia spun her staff up—the sound of wood meeting wood and a splintering as the arrow spi-raled into a nearby wall. Lydia lowered her staff once more. The crossbow dropped from Jak's fingers.

"All right, Vel," Lydia said slowly, her gaze trained on Jak, "we're going."

chapter 11

"You have one minute."

"Listen to what I'm telling you. The kid wasn't alone. That bitch shot down four of your policemen."

"Just one person. You should have been able to handle it. That was your job."

"Well, apparently you ran into the runt earlier, didn't you? At the bar. Why didn't you arrest him then?"

"You will not question me. I want an explanation for your failure. I recruited you to do a job and you failed."

"Didn't realize this was a trial."

"I was told that you took kindly to the boy on several occasions. Why?"

"I wanted him to trust me and follow me out of the place. What do you think? Sure, the guy's a hell of a lot cuter than you are, but don't think I'd stoop to that."

"Why didn't you apprehend him earlier? I made the urgency of this mission fairly clear, didn't I?"

"Why didn't you arrest him at the bar?"

"Jak, I have very little patience—I think you know that."

"All right, 'Your Honor.' I didn't want to worry about Mr. Till or any of the others. I set the trap, and I waited for him to walk into it. And he did. I had the police stationed in that alley a week ago. He would have been ours if that girl hadn't helped him."

"That girl doesn't concern me. Where is he now?"

"I don't know."

"I shouldn't have trusted you with this. And you should have communicated with us. We weren't even sure he was staying with the Tills."

"Next time, I'll let you know. You give me a few more men and

I'll track the kid down again. I'll catch him now that I know what to watch for."

"No. This is as much my fault as it is yours. I should never have trusted you with something this important."

"Hillor, don't give me that. You know damn well I almost had him. I ran the cure back for you, and I can get this boy."

"The boy may well be more important than the cure. Besides, you had personal interests in the cure, didn't you? No, I think this has gone far enough."

"What the hell does that mean? What are you going to do? Arrest me?"

"That is exactly what I am going to do."

"What?"

"Jak, you're under arrest—you'll be placed in the Southern Garr."

"No, you can't just lock me up. Who do you think you are?"

"You know who I am."

"You ever read Blakes, Justice?"

"Jak, this is—"

"Blakes's *Rebirth.* Chapter seventeen, second paragraph—"

"Enough. Take her away."

Lɣdia slammed the door. She drew the lock into place and turned to Vel, face dark in the flickering light. Ponce stood beside him, looking exhausted. Vel had insisted that Ponce accompany them, refusing to follow Lydia without speaking with Ponce first.

"You can both take a seat," she said.

As Lydia made her way around the small room, Vel rolled his jaw and let his eyes adjust to the dim candlelight. One by one she drew the three windows shut, sealing off the outside world. It was midday, but as the last window fell into place, Vel was once more inside a room where time had no meaning, where days could pass without passing. He wanted to leave, to go outside. Ponce said, "I still don't follow this whole protection thing. Why are you so concerned about Vel? Yes, he's great, but—"

"Sit down," Lydia said, facing him. Vel did not move.

Ponce said quietly, "I guess that can wait."

Lydia shrugged. "Fine. Stand."

She went to a side door and said, "Wait here."

The door opened into blackness, and Lydia was gone. Light traced shadows across the room—slivers of gray light slicing through the uneven window boards. The place smelled of sweat, and of people, as if it had recently been very crowded.

"Do you have any idea what's going on?" Ponce asked.

Vel said, "I told you what I know. She claims that she's part of some kind of underground organization that works against the government."

"Like the Tills."

"I don't know."

"Did she mention *why* she works against the government?" Ponce asked.

"No, not exactly."

"But she really did stop an arrow?"

Vel nodded, beginning to wander around the tiny room. It was modestly furnished with a pair of matching purple chairs, a circular table, several paintings, and a small bookshelf. It resembled Vel's house—the books reminded him of his parents. Everywhere I go people are stocking illegal texts, Vel thought. He had bandaged his wound and changed shirts at Ponce's house.

Ponce said, "So, she's sexy *and* she has superhuman reflexes. What more do you need?"

Vel studied the rows of books. Several treatises on government, and three volumes by Blakes. He had only heard of one of them, the *Rebirth*. The others, *Urizen's Return* and *A History of the Twilight*, Vel had never seen before. *Urizen* was as thick as the *Rebirth*, while *Twilight* was thin—perhaps less than a hundred pages long.

He picked up *A History of the Twilight* and said, "She also told me that my parents weren't my real parents."

"I think sometimes people are just trying to be confusing," Ponce said.

Vel opened the book to a section near the beginning.

It follows that science is the expression of a collective weakness; that the strong and the pure are subjected to "modern" blasphemy.

Lydia returned. "Be careful. There are only two other copies of that book in existence."

Vel stopped reading. "What is it?"

"Blakes's memoirs." She took the book from him, returned it to the shelf beside *Urizen*, and sat in one of the two chairs. Lydia's staff had once more become a small stick, fastened at her waist. As far as Vel knew, Blakes was the founder of Hope, a saint who had written the Church scriptures—inspired by God. He had also been the first King of Hope, but Vel had never heard anything about him writing his memoirs.

"Please sit down," Lydia said.

"How did you get one of the copies of Blakes's memoirs?"

"Sit," she said.

They finally did as they were told. Vel sat in the remaining chair, and Ponce sat cross-legged on the floor.

"It's been in my family for years. It's not the original—mine's a copy that my great-grandfather made. And he might not have even had the original."

"How do you know it's not a fake?" Ponce said.

Lydia glanced at the bookshelf. "It's real." And to Vel, "We may not have a lot of time, so I'll get started."

She wasn't looking at him. Lydia was staring straight ahead in the dimness. Outside, Vel heard people talking as they passed.

Lydia said, "Jak nearly had you arrested. My guess is she'd been trailing you for some time and set up that actual encounter a while ago. She wasn't in uniform, but it was fairly obvious that Jak was on the police payroll."

"No," Ponce said. "That doesn't make sense. *We* went to the Watchman looking for her, not the other way around."

"I know that," Lydia said, and she spoke to Vel. "Who told you to look for Jak?"

"No one told me to," he said. "I saw her with the Pox, and I kind of overheard that she had survived and was at the Watchman."

Lydia took a slow breath, considering that. "Then you were meant to overhear it." Vel started to object, and Lydia said, "Who told you to go to the house where Jak was staying? To Turn Tables, who gave you the address?"

"The owner of the Watchman told us about Turn Tables," Vel said. "We followed his directions."

"And you knew him well . . . ?"

Vel swallowed uncomfortably. "You have a point. I guess it's possible that was setup. But she was sick—we saw her." He looked at Ponce for support.

Ponce said, "Vel's right. We saw a girl who looked like Jak, who was sick."

"She didn't *look like* Jak, she was Jak. Come on, Ponce, we were both there—we both saw her. She had the Pox."

"Regardless," Lydia said. "Jak had it planned some time ago. She waited and played you, arranging that ambush in the alley. The Pox might even have been setup."

Vel shifted in the chair. "I know she was sick."

Lydia's face was dark and changing with the candle. She was really quite attractive. "But did it have to be the Pox? The symptoms are common, Vel."

"That's all I meant," Ponce said. "Didn't have to be the Pox. Could have been something that isn't fatal."

I've been wanting to believe that there's a cure, Vel thought, because I'm sick. Because my throat is starting to hurt—I don't feel normal. My joints ache, but I could be imagining this, couldn't I? Convincing myself that I'm sick.

Vel asked, "So Jak set that up just to catch me?"

Lydia nodded. "I think so, yes."

"Why?" Vel said.

Lydia thought for a moment, and then she said, "Hope was founded five hundred years ago, you both know that?" They indicated that they did. "It was settled by a group of people from another planet."

"There aren't any other planets," Ponce said.

"There are," Lydia said. "And people were living on one of them before they came here. God didn't just create the people on Hera five hundred years ago, it doesn't work that way."

"So, where did they come from?" Vel asked.

"There are references in Blakes to huge expanses of water and more people than can be counted on this other, first world. It was very different than Hera. They had thousands of cities, some much larger than Hope."

"What was the planet called?" Vel asked, and Ponce listened skeptically, but said nothing.

"I don't know," Lydia said. "It had many names. Merica-Urope. Eichland."

Ponce said, "How do you know any of this? Why haven't I heard this before now?"

"We—my order—knows things that are generally kept from the public by the Church and the government. The soldiers would send me to prison if they found these books—why do you think that is?"

"It's what they do," Ponce said.

Lydia nodded patiently. "But *why* do they do it?"

Where's Darden when you need him? Vel thought. "They do it," Vel said, "because books are supposed to contain lies against the laws and the Church. Lies lead to prison and damnation. *Life over Lies.*"

"Do you believe that?" Lydia asked.

Vel thought about it—he had never seriously questioned the government, always worrying more about taking its money when he could. The philosophy behind the system had never struck him as particularly important.

"I don't know," he said.

"Why do you think so little is known about the origins of Hope? And what is known is a collection of nonsensical scriptural accounts—why is that?"

"Doesn't make sense," Vel said. "Why would they do that? Why would they destroy it or hide it from us?"

But he thought, What if she's right? The official Church teaching is that God blessed Hera and created people to live in Hope under the government of His prophet, Blakes. Vel had never seen anything to prove that a God existed in the first place, much less one who cared about Hope.

"So, if the Church is wrong," Vel said. "What really happened—people dropped out of the sky on a meteor?"

"Something like that," she said, and Lydia told them about a group expelled from Merica-Urope, from Eichland, to Hera. She didn't know why they were banished, as Blakes's descriptions never explicitly said. She knew only that according to Blakes, Merica-Urope, though he never called the planet by name, had been infested with sin and had been condemned by God—in his own words, Blakes had been the champion of the Lord over their wickedness.

And so Blakes had landed on Hera and founded the city of Hope, destroying what he called his people's sinful toys, using only what he needed. Lydia explained that these original settlers had probably possessed a level of technology beyond what existed in Hope now, and Blakes had rejected most of this as the work of the weak—the slaves, as he called them—influenced by Satan, to control the strong.

Blakes established the city, convinced that if the old technology were used regularly, Hope would destroy itself. Lydia said that Blakes created the government originally as a dictatorship—giving himself supreme power. He made his position hereditary, intending that all of the future rulers of Hope would be his descendants. Over the past five hundred years, the King—Blakes's position—gradually lost power with the evolution of the Executive Council, so that today the King had a very limited control over the government, so that in terms of legislation, the King could do little more than veto.

Ponce asked, "So why did Blakes become a dictator?"

Lydia explained that there were references in Blakes's writings to him ruling similarly on Merica-Urope, before being banished to Hera. Originally, though, Blakes claims he took power to fight the Frill.

I knew this was coming, Vel thought.

Lydia said, "The Frill are mentioned vaguely by Blakes numerous times as vengeful demons. Apparently they helped to build some of the city before war started."

"The Frill aren't real," Ponce said. "They're make-believe."

Lydia continued, "There was a falling out between the humans and the Frill. Blakes never goes into the specifics of what happened, we only know that the Frill started to fight with the people, and the Frill were obliterated. That's why no one believes in them anymore; they shouldn't. The Frill have been extinct for over four hundred years. Blakes's work survives because he was in control and he won the war. He didn't want to die."

Lydia looked at Vel carefully. "Why *did* you go looking for Jak?"

Vel stiffened, as if she had suddenly slapped him across the cheek. "What difference does that make?"

"It had to do with your parents, didn't it?"

"It had to do with the Pox," Vel said quietly.

"Because your father had it before he died."

Muscles underneath his skin tightened. Tendons snapped against bone, and blood rushed into his arms. Vel's hands began to shake. "How did you know about that?"

"You think that's easy to handle?" Ponce asked her sharply.

Lydia ignored Ponce. "Calm down, Vel. I saw you the other night at the bar, remember? I saw you earlier, taking that policeman's money before the festival. Can't say I really blame you. But it *is* dangerous to hit a cop like that in broad daylight."

Vel scratched at the arms of the chair. "Who are you?" He glared at her. "Tell me why I should believe anything you've said—you haven't told me anything about *you*. It's always Blakes and the Frill, how important I am. Never *why*; you haven't said why any of this matters or what the hell is going on."

"Yes, that seems kind of important," Ponce said.

She thought for a moment and then said, "There's legislation in the Executive Council that's been around for a decade or longer. It hasn't been passed—even though it's gotten a majority several times—because the King has always vetoed it."

Vel said, "You going to tell me what it is?"

Lydia said, "Basically, it stops rationing. If it passes, all the food supplies in the granaries will be *sold*."

Ponce frowned. "That would mean that—"

"Yes," Lydia said, still staring at Vel. "It means that if it passes, the aristocracy and the members of the government and Church will own *all* of the city's food, enforceable by the police. Recently, the measure has gotten twenty-three votes in favor, seven opposed, and the King has vetoed."

They need twenty-five, Vel thought. "Those twenty-three are part of the aristocracy, aren't they?" Vel said.

"Yes, they are," Lydia said. "The seven opposed are from the poorer districts."

Vel thought, the representatives on the Executive Council are elected by the people in each district, and the council members have to live wherever they run for office. Meaning the poor vote for representatives who are probably poor themselves and who will most likely vote in their interest.

Vel said, "How much food is there?"

"Nobody knows exactly," Lydia said. "Enough for a few months maybe, if the rations continue."

"This is crazy," Ponce said.

"Yes," Lydia said, "it is." She watched Vel closely. "The King is the one who's important. He has the Pox. If and when he dies, the legislation will pass and half the city will begin to starve."

"And what do you propose we do?" Vel said.

"Vel, do you remember when I told you that your parents weren't really your parents?"

"I remember you said something like that, yes."

Lydia said, "You have a mark of founding on your stomach."

"A mark of founding?" Vel filled his lungs, and he pulled his shirt up casually. "It's just a squiggly line. Just a"—Vel's voice slowed—*"birthmark."*

Lydia stared at his revealed skin, straightening in her chair. "You know who else supposedly had a mark much like that on his stomach? Blakes."

Ponce shook his head, laughing. "This is a joke right? Vel's not the King's son."

"No," Lydia said. "You're right; the King doesn't have any kids. Vel is the King's nephew. He's the son of the King's dead brother."

There was a pause, and then Vel asked quietly, "So my dad wasn't really my dad?"

"No, he wasn't."

"What about my mother?"

Lydia said, "You don't have a mother as far as I'm concerned."

"What does that mean?"

"I don't know who your mother is, and if I did it wouldn't matter. There are no records of her ever existing; we don't know who she was. What matters is that you're the last in Blakes's line after the King."

Vel stood. "Come on, Ponce."

Lydia froze. "What are you doing?"

Ponce followed Vel to the front door, and Vel opened it, feeling a rush of cold air. He smelled something burning again, far off.

"I'm leaving," Vel said.

"You can't," Lydia said. "We need you—haven't you been listening? You're the rightful heir."

"What makes you think anyone will care that I have a pimple on my stomach?"

"Vel, I haven't told you everything. There *is* a system—you'll have access to information that even we don't know."

"All right," Ponce said loudly. "We get the picture. Bad things are coming, so Vel should suck it up, ignore the fact that his entire life has been a lie, and just go along with you. He should trust you, right? Is that pretty close?"

"I know how hard this is," Lydia said.

Vel turned to her, making no attempt to hold his frustration in any longer. "Oh, that's right. You *do*, don't you? You know every damn thing about me. You've been studying me and following me for days now, haven't you?"

"Vel—"

"Lydia, I don't believe you. You haven't given me any real reason I should."

"I'm going to protect you—you have to trust me."

"Like Jak, right? No, I don't have to trust you." He turned away from her. "I want to be left alone. Suppose I become King and the aristocracy kills me off—you going to fight all of them?"

"There's a tradition here, Vel," she said and rose. "You know that, and I can't let you leave." Lydia dropped one hand to the stick at her waist.

Vel hesitated.

Ponce said, "You're going to stop both of us then?"

"No," she said. "just Vel. You can go any time."

Color rushed to Ponce's cheeks, but before he could respond, Vel said, "Lydia, you don't know me, and I don't know you. I appreciate the thought, and I appreciate your help back there in the alley. But, I'm not a game piece. You can't just put me into position and wait to see what happens."

"I know what will happen if you're not there," she said.

"Lydia, I'm not interested. What do I have to do to get you to leave me alone?" She didn't respond, and he said, "Find some other way. I want to stay out of this."

"That's just it." She took a step forward. "There isn't another way. You're the last one, Vel. Believe me, there are plenty of people who would take your place if they could. You know what's going to happen if you don't take over?"

"That's not my problem."

"Winter has set in." Ponce moved outside, waiting for Vel to follow. "Winter has come early," Lydia said. "There isn't enough food—they never really started storing for the winter because it's supposed to be another four and a half years away. This has never happened before, Vel. It may be that the normal cycle will begin again—that winter will end—in the same amount of time that the summer harvest lasted, in six months. But that won't matter. Ninety percent of Hope doesn't have six months if the legislation passes. The rich *will* have enough to keep eating, while the rest starve. No one's starving yet, but they will when the rich buy all of the food."

"And if the rationing continues, we'll run out of food in a few months anyway," Vel said. "So what?"

"It's not that simple," she said. "Don't you think that once people realize there isn't enough food, some are going to take matters into their own hands? The government will break down. As soon as that measure passes, the city will burn. There's going to be fighting over what little food *has* been stored."

Vel indicated that Ponce should come back inside. Ponce did so slowly, and Vel shut the door. He stood for a moment, unmoving.

"There's going to be a war, isn't there?" Vel said.

"Maybe. Yes."

Vel sat weakly in the chair again, resting his head in the palm of his hand. Ponce remained where he was.

"How are we going to solve that?" Ponce asked.

"He's right," Vel said. "What am I going to do about that? Even if I do try to become King, and even on the off chance that they accept that, why would that solve anything? It might not even delay the war, and it won't stop it. There's still a food shortage."

Lydia put one hand on his shoulder warmly, and Vel tried to ignore the gesture. I need this, he realized. I need someone to let me know that it still matters. But I wish it didn't.

Lydia said, "Why did you look for Jak?"

Vel glanced at her. "What?"

"Why did you start looking for Jak in the first place?"

Vel looked away. "You know why, remember?"

The flickering of a candle. She'd struck one of the nerves running inside his mind.

"My parents were—I think I have the Pox." Vel's throat constricted. There is no reason Jak had to have had the Pox, he thought. None at all. "I don't know what I expected. It doesn't matter. So, I guess in a little while I'll be dead whether I save the city or not, won't I?" He tried to smile.

Ponce sat unmoving and lowered his head. Lydia touched Vel's hair, running her fingers through it. She traced the contour of Vel's skull. He remained for a time, unable to react. Then, slowly, he pulled away.

I'm going to die, he thought. It had become more real somehow in telling Lydia. My body won't be mine anymore, it'll be burned, just like . . . There were tears in his eyes, and Vel blinked them away. No, he thought. I can't break down like this.

"What's your point?" he said at last.

Lydia touched his chin. "My point is there may be a cure for the Pox."

He shook his head. "I don't think Jak had it."

"Whether or not she did, there are other people, besides Jak, who have survived it."

Vel thought, That's a lie. "Who?"

"Justice Hillor, for one."

"How do you know all of this?" Vel said.

"Right now, just trust me. And Jak probably *did* have the Pox."

"So where's the cure?"

She said, "Don't know. You talked to Jak, didn't you? Did she mention the ruins?"

Ponce said to Vel, "How much of this are you planning to listen to?"

"I'm sick, Ponce," Vel said, and he looked at his friend calmly. "I have the Pox."

"How do you know?"

"I don't feel well," Vel said. "Not like I'm dying, but like I'm starting to get a cold." Ponce was silent, and Vel said to Lydia, "What about the ruins?"

"Hillor survived the Pox, and he was seen going to the ruins several weeks ago. Now Jak survived it—"

"She had a pass," Vel said.

Lydia's face brightened. "You saw it?"

"Yes—she had it at Turn Tables. What do the ruins have to do with anything?"

"I don't know everything, Vel. But Hillor had the Pox, went to the ruins, and now he's well. You saw that Jak was sick—now she's not—and she had a pass."

Vel knew virtually nothing about the ruins, except that they were dangerous; every salvaging expedition—groups sent to collect wood, fur and metal—walked for hours to keep their distance from the stone ruins in the south, despite the fact that the woods were closest to Hope just beyond the ruins.

Ponce asked Lydia, "Do you know what the ruins are?"

She said, "They weren't built by people. I know that—Blakes connects them with the Frill."

"The Frill again," Ponce said.

She ignored his tone. "Yes, they may have been built before people arrived here."

"So, what are you going to do?" Ponce said. "Just explain to the perimeter guards that there's a magic cure at the ruins?"

"We don't have much of a choice, do we?" she said and went to the door.

"What?" Vel said. *"Now?"*

Lydia nodded. "You're sick, and the King is going to die in the very near future."

"This is insane," Ponce said, and slowly Vel followed her. "Vel, you're not going with her?"

"What do you say, Ponce?" Vel said at last. "You want to rob a cop?"

Ponce grinned. "With her? Vel, I'm still seeing straight."

Vel did not finish the routine, and he followed Lydia into the street. Lydia shut the door behind Ponce.

Ponce said, "This doesn't make any sense. Think about it. There are soldiers every twenty feet—you'll draw all of them. There must be hundreds."

Lydia said, "We're not going to fight all of them."

Vel said, "The last time I followed someone to the cops—"

"I'm not Jak," Lydia said, and they paused in the empty street. "Who was it that got you out of that, Vel?"

Vel said, "You don't think I could have taken them?"

Ponce was tugging at his shirt uncomfortably. He's afraid, Vel realized. Of course he is—we can't just fight past the perimeter wall.

"Lydia," Vel said, "assuming I agree to go with you, do you have something in mind besides marching up to the guards and getting killed?"

She tapped her small staff with one hand. "We don't have any other options." When Vel started to respond, she said, "Vel, there's a chance it will work. I've done things like this before."

"Against that many soldiers?"

"No."

Ponce laughed uneasily. "Come on, Vel."

"Listen," Vel said to him. "I think she's right."

"You have a death wish? Think about what happened to Darden."

Vel stiffened. "What happened to Darden? We don't know where Darden is."

Ponce spat. "He wouldn't tell you to go with her."

"I have the Pox," Vel said again. "What difference does it make if I die in another month or in a few hours?" Ponce didn't respond. "I'll get in touch with you in a few days."

"Think about it, Vel. Don't go with her."

Vel glanced at Lydia, waiting quietly, then back at Ponce. Loud enough for her to hear, Vel said, "I don't trust her, but she helped me in the alley, and even if part of what she said is true, I'm going. I'm sick. What else am I going to do? Go on, I'll be back in a while."

Ponce started to back away. "You're going to fight the guards?"

"I don't know," Vel said. "I'll see you."

Vel watched him go, neither of them speaking. At the far end of the street a fountain sat dormant, cracked ice filling the basin, and a small circle of children sat around it, watching.

When Ponce had gone, Vel turned to Lydia. "I'm going to regret this, aren't I?"

Lydia took his arm, leading him to an intersection. "Come on."

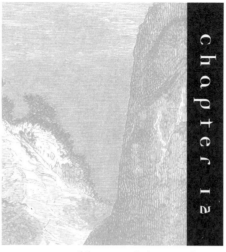

Justice Hillor led two columns of police soldiers down the center of the street. Don't these people know how to clean their own filth? Hillor thought, as they turned at a corner, onto a dirtier road with more garbage in the gutters. A band of raucous children ran past, but the soldiers did not stop them. The road cleared as Hillor approached, people stepping quickly out of their path.

Finally, the group stopped at the door of a large single-story house. Hillor knocked twice. No answer, and he pounded the wood again.

"Sir, they may be asleep, it—"

"No," Hillor said, and he motioned to three of the nearest soldiers. "Swords. Break it down."

Weapons drawn, the soldiers advanced on the house, attracting the attention of a handful of pedestrians. People stopped in the street to watch as the three soldiers attacked the door simultaneously, hacking it from its hinges. Hillor pressed past them, kicking the door apart as he stalked into the room. A group of five sat at a table in a small, barren room: two adults, three children.

"Mr. and Ms. Till," Justice Hillor said, and the police hurried to the door at the other end of the room, rushing down the hall, throwing doors open, grabbing children from their beds. Someone was screaming from the hallway, someone else crying.

"Justice," Mr. Till said, and he rose.

"Please," Hillor said, and police took Orula from her chair, quickly binding her wrists behind her back.

"No," she said, "you can't—"

More surrounded Mr. Till.

"You are convicted of subversive collaboration and treason,"

Hillor said, and several police returned from the hall, dragging two young girls and an older boy. One of the girls was screaming, her face puffy and red. The children at the table were ushered from their chairs, outside.

Orula said, "We haven't—"

"You harbor unregistered children for the purpose of subverting the government and the Church of Hope. We call it treason. What name do you give it?"

Mr. Till glanced at her, indicating that she should be silent, and said to Hillor, "Sir, I swear to you, we haven't—"

A soldier rushed from the hall with three books under his arm, and he handed them to Hillor.

"Not subversion? You haven't been committing treason?" Hillor said, and he took a torch from one of the cops. "You, Mr. Till, will be sentenced within the next few days." He ignited the books, watching the paper curl and smoke in the flames. Still Hillor held them, as the flames spread closer to his fingers, dropping blackened pages to the floor. To the soldiers: "All of these children are to be placed at the Southern Garrison. They are Hope's property now."

Orula struggled as more children were forced from her house.

"Please," she said. "Don't do this. They haven't done anything."

"I will decide who is guilty here," Hillor said, and he threw the remains of the books down in an explosion of hot ash. They smoldered on the wood floor, scorching it. "The woman dies, the man to the Palace prison."

"Yes, sir." And the soldiers pushed Orula up, still holding Mr. Till behind the now empty table.

Hillor approached Till, and two of the soldiers stood on Till's kitchen table, cutting holes in the wooden ceiling and winding a piece of coarse rope through it.

"Don't do this," Orula said. "Please."

A soldier carried a limp boy through the room and out, onto the street. Orula fought her captors, her face reddening. "Let go of me, this is against the law, we haven't—" A soldier kicked her to the floor, and they finished with the rope, tying one end into a noose.

Mr. Till stared at it, paling.

"You were a city clerk weren't you?" Hillor said. "And now you've turned to *this.*"

"Not my idea," Till said quietly.

Orula looked up, touching her side where the soldier had kicked her. "We haven't done anything. You can't—"

"Resisting arrest," Hillor said. "Should I explain the concept of a black market to you? What about treason?" He motioned to the soldiers, and they moved the table away, knocking it onto its side in one corner, sliding a chair under the noose.

"No," Orula said, and the soldiers lifted her roughly by the armpits. She looked at Mr. Till desperately. "Don't let them do this!"

"It's done," Hillor said, and two soldiers held her as a third cut open the front of her dress. She screamed, fighting with them, large breasts and stomach heaving. The third soldier drew a long, pointed dagger. Orula sobbed, shuddering, her legs slackened, and the third soldier kneeled in front of her, the dagger to her stomach.

"No, no, no . . ."

And then Orula screamed again, kicking and clawing at the soldiers as he cut words into her flesh. Hillor crossed his arms across his chest and studied Mr. Till.

"I hate doing this," Hillor said, and Mr. Till stared at the floor, jaw tight. "You understand, I'm sure."

And Orula began to cry as they forced her toward the chair, ripping away the rest of her dress.

Hillor said, "Perhaps something can be arranged—where is the boy named Vel?"

The soldiers tightened their grip on Till's arms, a sword pressing into his back. Orula's legs dragged as they pulled her closer to the chair, and she shook her head, begging them to stop. Naked, she was lifted onto the chair, head forced through the noose, the cord tightened.

"Tell you everything I know," Till said.

Hillor smiled.

Orula sobbed, "God, no. Honey, *please.* Please, look at me. Love you, oh God—"

A soldier kicked the chair away, and Orula stopped speaking, legs reaching and kicking, less than a foot above the floor. She turned in a slow circle, still fighting.

Hillor motioned the soldiers to take Till from the room. They walked past Orula, her legs and torso still spasming. Blood dripped—from torso to navel and down her legs—from the words *Life over Lies.* Hillor left the room, burnt pages crunching under his boots.

A moment later the last of the soldiers returned from the back rooms. "No more, sir. Eighteen total."

Eighteen, Hillor thought. The arrogance of thinking that they would be overlooked—or was it stupidity? Ignorance?

Hillor said, "I want this house leveled. Burn it down."

Almost there, Vel thought, as they continued toward the edge of the city. Closer to the farmers' fields and the granaries and the perimeter wall. Vel and Lydia both wore packs, filled with food and water supplies, along with several torches and tinderboxes.

As they walked, more trash filled the spaces between the buildings, and people sat in the cold, watching them. A squad of police stood talking in the center of the street ahead, and children kicked a brown ball against the wooden wall of their home, the entire house vibrating with each hit. They sang a song as they played, something Vel had never heard before. All of these people, he realized suddenly. All of these people are going to starve. There won't be enough food, and the poor will go first.

The soldiers nodded to Lydia and Vel as they passed, and Vel pretended to be distracted, reading black graffiti on a medicine shop at the corner. Murderers and Fire Is Hot, But Only If You Lite It. Vel knew the way the doctors healed. They cleansed the bad blood and fluids from a person's body with bloodletting and sweat. And oil that washed everything out of the stomach. All illness could be healed that way, except the Pox. Vel had never been sick enough to go to the doctor, but he had heard from Ponce and Darden about the way they worked.

Soon the houses thinned, and past the last rows, Vel saw the plots of irrigated farmland, the squares of withered grasses, and then beyond rose the black perimeter wall. Yes, Vel thought, one soldier every twenty feet. This cannot be done—I should have listened to Ponce. Lydia crouched in the dirt, unhooking her staff, and Vel fidgeted with his sword handle.

"We're going to do this fast," Lydia said.

Vel's pulse pounded under his rib cage. "How?"

"Rush them. Let me go first. When I give you a signal, I want you to run for the wall and get over and into the grassfields as quickly as you can. Stay low."

"Lydia, why can't the rest of your order help us?"

"There's a lot happening now, Vel. Believe me, I wish they could."

We can't do this alone, Vel thought. We can't fight this many soldiers. Even at this distance, Vel could see that the guards were all armed with both swords and crossbows. It won't work, he thought.

He asked, "There's no other way to the ruins?"

"Not that I know of. Supposedly there were once tunnels, but I don't think they really existed."

"They do," Vel said, and he backed away from the fields. Blue light through fence beams.

"What are you talking about?"

Not a coincidence that I saw that so close to Jak. That hadn't been chance, Vel thought, at the cemetery. He told her about the blue light he had seen through the open hole in the cemetery dirt.

"That doesn't make any sense, Vel."

"Unless there's a tunnel under the cemetery."

Lydia watched the perimeter wall, as if she wanted to try and fight them rather than look for an easier way.

"There are soldiers at the cemetery too," she said at last.

"But not many. Let's take a look," Vel said, "all right?"

Lydia agreed, and it was dark when they had reached the cemetery. Soldiers and women cluttered the streets nearby, lounging outside the rows of bars and brothels. Through the fence, Vel saw only darkness.

Lydia pointed out two soldiers patrolling the cemetery grounds near a fresh grave. "I don't see anything, Vel."

"It was there," Vel said. "Near the older headstones."

"Near Blakes's tomb?" Lydia asked, and they moved along the fence, soldiers passing in the street behind them. Another soldier crouched near Blakes's grave, arranging flowers in the dirt.

"Close to it," Vel said. "Yes."

Lydia frowned at him. "You're sure you saw something in the

ground that wasn't just a body wrapped in cloth?"

"Yes."

"All right," she said, and jumped the fence in one movement. Vel clambered after her. Lydia drew her staff and advanced on the soldier near Blakes's grave, crouching across the cemetery grounds. Vel made a sound landing from the fence, the soldier turned, and Lydia took him down—hitting him hard in the throat with her staff. She indicated that Vel should wait where he was, and then she went after the other two. Vel lost sight of her in the darkness, and a moment later she returned, still holding her staff with one hand.

"It's all right," she said. "Come on."

They took shovels from the mounds of fresh dirt at the new grave sites and started to dig a dozen feet from Blakes's tomb, where Vel remembered seeing the light. Several strokes into the dirt—and Vel's shovel knocked away a layer of dirt, and he caught himself in the grass, almost falling in. Through the small hole Vel had exposed, the same blue light glowed. Lydia knocked away more of the dirt, widening the hole, and crouched closer, struggling to determine how deep it might be.

"Wait," Lydia said, and she fit her staff back onto her waist, set her shovel aside, and dropped into the hole—she hit a stone floor less than twenty feet below.

"Not as deep as I thought," Vel said.

"It goes on in both directions," Lydia said, and she took out her staff again. "Try and cover up the hole before you come down."

Vel shoveled some of the dirt back over the hole, but it would not stay in place as it had been. Finally, he gave up after concealing the sides of the hole and jumped down after Lydia. The tunnel was smoothly cut from black rock, and the walls and ceiling glowed a perfect blue.

"Where is that light coming from?" Vel said, and he followed Lydia, as she started walking. "What is this?"

"I don't know. Stay close to me, Vel."

After an hour of walking—the tunnel always continuing in a perfectly straight direction—the passage ended. Uneven steps, small, as if they had been cut for a child's feet rose to another hole. Lydia went first, and soon motioned Vel to follow. The hole opened in the ground in the middle of the wild grassfields; they were outside.

"Didn't have to deal with the perimeter wall," Vel said. "I felt something in that tunnel—like I'd been there before. What does that mean?"

Lydia paused to find which way was south, and then turned to Vel. "Doesn't mean anything. Let's just hope you get to go down there again."

chapter 14

Lord Denon motioned the Religious Guard soldier closer to his chair. Denon sat in one of the three seats at the balcony of the Cathedral, overlooking the altar and empty pews. Candles flickered below. A priest approached. "Go ahead," Denon said.

The priest offered him a folded paper. "Lord Denon, reports from the granaries have arrived."

"Food shortages do not concern me now," Denon said softly. "God will provide. What did I hear from the cemetery? Police soldiers wounded?"

"Dead, Lord; three dead. The police do not know yet—the cemetery is unmanned at the present and—"

"Send a team of Religious Guard to the cemetery. They'll find an open hole near the prophet's grave. They are to take this passage outside of the city and find the boy who has escaped. This boy is important."

The priest started away. "Yes, Lord Denon. Should the police be notified?"

"No. Let them discover in their own time."

"Yes, Lord." The priest paused. "Pardon, Lord, but a boy couldn't have beaten three soldiers, could he?"

"Send the team now," Denon said carefully, and he folded his hands. "He isn't alone."

"HOW much farther?"

A corridor of high-reaching grass rose into the air a foot over Vel's head. Blades of grass. The stalks frayed off at their peaks into billows of burnt color. In the summer, the fields were a healthy green, now dried brown and black. When the grass turned green, it yielded fruit under the soil. That was how grassfruit was harvested—in planned plots within the perimeter wall; rows of high grass stalks evenly spaced yielded bigger fruit than the wild grassfields outside the wall.

"Come on, Lydia, how much farther?" Vel asked again.

Vel stumbled, snapping the stalks in his path. They scratched at his cheeks and raked at his clothing. Lydia fell in and out of the grass in front of him. She appeared, and then was gone a moment later.

"Don't know. We should come to a place where we can stop," Lydia said, still gliding forward, "if you're tired."

A dark sky winked at Vel as his cheeks flushed red in the cold. He took a dry breath that went down his throat and into his lungs. Lydia moved on ahead. The grasses concealed everything, save a distant horizon of black outlines and the pinpoints of light overhead.

"I can't see anything," he said.

Vel imagined that she nodded in agreement.

"I know. You aren't supposed to. The grasses go on for miles like this. Real easy to get lost without the sun."

"Or someone tall."

Vel grabbed at the pack fastened to his shoulders as a loose strand of grass caught under it. The grasses made a scratching whistle as they went on. The blades grabbed at Vel's hair, and he cursed under his breath. Once or twice he thought that he saw things scurrying out of his path in the blackness. He kept moving.

Over an hour had passed, possibly much longer, since they had left the tunnel. Now the moon hovered in the cold air, and Vel shivered, feeling more and more lost as they pushed farther from Hope. He had never been outside the city boundaries before, and this wasn't what he had expected. He felt vulnerable, exposed.

What if something happens to Lydia? he thought. How would I find my way back? Wait for light and then head north.

Abruptly, the grasses vanished and Vel stepped into a clearing behind Lydia. The clearing was twelve feet across, in an uneven circle; the grasses beaten down, writhing into the dirt. The stalks had been snapped, and some looked shredded, as if run through a razor.

A smell—like rotten fruit, but it wasn't fruit. The smell sunk into his mind, and he shivered. Darkness stained sections of the wounded grass, and across from Vel there was a large break in the grass wall. Something had ripped through the grass—into the clearing—bending the blades. Torn fabric, also stained, lay scattered across the ground.

"Someone died," Lydia said.

Vel watched as she examined several lumps on the clearing floor. He looked across the surrounding grasses. A cool wind rushed over them, and the sea rippled in loose waves of brown.

"Looks like someone got eaten," she said.

Vel's mouth went very dry. He walked behind Lydia and looked at the mess in front of her. Stronger scent of rot, and small white insects crawled in and out of the decaying flesh.

Lydia said, "My guess is, a couple of people came out here— probably wall guards or people with the last salvaging expedition. Whatever happened, they got ripped apart right here. Looks like one was killed, although parts are missing, and the other was dragged off," she hesitated, and then motioned to the gap in the grasses, "that way."

Vel's voice shook slightly. "How do you know a person died? Aren't there animals that live out here?" Vel had heard of rodents and insects beyond the perimeter wall, but nothing this large.

Lydia wiped her hands unceremoniously on her pants and unhooked the staff from her waist.

"One of them was wearing a ring," she said. "I've never heard of animals that wear jewelry."

A tightness crept into Vel's chest. The dark lumps on the ground gradually became a sticky mass of blood and tissue, splattered and shredded across the floor.

"You mean there's a hand in that?"

Lydia nodded, and she dropped to one knee. After a moment, she motioned to a dark splotch.

"See?"

Vel squinted. At first, he saw a simple blot. Then the shape began to register in his mind, and Vel backed away. There were definite fingers—a hand that was half eaten, but still a hand— and on one of the fingers Vel saw a faint golden glimmer.

A ring.

"What could have done that?"

Vel, honey.

He spun, and Lydia looked at him.

"What was that?" he said.

She stared at him. "What?"

The grasses waved, and darkness broke through their ranks. Silence sunk into Vel, filling the empty spaces in his chest and stomach.

Lydia stood back up. "How does the cycle work? Twenty years of normal weather, then five years of summer and five of winter."

Vel stared at the grass.

"You tell me," he said quietly.

"I think other things might come with winter besides the weather. You understand?"

He nodded hurriedly. "Yes, I get it. Good harvest, bad winter, and people are going to die. Whatever did this might still be around, and I don't want to get eaten."

"These people have been dead for days."

"Can we get the hell out of here, please?"

Lydia smiled to herself. "Yes, Vel."

She walked away from the broken hole in the grass, stepping carefully around the mounds. The grasses closed around them again, and they continued toward the ruins.

"We're going to get there tonight, aren't we?"

"We should," she said in between the whispers of the grass. "I've never been there, but the ruins aren't more than a few miles away."

"The grasses don't grow around them, do they?" Vel said.

"I don't think so. Part of the ruins is overgrown with woods, and the grass thins as it gets closer to the trees."

Lydia kept walking. Vel had only seen the tiny trees that grew occasionally at the riverside in Hope—he tried to imagine the woods. With long tufts of fur moss hanging from their branches, the trees of the southern forest were supposed to grow taller than the largest buildings in Hope. But still small compared to the ruins.

Eyes.

They shimmered between the layers of grass. Vel stumbled, and Lydia disappeared into the darkness. He was alone.

"Lydia."

The word was a rasp, barely audible in his own ear.

Darkness. The eyes were gone.

"Lydia," Vel said again.

Something was out there, watching him. He backed away from where the eyes had been. Those two slits of yellow on red. He felt whatever it was staring at him and imagined he could hear its muscles tensing in the blackness.

"Lydia."

Vel's voice shook, dying briefly. A moment later he wasn't sure that he'd said anything.

A whisper to his left. Movement. Vel spun and staggered back, drawing his sword. He held the weapon in both hands, backing farther from the noise.

Something out there was staring at him through the grass. God, I can't see anything, he thought. And the grass was scratching against his cheeks. It raked across his clothing, as he backed through it. Vel glanced over his shoulder. Where was the damn thing?

Darkness.

All around him, darkness.

Come on, bastard.

Why wasn't it attacking? he wondered. What was it? Why was it waiting?

Oh, God.

Vel's heart drummed louder in his ears. It pulsed up through his neck and down his wrists. What if the eyes ripped him apart? What if they did to him what they had done to those other people?

Grass snapped to his right. "Vel?"

The voice was incredibly close. He dashed blindly through the grass. Blades flashed up and into his eyes, ripping his shirt and pants.

"Lydia!"

Something charged behind him. Grasses broke and shattered in his wake.

"Vel?"

Closer now—he was so close to her. He couldn't run any faster. Sweat poured into his hair and went streaming down his face, and he chopped at the grass, hacking it wildly as he tore a path.

"Vel—"

Vel heard the voice to his right and turned, diving forward, and he crashed into Lydia. They both went down, and Lydia held Vel about the shoulders, his chest heaving again and again.

She stood. "Vel, what—"

"There's something out there. Something's following me."

Lydia ran a hand across Vel's face. She held her staff casually in one arm and wiped a stream of sweat from his eyes.

"What happened?"

He grabbed her by the arm. "We've got to get out of here, Lydia."

Lydia shook her head. "What are you—"

Behind them—movement flicked into the corner of Vel's vision.

Lydia yanked him forward, and something caught her ankle— Vel staggered back—they fell, images dancing in his mind, and the grasses whispered. Lydia rolled to her feet and swung her staff blindly.

"Lydia," Vel said. He stood and the sea shimmered around them. Blackness and the wind whistled in Vel's ears. He waited, looking from Lydia to the grass, then back to her again.

"What is it?" he said.

She stared at the moving grasses. They fluttered, shifting to one side, so that the entire world seemed to tilt.

Something huge snapped forward, lancing at her. Moonlight hit a curved shape, a sharpened, attacking crescent—a pincer. Large enough to chop them in half. Lydia spun back, and her staff connected with the pincer's side, it clicked at her, and she ducked another attack, ramming her staff into the side of it again. And it was gone.

The pincer had come from the grasses themselves. Lydia's arm shook, and she backed away.

"Vel," her voice was low. "Vel."

"Yes?"

"When I say, start running."

Sweat trickled into his ears, and Vel's heart thudded loudly in his forehead. What if it heard his heart? We're going to die, he thought.

"All right," she said. Lydia stepped beside him, and the grasses waved. It could have been two feet in front of him; Vel wouldn't have seen it. Too dark.

"Go. Now."

Lydia pushed him, and, they ran. Strands of darkness lashed at him, scratching his skin and shredding the sides of his sleeves. The night resonated in his blood, in the beating of his heart.

Gradually, they slowed. Panting, Vel said, "How far—how far are we from the ruins?"

Lydia looked back the way they'd just come.

"Testing us," she said, and Vel realized that she had not broken a sweat. "Wasn't trying to kill us or it would have—just testing."

Vel said, "Shouldn't we—"

Trip, trip, trip into the world.

Vel recoiled at the sight. She was dressed entirely in white, staring at him through the grass. Her bare, upturned arms ran red.

Vel. His mother smiled with blue lips. *Vel, I—*

Lydia's hand caught his wrist. "Vel?" He jumped.

"Vel?" Lydia said again. She was watching him. "What is it?"

An empty field.

"I don't . . ." He stared at the grass.

Lydia said, "What just happened—you saw something?"

"No."

"You've got to tell me if there's something that—"

"I didn't see anything," Vel said. "Let's keep going."

They started moving again.

A voice sang to Vel between the grasses—it could have been the wind. He could have been imagining it. The song resonated in the whisper of the field, the song hissed at him.

Trip, trip, tripping . . .

Vel kept going.

The voice died, then rose again, more loudly, sounding sad and beaten. Vel pushed it away. Not real, he thought. I'm going crazy. She's dead; my fault, but she's still dead.

Trip and we'll be merry.

The song ended, and still they had not reached the ruins. Should be there by now, Vel thought. Where are they?

"Lydia, shouldn't the ruins . . . ?"

The grass ended.

Blending with the night sky at their summits, mountains of black stone towered over them. Vel couldn't move; his mouth became very dry. At first, they really *were* mountains—as if someone had cleared away all of the dirt from an irregular mountain range. But gradually Vel understood what he was looking at, or thought he did. A city just like Hope, except that in the place of aligned wooden houses, black stone towers stood. And yes, there were streets—dirt paths—between the towers, not much wider than the roads of Hope.

Vel spotted several doorways on the nearest stone building, fifty meters away. These *are* buildings, he thought. They varied in size, some rising hundreds of feet to multiple spires, while others looked more like random chunks, cracked and broken. No real pattern to any of it that Vel could see—except the streets. It looked as if most of the buildings had been worn smooth around their edges by centuries of wind and rain.

Vel followed Lydia closer, and they did not speak.

Black rocks crunched underfoot, and Vel realized that some of the small buildings might actually be *parts* from the taller ones, long since fallen away, leaving uneven gaps in the strange stone mountains. Drawing nearer, veins of brown and gray traced the nearest ruins—vines, slinking up from the dirt. Trees grew randomly in the street and around the buildings, thick strands of what looked like brown hair drooping from their branches—fur moss. It was where all of their clothing came from.

Vel had reasoned through all of this before. He had rationally thought about the size of the ruins—they could be seen from Hope, after all—and the idea that they were some last monument to something that had once been alive, but that was now very dead. All of that meant nothing now. The ruins were simply *too large*. Looking all the way up brought a feeling of vertigo, an uneasiness in Vel's stomach.

It meant nothing to *think* that the ruins were old—they actually *were.* Is this place older than Hope? Vel wondered. It had to be. In places, Vel saw the human carvings, the markings and graffiti people had left in their presence over the past few centuries. Names, initials, mostly indecipherable.

Vel motioned to a number carved into a block ten feet away. A proud swa—the "spinning cross"—with another symbol that resembled a fist were carved above the clear writing:

Hera—2402 A.D.

"What does that mean?" Vel asked.

"I'm not sure," Lydia said. "I think that by another calendar, that's the year people arrived here on Hera."

"They arrived *here*? At the ruins?"

Lydia shrugged. "They could have."

"You were serious about people coming from another planet."

"Yes."

Vel said, "Two-four-oh-two what? What does it mean? What's *'AD'*?"

"I don't know," Lydia said. "Maybe they picked an event in their own history—on Merica–Urope—and agreed to count from that."

"But . . ." Vel's mouth went dry. "Hope is only five hundred and nine years old. People were around for two thousand four hundred years *before* that?"

"Blakes doesn't go into it," Lydia said. "But, yes, they probably were."

"Then that would mean it's something like 2911 now?" Vel said, and he started to laugh. "By their calendar. What the hell is going on? This is insane. Suddenly everything's more complicated."

"That happens," Lydia said, and she patted him on the shoulder. "I wasn't lying to you, Vel."

After a pause, he said, "I don't understand. Who built these? Blakes and the first people to land here?"

The nearest ruin rose thirty feet in the air, running horizontally for another fifty. The building's top was crumbling, and loose bits of black stone scattered across the ground.

"No," she said. "I don't think *people* built these. My guess is, it was the Frill. You can see where some of the bigger chunks are missing—where they probably took the stone to build the Palace, Church and Garrs."

Vel saw only a mess of enormous stone ruins. They all seemed to be missing sections.

"This was a city?" Vel asked. "The Frill had a city here?"

"I don't know."

Something small slithered away in the moonlight, and Vel drew in a slow breath, feeling more and more uncomfortable away from Hope.

"All right," he said at last, turning to her. "Now what?"

chapter 15

When the police soldier called to him, Justice Hillor did not pause. He continued up the main staircase, the carpeted steps creaking loudly. The hall was dark but still manned, as it always was, even in the middle of the night.

"Sir," the soldier called again, and rushed after Hillor from the main entrance hall below. Hillor gripped the railing hard and finally paused. There will be a hanging if this is not urgent, Hillor thought. I haven't slept in almost two days.

"Yes?" Hillor said.

The soldier saluted at the foot of the stairs and said, "Sir, dispatches from the cemetery post."

"The cemetery post," Hillor repeated, and he took the sealed paper from the soldier. Hillor opened it, quickly reading the message. Three men dead, he thought, and now the Religious Guard were seen entering, but not leaving. Denon, you would love to slide into the advantage, wouldn't you?

Hillor crumpled the paper in one hand, then stopped and wrote a quick note on the back, ordering a company of police soldiers to find a certain tunnel in the cemetery and to follow it outside of the city—until they had captured the boy, Vel. That's what this is, isn't it, Denon? Hillor thought, and he gave the note to the soldier, dismissing him. The boy's fled the city, and you want to beat me to him.

With the message sent, Hillor continued to the top of the stairs, and he headed for the King's bedroom toward the end of the hall. Everything depends on that boy, Hillor thought, but so long as the King is alive, I have time. Should never have given Denon a part in this; I trusted him too much years ago, and now he's lost his nerve. My mistake to rely on him.

Hillor knocked on the King's bedroom door, and without waiting for a response, stepped inside, past the guards stationed in the hall. The room was entirely dark, and Hillor shut the door behind him.

"Your Majesty, the situation is getting more complicated. I wish to speak with you about the Church."

No reply, and Hillor walked tiredly to the side of the large bed. The King was sleeping on his side. Wake up you old fool, Hillor thought, and he kneeled at the bedside.

"Your Highness, we must speak. I'm sorry to wake you, but it is necessary."

Still no answer, and slowly Hillor touched the King's throat with his fingers, moving the soft flesh closer to the bone to feel for an artery. Hillor waited a moment, and then he stood over the King, thinking.

No pulse, and Hillor said, "Your Highness, you are the most damned stubborn human being I have ever met." And he covered the dead King with the blanket.

vel shivered, pulling his blanket farther up his chest. He rolled onto one side, and closed his eyes in the darkness. Nearby, the first of the ruins began, crumbling up from the cracked ground. Cold night winds whispered across the grasses, ruffling Vel's hair. He tried to yawn, but the feeling died. Lydia lay nearby on his left, in the direction of the ruins, away from the grass field.

She was curled into a ball, her gray blanket wrapped around her neck. Vel shifted so he could watch her side rise and fall as she slept. Stars and the moon, and Vel wondered why he had never really thought about them before. Heaven was up there, wasn't it? Isn't that what the Church said the stars were? God's light piercing the darkness, and the moon His watchful eye.

Vel looked at the wall of grass. He saw eyes again. Nothing. Gone. Vel's mind remained calm, incredibly so, and he told himself that he hadn't seen them. They weren't really there. The grass shifted and danced in the moonlight, and a humanoid figure peered out at him.

You have a sword, don't you Vel?

The voice was too close, and he started, rolling away from the grass—into his mother's legs. She stood over him, her eyes sunken and discolored. Blood dripped from her arms into the palms of her hands, onto Vel. He couldn't move.

"Mom."

She smiled. *Your sword is on the ground there.* She motioned weakly. *That girl is using you for her disease. She has the Pox too, Vel. She wants to find a cure for herself. Not for you. Not for your father.* Vel stiffened. *It's a very simple thing, Vel. If you love me, you'll do this for me. Do it for me, please.*

He shook his head and felt his arm straining as it searched for the sword.

"No!" He grabbed the handle loosely. "No!"

Vel rose from the ground, and his mother smiled, a cold hand on his cheek. Wet.

That's right, Vel. Thank you. Now, do this for me.

He turned, and Lydia was watching him, eyes wide. Vel froze. His mother danced back and out of his vision. *Trip away with me.* And she was gone.

"Vel?"

He stared at Lydia, his muscles shaking, and dropped the sword. Vel's legs trembled, he lost his footing and went down, landing roughly in the dirt and stone. The tiny black pieces bit into his palms.

Lydia drew closer and Vel tried to wipe the small stones from his hands. His arms shook uncontrollably. They wouldn't stop.

"Vel—"

Vel's voice was not his own, hoarse and low. "Didn't want to."

Lydia nodded. With one hand, she touched him quietly across the folds in his back.

Vel jerked away from her. "Stop it. I'm going back to sleep. I'll just sleep."

"Vel," she said, "what happened?"

He pressed his hands together to still them. "I'm sorry."

Lydia leaned closer to him. "What's wrong?"

"Nothing," he said. "Let's just go back to sleep, all right?"

He was shivering.

"You talked to your mother," Lydia said softly.

"No, I didn't."

Trip, trip, tripping . . .

"I'm sorry, Vel." She took his hand gently. "I want to help you. Tell me what happened."

"Not now," he said.

"I don't know if you've noticed," she said, "but we're not safe out here. I need you to work with me."

"I don't want to do anything to you, Lydia. I think I'm going crazy, so leave me alone, all right?" He looked at the grass. "I want to go back."

"I think what we saw back there was the Nara—don't know what they are exactly, but they're dangerous. And some people think they live in the grasses."

"Great." Vel felt exhausted, as if everything that had been happening was just becoming real. "I want to go back to Hope."

"You can't," Lydia said. "Remember that clearing we found? It may not have been a good idea to come here, but we're here now, and tomorrow we'll find a cure for the Pox if there is one."

Vel shook his head. "I don't particularly care anymore. Both of my parents are dead, and before too much longer, everybody else will be too. I don't care about saving these people." Vel waved his hand at the city on the other side of the grass. "Tell me why I should. Let them save themselves—the only thing I've ever done is steal from them. Why should I suddenly care?"

Lydia stiffened, becoming serious. "You're giving up?"

Vel shrugged. "Can't give up if I wasn't trying in the first place."

Lydia said, "You stole because you didn't have enough to eat. You stole to survive, Vel. That isn't your fault."

He started to laugh. "It's society, right? I stole *before* the rationing began, Lydia. You think I spent all of that on food? Don't know who you were following around, but it wasn't me. I've conned people out of their money my entire life, and now you want me to save them, as if I have a right to save them."

"It's an obligation."

"Screw that," Vel said, shaking his head. "Ponce was right. Why should I do any of this? I'm just going to get myself killed."

Lydia's voice was distant. "We need you, Vel."

"What if I say no?" He looked at her, waiting. "I don't want to be King. You think I have any idea how to stop the city from destroying itself? The cops will poison me the first chance they get."

"That isn't true, Vel."

"How do you know?" He glared at her. "What makes you think that you've got everything figured out, Lydia? You're not much older than I am. You think you've seen so much more than I have—and you use it like a card over me. 'Follow me, Vel, I know the way.' My secret order knows every goddamn thing, but I'm only going to tell you what's convenient for me to tell you— enough to get you to follow me. How do you know Hillor had the Pox? How do you know he came to the ruins?"

"You have to trust me," she said.

"Actually, I don't. I want specifics: How do you know?"

"Someone in my order saw him leave sick, and someone else saw him return well." She crossed her arms. "Satisfied?"

"No. How do I know you're not working for someone else?"

"What do you want me to do?"

Vel rubbed his eyes, and his head began to ache. His skull was too hot, and sweat beaded on his forehead. He stared at the ruins, his heart quickening. "I want you to let me go back to Hope."

"Vel—"

"The Frill built these?"

Lydia nodded. "I think so, yes."

"But they're extinct now."

"That's right."

Vel turned to her simply. "Then we're worried about the Nara— the pincer-things, right? Not the Frill or anything else."

Lydia smiled slightly. "Yes, Vel, we're worried about the 'pincer- things.' That's why I'm with you."

Vel pointed to her staff. "How long have you had that?"

"Since I was three."

"Your family just let you train with this mysterious order?"

"My family is the order." Lydia's eyes seemed to go out of focus, and she looked past Vel, into the sky. "Both of my parents died when I was a child. The order found and raised me. I've trained to fight since I was old enough to walk."

"That's all you do?"

"No," she said. "That's not all."

Vel waited, but Lydia did not go on. Finally, he said, "I'm sorry I woke you."

"It's all right."

They sat in silence for a time, and Vel asked, "Do you have any friends?"

This time it was Lydia who laughed. "What?"

"Friends," Vel said. "You know, other people. Do you have people you can talk to?"

"Do you?" she asked.

Vel shrugged. "I used to." He scratched his head. "I don't know what's going to happen now." To her again, "What is it like?"

"What do you mean? The training?"

"All of it. Is it lonely? No one knows you exist."

"That's not entirely true."

"You know what I mean." He reached for her hand, and Lydia watched as Vel took it in his. Her fingers were trembling. "I'm sorry I yelled."

"You're forgiven."

He watched her, and Lydia looked away deliberately.

"You didn't answer my question," he said.

"What?"

"Is it lonely?"

"No, it isn't," she said.

Vel began to trace along her knuckles, and Lydia closed her eyes, shuddering involuntarily.

"Don't," she said softly.

"Why?"

"Please, Vel, don't make this harder than it is."

"Make what harder?"

Lydia looked directly at him, away, and then back again. Her voice cracked as she spoke, "I've been watching you for weeks."

"What does that have to do with anything?"

"I care about you. But this is a job."

He swallowed. "I'm hard work, aren't I?"

She nodded. "You said it, not me. But, yes, you have a stubborn streak. A tendency to be negative."

Vel pretended to be insulted. "No, I don't."

She smiled slowly. "Thanks for coming with me."

"Didn't actually have much of a choice, did I?"

"Well, I could have put you on a leash. You were more agreeable than I thought you'd be."

He grinned and touched her cheek lightly. "Don't think we should buy matching funeral pyres just yet."

"Seriously, Vel, I'm here to look out for you," she said, and her hand ran across his shoulder. "I'm not going to die and neither are you."

Trip, trip, tripping . . .

A cold wind rolled through the ruins, hissing against the stone. The temperature was still dropping, and Vel's toes numbed. He wiggled them uncomfortably and tried to ignore what Lydia had just said.

"I know I'm not going to die," Vel said, trying to sound casual. "I'm invincible, didn't you know?"

Lydia said, "I won't die."

"Lydia . . ."

They kissed. It happened so suddenly that a moment after Lydia had pulled away again, Vel wasn't sure how he was supposed to react or whether or not it had actually happened at all.

"I'm sorry," Lydia said, and she rolled onto her side again, away from him. "You were right—we should sleep."

What just happened? Vel thought. "Lydia?"

Without moving, she said, "Go to sleep, Vel."

Is this to keep me from running away? he thought, and he could still taste her lips. His heart was beating faster. Vel slipped back under his own blanket, and Lydia said quietly, "Remember what I said."

What? Vel thought, and he knew what she meant.

I won't die.

chapter 16

"Then you don't know where the boy is?"

"No, Justice, I don't. I told you that. Probably in hiding. You don't think they'll find out about the King sooner than you've planned?"

"No. They'll find out when I decide that they'll find out."

"Be careful. It's very difficult to shake hands with a clenched fist."

"Don't patronize me. We're both lucky that people don't think, aren't we? The situation with the King is under control, but we need that boy. You know, the Frill will kill him if he goes to the ruins."

"Maybe. What makes you think he's at the ruins?"

"I don't know, Denon. He must stay alive long enough to speak with Blakes."

"Of course. We'll find him."

"But alive."

"Yes, Justice, it will be finished soon."

"In a way, this is turning full circle, isn't it? I only hope the boy survives long enough to be executed."

The ruins were very quiet. Vel trailed after Lydia down the "street" between several of the larger black towers. He had been awakened at first light, much sooner than he would have liked, and now they were wandering, searching for some sign that Jak and Hillor had come here. So far nothing.

Vel ducked the branches of a tree that grew in the center of the dirt path, soft moss brushing his cheek, and something buzzed past his right ear. The tree was a complex maze of branches twisting and writhing high, all draped with brown and gray moss. The vines that snarled up the ruin walls had grown so thick in some places that the stone was entirely covered in vegetation.

Lydia approached a pile of burnt debris outside a small building nearby.

"See this?" she said, blowing onto her hands to warm them.

Vel knew perfectly well what he was looking at: someone had built a fire here. The closest ruin opened onto the street with a huge weathered doorway, and Vel followed Lydia closer. Inside, the black walls were carved with spiraling symbols that continued unbroken around all four walls and up the domed ceiling.

"Frill writing?" Vel asked. Uneasiness tightened into a cold knot in his stomach.

"I think so," Lydia said, staring at the symbols. In places, they had worn away into smooth stone, and in other areas people had carved their own graffiti over them. Vel saw the words *God's Wrath on the Devils* covering a line of spiral writing.

Lydia headed out onto the street again. "Come on."

They started away from the fire remains, approaching a long black pole that stood in the road ahead. A tiny trail of blackened fabric hung from the tip, and the pole was cracked midway up, so that it seemed ready to snap in half at any moment.

As they passed, Vel noticed more strands of fabric clinging to the pole near the top, as if a tapestry or piece of cloth had once hung from it. Lydia picked up a black rock from the dirt casually and handed it to Vel. He was about to speak, when he saw tiny writing on one side of the stone. Not sentences, just a single word.

DIE

Vel chucked it into one of the towers, and it smashed in an explosion of black dust, leaving a crack in the wall it hit.

"Lydia . . ." Vel was alone.

He spun—the road was empty. No, he thought, don't do this again.

"Lydia!" Vel waited, and when she didn't respond, he started back the way they had come. No sound as he walked, and Vel shouted again, "Lydia!"

This place is dead, Vel thought. There's nothing alive here,

there's no cure for the Pox. We shouldn't have come. The buildings looked different here, and Vel began to wonder if he was
following the wrong path. Noticing a large stone the size of his
house in the road ahead, he stopped. That wasn't there, he
thought. Vel turned back—movement flashed in the corner of his
eye—and Vel spun again, the shadow flicking away.

Vel heard his heart, and tension constricted his chest. Nothing,
the road was still empty. Sweat on his scalp, and Vel touched the
handle of his sword.

"Lydia!"

Vel pivoted—something caught the back of his foot, he flipped
off balance, and a sharp pain exploded at the back of his skull.

And he was awake again, blinking in darkness, not sure how
long he had been unconscious. Vel felt cold stone under his back,
pain rolling through his vision in bright waves. He breathed moist,
thick air, feeling almost as if he were underwater—but he *could*
breathe, so where was he? Underground, Vel thought, and he felt
around in the darkness.

Something clammy—cold—and hair: a face. Vel recoiled, ball-
ing his hands into fists. A dead face, and Vel tried to stand, his
hand bumping against lumpy fabric, and more flesh. Bodies. Vel
steadied himself. What the hell is going on? he thought. Where
am I?

Red slits flashed, like eyes. Darkness.

"Lydia," Vel said, but he didn't move, not wanting to trip on
the corpses, not knowing where they were. "Please, I—"

Die.

Stinging pain, and then blackness again.

vel woke near the grassfield, Lydia sitting nearby, watching
the darkening sky. It smeared an orangish red as night approached, and Vel pressed his hands to both sides of his head.

"God, how long was I gone?"

"All day," Lydia said, and she moved closer, looking subdued,
as if the sky had relaxed some of the tension usually behind her
eyes. "I found you out here, unconscious." She studied him.

"Looked around all of the ruins before I finally came back here. What happened, Vel?"

He tried to make sense of what he could remember, concentrating on the red sky. "We were separated."

"I know. One minute, you're there, the next you weren't— Where did you go?"

"I didn't go anywhere. You were gone."

"Vel, that isn't true. I just looked back, and it was as if you'd gone sprinting in the other direction."

Vel thought about it. "After you handed me that rock, I was alone. Then something hit me and I woke underground, and there were bodies."

"Bodies? How many?"

"I don't know, it was completely dark." Vel's stomach growled, and Lydia heard, offering him a piece of fruit from her pack. He thanked her and broke it open. Between bites, Vel said, "There were red eyes, and then something hit me again, and now I'm here."

"You saw eyes in the field just before we were attacked, didn't you? Was it the same thing?"

"No," Vel said. "These were different. I don't know how to explain it. And I heard someone say 'Die,' except I don't know if they actually said it. I might have just imagined it." He sighed, frustrated that he couldn't explain or remember it more clearly.

"You're sure you saw these things? There were really corpses?"

"I didn't see the bodies, I felt them. Yes, they were there," Vel said, and he finished his fruit, crossing his arms across his knees. "We have to get out of here, Lydia. Whatever it was, there's no reason it can't do that again. I think that was a message, with the bodies. We aren't supposed to be here."

Lydia said, "You might be—"

Movement in the grass brought both of them to their feet. Vel stumbled backwards, pulling away from Lydia. Vel drew his sword, and Lydia unhooked the staff silently from her waist. It hissed, and her cheeks flushed as the weapon assumed its full length. They stood side by side, watching at the edge of the grass-field.

Nothing.

Lydia turned in a slow circle. The nearest ruin sat less than ten feet behind them. It was a small structure—maybe a piece of one of the larger ones—with a flat roof.

"Did you see it?" Vel said.

His heart drummed through his neck and skull.

Lydia didn't answer, intent on the ruins. A moment later, she focused on the grassfield again. Vel felt foolish standing in the open, waiting.

"Did you see it?"

Again, she didn't respond.

Vel said, "They're out there."

Lydia readied herself, planting her legs exactly as she had in the alley—a defensive stance. Vel motioned to the grass in confusion. "Lydia, we don't know what these things are."

"Nara," she said. Then she asked, "The things that took you underground—tell me what they looked like."

Movement in the grasses.

Vel said quickly, "I didn't see them, Lydia. Just red eyes."

Something drew closer.

"It's possible not all of the Frill are extinct," Lydia said. "That might be what you saw. But, the Nara are altogether different than the Frill—you may have been right after all."

"About what?"

"Maybe we should have gone back."

Vel's hand was shaking, and he gripped the sword more firmly. Sweat ran down his brow and hair, falling into his eyes. The Frill, he thought, that must be what the eyes were. They're not extinct, and they're going to kill both of us.

"Not too late to run," Vel said. Something emerging from the grass. "We can—"

Then it was too late. Vel raised his sword.

"Both of you stay where you are."

A man, clad entirely in white, walked forward. He wore a swa armband on his left arm—the Religious Guard. Large and well-muscled, the priest indicated that they should drop their weapons. Vel stared uncomfortably at the receiving end of a long wooden crossbow.

"Lydia . . ."

Lydia shook her head, silencing Vel.

Behind the lead priest, a wave of men stepped out from the grass, dressed identically in suits that shined like the moon, all wearing swas on their arms. Ten men in all. They fanned out in a loose line. Vel counted four crossbows, and every one of them wore a sword at his side.

"Ideas?" Vel said under his breath.

"What's going on?" Lydia said to the priests.

The leader came nearer. "Drop your weapons."

Vel glanced nervously at Lydia.

"Drop yours," he countered.

They paused and watched in amazement as Vel pointed his sword at the leader.

"Lower your crossbow," Vel said.

Lydia watched Vel tensely.

"I don't think so." The leader was not amused. "I'll shoot you if I have to. 'Alive' does not mean 'intact'—there's no rule against taking a leg."

"Listen to me," Vel said. "If you don't do as I say, every one of you will die out here."

Impatiently, the leader lowered his weapon, aiming at Vel's leg. "Enough."

Lydia sprang at him. At the same instant a creature, with segmented legs and a muscular tail that curled onto its back, broke through the edge of the grasses. The leader fired his crossbow at Lydia. A wooden shaft flashed, and she sidestepped it, the bolt hissing under her right arm.

Sweat formed in Vel's palms as the monster snapped at the circle of priests, slicing cleanly through one man's neck. What the hell is that? Vel thought. Its tail was the same pincer Vel had seen in the grasses, and its body was hung with black hair—its head, a snout of teeth. It killed another priest.

Lydia swung up with her staff. The leader ducked, swinging his fist and Lydia caught his arm, her staff crashing against the back of his skull, and he toppled. She rolled, springing to her feet. The leader's body lay motionless in the dirt. She touched his throat and nodded at the lack of sensation.

"The Nara," Lydia said, as the monster tore a third priest apart.

"Lydia, I think . . ."

A quick cry of pain as a fourth man fell, and the creature's tail withdrew onto its back. Dark wetness drenched the ground.

"I think we need to . . ."

The remaining Religious Guard formed a loose circle around the Nara. It made a slow, scuttling turn as they shouted to one another. The pincer curled on its back, ready to strike. Crossbows discharged, arrows firing into its side, but the Nara gave no indication of pain, nothing to indicate that it felt the shafts at all, or that they had even hit their mark—and they had.

"Come on," Lydia said.

She grabbed Vel's shoulder and pulled him away, to the nearest building with a flat roof, twenty or thirty feet high. Vel hesitated as they approached the large doorway, and Lydia pulled at his arm.

"Not inside," she said.

Bones cracked behind them, men shouting. Vel spun. Bodies lay strewn about the dirt like discarded toys. Six of them, only four Religious Guard left.

"Up!" he shouted.

The Nara killed another priest-soldier with its pincer-tail, striking him almost leisurely. The remaining three gave up trying to fight and scattered into the grasses, disappearing behind a wall of burnt waves.

For the briefest moment, the Nara froze, as if uncertain which direction to charge. It scuttled to one side, clicking the curved points of its pincer, as if in thought—then it made a decision.

"Go!" Vel shouted. "Up the side!"

The Nara bounded toward them, its pointed legs racing, brushing against the random clumps of hair that hung from its sides and belly.

Vel sheathed his sword and pulled himself onto the wall. The Nara was a fast clattering of legs, drawing closer. Lydia tossed her staff onto the roof, and jumped to grab a crack, pulling herself ten feet in the air. Vel stared up at her, his eyes widening. He reached for another crack and pulled. Stone broke, and the wall shook as a pincer crashed and snapped inches below Vel's foot. A second earlier, and his leg would have been severed at the knee.

Lydia glanced back, and sweat formed along Vel's palms. He didn't let himself look down. Another crack, and Vel hauled himself up, closer to the top.

The Nara pressed its body against the side of the building in frustration, and its tail rose again. This time, Vel had almost a foot to spare, the pincer clapping in the open air below him.

Lydia grabbed a higher crack and rose easily, several feet from the top. Snapping below, and the sound of the Nara shuffling in irritation. She ran out of cracks. Wedging her feet in between two smaller spaces, she pushed off and managed to grab the ledge of the building's perfectly flat roof.

Lydia's muscles shifted, and her body rolled, panting, onto the surface of the building. Vel stared up, the Nara still snapping below him. He hadn't moved. If he lost his grip, that thing would rip him apart.

"All right," Lydia said.

She brought her staff into view, extending the tip down to Vel. It hovered, six inches above his head. His eyes focused on the end of her weapon.

"That's as far as it'll go, Vel. You'll have to—"

Vel pushed off violently. His hands rose, toward the end of the wooden pole—his fingers caught against the tough surface, slapping it, struggling to maintain a grip. He clawed.

Vel's right hand caught the pole, and he struggled with his left. His fingers slipped and would not hold. And Vel was left hanging by only his right hand, from a long, wooden pole, held by a single woman on a rooftop, above the Nara.

Sweat ran into his eyes.

Vel's voice was a growl, "Great."

His arm stretched, and the pole shifted as Lydia strained to hold up his weight. Vel pulled, muscles cording and running sore under his skin.

Hold on to the pole. Just hold on, and pull up.

He grabbed at the surface, the fingers across his right hand beginning to lose their friction as sweat built up in the joints.

"Vel, you pull up now!" Lydia said viciously.

Snapping below him.

The damn thing was still there, waiting for him to fall.

"Pull up, goddamn it!"

Vel's vision began to blur red. "It isn't as easy," he snarled, "as it looks."

His left arm throbbed as he forced it up to grip the pole. Veins pressed at the skin of his right arm.

Fingernails digging into the pole, and Vel's head beat rhythmically. Blood rushed underneath his skull. His vision shook, and Vel strained, closing his eyes tightly as he pawed up the pole. Slowly.

Don't think about the snapping. Don't think about the way it split those men in half. He began to shudder, fear finding a hole inside him. I am going to die, he thought clearly. He could concentrate on nothing else. I have to stay alive.

A head spiraling off, and blood spraying in a fine red mist.

No.

His hair was sticky with sweat now, and Vel's chest filled with tension. He pulled against the staff. Reaching farther up. All of his weight was focused on the pole he held tightly in his hands.

The rooftop was so close to him now. Just a few feet away. Lydia's eyes were tightly drawn shut, and Vel saw her crouched, straining against his weight. He pulled down, hauling himself farther up. Closer.

Snapping.

It didn't matter now.

Vel was out of its range. The damn thing couldn't jump, and Vel was almost there. He grabbed at the edge of the rooftop. Slippery. As he reached out for the building, Vel lost his grip, and he twirled, kicking out, searching desperately for a foothold on the outer wall—he fell. His toes caught in a crack, and Vel's hands slid down the end of the pole. As his knees jolted, pain rushed through his nerves.

He stopped, less than two feet from the top. His hands pressed against the smooth surface of the building. The only thing holding him up now were his feet. His toes, wedged into those tiny cracks, and his body pressed against the side of the building, hugging it.

Lydia extended her staff down to him again. "Grab onto it, Vel."

"It's too slippery. My hands I mean. They're too slippery."

Don't look down.

It was still scuttling beneath him, snapping its pincer in anticipation. Why does it want to kill me? he thought. It hadn't eaten the bodies. It just left them there, decapitated, ripped apart on the ground.

"Vel, there aren't any more handholds."

He took a slow breath and closed his eyes. "I'm very aware of that, Lydia. What would you suggest? Other than grabbing onto your staff again."

"We might have done better fighting it."

"Well." Vel remained motionless against the surface of the building. "I don't think this is that good a time to discuss what we should have done. All I want to do is live."

"All right, Vel. Look to your left."

Vel's eyes opened, and he looked. Scratches against the outer surface of the wall.

"Do you see it?"

Vel stared. Cracking below him. The thing was still waiting.

"See what?" he said.

"A foothold. And a handhold. See it?"

Vel's stomach churned. "No, Lydia. I don't."

"That crack that runs all the way down from the very top. You see where it starts? You're close enough that if you get a grip, you can push off and grab onto the ledge up here."

And then he saw it. A slight imperfection in the worn surface of the wall. Bits of dark rock were chipped and crumbling around the gash. It was narrow, but sure enough, the rip ran up several feet to the roof's edge.

"You're crazy, Lydia."

"Try for it."

"Look," he said quietly, "that crack isn't big enough for my thumb. Let alone my foot. I'm not going to reach over there, and then get slashed by that bastard down there, below me. Find something else."

"Vel, if you can get in there, you can rise enough that I can reach you."

"Yes, and if I can't, I meet an untimely demise."

"What choice do you have?"

"I can say no."

"And you can hang onto the wall until you get tired, right?"

"You got a better idea?"

"That crack—"

"—is too small."

"Goddamn it, Vel. Listen to me—you can do that! Now grab onto—"

Before his mind could object, his body was acting. He shot to the left, his foot driving hard into the crack, desperately searching for traction. Bits of black rock broke and fell away. Vel's hands scrambled above him, and he grabbed at the wall, ripping deep gashes in his palms. Pain was no longer an issue.

The rock crumbled away, and Vel's fingers strained in the tiny handhold, tossing away bits of loose stone, as he struggled to rise.

Just a little farther.

Lydia caught his wrist. Vel pulled and kicked, his pants fraying, legs sheering against the side of the building, and he reached the top.

He was laying on his back. Vel's chest heaved wickedly, he coughed, rolled onto his side, and groaned. Fingers touched Vel's hair, brushing it out of his eyes, Lydia sat beside him, her cheeks flushed red. Streams of sweat created paths of moisture down her chapped skin.

"Thank you," Vel said slowly.

Lydia rolled her staff away and embraced him. She pulled Vel close, but his heart refused to slow down. Below, there was a final snap of resignation, and the sound of the Nara scuttling away. Vel closed his eyes, listening to the pounding of Lydia's heart through her shirt.

"Take a look at this, Vel," she said softly.

He refused to let go of her. "Give me a minute."

"Look."

Vel pulled his head up, blinking away tiny pieces of stone from his eyes. At first, he saw nothing out of the ordinary; a perfectly flat rooftop—and there, across the eroded surface, Vel saw scribblings. Dark, curling pictures, carved into the stone, somehow still visible on the weathered rock. At the opposite end, a small circle of blue had been colored, perfectly round. It almost looked new.

He shook his head. "What's this?"

"I don't know," Lydia said with a smile. "Different than anything I've ever seen."

Vel glanced at the empty ground below, where the Nara had been. "That thing down there . . ."

"Was a Nara."

"Nara," Vel repeated. A story came back to him. Something his mother used to read him as a child. Something with a young trader and the lessons he needed to learn from the world, and the evil Nara that were always there. The demons that punished the wicked. In the story, they had been very similar to the Frill; both evil. It had been a religious story.

"But, what was it?" he said.

"You saw it as well as I did, Vel. Maybe the winter is changing Hera—waking up things that are usually dormant."

"The Nara are big insects, right? Mindless demons that parents make up to scare their children."

Lydia's gaze flickered. "Apparently not."

She lowered herself to inspect the surface of the roof.

"I was afraid for a moment there," she said. "You almost didn't make it."

"I noticed that too." He hesitated, then turned away. "Thank you. How many times have you saved my life now?"

"You saved yourself there, Vel. You pulled yourself up."

Vel sat and took a breath, his pulse finally beginning to slow.

"Still," he said. "I think we work together pretty well."

He watched her as she studied the inscriptions, and Lydia blew him a kiss.

"Seriously," he said.

"I didn't think you took anything seriously."

He said, "I don't."

Lydia said, "Well—as long as we're both being serious—yes, I think you're right. I think we suit each other well."

"I still don't want to buy matching plots just yet," he said.

Lydia smiled. "Well, stick with me and we won't have to."

Because you won't ever die, he thought, but he said nothing for a time, and then simply, "Thanks."

Lydia said, "You're making me care about my work too much,

you realize that. What is it with you, Vel? Danger seems to have a way of finding you, doesn't it?"

Vel said, "You found me."

"So much for that theory. I don't think love and danger are exactly the same thing."

Vel started to respond and realized he couldn't.

She said, "So?"

"So, I don't know what to . . ."

She winked at him again, and said quietly, "You heard what I said."

And they kissed.

CHAPTER 17

SHADOW AND SKY

Born of Shadow and Sky.
Without understanding,
   all is lost.
Heat binds wounds that
   separate,
And snow feels like cold
   ash.

—Blakes's *Rebirth*,
Chapter 9

"Why wasn't I notified?"

"I tried to contact you, Justice. Please, we don't have time for these disputes."

"At the ruins—you realize what this means? How could the boy have found a way to the ruins? Why would he go there?"

"My men have not reported back, Justice. Have yours?"

"Yes, and they haven't reached the ruins yet. Is it the Frill, is that why your men are missing?"

"I don't know. It's still too soon to know."

"The Frill may retaliate, you realize that. We told them the boy was dead; just his being there could—"

"I understand the significance, Justice."

"No, I don't think you do. You underestimate just how important he is. If the Frill take him, they take the code, and more than that."

"I'm afraid that if the Frill find him, they won't *take* him. They'll grind him into powder, Justice. The Frill will kill him."

"We shouldn't have made the deal with them, should never have agreed to any of this. And you're wrong. The boy is just as important to them as he is to me, to us."

"Means to an end—you knew the risks. We must remain in communication until it's finished."

"Assuming we live that long."

The soldier outside his cell nodded. "Yes, I remember you. You worked the eastland district, didn't you? When I was working that side of the force, you were real fair with the taxes. I remember that."

Till's arms and legs were bound with heavy links of chain. "This is a mistake," he said.

The soldier shrugged. "I remember you. I don't forget things like that; you were a good clerk. Not like some of them these days."

"I will take your post," Till said. "No one will know. Twenty percent."

The soldier grinned a set of dirty teeth, and he said, "Smart, aren't you? You want twenty percent so I don't have to work? You'll deliver me my money?"

"Yes. I need the twenty to live."

"Fifteen."

"Done," Till said, and the soldier let him out of the cell, unlocking Till's arms and legs.

"You'll have to find your own uniform."

"Thank you."

"Never heard of anybody who could argue with someone doing his job for him. And it sure as hell beats sitting in that cell, doesn't it? Don't get these chances often, do I? You're a clerk, I know you."

"Yes," Till said. "You do."

Lydia recovered their packs from the ground, and they both settled onto the rooftop, light fading from the sky rapidly. It was almost dark now.

"So they know we're here," Lydia said. "The Church does at least. And that might've gotten out."

Religious Guard, Vel thought, and he said, "Why would they come here—do they know I'm the next in line for the throne?"

"I would assume so, otherwise you're just someone breaking the perimeter law, and that's the police's responsibility, isn't it?"

"Why would the Church care?"

"I honestly don't know, Vel. It's possible they've been working with the police and government, but there's still no obvious connection, is there?" She opened her pack and retrieved a black book of notes she had made since they arrived, along with her writing rock. Lydia had admitted that she couldn't understand the Frill carvings, but she was still fascinated, copying as carefully as she could the few patches of surviving spiral-writing. And even now she prepared to start working.

Vel stared in amazement. "You're not going to write now, it's too dark."

She shook her head and readied one of their two torches. "No it isn't."

"If we start lighting fires, won't people know where to find us?"

Lydia looked at him. "They don't already? Vel, we don't have much time—the Nara might keep them away for a while, but we can't count on it. Besides, they have other things to worry about."

"What other things?" Vel said.

She took out a pair of silver rocks and struck them together. A sharp crash of metal, but no spark.

"You didn't see the smoke?" she said.

He stepped away from her as she slammed the rocks together a second time.

Vel sniffed in the cold. "Where?"

Lydia hesitated, and tiny sparks flashed onto the torch. It gave a crackling hiss, and she set the stick up, removing a wooden base from her pack. Lydia blew gently onto the waft of white smoke that rose from the torch's tip, and the flame grew, eating at the wooden torch.

Lydia stood, satisfied, and squinted in the night. She scanned the black horizon for a moment, and then pointed.

"There," she said.

Vel struggled to see in the gray moonlight. He stared blindly at the grassfield. "What am I supposed to see?"

"Look just above the field. On the horizon—you see it?"

Darkness.

"No."

"It's harder to make out the further up you go, because the northern hills obscure everything, but it's there."

Finally, Vel gave a disgruntled shrug. He yawned, his eyes watering in the cold, and walked back to where his blanket lay. The torchlight flicked on the carvings.

Lydia smiled, studying the roof closest to the light. "Thought this might work."

Vel wrapped the blanket around his shoulders and shivered. "Aren't you cold?"

She shrugged casually, lowering her head to the carvings. "Should I be?"

"Well, it's pretty damn cold out here, and you aren't even . . ."

Vel's voice died. Pale skin. And sweat. A sickening lump dropped into his stomach, and he tried to ignore it. He slowly went to her—Lydia smiled sadly.

"Vel, it's all right," she said.

Even as she said the words, color drained from her cheeks. He put his hands around her shoulders, drawing the blanket closer to her. No, he thought. Not now.

"Vel—"

"Lydia, you're sweating."

She pulled away from him. Vel pressed her forehead—hot to the touch, as if steam should be drifting up from her. He recoiled, and he smelled sickness. Why didn't I notice it before? he thought. Why now? He had to hear her say it. This wasn't happening.

"Lydia, what's wrong?"

He held onto her shoulder, and she lowered her head, away from him. Shadows flickered across her cold cheekbones. Dark circles beneath her eyes, and a fine lapse of black on either side of her jaw. This isn't real, he thought. I would have seen this earlier. Why didn't I see this? Vel stared and the smell reminded him of his father.

"Didn't want this to happen," she said. "I'm okay."

Vel's throat went dry, and he pulled her closer. She let herself be moved.

"Calm down," she said.

He saw himself screaming, moving rapidly and breaking his hands against the wall in a fury. Vel saw it in his mind.

"Calm down," he repeated. "You're all right. Just tell me what's wrong."

Her voice dropped. "It's okay, we need to find something about the cure."

"What's wrong?"

She met his gaze. "I'm sick."

He shook his head. "No. You're not." Vel managed a smile. "You're not sick, Lydia."

"Yes," she said. The smile twisted, and Vel's body froze. He stopped moving, and his eyes steadied. No, you are not doing this, he thought. No. My father was sick, he thought. Not you. The darkness stared down at him, and Vel backed away. His skin bristled.

"If you're sick, you might die—you said you wouldn't."

"Vel—"

"How long?"

Lydia groped to her feet and reached out for him. He staggered back.

"Stop," he murmured. "How long have you been sick?"

She touched him, trying to keep serious emotions away. "We'll find a cure, Vel. That's why we're—"

"How long," he said softly, "have you been"—his legs shook—"sick?"

Lydia backed away. "Several weeks."

Vel nodded. "Of course you're sick." He let go of her. "Why wouldn't you be?"

Lydia's throat caught, and her face hardened, her eyes becoming cold, as they had been when she had fought Jak in the alley, when she had killed the lead priest. Vel smiled, stumbling away from her.

"It wouldn't make sense if you weren't sick," he said. "Would it? Why did you tell me you wouldn't die? Why did you say that?"

She said calmly, "There's a cure, Vel."

He sat, curling methodically into a fetal position. Fire burned, spouting misty discharges of smoke into the night. Their shadows danced together. Nothing moved.

"There's a cure," he repeated.

"I care about you, Vel."

Silence. He refused to meet her gaze.

"No," he said. "That's bullshit. If you cared, why didn't you tell me? 'I promise—I swear—I won't die, Vel. You can trust me.' "

The words hit her, and she sat quietly at the carvings. Lydia picked up her book and writing chalk. "I'm sorry. I probably should have."

"No, that's all right," he said. "Doesn't matter that if I didn't have the Pox before, I have it now, does it?"

"You *do* have the Pox," she said.

"I do now."

She was silent for a moment, working in her book. Then, she stopped. "You wonder why I do this—why we're here, why I give a damn about you? You think about that? Why I'm looking out for you?"

"Looking out for me."

She said, "This is why I'm doing it, Vel. For hope."

"How goddamn noble of you," he said. " 'For hope.' What the hell does hope have to do with anything? What's hope done for me again? Why should I care? Hope didn't seem to save my parents, did it? I think it worked the other way around—it killed my parents. God, Lydia, why did you say that?" He looked at her. "You didn't have to lie to me. I'm supposed to trust you now?"

"Vel, I didn't lie. I *won't* die on you."

"Stop it. Why should I give a damn what you say now? You kept things from me—you don't care about me, that's part of your plan too, isn't it? You care about your greater good, and all I do is serve a purpose. I've got important blood, right?" She didn't answer him. "It doesn't matter who *I* am, it's who my father was." Vel rose.

"You don't understand," she said. "What's happening now is bigger than you—*everyone* is going to die if you don't help. Everyone."

"Maybe," he said. "But then again, maybe not. Maybe it will be better if one percent survives, rather than all of us dying. The government's coming apart, and I'm going to magically fix that, right? I think you're wrong, Lydia. Whether or not Hope ends has nothing to do with me."

"If you die," she said, "Hope dies."

Vel sneered, looking away. He rolled his head back and spat over the side. "Everything's so important. To be honest—because we've been so honest with each other, haven't we?—I don't think I care right now whether we win or lose. I should have listened to Ponce." He tightened his fists, the words flowing over one another. "Only I can't leave now, can I? Because it's too dangerous to go anywhere, because we're stuck in the goddamn ruins, and everyone's trying to kill us." She didn't respond. "Something's burning over there, right? And there are dead men in the dirt; and there are things called the Frill running around out there; and the Nara which isn't real, but 'oh, by the way, yes that's trying to kill you, too.'

"And we're sitting on a rooftop in the middle-of-nowhere ruins, scribbling about pictograms that don't mean anything. Hoping they'll give us a solution to our problems. You don't need me Lydia, you need a miracle. Oh, and by the way, that city, Hope—" He stood in the darkness. "—let's be honest, it isn't worth saving, is it?"

Vel shook his head. First one leg rose, then the other—he walked away.

"Where are you going?" Lydia said.

"I'm getting down. Find your own answers because I can't do this anymore. At least in Hope, I know where to hide."

He kept going. Lydia touched her staff with one hand, but she didn't move.

"The only way down is the way we came up," she said. "The wall's the same over there."

"Listen to me." And when he saw that she was holding her weapon, he grinned. "You know what? I don't care. I don't care about you. And I don't give a shit if you want to try to stop me. I'm not staying here. You understand that? You sit here and copy these." His shoulders trembled. "I don't care. I trusted you—I came with you—and you didn't even tell me you were sick. You lied." The words lingered. "Lydia, these writings aren't going to reveal some secret cure for the Pox." He started moving again. "And they aren't going to magically transport us—"

He disappeared. Lydia dropped her writings and stared—nothing.

The rooftop was empty.

chapter 18

Lord Denon led a prayer, the Cathedral pews full of priest-soldiers, all chanting at the appropriate times, kneeling at others. Denon bowed to the altar, saying, "We give thanks and praise in hope of the glorious return to our past."

Then the congregation: "Praise be to God."

"Lord, you sent your prophet Blakes to a new Eden in the dawn times."

"Lord have mercy."

Denon said, "Lord, through his hands, you worked the creation of a Divine state on this Eden of Hera. Our laws are God's laws, the state's laws are our laws, and Blakes's law will never be forgotten."

"Glory be His name."

Denon held up the book of holy scripture, the *Rebirth*, and kissed the worn cover. He set it carefully back on the altar between candles, and picked up a sacred relic from the altar, a small black tube with tiny writing on one side, near a white circle. It read: *Rechargeable Solar Cell, Model 810.* Denon held up the tube and said, "Blakes's memory will remain, until the day of our glorious return to our past."

Denon pressed the white circle, and light shot from one end of the tube in a continuous stream, lighting a circle on the black ceiling far overhead.

The entire congregation fell to their knees, heads bowed in reverence. Denon held the tube over his head and faced them solemnly. As he spoke, he shined the light on each of them in turn.

"Lord, we remember that Blakes fought the wickedness of Eichland, and the demon's name was Urizen and your power, which is everlasting is our model from the dawn times, when this was given to Blakes, eight hundred and ten years before the coming of Hope and Hera. With the eternal light, we remember that once it filled all of existence—as tradition tells us. This light that you gave to Blakes while he was imprisoned in a cell in the land of Solar, in the prison, Rechargeable.

"And Blakes used your power, oh God, to bring light to the barren darkness of our new Eden, to Hera, and thus Hope was born. And though the light is diminished, it will someday return, and we will be saved. Thus the sin of temptation and lies is traded for life through His name. Glory be to God."

"Praise Blakes His prophet," the congregation said, and they rose together. Lord Denon pushed the tube's white circle again, and the light blinked out. He returned the holy relic to the altar, facing the congregation again.

Denon said, "Let us remember holy sacrifice in these dark times, and let us never forget the word of the Lord and His scriptures. Life over Lies, my children."

The Religious soldiers said, "Praise be to God." And Denon ended the mass, bidding them all to go in peace. They filed out of the Cathedral in silence, several heading to the altar to return the relic to one of the chambers deep beneath the church. These private masses were held three times daily for the members of the Religious Guard, and they were generally identical to the masses held at the end of each week for the general public. Except that the sacred relics were never displayed before the populace, of course.

Greater devotion was required for those within the hierarchy of the Church, and when he was alone, Lord Denon stood behind the altar, tracing the edges of the *Rebirth*'s old cover with one hand.

Justice Hillor is becoming dangerous, Denon thought. What will happen if the boy dies? A coup? Denon flipped open the book, glanced at pages of text, but he did not read the words. More Religious Guard had been sent to the ruins, and Hillor had dispatched police soldiers as well. If Hillor finds the boy, Denon thought, I won't hear of it, will I? And yes, Blakes's teachings are still very much alive, aren't they?

Dark revolving in silent activity:
Unseen in tormenting passions.

Lord Denon thought about the decision they had made years
ago, when they were both younger. Hillor had been so strong
then—but he's still powerful, Denon thought. He just sees the
reality of the situation now. He's nervous; he sees the possibility
that everything may fall apart. The boy is too important. But I'm
not sorry we made the deal, Denon thought. The Frill are treacherous, yes, but even demons can be used toward His end. We
knew the boy would someday be this important when we made
the deal, when we agreed to their terms. But we didn't understand, did we? We didn't really know what we were doing. I
should have seen this happening, Denon thought. But the seasons
hadn't even begun to change years ago, and now it's all happening
so quickly. So complicated.

Denon bowed his head, closed his eyes, and leafed through the
Rebirth, as he did when he needed guidance. He opened a page
near the middle of the book. It read:

*Millions have died for His purpose, for the purpose of
individual greatness, and sometimes the hypocrisy of mass
slavery can only be challenged through a holy act so bloody
that it must be righteous. Science is the tool of the weak,
who want only to remain as slobbering animals. I have seen
angels, and I know that man can someday become as God:*

*As I looked, the shape dilated more and more: he waved
his hands; the roof of my study opened; he ascended into
heaven; he stood in the sun, and beckoning to me, moved
the universe. An angel of evil could not have done that—it
was the archangel Gabriel. I saw him, and someday I too
will have wings.*

Denon thought, Praise be to God. And he closed the book.

A faint blue light and the stench of dust.

Vel shivered in the pale illumination. Near darkness and the sensation of being submerged. A kind of moisture clung to the air. Something Vel could not recognize, and yet his body told him at once what the feeling meant: he was underground. He *remembered* the light. It was the same blue from the cemetery tunnel that led past the perimeter wall, but Vel had seen it somewhere else . . .

In the wide expanse of blue, he saw very little. The musty light originated at no single source, and yet it filled out to give the room shape. Long, high-rising walls, smoothly cut and cluttered with dark symbols. More of the pictograms. The room was perfectly square, rounding off in a dome, fifty feet above his head.

Across the surface of the ground, Vel saw a distinct layer of film. A buildup of dirty residue, like old dust. Objects lay scattered about in dark, meaningless clumps along the four walls. They could be anything. Vel's heart pounded.

Silence—as complete and consuming as a loud symphony of noise. As he approached one of the shapes, Vel's feet sank into the layer of dust across the floor. And he stopped.

Footprints.

Deep and fresh in the dust, a set of footprints, originating exactly at the spot his own did; in the center of the room. Both his and the other prints began in a large circle, worn and colored a dark blue, where Vel still stood. Vel lowered himself to the ground and stared at the tracks: a long, slender shoe, like a woman's foot. Jak.

He stepped off, into the room. And he thought of the rooftop.

The blue circle was identical to the one he'd seen colored on the roof. Where the hell am I? he wondered. Vel stepped back onto the shape, pressing his feet firmly onto the circle. He stood completely on the blue surface, obscuring the other breaks in settled dust.

Nothing.

What if I can't get back? he thought. Vel glanced at the shadows in the corners of the room, and noticed a large doorway in exactly the direction the female footsteps led. Those tracks did not return this way; they disappeared into the darkness, meaning there was probably another way out. This blue circle wasn't an exit, it was just an entrance. Vel started for the doorway.

The world blurred white, leaving spots in his vision, and he stumbled.

"Vel!"

Hands touched his shoulders. Lydia stood before him, and Vel snapped back, away from her. On the roof again. Still dark, nothing had changed.

"You all right?" Lydia's eyes were wide, and she was sweating. "What happened?"

"I'm not going to leave," he said.

She said, "Vel, I'm sorry. You're right, I was wrong not to tell you."

He shook his head. "There's something you're going to want to see."

"What happened?"

"That," Vel pointed to the circle, "took me someplace else. Onto another circle in a cavern somewhere—like the tunnel, except it was a room. And I saw footprints." He smiled. "Female footprints."

Lydia froze. "Jak?"

"Maybe. This could be the way she came. Someone's been there."

"What's in the room?"

"Don't know." He shook his head. "I wasn't gone long, was I?"

"No, you weren't."

"Lydia." Vel looked at her. "You need someone down there with you. Sorry, I said things so quickly. I didn't mean . . ."

Lydia touched his hand, and reluctantly he accepted the gesture.

"I should have told you," she said. "I was afraid, and we're here to find a cure."

"It's all right." He hesitated. "This is a hell of a time for this, isn't it?"

She moved closer to the circle. "We'll find the cure, Vel."

"If it's down there." But he'd begun to sound more confident. "That's a big *if.* Do you have any idea what *it* is exactly?"

"No, not really. Could be a magic river, directions for a special kind of bloodletting—I don't know." She seemed hesitant to step onto the circle. "What's it like?"

"It doesn't feel like anything. One minute you're here, the next you're somewhere else." He paused. "I'm an idiot."

She pursed her lips. "You might be." She kissed him. They remained together, and, finally, she let go. Lydia stepped onto the circle, bracing herself.

A moment later, she looked around in confusion. "I thought you said it would—"

"Step away from it."

She did.

A brief flick of her figure, and the roof stood silent. Vel stared at the empty space that Lydia had occupied moments ago.

Vel took a breath and walked away from the circle, picking up her book. What am I doing? he thought. She's sick. Lydia will be dead in a matter of months, if not sooner. The thoughts brought a stab of unwanted aggression into him. And so will I.

Vel got back onto the circle. If Lydia had to die—and she wasn't going to, they were going to find a cure—then Vel would somehow kill the disease that had done it to her. If there is a cure, I will find it, he thought. Jak and Hillor had both supposedly come here, but then why was there only one set of prints?

Vel stepped off.

With a surge of brightness, the world constricted into blue light and darkness, leaving spots that Vel blinked away. This time the room appeared more distinct than it had earlier. Lydia stood nearby, watching the lone doorway.

"You see that?" she said.

Vel coughed. The sound soaked into the walls.

"What?"

Some of the objects across the floor took on shape and definition.

"When you came down, it got a little brighter. That blue light must be triggered by the number of people in here at a time. Was it this bright when you were here?"

Vel shook his head, moving to one of the forms against the wall. "No."

Vel knew damn well what it was. Its surface was broken, and pieces had long since eroded into nothing. The entire shape turned a moldy black with age. A skeleton. Vel stopped, unable to move. Lydia's footsteps behind him.

"What happened to him?" Vel said.

"It's pretty clear, isn't it?" Lydia's voice was quiet.

Braced against the wall, the skeleton was missing one entire arm, its remaining hand gripping a small black device. Just like Hillor's weapon, Vel thought. My God, it's another one. Discolored bone, and cracked teeth smiling up at them. The right side of the skull was pounded in, almost ripped in half, with a fractured hole.

"I'd say he's been dead for a while," Lydia said. "Maybe a few hundred years old."

"Who is he?"

"I have no idea, could be one of the original settlers. I told you they fought with the Frill."

Vel turned away and moved back to the circle. "You said they wiped out the Frill."

"They did, but that doesn't mean there weren't human casualties."

"Earlier," Vel said, "when I was taken underground—that was a Frill's eyes I saw. They aren't all dead. This is a bad idea. We shouldn't be down here."

Lydia looked up. "We'll find the cure, and we'll leave, okay?"

"You think the Frill did that?" Vel said. "Broke open his head?"

"He's been dead for a while." She leaned closer, inches from the skull, and picked up something from the dust nearby. Some kind of bracelet, with a circular piece of metal on one side. Lydia showed him the bracelet, and Vel studied the markings. Numbers from one to twelve, and tiny lines.

"I don't understand," Vel said.

"Probably a charm," Lydia said, and she set the bracelet back where she had found it. "I think the numbers have something to do with religious laws—Blakes calls them Commandments, but he never actually explains them. I think there were around twelve of them."

Vel pointed to a rotting collection of papers revealed by the disturbed dust. "You think those were his?"

Lydia examined the pile, without touching it. " 'Gainst the sin of technology,' " she read, and then gingerly moved the top pieces aside to look at others. " 'Thoughts of Chairman Mao.' "

Vel frowned. "What?"

"I don't know—that's what it says." Lydia sighed. "Most of these are too old to read, and I'm afraid to touch them. They look like they might blow away, don't they?"

"Or fall apart."

"But, look at this." She held up the perfect, black object; just like Hillor's. Vel stiffened.

"I've seen that before," he said.

Lydia nodded. "So have I. It's the same thing Justice Hillor carries—he uses it instead of a sword. And he's the only one who has a working model." She seemed to be talking more to herself than to Vel. "Supposedly the Church gave it to the first Chief Justice several hundred years ago. It's a weapon. You saw Hillor at the Watchman, didn't you?"

Lydia held it in the palm of her hand, looking quietly into its side. This one was considerably smaller than the one Hillor used, but it still looked the same. She clicked a portion of the object out, and a compartment dropped into exposure.

Vel said, "It almost looks new. Why isn't it worn away like the rest of this stuff?"

"I don't know how they made these," Lydia said. "But the founders made their weapons to last."

"Then, it's the same hand-crossbow Hillor carries?" Vel asked.

"Not a crossbow," she said. "It's called a gun, but it doesn't make any difference that it's in perfect condition—it's out of ammunition."

"How do you know what it is? Most people think Hillor's is magic, like God's fire or something."

"Blakes mentions guns in some of his books—he condemns them."

She tossed the small gun to Vel, and he caught it, holding the metal tenderly, as if it might break at any moment.

"So how does it work?" he said. "What do they do? How did Hillor kill that man at the Watchman? He just kind of pointed the thing at the guy, there was a noise, and the guy's face exploded. How does it work?"

Lydia touched the wall directly behind the skeletal body.

"It fires a projectile," she said distantly, looking at the stone, one hand tracing a path through the symbols. "A little piece of metal shoots out of the end of it. According to Blakes."

Some of the pictograms had been scratched out and crudely carved over with a swa and the words:

Sieg Heil
Unser Führer Blakes

"You see this?" Lydia asked.

Vel indicated the skeleton. "You think he wrote that?"

"Don't know."

"Looks like gibberish." Vel strapped the gun into his belt, beneath his shirt. "So, how do guns shoot metal?"

"I don't understand it myself." Lydia picked through more of the rotting debris. "I didn't invent them, Vel. Hillor might be the only one alive who knows how they work, but even he might not really know the specifics. From what I understand, most of the things from the beginning of Hope were destroyed in the war against the Frill. If you have a crossbow, you have to keep getting more arrows if you want it to shoot, don't you? I think guns were the same way—run out of little metal ammunition and it won't shoot."

"So where does Hillor get his?"

"The Church maybe?" Lydia shrugged. "I don't know." She held up another piece of rotting paper. "Look at this—"

Movement behind him, and Vel spun.

An expanse of dust separated him from the doorway across the room.

"Vel?"

I heard something, he thought. Something's here. Without turning, Vel said, "What does it say?"

A heartbeat passed in silence, and for a moment Vel wasn't certain that she'd heard him. He opened his mouth, and her voice struck out at him: *It says things that everyone knows, about your parents.*

Vel looked at the back of her head.

"What?" he said.

It wasn't her voice, it wasn't Lydia. He tried to back away, but his legs refused to obey.

It says that we are going to die down here. That people are doomed to repeat what they have already repeated and that killing is wrong. The voice flowed from his own skull, as if his thoughts were bouncing back at him through her mouth. *It says that you're a bad person, Vel.*

A chill rushed into the top of his head.

"Stop," he said.

Because you let your parents die.

"Stop it, Lydia."

She turned to him, it wasn't her. The face had sunken into white lines of flesh, struggling to hold onto the bone, deep grooves beneath swollen eyes.

His mother was smiling at him.

Vel couldn't move. "You're dead."

Lydia frowned, and Vel stumbled away, his arms flailing. There was nothing to hold onto. Just like that. Just a quick flicker, and he was back in the real world.

"Who are you talking to?" she said, still holding a fragment of paper.

"I don't know." He stared at her, willing the image to return.

Lydia studied him. "I take it that's what you meant? Earlier, about your mom—you saw something, didn't you?"

He nodded. "I saw my mother. I saw her there."

"Where?"

"She was you," Vel said. "I mean, you looked like my mother. You weren't you."

Lydia glanced back at the wall. She ran her palm across the swa and more words written over the original carvings—the words looked too small to read. "This writing is bad."

"What do you mean?"

"Most's illegible, but look at this: 'Destroy them all, until Blakes returns for his judgment.' And here—" She indicated another section of writing. "More of the 'Sieg Heils' and then it says, 'Blakes will pour their blood into the riverbed, and Hera will die. Mankind is damned, despite God's love.' "

They looked at the corpse.

Vel asked, "What about the paper?"

She set it back on the floor, looking weary. "More nonsense."

"You were going to tell me something—what did it say?"

Lydia backed away from the skeleton and smiled weakly. "I wondered if you had heard of something called a 'Khmer Rouge'? It was some kind of prophecy, like the ones on the wall. Not important." She took a breath. "We're looking for food and a cure."

He nodded and said, "I feel like I'm part of this. I was right earlier, wasn't I? We are underground."

"Yes, I think so. But these tunnels might go on for miles. The best we can do is follow Jak's footprints."

Vel shook his head. A part of him, some limb that had been sleeping, began to awaken.

"I don't think so." He walked closer to the doorway, and a bluish tint illuminated that part of the room. It surrounded him, bleeding out of the walls, and the section Lydia stood in grew significantly darker. She followed, and a separate light tracked her.

"I don't know how," Vel's voice was distant, "but I know this place. There are things down here, things in these ruins that I know. I know the Frill liked purple flowers."

Lydia shook her head. "What are you talking about?"

He hesitated. "I know things I shouldn't know. What the hell is going on? I understand this entire layout. I know the tunnel system."

Lydia came closer. "You have a map inside your head?"

Vel walked to the doorway. "No. It's different. It's like trying to remember a dream, and then going to a place in your dream in real life, and as you walk around, things start to come back to you."

She watched him, eyes wide. He kept walking, then hesitated, facing her.

"Lydia," Vel said, "I'm not going crazy."

"How?" she said. "How can you possibly know the layout of this place? You've never been here before."

"I don't know how I know." He looked at the footprints. "I just do. We follow these. You were right—follow the path Jak took."

Vel stepped into the corridor and the light followed him. Lydia did the same. Walls, covered in that same deep-set pictograms, continued into the hallway, periodically scratched out and drawn over with swas and graffiti. The passage branched into fragment after fragment.

They turned and followed the hall through a series of jagged breaks—and stopped. There were two mounds on the floor ahead, bodies. Jak's footprints wound around the piles, continuing on ahead.

"Lydia—"

"I see them." She drew her staff, and it lengthened. "Stay here."

After examining the corpses, Lydia said, "It's all right, come on."

More skeletons, but these smelled, and Vel stepped over the scattered limbs, trying not to look. The toe of his boot caught on something—a leg—and he dropped, dried flesh—like frozen, decaying fruit—on his hands, against his arms. Vel struggled, his fingers running through dead hair, a clump came away, and Lydia grabbed him, pulling him back up, away from the bodies. The blue light followed.

Vel was panting, cold sweat across his back. "They're—they're . . ."

"They were soldiers," Lydia said, and she guided him away from the dead, finally stopping out of sight.

Vel could smell the rot under his fingernails, and he wiped both hands hard on his pant's leg. "Goddamn it."

"They died around twenty years ago," she said. "Maybe not even that long."

Vel started walking again. "I don't care when they died. What the hell did that to them—they were ripped apart, like something just . . ."

"I know."

They finally came to a halt at a solitary wall. Dark symbols and pictograms, partially obscured by swas, pointed to a central focus: a blue circle in the exact center of the wall, barely four inches in diameter.

"I think this is it," Vel said. "I know there's a cure here."

Before Vel could continue, Lydia thrust her hand into the circle. It disappeared up to her elbow, vanishing in the stone. Lydia frowned and shook her head. "Something's wrong."

Vel hesitated. "What?"

"There's nothing there."

"Let me try."

Lydia withdrew her hand, unchanged, and Vel put his in, arm passing through the colored rock as if it wasn't there. Nothing. Vel pulled his arm back out and said, "I *know* it should be here."

"How?"

"Lydia, I don't know how—the same way I know these tunnels. Jak must have taken it. Someone has it."

Lydia started back without answering—she vanished. Vel stood alone on a blue circle. They hadn't noticed it.

How many are there? he wondered.

Vel glared at the small circle in the wall. Something's supposed to be here, he thought. Goddamn Jak. Vel went through.

"WHAT THE hell is that?"

Lydia looked back at Vel. They were in a miniature version of the first room. Walls covered in markings, some drawn over with even larger swas and more writing. There were two doorways, the footprints heading down the one on the right—then back again—appearing to finally decide on the left doorway.

Apart from a single statue between the doorways, the room was empty. The statue's silver side glimmered in the light, and Vel's twisted reflection bounced back. A deformed body of armor more than twelve feet high, its "head" nearly touching the slanted, domed ceiling. The armor was a thin, humanoid shape with a huge, distorted headpiece, elongated as if for a snout. Two arms hung stiffly, three definite joints in each arm, marked off by segments in the armor.

No fingers at the end of the arms, just rounded, somewhat compressed hunks of metal. Four legs dropped in a precise pattern below the torso, and at the bottom of each leg, the segments split again, into three miniature stalks supporting the legs.

Lydia crouched in front of the thing, running her fingers across a block of metal at its feet. A marker.

"Do you know what it is?" she said. "Does this have to do with the Frill?"

stephen chambers

Vel stared, unmoving. "I don't know." He motioned to the marker. "What does that say?"

"It's nothing I've ever seen before," Lydia said. "There are definite sounds. But, it's gibberish."

Vel smiled. "A name."

Lydia stood. She frowned and brushed off her legs. "That might be it."

"Maybe it's a monument." He stopped. "No. It's more than that." He turned, moving to the first doorway.

Blue light flooded his passage.

"Vel." Lydia extended her hand tiredly. "Give me a second."

The hallway was a dead end—stopping at a strange, transparent wall, like glass. Vel drew closer. Through the wall, a giant room stretched out, dimly visible in a shadowy blue, filled with grassfruit, all fresh. The layers of food extended farther than Vel could see, and several large cylindrical monuments had been placed among the fruit. Vel squinted, and there, written on the monuments between perfect swas were the words *Refrigeration/ Freezing Agent–38011.*

The words meant nothing to Vel, but the food looked untouched, somehow preserved.

"My God," he said. "Lydia—"

The lights were gone—a crash, and a muffled scream.

"Lydia!" he shouted.

Vel ran, drawing his sword blindly. No, he thought. This can't happen now. Into another room, and he felt along a wall, searching for a doorway.

"Lydia!"

No response. Into another hall, and Vel paused.

"Lydia!"

A distant blue light was visible at the end of a long hallway. What causes that? Vel thought. That same light. He could almost see the outline of the passage in the dimness.

Vel was alone, and he stalked forward, his sword still drawn. Something knows I'm here, he thought. An unsettling feeling formed in his stomach, as if he had just eaten something not entirely cooked. He walked toward the light. Vel moved through a doorway into another hall unlike anything he had ever seen.

He called, "Lydia?" No answer.

Faces and body parts protruded from the walls, as if statues had been sealed partially into the foundations of the tunnel, so that only parts of heads and reaching hands and legs could be seen. Vel stopped at the first carving. It was a young woman, her head tilted and mouth open, as if singing. The walls in this corridor had no writing on them, only these perfect, stone extensions.

Vel touched the woman's cheek. It's stone, he thought. These are not real people. These are works of art. He walked past the woman and saw a man and part of a young boy smiling and holding hands, the boy's arm high above his head to reach the man's. One of the man's legs stuck out of the wall, as if he was dancing, and Vel could imagine his other leg and the rest of his body encased in the stone.

On the opposite wall, an angry-looking man with a beard stared at Vel, both of his arms raised above his head, protruding from the wall into perfectly constructed fists. His legs were not visible, only the tip of one of his knees. His mouth was closed, and he seemed to be concentrating on Vel. Vel drew nearer.

He stood directly in front of the statue and touched one of its fists. The man was exactly his height. Stone, Vel thought, his heart pounding. It's not real. Vel began to walk again, the motionless people laughing and shouting silently at him as he passed. The light was coming from a door in the center of the far wall. What is this? Vel thought, and he moved closer to the door. It was black—but not stone.

Where there should have been a doorknob, there was only a stained square. The door was cold to the touch. Not stone. What was it? Almost as if the entire door was built of a kind of metal— like his sword—but large enough to create an entire door. This door was more perfectly formed than anything Vel had ever seen. No imperfections; the edges were flawlessly aligned.

Vel touched the square with his palm, there was a click, and the door opened in. The blue light vanished, but Vel could still see. A different kind of light came from the crack the door had created, and Vel felt warm air from within. He pushed, and the door opened easily, revealing a small, metal passage. Over a second door, in capital letters were the words:

WELCOME ABOARD!
PLEASE VERIFY YOUR CLEARANCE ID NUMBER BEFORE
PROCEEDING.

Not knowing what else to do, Vel touched the door.

From somewhere above hummed a soft female voice: "Identification number, please."

"What?" Vel said. "I don't understand." He waited, staring up at the ceiling, but again he was left in silence. Vel pressed his hand against the door again.

"Identification number, please."

Vel jammed his finger at the door again, harder.

"Identification number, please."

"What do you want?" he demanded, frustrated. "What do you want? What?"

Silence.

Then, *One . . . three . . . two . . . one.* A voice, but not the same modulated female voice. This was a voice from inside his head. A sudden chill raised prickly sparks on his scalp. Vel touched the door again.

"Identification number, please."

Vel said, "One . . . three . . . two . . . one."

There was a pause. Then came the voice, brisk and reassuring. "Thank you, Commander Blakes. And welcome aboard."

chapter 19

The Executive Council stood as Justice Hillor entered the room, all twenty-nine of them. Most were aristocrats, signs of their wealth visible in their large bellies and expertly cut clothing. Several of the women even wore jewelry, glittering pieces of metal in their ears, rings on their fingers.

Candles burned on the long black table, past alternating tapestries of Church swas and government stars. Lord Denon nodded as Hillor passed him, and two police shut the door to the room. Hillor took his seat near the empty chair at the head of the table. The rest of the council sat, filling all but one seat—the King's place.

One of the older men started speaking, asking for suggestions on the repairs that were needed for the eastern districts. Hope's only public park—a small enclosure of paths and trimmed grasses—had been vandalized recently; what was to be done about heightened security? Others argued that the police did not have soldiers to spare, and the discussion turned to a new tax on liquor and whether or not a law ought to be passed requiring checkpoints for permits at all of the city bridges.

The tax passed, but the other issues remained undecided, and Hillor said, "Motion for announcements on the floor."

"Recognized," someone said from the opposite end of the room.

Hillor said, "I will be brief. The King is dead."

A handful of the council looked surprised, but most remained exactly as they were, waiting for Hillor to continue.

He said, "He died without a direct heir, and we are left in a fragile situation."

One of the poorer members of the council, a man named Orik, said, "What's being done about the food rioting?"

"The police are maintaining order," Hillor said. "I'll speak to that in a moment. First, I have good news. While the King did not have an *immediate* heir, we have located the next in his line, his nephew. The King's brother had a boy named Vel who is now legally King of Hope."

"Where is he?" a woman asked.

"As we speak, he is being located by police soldiers who will bring him here, to the Palace."

"The King's death must be publicly announced," Orik said, and Hillor shook his head.

"I disagree," Hillor said. "We should wait until Vel is ready to be made King. An early announcement will cause panic."

"Justice Hillor is right," one of the older men said, and several of the wealthier members of the council agreed. However, those around Orik objected, shouting that the people had a right to the information, regardless of what *might* happen. Only Lord Denon and a handful of others watched the dispute silently.

Hillor said, "The city is not ready to know that the King is dead."

"They'll learn sooner than you think—and unless it's announced formally, they'll think we're afraid," Orik countered.

"We'll have the new King shortly; the people are perfectly capable of waiting until then."

Orik said, "But they won't. And they shouldn't have to."

One of the women on Hillor's side said, "Orik, you're taking this too far. We're not talking about anything unreasonable here—Hillor isn't going to keep it secret for longer than is needed."

Hillor nodded. "Several days."

"It will get out," Orik said. "Whether you think the people have a right to know if their King is dead or not, they *will* know."

"How? Will you tell them?"

One of the men near Orik, came to his defense, saying, "We'll put the secrecy to a vote, and if it fails, the people will be told."

"No," Hillor said. "We'll put the decision *to tell them* to a vote, and if *it* fails, the King's death will be kept secret." Nothing will pass now, Hillor thought. Whatever is voted on will be defeated.

They argued, and finally Lord Denon raised his hand, the voices slowly quieting.

"The King has been sick for months," Denon said, and he

looked from Hillor to Orik. "The people know, and yes, they will learn of his death whether they are told or not. But it won't be real knowledge, it will be a rumor that the King was murdered, that his death is a secret for the purposes of this Council. We must keep the loyalty of the people." Denon looked at Hillor, and Hillor's jaw tightened. "I'm sorry, Justice, but the councilman is right: the people should be told. Not because they need to know, but because they *will* know, regardless."

Hillor glared at Denon and said quietly, "I disagree."

"We will put the decision to tell them to a vote," Denon said. "Who is opposed to that?"

It won't pass, Hillor thought.

"All in favor of telling the city that the King is dead?" Hillor asked.

Seventeen members of the council raised their hands, including Lord Denon. They needed sixteen to pass. Damn it, Hillor thought, and he said, "All opposed."

Thirteen opposed. The votes had to be counted, regardless of whether the measure had already gone through. Hillor thought, Why did you fight me on this Denon? You work with me when it's for your own benefit, don't you? And when it isn't, we're enemies.

"It is my decision that the proposal to formally inform the city of the King's death has passed," Hillor announced, and he stood to leave. "Council is dismissed."

vel stood at one end of a short metal hallway that flowed into a darkened room. He had the strangest feeling of being able to taste the air, and small, perfectly aligned holes in the ceiling over his head hummed. Air blew down at him, tossing his hair, and Vel walked forward slowly, the door shutting behind him. Lights came on at regular intervals on both sides of the hallway. They too, gave a weak hum, and Vel held his sword with both hands.

In the new light, Vel could make out several forms in the room ahead. The entire structure was built of dark metal, and Vel saw what looked like three metal chairs that rose from the floor in front of a metal counter and smooth squares that might have been one-sided glass. Vel stopped walking, and he leveled the sword to the chair on the right. Someone was sitting in it. If there was more light . . . But by the light of this hallway, he could definitely see someone in the chair on the right—and on the left. Only the middle seat was empty.

"Hello?" Vel said.

The dark shapes did not move or answer. The room was larger than he had thought, and Vel took several steps closer, spotting a hole in the far ceiling and a metal ladder attached to the wall, extending up, through the opening.

"Hello?" Vel said again. "I see you sitting there."

The forms in the chairs remained. Vel walked closer, entering the doorway of the room. As he entered, air shook his hair, and lights flickered, gradually illuminating the entire room. It was broad and round, with a sealed door at the rear wall and several empty chairs placed along both walls, facing more metal counters and squares of one-sided glass. The counters were riddled with circles and slots, cracked and covered in a thick layer of dust and mold.

"Turn around," Vel said to the occupied chairs. No answer, and he approached, walking quietly around the left chair, with his back to the wall. The room, the walls, everything was silent. Dust rose as Vel moved—and froze, keeping his sword ready. Jak hasn't been here, he thought. No one's been here.

"Goddamn it," he said. "Is *everyone* dead?"

Skeletons smiled back at him. The nearest one was dressed in rotted black fabric, and in one hand, resting on its lap, was a small object, about the size of its palm, with a tiny square of the same dark, reflective one-sided glass. The farther skeleton rested one hand on the ancient counter in front of it, its chin sitting on the top of its rib cage. In this skeleton's free hand it held another one of the guns, and on the floor, around the skeleton's rotted boots, Vel saw a collection of tiny metal nuts. Ammunition? he thought. That's what Lydia was talking about—they fire pieces of metal. Diagonal holes had been cut in the backs of both skulls, as if they had been stabbed hard.

Vel stared without moving. He sheathed his sword, and moved closer to the nearest body, taking the small oval object in both hands. It slid out of the skeleton's fingers. "So what the hell is this?" Vel said, and the tiny screen came to life.

On the screen—filling the one-sided glass—an attractive woman with long, red hair was shouting . . . at him, Vel decided. She appeared from the shoulders up, and from behind her there was a loud, scraping, smashing noise.

"Get out of here!" the woman shouted, and Vel dropped the device, stumbling away from it and drawing his sword. He spun to face the room behind him—nothing had changed. The small device had landed on the ground nearby, with the screen up, so that the tiny face of the woman was still visible, shaking her head and glancing over her shoulder. "We're wrong!" she said. "Never any rescue ship—you bastard, we're all going to die. There's no way out of here."

Vel stood over the small device, and on the screen the pounding in the background grew louder, and the world moved quickly to show a lean man in a nearby chair, frantically pressing the circles—buttons. The glass square in front of the man was lit in a bright white light, and numbers flashed rapidly across it. The man turned, raised a pistol and fired three times off screen. "Damn 'em," he said with an accent like nothing Vel had ever heard. "And damn you for puttin' us in this position, Blakes!" the man shouted at the screen, and he fired again, hitting keys with his other hand. "Close, damn it!"

The woman appeared on-screen again, and she spoke directly to Vel, struggling to ignore the flashes of gunfire and metal pounding in the backdrop. "Listen to me," she said, "you find this, Blakes—you get out of here. Hope won't last. You can't use these creatures like you think you can. They'll kill you—you can't shoot them! Do you hear me? Get out of here! It isn't—" She broke off, and the screen twirled. On-screen there was only the ceiling, and then a snapping sound, accompanied by a short scream, and a second snap that was louder than the first, and the screen shifted slightly, and was still. It went dark.

Vel looked back at the bodies, and he picked up the device, his hands wet and shaking.

That is this room, Vel thought, looking at the nearest skeleton. It smiled blindly at the console in front of it, and Vel walked behind them to examine the openings in the backs of their heads. What could have done this? he thought. I have to get out of here.

He stared at the room, at the ladder and the other door on the opposite wall. Vel walked away from the bodies, leaving the strange device on the floor. He thought of the woman on the screen. *You died a long time ago. You were warning someone.* Vel's mouth had gone very dry. *You were warning someone else: Blakes. Your message was for Blakes, not me. Who the hell were you, Blakes? What did you do?*

Vel walked toward the closed door at the other end of the room. *How long had these bodies been here? How long had it been since they were killed?* On the ceiling near the door was a long, shredded tear in the metal, and the wall was nicked and blackened with holes. Black strings of different sizes hung from the ceiling wound, frayed at their ends, and as Vel walked beneath it, he looked into the opening. The hole was deep, and Vel could see levels of metal, as if he was staring into a grassfly hive.

He touched the strings—wires—uncomfortably and glanced back at the bodies. *What was in here? What the hell is this place— what are these glass squares? Do they somehow remember what's happened here?* Vel went to the nearest dormant box and pressed the one-sided glass—nothing happened. *This isn't magic,* he reminded himself. *But, then what the hell was that scene on the tiny glass?*

Vel.

He stopped. Vel let go of the wires, and readied his sword. The voice had come from behind that door. *I heard you,* Vel said in his mind. It had been Lydia's voice. But, something about it had been wrong.

The room was quiet. He walked closer to the door and spotted another red square where the doorknob should have been.

"Lydia," he said.

I'm here, Vel. It was her voice, it was Lydia. *Open the door.*

They're doing this, he thought. *That isn't really your voice.* The sound was right, but Lydia wouldn't say that—she would speak differently, use different words.

Touch the door, Lydia said, and Vel moved closer, keeping his sword steady.

"Why?" Vel said. "Why should I open that door?"

Vel's breathing quickened, and he looked briefly around the

room, turning back to the original hall, the way out. What is this place? Did the first people on Hera build this—did Blakes?

Vel—

"Stop that!" Vel said. His heart pounded faster, and he turned slowly to the ladder instead. "Why through the door?" he said. "Why do you want me through that door, *Lydia*?"

To the ladder, and Vel held his sword in one hand, slowly climbing. One rung, and another, until he had passed through the metal ceiling and stepped away from the ladder into another, smaller room—on an opposite wall there was a hall with more closed doors. Behind a table, lying against the wall, on its side, sprawled another skeleton, its jawbone fallen away from the rest of its skull. In its hands, it gripped another gun, this one much larger than the others, even Hillor's. It was differently shaped, but yes, Vel thought, still a gun. The skeleton's rib cage had been shattered completely on the left—turned to a mess of sharp fragments— and whatever had caused the damage had gone on to break the spinal cord in half, severing the bottom of its body from the top.

On the table, in front of the body, sat an open metal box, filled with rows of intricate glass items, some with sharp ends, filled with liquid, others nothing more than capsules the size of Vel's fingernail. All perfectly arranged.

There were rectangles of paper with pictures on them attached to the walls. All were faded, but still legible: the first contained a giant red swa above more of the gibberish writing:

Deutschland
Was bietet Deutschland?

The second poster was a precise drawing of a strange-looking man with squinting eyes and dark hair, smiling, dressed in a brown uniform. There was some kind of writing above the picture unlike anything Vel had ever seen. Elaborate crisscrossings and almost-pictures, the red writing seemed closer to the Frill pictograms than the language of Hope—Enish—that Vel had learned to read. The more Vel looked at the drawing, the more unsettling it became—the smiling face was *real*, as if it had been captured on this paper.

Before examining the third poster, Vel approached the table, spotting something bright—a cross with a tiny form of a man sleeping on it, arms spread over his head. Vel had never seen a simple cross before; the Church symbol was the swa—the wheel cross that seemed to be spinning to the right—just like the ones on the first poster. This was something new.

Vel picked up the tiny piece of gold. The four lengths of the cross were not even, as they should have been, but seemed to be altered to accommodate the tiny sleeping man with only a cloth over his groin. Vel felt grooves on the back, and, holding it up to the light, he saw a tiny inscription in ornate writing that was almost too faint to read:

Hernán Cortés

The letters were real letters, but what did Hernán Cortés mean? Vel pocketed the cross, trying to ignore the building frustration. Nothing meant anything here—the original people were mad. Vel understood none of it.

"What the hell is this supposed to be?" he said aloud.

The third poster was black and white. A whitish gray plume rising on a tower of white—what might have been smoke—against a black backdrop. It looked like a cloud shaped as a stalk or a tree trunk with a puffy top, almost perfectly ovoid. Vel stared at it. He had never seen a cloud like this, but maybe they had them on Merica–Urope. If it had been in color, Vel might have said it was beautiful, but as it was, it looked more like his fake dirt paintings than a real cloud.

Vel left the posters, heading for the hallway, and lights hummed nearby, brightening. What is this place? he thought. Vel stopped at the first set of doors in the hall, one on the left wall, one on the right, facing each other. There were red squares on both doors. Something fell into place, and Vel's hands began to tremble as he held the sword. Lydia had said that people didn't begin in Hope. They came from somewhere else and founded the city. This, he thought, looking at the perfectly cut walls, this is where they came from. What is this? This isn't from Hope—it isn't even from Hera, is it?

Learn to run.

He stiffened, refusing to back out of the narrow hall. Vel glanced back at the ladder, and he looked at the doors again.

"What—"

You don't listen. You belong to us, boy.

The lights hummed, and Vel stepped back. The hall and room flickered.

"Stop," he said.

Stop?

The lights continued to flash, and Vel ran back into the smaller room, bumping into the table. The metal box and its glass contents rattled noisily. One rolled out, and Vel heard a tiny smashing as whatever it was hit the floor.

Stop?

Vel tried to keep his eyes focused on the ladder. *Deutschland* . . . the room darkened—*Was bietet* . . . blackness again—*Deutschland?*

"Let me out of here!" Vel said.

The room went dark, and the light did not return.

No.

Vel staggered blindly, waving his sword at the blackness.

Now, boy.

"Who are you?" Vel said.

Two glowing red slits in front of him. He raised the sword, and more appeared—and more. Vel spun in the darkness, and they were all around him. Red slits, perfect red eyes, watching him. Vel kept the sword raised, and he tried to back away, but there was nothing in the darkness, no way out.

We are fire and we are shadow.

Vel heard his own breathing, and he gasped at the air, unable to see his own arms, unable to feel anything but the sword handle.

We are the end of you.

You are the Frill, he thought. You're not dead. My God. How many of them were there? He saw dozens, and maybe more than that. Vel tried to focus on one pair of the motionless red slits, keeping the sword raised. They were everywhere.

"Stop it!" Vel said, his voice disappearing in the darkness.

You belong to us, boy. We are the same. Traitor.

Vel's legs shook, and he dropped to his knees in the center of them. The eyes around him did not move.

"I don't understand."

We will have our justice, and we will collect. Heat binds wounds that separate.

Vel closed his eyes and shook his head, beginning to rock slowly back and forth. There were too many of them. He wanted to make everything, even the darkness go away. Stop pushing me, he thought. Stop it. What do you want me to do?

Remember.

Vel dropped the sword. He heard it rolling across the metal floor, and he pressed both hands to the cold surface.

"No." Vel trembled, and he felt the air changing as they came nearer. "No."

There is heat in birth. The cure to your disease is the blood of a plant. We made that—we are death.

Vel fought the urge to shout and run through the darkness. He wanted to charge them—why had he dropped his sword? He was helpless.

You're right, boy. We had a deal.

"What do you want?" Vel said softly. "What is this place?"

You will see. There are things to be done.

"What things?"

If you cannot survive, you're useless—we will not interfere when you are gone. But, we will collect, do you understand? The wound shall be united.

"What are you talking about? No, I don't understand!"

Something hovered above his head, and Vel tensed, knowing that they were finished with him. These are the Frill, he thought. The Frill are alive.

You came to us, you will see what we are, and then you will tell your people what will happen to them. Tell them that the winter will destroy them, that they're foolish to think that we would forget. Our prophecies are ours alone. We will not interfere. We will not intervene—and tell them that justice will be served where sky and shadow meet. They're all going to die. But now, you will understand.

And then nothing.

Denon was nearly asleep when someone knocked on his bedroom door. His quarters were simply appointed, with several swa paintings, a bed, and a neatly folded pile of robes and vestments. Situated in the recesses of the Church, Denon's room was always guarded, and it was well known that he was only to be disturbed for matters of great importance.

"Yes?"

"Lord Denon, a prisoner."

Denon remained on his back, watching the dark ceiling. "The boy?"

"No, Lord. A girl, she was seen with him."

"I will deal with her at first light," Denon said. "Goodnight. God go with you."

"And with you, Lord."

Denon closed his eyes, knowing that God would grant him little sleep tonight. Too much to be done. The girl might be persuaded to take his side against the opposition, if she understood just what was happening, just how important the boy was. I have the advantage, Denon thought, and I intend to keep it. So long as the Frill don't find the boy.

Vel woke with one thousand fingers touching him, dancing across his body, and he stood, the sensation suddenly gone. Vel remained in total darkness, closed his eyes, and he checked his sword—still hung at his side—then feeling blindly, he touched only air in every direction. It tasted moist: still underground.

Hesitating, Vel wondered what Lydia would tell him to do. His stomach became an uncomfortable ball of ice, and his heart quickened as he felt slowly forward in the blackness. Could be a cliff, he thought. No reason the stone floor might not suddenly end. Still, Vel felt nothing, no walls. He blinked his eyes, struggling with the complete darkness.

Where am I? he thought—snap of light filling an enormous black cavern and hundreds of creatures around him, in metal masks with twin slits where their eyes should have been, so close that he should have felt them when he moved—and blackness. Vel froze. Not real, he thought. They're all around me, and Vel extended his arms in both direction, and felt nothing. Moving back when I try to touch them, Vel thought. They had been so close, all nearly his height, with thin black bodies, triple-jointed limbs, braids, like hair, from the tops of their metal faces, and tubes from the bottom connecting with tiny metal breastplates. The images remained on the inside of his eyelids in the blackness. The Frill, he thought.

Red slits directly in front of him.

Vel turned, and more behind him, and more, and soon the red pairs surrounded him. Hundreds of them. Then only darkness.

Vel said softly, "What do you want?"

We are going to kill you.

Please, Vel thought, I don't understand what's happening.

All that you touch will burn.

Vel saw a stone table, and there, arranged in a circle around the outside of the table—blackness. He had seen heads. Severed faces looking out, dozens of them, like old fruit, arranged neatly around the perimeter of the circular stone table.

"What is this place?"

Hell.

"I'll go away, please, I don't want to fight you."

You cannot fight us, boy. We are the same. Now listen.

And Vel heard a trembling voice, like someone screaming a song—it was unlike any voice he had ever heard. As if all of the pain of generations of people had been compressed into overlapping syllables, the wordless song continued, growing louder. But it wasn't a human voice. It sounded as if the rock was cracking carefully, exploding to create a voice that wasn't a voice, but the ground crying. Vel shuddered uncontrollably.

"Stop."

The noise stopped.

Longer ago than you will ever understand, our gods left us here. They created us, not in their image, but in the image of warriors and caretakers. This world is the world of our gods, not ours and not yours. We were to preserve this land, keep their animals from running wild, and wait for their return.

But the gods have not returned, and there are two factions now. And the gods' city decays on the surface, their animals run loose, and half of our number have lost their faith that the gods will ever return. They believe we are damned, that the gods never meant to return, but left us here in punishment for our failure. But some of us still believe the prophecies of the shadow and sky, and we know that our factions will someday be united when the two meet. That is why you are here.

"Why?"

Someday you will unite us. That is why we accepted the agreement that your people broke. You belong to us.

"What are you?" Vel said, still seeing only darkness.

We are the Frill, and we are your death. We are the instruments our gods left to safeguard this place. We are alive, but we cannot give life. We are unending and have no natural death, and none but the gods have been able to kill us. We were created by the gods to watch over their city until the day that they return to this place you call Hera. We are the same, boy.

"The Frill died when people first came to Hera. I'm imagining this."

We are alive, boy. No Frill has ever died at a human hand. Blakes was a traitor, and we will destroy him someday. Do not forget. Without unity, everyone is going to die. Our gods created a great city, and now we are left to live in its shadow, but someday they will return. And we will be united.

Two groups of Frill, Vel thought. Creatures living underground—beneath the ruins. The Frill didn't build the ruins, but they were *created* by the creatures that did. How could they have been created?

The gods created us, and their birthing chambers exist today, so that any Frill who might die unnaturally can be replaced. So that our number remains constant. Except it has not remained constant, it has grown very slightly.

"What do you mean?"

You do not ask questions, you answer them, and you listen. A plague was created as retribution for your treacherous leaders; after years of work, it was finished and released by the other Frill. And now our cure has been stolen by the same traitors who caused the disease's creation. We would have given it to you, that is why we created it—but you took it. So we will not help your city. And Hope will die.

Vel tried to focus on what they were saying. Two groups of Frill, and one created a disease—the Pox?—as punishment for something the people did years ago, and the *other* Frill, this group, created a cure for the disease that they intended to give to the city to use against the rival Frill's plague. Except that the people didn't wait, and they stole the cure.

Yes.

Vel's chest constricted, and he felt around uselessly in the blackness again. "You heard that?"

Yes. You belong to us. And we'll decide when you die. We will destroy everything that you will ever have.

"You said something about helping me—about me uniting you or—"

You do not ask questions. Everything we've said is true. Hope will die, and we will have our vengeance on the murderer Blakes. The gods left us alone in damnation, but the Frill will be united or everyone—Frill and human—will die. Do you understand? You are important in this.

"How? Tell me—"

And something flashed white, leaving traces of light in Vel's vision, and he was laying on his stomach, tasting dust in a pale blue light. Across the room, an armless skeleton grinned at him, and Vel sat up painfully, coughing too loudly. He stared at a blue circle in the center of the room, noticing several sets of footprints.

Back here, he thought, glancing at the doorway that he knew led to the hall full of bodies. Terrific.

chapter 21

Lydia felt groggy as she woke, wrists bound in front of her—but nothing on her ankles, and she was sitting in a chair at a table set with plates of garnished fruit and tiny meats. Four Religious Guard stood sentry behind her, all armed, and Lydia stared across the table at Lord Denon. They were alone, except for the Religious Guard, the other chairs all empty. Church tapestries hung on the four walls, between sealed doors. Lydia spotted one door with more internal locks than the others; a door to the street. Denon looked tired, both hands set evenly on the table in front of him.

Drugged, Lydia thought slowly. They drugged me, and took my staff.

"You must be hungry," Denon said, and he nodded to the plate in front of her. "It's perfectly good food. I suggest you eat."

Only four, Lydia thought, and my legs are free. Mistake. Must do this quickly.

Denon said, "Obviously, I'm interested in knowing where the boy is. And anything else you might know." When she didn't answer, he continued, "My intentions are correct. I do not—"

Lydia pushed her chair away from the table. "I'm leaving."

In one fluid motion, she grabbed her metal plate and smashed it in the nearest guard's throat. As he dropped, she hit another hard in the nose with her fist, and spinning, broke another's groin with her knee—and the fourth guard had drawn his sword. She kicked it away, caught the weapon as it fell, and sliced open his stomach in three steps.

Denon had not moved.

Lydia glanced back at him, bloodied sword in hand, and she chopped away her wrist bindings.

"I'm sorry," she said, "but I don't have time to deal with this."
She went to one of the doors and clicked off the locks.

"Please," Denon said. "You do not understand."

"Yes," Lydia said, "I do."

She threw the door wide, stepped out, and froze. A column of
thirty-four police soldiers stood at the far side of a narrow street,
less than twenty feet away. Their officer immediately reacted,
raised one arm—"Steady!"—and ten of the soldiers raised crossbows. The others drew swords and advanced.

People scattered from the street, and Lydia retreated to the
door, but didn't go in. She heard shouting behind her, the Religious Guard. She glanced back—Denon still sat at the table,
watching, and priest-soldiers hurried from the side corridors,
weapons already drawn.

The police officer motioned to the archers—"Aim!"—and ten
crossbows focused on Lydia's head and torso. The other soldiers
closed the distance to the Cathedral, swords poised. Ten feet
away. No time, Lydia thought, and she slammed the door behind
her, diving at the nearest policeman.

"—ire!"

Her sword went up, knocking his back, and she ducked *into*
the soldier, using his body as a wall against the barrage of arrows.
Two police dropped in the volley—including the closest one—
and a shaft shot past Lydia's throat.

"Steady!"

Lydia charged more police soldiers—sword flashing in a quick
thrusting spin that twisted through another man's defense, into
his chest, and then across another's throat, opening a deep
wound.

"Aim!"

The soldiers fell back, cursing, into a sudden wall of extended
swords, dropped to their knees in the street, and there was no
time to attack.

"Fire!" Arrows lanced over their heads, at Lydia, and she sidestepped into a roll, the clattering smash of arrowheads on the
stone of the Cathedral, and in the hard dirt, and then a fire in her
leg—and Lydia flipped into a stance, the crossbowmen already
reloading: "Steady!"

She wavered, a low cut along her left calf. No direct hit, she thought, and the police tried to surround her, to form a circle, pinning her— She backed to the church wall, and the door opened.

Lydia spun, deciding to fight the priests rather than the soldiers—"Aim!"—and the door slammed against her arms. Coursing pain in both forearms—"Fire!"—and Lydia instinctively dropped into a fetal position, arrows hammering the door around her. Shaft in her shoulder, another in her leg, again in the leg, and she cried out, forcing herself to stand again—to face the police as they closed on her. Pain blurred her vision as the soldiers attacked, and she knocked away their swords, almost too slowly.

"Steady!"

No, she thought, no more arrows, and the soldiers hacked at her again with their swords, and this time Lydia couldn't stop them all, and they knocked her to the ground, kicking the arrows deeper inside her, kicking her teeth loose, so that she tasted them in her throat, breaking her nose and fingers with their boots.

I'm sorry, Vel, she thought. And stopped struggling.

stepping away from the blue circle, with a white flash, Vel was on the stone rooftop again. Midday, he thought, examining the surroundings. The dead Religious Guard still lay where the Nara had killed them, near the edge of the grassfield, and Vel saw several of his supplies scattered haphazardly on the roof. I left them here when I was going to leave, he thought, and went to the edge of the roof.

"Lydia!" he shouted, and waited, not really expecting an answer. Not the Frill's city, Vel thought, looking at the stone mountains that had once been buildings. But they were watching it now. I have to get back to Hope, I have to find Lydia. And Ponce.

He thought about what the Frill had said as he searched for an easy way down. Finding none, Vel lowered both feet over the side and dropped, hurting his ankle as he landed. It burned slightly when he walked, but Vel tried to ignore it, heading for the grassfield.

The Frill had seemed to know what I was thinking, Vel

thought. As if I were saying it out loud—and I didn't really hear them speak. It almost sounded like my own voice, but they *were* talking. How many did I see down there? Vel entered the edge of the grasses, the whistling rush surrounding him again.

Hundreds of Frill, and all of them just waiting underneath the ruins. Just protecting the ruins that their gods built—but why were they ruins? Why hadn't the Frill been able to do a better job? And I'm connected to them somehow, Vel thought. They said that I belong to them. What does that mean? No one owns me, what were they talking about?

Vel spotted something white between the grasses ahead, and froze. No, he thought. You're not really here, you're dead. Don't do this now. The grasses rustled and swayed around him, and Vel's hair fluttered in the breeze. But what if someone was really—

A cord caught his legs, and Vel shouted as he was yanked off his feet, the ground slamming the air from his chest and stomach. Vel coughed, reached for his sword, and someone in a white uniform, with a swa armband, stepped over him. Vel started to speak, and the man hit him hard across the back of his head. Vel tasted blood, the world spinning, and he heard himself cursing, and then another blow and it was gone.

chapter 22

"What do you want?"

"You were taken prisoner by the Religious Guard, weren't you? And then you escaped, and in the process, were captured by city police soldiers."

"Yes."

"Where is the boy?"

"As far as I know, he's still at the ruins."

"And the Church is looking for him?"

"Yes, I suppose so."

"You're lucky to be alive, you realize that? You should have been hung."

"Yes."

"You're alive because the Church is overstepping its bounds. You need to understand that you are only important so long as the possible benefits of your breath outweigh the desire of my soldiers to have you executed. That may not last long, unless you can tell me exactly where I can find the boy."

"I can't."

"And if you could, would you?"

"No."

"If the boy survives, will he miss you?"

"I don't intend to die."

"Most people don't. Will he miss you?"

"He knows what he's doing. You're not going to catch him. And I won't die."

"Maybe not. But, you will hurt an awful lot in the meantime."

A throbbing pain coursed into Vel's wrists. As awareness returned, his stomach churned. His head rang with a pulse that resonated at the base of his neck and snapped into his brain. Vel's mouth was dry, and he felt cold. A hard stone surface beneath him, and dampness pressed against his clothing and skin. He tried to change positions. He'd been here for sometime.

Darkness.

Wherever here was. Total darkness. For a moment, Vel wondered if he'd opened his eyes at all. The ringing in his mind told him that he had indeed woken up. Vel sat against a wall, breathing moist, cold air that smelled of rotten things and wet mold.

Somewhere . . . a dripping. A steady beat of water, falling from somewhere above, to connect with stone. Vel leaned away from the wall, but heavy chains caught, pulling him back. They clanked in the blackness, twisting and scraping against stone. Vel's wrists and ankles were bound in metal clasps connected by a single length of locked chain. This same binding linked with another series of chains, fastened to the stone wall, keeping Vel from moving. He managed to climb awkwardly to his feet. He could stand, but just barely.

At first, he remembered nothing. And it came back. The Frill, he thought. And then the man in white—religious soldier—and somehow I lost track of Lydia long before that.

"There's food there, you know."

Vel spun around in the dark. "Where am I?"

"Where do you think?"

Vel cleared his throat, feeling around the floor for the food. "Who's holding me?"

"The Church. By the orders of Lord Denon himself . . ."

"Who are you?"

Half of a round object.

The voice ignored the question and asked, "Why are you here?"

Vel picked up the fruit and took a bite. Grassfruit. He'd seen that at the ruins, hadn't he? Preserved food—enough that it might save the city.

"Don't know why I'm here," Vel said. "Don't even know where *here* is, do I? Just have your word to take for that."

"You've been out for a while, they drugged you. Wearing off now. They don't need it, now that you're down here."

Vel experienced an unfamiliar lightheadedness. His thoughts

weren't responding exactly as they should have been. The sensation began to gently recede.

"How long have you been down here?" Vel said.

"Me? Why don't you worry about yourself? The guard'll check on you soon. Bring you more food tomorrow."

Vel continued to eat. "Why am I alive?"

"Church is keeping its options open, probably. You're dangerous—someone they're afraid of or you wouldn't be here."

"Where are we?"

"Below the main Cathedral. Near the river."

That dripping continued, echoing.

"In Hope?"

The voice chuckled. "Where else would you be?" A brief silence. "So, who are you?"

"My name is Vel."

"What's the Church want you for?"

Lydia's words trickled back into his mind. They wanted to put him out of the picture, or in the center of everything, but was that the Church or the government? The two *were* separate, although they overlapped, reinforcing one another with doctrine and law. Why was I never told that I'm the heir? Vel wondered. Didn't my parents know? But, they weren't even my real parents.

"Don't know why anyone's after me," Vel lied. "Is there any way out of here?"

"Certainly," the voice said. "A door to your left leads to stairs. Stairs'll take you up to the back rooms of the Church, to Reich Hall. And from there, a door opens onto the street."

Vel smirked. "You sound like you've gotten out of here before." He finished his fruit.

"I have."

Vel dropped the rind. "Really? Why are you still here?"

"I like it in here."

"What—"

Light flooded the room. A door, set on a level above them, opened. A man in white stood in the entryway. The prison room was small, with old, stained walls. Masses of chains, identical to those that bound Vel, hung at regular intervals, and a man with long hair and a bare, scarred chest lay at the opposite corner—

the voice. The bright figure descended into the cell, leaving the door open behind him.

"You need more water?" he asked. His hair was closely cut, jaw cleanly shaven. "Either of you?"

The longhaired man nodded. "Yes."

"You?" The priest-soldier looked at Vel, drawing closer.

Vel hesitated.

"Well?" the priest said.

Vel shook his head, wincing. "My hand is broken."

"What are you talking about?"

Vel nodded to one of his limp hands. It hung in the chains, unmoving. "You bastards broke my hand, putting me in these chains."

They'd taken Vel's sword, along with his daggers and the tiny pouches of money in the lining of Vel's clothing. And the cross he had found at the ruins. The priest wore a sword at his waist, a swa on his left arm.

"Enough. Do you need water, or not?"

Vel swallowed. "Need a brace for my hand, so that the bone will heal." His jaw tightened. "And so my joint won't swell. I need a doctor."

The man shook his head. "If your hand was broken you would be in more pain than this."

"Yes, I know," Vel said. "That makes me think I've been drugged. You numbed me, so that I didn't even notice when you cracked my hand. But, now that it's wearing off, I notice. I notice quite a bit."

The guard leaned close to inspect the hand.

"That one?" He nodded to Vel's limp palm.

"Yes. That one. Will you get me a brace or something?"

The man shook his head, reaching into a long pocket. Out came a jumble of keys, and Vel tried to steady the sudden quickening in his chest. Grab his sword, Vel thought.

"I'll look at the hand myself," the priest said, drawing close, and Vel held his breath as the key fit into the tiny hole in the metal. Vel winced as the priest grabbed his wrist.

"Where's the broken bone?"

"Right here," Vel said, and he drove both of his knees up between the priest's legs, kicking hard—the priest doubled over, dropped the keys, and Vel grabbed them, unlocking his wrists. Vel took the priest's sword from its sheath, unlocked his ankles, and kicked the priest again to make him stop groaning—the priest moaned louder.

"Help me," the other prisoner said.

"Here."

Vel kicked the bindings off his legs and tossed the keys. They landed in a clump at the prisoner's feet, and Vel ran from the room, taking the stairs three at a time.

A door opened a crack at the top of the stairs. Low voices beyond that. No time to consider it. Just move. Vel pushed, throwing the door wide to an open room, fashioned of black rock with a long stone table adorned with plates and silverware, set with chairs. Two more Religious Guard by the chairs, each dressed in the same white garb, each wearing a sword and armband.

The back door. Vel turned quickly. A long passage—Reich Hall—and opposite that, to his immediate left, a simple wooden door, shut and locked from the inside. Vel threw it open, and a third figure stepped into his path.

"Stop him."

Men shouted, and the world began to blur.

Vel stabbed the priest in the chest, blade sinking in without any effort at all, dropping the priest in a bloody heap. Crimson drenched his white garments, bleeding from the wound. Vel ran, and behind him people shouted orders. Footsteps chased him onto the street.

People hurried by, and a rush of bitter air passed across him—smoke, thick in his nostrils—and Vel bounded across the street, into an alley.

Voices behind him.

Vel kept going. He changed directions, backtracking at a corner, weaving in and out of houses. The people he passed swirled together in a meaningless collage, and still Vel kept running, sides burning with the effort. Finally, he stopped, panting, in a side street somewhere in the heart of the Old Town, one of the poorer districts.

Sweat ran down Vel's forehead and cheeks. Were they still

following him? He pressed his head against the warped wood of a house, listening, catching his breath. Wind blew through the street, tossing loose trash and making Vel shiver in the dry air. He could still smell smoke.

Where am I?

Vel examined the road; houses smaller here, little more than shacks. They leaned against one another to remain standing, rattling with the wind, as if it might blow them apart at any moment.

He started walking. Nearby, a young boy with a shaved head lay curled on a pile of broken wood and garbage. His side rose and fell gently, torn clothing shaking as he dreamed in a quiet sleep. There was dried blood along his scalp, and he stank of feces. Vel looked away as he passed. And paused. His legs refused to go any further, and Vel hooked the sword onto his belt. The priests had taken his sheath, but the blade would still rest.

Vel stared at the boy.

A sudden anger welled up inside him. It ignited deep in Vel's chest and spread out to the ends of his body, tightening his fists. He'd been inside a stone building, and here was a boy sleeping on the street. Sleeping alone in the cold. And no one was doing a thing.

Vel drew closer to the boy, leaning down. He stopped—recognition snapped into his mind.

Darden.

The boy rocked in his sleep. Vel stepped away. Darden. No, Vel wanted to say. Darden's hair is long and well groomed, and he's strong and brilliant, not small and pale like this. This isn't Darden, Vel thought. What the hell is going on?

"Darden . . . ?"

The boy rolled, eyes opening reluctantly. He sat back, propping himself against the wall. He looked from Vel to the alley.

"What do you—"

Darden stopped.

He looked at Vel for a long time, studying Vel's face, hands, and the bloody sword at his side. A large scar ran the length of Darden's left cheek. A fresh wound that had yet to fully heal; the skin was still soft and red.

"Vel," he said.

"My God," Vel said, his voice quickening. "You're really here. You're alive." Darden rubbed his scalp uncomfortably and did not respond. "What happened?"

Darden watched the alley floor. "What do you want?"

"I want to get you out of here. Come on, you can't just lie here."

"Go away."

Darden wasn't looking at him, and Vel noticed dark gashes along his exposed skin. Deep cuts and burns.

Vel said, "Did the police—"

"Leave me alone, Vel."

"I'll take you to a doctor," Vel said.

Darden stared at him, but something about the way his eyes focused was not right. Darden was looking at Vel—but, no, he was looking *through* Vel.

"Did you know that they planted seeds inside my brain," Darden said. "They're growing food inside my skull. Did you know that?"

"What?" Vel expected him to laugh and turn the remark into a joke. He didn't.

"They're watching me," Darden said. "And did you know they cut off my dick? Did you know that? They cut it up and fed it to me. They called me all kinds of names, and they wanted me to fight back so they could kill me. I should have. I wanted to, and I should have."

Vel felt weak, and he caught himself on the opposite wall, still watching Darden.

"You're not joking, are you?" Vel said.

Darden seemed not to hear. "You know they cut off my hands, too." Darden waved his hands in the air in front of him, shaking his head sadly. "They chopped my hands up and planted them in the ground to grow."

"What are you talking about?" Vel said. "Your hands are right there. Stop it, Darden. Your hands are right there."

"I wanted to fight back," Darden said, and he began to cry softly to himself. "But they laughed in my face. They spit on me."

"Stop it!" Vel shouted at him. "What's wrong with you?"

"They made me do things," Darden said, and he began to

scratch at his head, opening scabs with his fingernails. "I wanted them to kill me."

"I'm sorry," Vel said, and he backed away.

Darden leaned against the wall again, suddenly quiet. Time passed, and Vel watched, waiting for some final comment, something to indicate that Darden was not gone. He said my name, Vel thought. He called me by name. Please, Vel thought. Say something. What did they do to you? Darden rolled onto his side and closed his eyes, beginning to sleep again.

My God, Vel thought. What the hell is happening? I've got to find Ponce. But, Ponce had been right. Darden is dead, and he died the moment we left him at that table. The moment I stood, Vel thought. But it's not my fault. Darden had been drunk. Vel thought, If I had tried to save him, they would have caught me too. It's not my fault.

Vel exited the alley, and his eyes began to twitch. He steadied himself, closing both eyes. There was pressure in his chest. No, he thought. It was not my fault. Behind him, Vel heard someone loudly sobbing. I'm sorry, he thought.

Vel left without looking back.

chapter 23

"I know this hurts. But, I haven't started leaving marks yet. I want you to think very carefully."

"God, stop. Please . . ."

"Where is Munil? I know you know who I'm talking about. When the boy comes back to the city, that's where he's going to go, isn't it? He'll want to find you, won't he? Where is Munil?"

"God . . ."

"How much do you want to hurt? I will learn what I want to know. Tell me now, and I won't begin to take fingers or . . . other pieces. Where can I find Munil?"

"Don't do this—oh God, don't . . . please . . . all right—just stop . . ."

"Where is he?"

"I'll tell you."

"Yes. You will."

vel knocked, and a moment later Ponce answered. He raised his eyebrows, joining Vel inside.

"Ah, the adventurer returns from battle," Ponce said.

They headed toward the river, the streets empty.

"Anything interesting happen while I was gone?" Vel asked.

"While you were gone?" Ponce said. "I figured you had been preparing the way for a bunch of little Vels in some quiet backroom of a hotel." Vel pulled his clothing to him more tightly and smiled. Ponce said, "I take it that's not what you were up to?"

"Not exactly," Vel said.

"No sign of Darden," Ponce said. Vel swallowed and didn't answer. "So where did you go?"

"Lydia took me to the ruins."

Ponce nodded, as if he had expected that answer. "Yes, I guessed as much. I've never heard it called that before, but all right. I meant what were you doing while you were awake?"

"I'm serious, Ponce. We went to the ruins. There's food there, and there might have been some kind of cure for the Pox—someone has it."

Ponce motioned to a nearby alley, and they stopped between the buildings. He glanced back uncomfortably.

"You shouldn't have come back," Ponce said.

"Why?"

"Things are getting worse. There have been riots, and the entire neighborhood around the Western Garr was torched. From Sixth Street to the river, they've been trying to loot the granaries."

Vel blew onto his hands. "What about the King?"

"Dead," Ponce said. "They announced it last night, and there were more arrests. And public executions." Ponce shook his head tiredly. "I think half the city might be in prison."

"That's reassuring."

"I'm telling you, things are getting worse. You should have stayed away. How'd you get past the sentries?"

"A tunnel," Vel said. "Remember that light we saw at the cemetery?"

"No."

"Well, it led outside the perimeter."

Ponce snorted. "That figures." And his eyes narrowed. "The cemetery, right? And there's food at the ruins? We can get out of here—"

"No," Vel said. He had passed the cemetery before finding Ponce. "We can't go back there, it's guarded now. No way we can fight past the cops."

Precise footsteps approached in the street, and they both reached for their weapons, moving reflexively to the side of the building. The footsteps stopped. They waited, and Ponce shook his head.

"But as you can see," he whispered, "not *that* much has changed."

They waited.

"I don't think this is anyone we know," Vel said softly.

"You know," Ponce said, "you might be on to something."

The footsteps resumed suddenly, and a man with a ponytail and goatee—mid-thirties—stood before them, dressed in black. At his side, he wore a curling, black sword, differently shaped than any sword Vel had seen. It arced at the end in a crescent. He motioned to Vel.

"You're Vel?"

They both remained where they were, swords drawn. Ponce had begun carrying a blade.

"Why?" Vel said.

"It's all right," the man said. "You can trust me. My name is Tiber."

Ponce said, "If we all wore name tags we wouldn't have this problem with awkward introductions."

Tiber shifted, popping his knuckles, and he said to Vel, "Understand you met with Lydia. I'm a friend of hers."

"How do you know my name?"

"I know more than that, Vel."

Vel leaned forward.

"Let me guess," he said. "You know everything about me—you know all about my life and my parents, and who I really am, and what's happening with the city—you know all of it, right? You have all the answers if only I'll help you. But I'm the only one who can do it."

Ponce whistled and said to Tiber, "We've done this before."

Tiber said, "I don't know everything."

"Who are you?" Vel asked.

"I told you, I'm—"

"A friend of Lydia's." Vel cleared his throat. "How do I know that?"

Tiber hesitated. "What do you mean?"

Vel smiled. "The order you belong to, what does it do?"

Tiber watched Vel differently, suspicion in his eyes. "What's needed. If I was against you, why would I bother asking you to come with me?"

"Because we've got swords," Vel said quietly.

"The boy's good," Ponce said.

"What do you want?" Vel asked.

Tiber said, "What did Lydia tell you about the information system?"

Vel stared at him. "Information system?"

"That much?" Tiber said. "You'll need to come with me. Please."

Vel didn't move. "Where's Lydia?"

"That's not important."

Vel's jaw tightened, and Ponce started to say something, but Vel cut him off. This time his voice snapped out viciously, "Where is she?"

"She's alive," Tiber said.

"Where is she?"

Vel stared at him, unwavering, and Ponce said, "You have a problem with just giving out answers, *Tiber*? Is there something important about these mindless little games?"

Reluctantly, Tiber gave in.

"She's in prison," he said softly. "She was taken by Church officials, escaped, and then captured by the police. They've got her imprisoned at the Palace now."

Vel's face darkened. "How is she?"

"She's alive, Vel," Tiber said pointedly. "It's time you learned what all of this means. There's a great deal of risk involved in every step we make, and it's important that we get started right away. We can't stay in the open any longer."

Vel and Ponce put away their weapons and followed him down the street. They moved in silence for a time, and then Vel said, "We need to get one thing straight before I agree to anything."

"What?"

Vel said, "I'm not coming along because you asked me to, or because I want to do any of this. I'm coming along because Lydia's in prison. I'm coming along to get her out of there."

Tiber shook his head shortly. "Vel, we're not—"

Vel glared at him. "Do you understand?"

Tiber put his hands behind his back. "Yes."

"Now *that's* a negotiation," Ponce said.

Tiber motioned to Ponce. "You're not involved in this."

Ponce tensed, flushing, and Vel said quickly, "Yes he is. He comes too, or *I* don't."

"This is critical, Vel. What you're about to learn is too important to risk losing."

"Why?"

Vel said. "Because people need to be kept ignorant? Because it's better that a small group hoards its knowledge rather than sharing it with the general populace? No," he said. "Ponce comes."

Tiber was silent, and Ponce frowned at Vel.

"All of this nonsense, and you're calling *me* ignorant?"

"sit down."

Vel looked around the room—a table full of a dozen people, all in black—and Tiber closed the door behind them.

"What the hell is this?" Ponce said, and Tiber silenced him quickly.

"Speak again, and it will be the last time."

A pair of candles flared, brightening the room in a flickering of faces and shadows. The group watched Vel approach, their faces grave, as if they had expected someone else and were disappointed.

Vel lowered himself into the last remaining seat, beside Tiber, and Ponce sat on the floor in the corner. The oldest of the group, a large, balding man with a thick walking stick, rose from his seat and began to walk around the outside of the room.

"It's good that you're here," the old man said.

Vel didn't respond.

"My name is Munil, and I am the senior officer here, among the organization."

"Officer?"

Munil nodded. "That's right. It is important that you understand your significance is in all of this, Vel."

"I know," Vel said. "I'm the heir to the throne."

"That's correct. But, there's more to it than that. The origins of Hope date back over five hundred years—before that time, we lived on Merica-Urope." Dark splotches shifted beneath Munil's eyes. It looked as if he hadn't slept since he was young. "Not much else is known about that place by anyone now living. Most of our history was *purposefully* lost—the founder of our city was a prophet who believed in the present at the expense of the past."

"You're talking about Blakes."

Munil smiled, as if pleased that Vel knew the answer. "Yes. Blakes consciously erased the past. That's why he came to this planet, because his vision could not survive in a world with a history."

"I don't understand," Vel said.

"Do you see this?" Munil motioned to his cane, and then he turned it so that Vel could see an inscription on the side:

Die Götzen—Dämmerung
1870
Friedrich Nietzsche

More gibberish, Vel thought, and he sighed.

"That is a name," Munil said. "Nietzsche was a man, like Blakes, with vision. We know very little about this Nietzsche, except that Blakes identified with him; Blakes collected fragments—pieces— that he believed linked him with the visionaries of history. And Blakes was unique because he rejected that history." Munil looked sad. "And since then we have struggled to preserve it."

What does that mean? Vel thought. How could Blakes have erased history?

"He was expelled from Merica-Urope. Why? We don't know, his writings don't tell us. All of their technology was specifically hidden or destroyed on Blakes's command after the founding of Hope. Blakes did that—it was not an accident."

Vel remembered the posters he'd seen, and he thought of what the Frill told him. "Why?"

Munil paced with his heavy cane. "Purity? Blakes writes that technology had corrupted mankind, that it was given to us by Satan. It's all very complicated, Vel—but Blakes saw technology as a chain, limiting human potential."

"So he became a dictator."

Munil's face brightened. "I see you spoke with Lydia. Did she take you to the ruins?"

"Yes."

"What did you find?"

"What were you saying about an information system?"

Munil held his cane patiently with both hands. "You first."

Vel told him about the storage of grassfruit, the bodies, and briefly about the Frill and original rooms with posters and more dead.

When he'd finished, Munil said, "Some people would like nothing more than to level the ruins and wipe out what's left there—but the Frill stop them."

"Lydia didn't act like she knew they were alive; she always said they were extinct."

"She probably thought they were," Munil said. "We've suspected that the Frill might be the reason the government stays away from the ruins, but we've never known because of the perimeter wall."

Vel thought about it and asked, "What about the information system?"

Munil chewed at his lip, as if wondering how best to start. Finally, he said, "All right, Vel. Imagine you've got a system that can save, can remember, anything you want it to. That system isn't mechanical, it has to be taken care of, because it's partly biological, like you and me. The way it remembers things—the way it works—involves blood and mucus and flesh, just like we do."

Ponce said softly to Vel, "Are you imagining?"

"All right," Vel said. "What about it? I think I understand the kind of thing you're describing—I understand the concept. So what?"

Munil looked at him seriously. "That's what they had, Vel. When Hope started, they had a system that could do that. Genetically engineered biology, living computers."

"What? You lost me."

"That's what they called them, computers. They had at least one of those here, along with other technology that could replicate people, that could mix genetic material."

Vel tried to ignore the bits he didn't understand. "So they had this . . . computer . . . and?"

Ponce chuckled, obviously not believing any of it.

Munil looked around suddenly. "All of you disperse."

Silently, they got up from the table, moving from the room through various doors. A moment later, Vel and Ponce were alone with Munil. Ponce remained where he was, and the older man touched his chin thoughtfully.

"The computer still exists," Munil said quietly.

Vel shook his head. "I thought Blakes tried to hide or get rid of all the technology."

"This was one of the exceptions. The system exists and is . . . online . . . working. It contains *all* of the information, all of the history and the scientific data possessed by the original settlers."

Vel asked, "So why don't people access it?"

"They do," Munil said. "Or rather, they've tried to. But Blakes left a fail-safe to preserve the system of government he set up. You know he was the first King, with absolute control." Vel nodded, and Munil continued. "Blakes altered the computer so that it could only be safely accessed by his descendants."

"I'm beginning to see why you're so interested in me," Vel said dryly.

"Recently, there have been problems—we don't know why— between the government and"—he paused—"after what you've told me, I would have to say the antagonists are the Frill."

"What do you mean?"

"For whatever reason, I think—I don't *know*—that the Frill created the Pox. And they infected the computer system with it, so that after the tainted system was accessed, the Pox could spread normally, like any other disease. The system's biological, so it *can* get sick."

"What does it look like?" Vel asked.

Munil frowned. "I only saw it once, years ago. It was small, sealed inside a metal box with a wire that transports blood in and out of it—letting it alter some kind of output to match genetic signatures in brainwaves."

Ponce let out an uneasy breath.

"This is nuts," he murmured.

After a brief pause, Vel said, "So why is this so important?"

Munil clicked his thumbnail on the top of Nietzsche's cane. "What do you mean? I told you that—"

"Let's assume there's something to this beyond the noble intentions of preserving history and science and all of that—why would it be so important for me to access this thing?"

Munil seemed caught off guard for a heartbeat, but he quickly concealed it with a proud smile. "You're smarter than I realized."

"So what is it?"

"The Church has a code," Munil said. "No one knows it any-more—not even the priests themselves. Without the code, their artifacts are sealed in unbreakable vaults."

Vel said, "You're talking about guns."

"Yes." Munil shrugged, as if Vel had just seen through him. "Among other things. But the guns are probably what certain pow-ers in the government are most interested in."

"So they want me long enough to get the code. What do you want?"

Munil hesitated. "If you assume the throne, now that the King is dead, you may help stop a civil war."

"That's damned honorable of you."

Munil's eyes hardened, and Vel's stomach curled. This man is dangerous, Vel thought. He's old, but this is his life, and it's more important to him than breathing, isn't it?

"Sorry," Vel said.

Munil said, "You can free Lydia, and as King you would have the power to remove the parts of the government that are pushing us toward war."

Just remove them, Vel thought, and he said, "You make it sound easy."

Munil nodded. "It can be done. There's very little standing in your way now."

The door burst from its hinges in a fury of splintering wood and sheering metal. The long table flipped onto its side, and Vel was thrown to the ground as broken boards crashed across his back. Munil stumbled, refusing to fall. Candles dissolved into wisps of vanishing smoke.

A figure strode into the room, flanked on either side by police. One cop quickly bound Ponce, dragging him from the room, but Vel was too dazed to move. The figure was tall and wore a long, dark coat that dropped to his shins. Justice Hillor. Thick eyebrows and dark hair, slicked back to grip Hillor's skull tightly. His cheeks were worn and deeply lined, prematurely aged. Vel rolled onto his side, away from Hillor, but the police were blocking the exits.

Munil backed away. "Hillor."

"Hello, Munil." Hillor reached into his coat and took a single step forward.

His large hand rose, in its grip the long stem of a black revolver. He leveled the gun to Munil's chest.

"You're afraid, aren't you?" Munil said, refusing to move away from the weapon. "Afraid and too stupid to understand the drawbacks of using force."

There was an explosive blast, and the old man dropped, choking sharply as his innards sprayed across the wall.

Hillor moved closer, stepping over the debris. He lowered the gun to Munil's head and fired it again. Vel shuddered with the sound, and Hillor faced him.

"Now then. You're the one called Vel?"

Vel froze. "Yes."

Hillor smiled. "Your Highness is under arrest."

chapter 24

Vel followed Hillor into a large, well-furnished room with red walls draped in tapestries with the government symbol of a five-pointed star. The length of a single bed was lapped in glittering metal, and a mirror hung nearby, full and imposing. Its round surface was outlined with the same metal, fashioned into waves, stars and swas. Hillor nodded to a lone chair, out of place at the foot of the bed, and motioned to Vel. Police paused in the doorway, hands at their sides.

"Dismissed," Hillor said.

The men nodded, and backed out. "Yes, sir."

The door shut noiselessly, and their footsteps droned mechanically in the hallway outside. Hillor and Vel had come through the front entrance of the Palace, down the entrance hall, up the stairs to the second level, and now to this room at the end of that hall. The King's Chamber. Vel lowered himself to the chair, folding his hands.

"Why did you bring me here?" he said.

Hillor looked at the mirror. "You'll have to get used to it, I suppose," Hillor said. "But these *are* your rooms now. I apologize for the scene I created—Munil was a criminal."

"What did he do?"

Hillor looked down at him. "Vel, we know each other. I've heard of you, and you of me. Let's try and get off to a good start, all right?"

Vel lowered his gaze. "I know about you."

Hillor smiled. He walked to the bed and sat on the end of it casually, as if they were good friends or relatives. "And what do you know about me?"

"You're on the Executive Council. You're also the head of the police force, and you're in charge of the district courts."

Hillor nodded patiently. "True enough. What else do you know?"

Vel shook his head. "You think you're stronger than you are."

"Really?" Something in Hillor's voice changed. The artificial smile faded, and in the folds of his large overcoat, Vel saw the handle of his gun. Hillor followed Vel's gaze, then grinned. "Yes, I expect you're a little curious at that, aren't you?"

Vel said nothing.

"It's God's Justice, not mine. This weapon is a part of your heritage—it's a tradition that maintains Hope's order. You understand that?"

I understand, Vel thought.

Hillor's hand blurred to his waist, and back up. Vel stared into the barrel of a revolver.

"You see?" The smile returned. "It makes me powerful, because it is God's will that I am powerful; otherwise I wouldn't be powerful, would I? The strong succeed because they are meant to. True, I would be powerful without it, but with it, I am invincible. You see? The police help to enforce that."

Vel clicked his teeth together. "What do the police have to do with that?"

"They keep the city alive, Vel. Everything I do keeps the city alive, and that's why I do it. You're smart enough to realize that. Anything—even tyranny—is better than anarchy, isn't it? It is necessary for me to have this power."

Vel asked, "Why am I still alive?"

Hillor holstered his pistol and after a pause, he answered, "You know how easily you could be killed, don't you Vel? You know how easily I could arrange that? There are any number of ways. I could shoot you right now, and every person in this building would acknowledge that I was only acting in self-defense. You're a criminal, aren't you? Like your *parents* were." Vel remained silent, and Hillor shook his head. "Are we agreed then?" He sat on the bedside once more.

"Agreed?" Vel said.

Hillor nodded. "Yes. Are we agreed that your life rests in my hands? I want to work with you, not against you."

Vel looked away. "You aren't invincible. And we aren't agreed."

"Think before you say something you'll regret," Hillor said softly.

Vel thought of his parents—this bastard had laughed about them. Criminals.

Hillor said, "You'll find as you get older that authority deserves more and more respect." Hillor's face was expressionless. "Do you know why that is?"

Because we've been living with it—we're too tired to do anything but work. Vel said, "My parents didn't think like that."

"Oh," Hillor said, and he looked as if Vel had returned to a particularly boring subject. "Obviously they weren't your parents, though, were they?"

"They weren't criminals."

"I see no reason to debate this with you," Hillor said. "You know that you're the next in line to the throne, and it is my desire that you become King. That's not terribly complicated, is it?"

"Is that why I'm still alive?"

There was no sarcasm in the reply. "Yes."

Vel looked at him and could read nothing from his face. Hillor sat, one leg on the bed's surface, one hand visible, the other beneath the folds in his coat.

"Why should I become King?"

"You have a birthright. You're the only surviving relative."

Vel nodded. "Yes, I know. What makes you think I want to be King?"

"It's your duty. There are plenty of people who would kill for the opportunity you have."

"Let them. What difference does that make?"

"You *are* stubborn, aren't you? I don't think you understand the situation. Do you know what's going to happen to this city if we go any longer without a King? He died not even days ago, and the social order is already beginning to fall apart. Our stability is based on tradition, Vel. A tradition that has been maintained for five hundred years."

"Things are falling apart because no one has any food," Vel said, "not because they don't have a King."

Hillor grinned, impressed. "Take your place, Vel. I'll teach you everything there is to know. Listen to me carefully. In the next hour, the Executive Council will meet, and you will be there. Then, in another few hours there will be a formal ceremony with the aristocracy." Hillor spoke very deliberately, "There's a code I need you to retrieve for me. In exchange for those numbers, I will let both of your friends go."

Just like that, Vel thought. He's not wasting any time—Munil was right.

"You're a liar," Vel said. "And let me tell you something, you make me King and I'll repeal the measure you just passed on the stored food."

Hillor's breathing stopped. Vel stood defiant, less than three feet away from him. It's happened then, Vel thought. I wasn't sure, but it must have just passed, they've given the food to the rich. For a long time there was no sound, and it was impossible to read anything from the Justice's face.

"Vel . . ." He shook his head in amusement—and punched Vel hard in the chest. Vel staggered back, grabbing onto the wall for support. He couldn't breathe. The world twirled, and Vel dropped to the ground.

Air rushed from his lungs, and Vel doubled over, gasping for breath. Nothing would come to him, and he tried to cough in the tightness of the room.

"I can dimly remember the last time there was a situation similar to this." Hillor's voice was no longer the quietly amused tone it had been. "You're fortunate you have importance, Vel. The last time someone forgot that I was in charge, I cut his throat not far from where you lay."

Vel rasped at the air, his cheeks reddening. Hillor stood over him, looking down.

"I should have that girl killed," he said. "Along with your friend Ponce."

Vel's eyes watered, and he looked up. Air came gradually to him, and a burning crept through his upper torso.

"You," he coughed, "stay away from them."

Hillor shook his head.

"No," he said. "I don't think I will. I didn't know they were *your* parents at the time, but I ordered their deaths. We were having problems with a bastard-thief. His mother was supposed to be kept alive, so that we could use her again if we needed to." Hillor paused. "I suppose she killed herself because the soldiers told her that her darling *son* had been executed. Book ownership *is* illegal, I'm afraid." Hillor smiled. "But, thank you for the advice. Your Highness."

Hillor kicked Vel's face with the point of his boot. A sharp flash of pain, and the world twirled. Vel was thrown backwards, blood spurting from his nose.

Hillor said, "You have potential, Vel. Understand that this is being done for your own good. We can work for each other, rather than in opposition. It's up to you. We don't have to be enemies."

His coat swirled as he left, and Vel tasted blood. Hillor paused to speak with the guards outside Vel's door.

"See that he doesn't leave," Hillor said. He walked away, and then paused, something occurring to him. Hillor turned to them, a wicked smile filling his lips. "What cell is that girl being held in?"

"Fifty-three, sir. The west wing," one of the guards said.

Hillor nodded. "Very good. Thank you, Sergeant."

"Yes, sir."

And he was gone.

chapter 25

In a rear section of the Palace, the Executive Council convened. Elaborate portraits hung from the stained wooden walls, and the thirty members sat around a large rectangular table, carved entirely from black stone. They were all dressed differently; some in dark suits, others in brightly colored vests and pants, and still others wore the plain, moderate clothing of the city workers. Government flags—five-pointed stars—hung evenly from the walls beside Church tapestries with large swas.

Hillor led Vel into the room through the main entrance, and immediately a pair of soldiers sealed the chambers behind them. The council members took their seats, as Vel followed Hillor around the outline of the table toward a pair of empty chairs at the opposite corner. Torches smoked on the walls, and candles burned from a collection of thin silver candlesticks in the center of the table. As they walked, Hillor nodded and smiled at the other council members, and Vel drew names from memory to match some of the faces.

One man in a bright white robe with a swa across his chest stared at Vel from a seat nearby. This man's eyes were dark, and his hair fell long down his back. He wore a pair of green earrings, his face entirely unreadable as Vel drew closer. Lord Denon, Vel thought. He's the only member of the Church on the Executive Council. Not only is he a part of the Church, but he's at the top of the hierarchy; Denon is the head of the Church of Hope. Just as Justice Hillor is in command of the police force and was also elected to the council.

The other twenty-eight were a mix of middle-aged men and women, the large majority from the aristocracy of the city. Some of the men wore beards, and they were all somewhat fat—signs of wealth. Most of these people probably owned—inherited—the major guilds that controlled the commodity factories, where blacksmiths, carpenters, distillers and weavers worked to supply the government and the rest of Hope with what it needed to survive.

Hillor showed Vel to a vacant chair, a step higher than all the rest, then sat beside him. There was a long silence, and they all watched Vel, some shaking their heads, others simply staring.

"Motion on the floor," Hillor said at last.

Someone answered mechanically, "Motion recognized."

Hillor smiled, both hands on the table as he leaned forward to address them. "The Executive Council of thirty has thirty-one again."

Chuckles around the table, and a red-faced woman on the right waved a meaty arm at Vel.

"Who is this boy, Justice Hillor? He doesn't look nearly old enough to be crowned."

"His name is Vel," Hillor said, and he indicated that Vel should stand. "He's the one I mentioned, the only heir." Hillor shrugged playfully. "We make do with what we can get, don't we?"

More uneasy laughter.

Lord Denon eyed them all calmly, and then stood without a sound. "The boy is legitimate."

One of the more poorly dressed representatives said, "Lord Denon, then you approve of a new Executive Council session, as is customary? A new King reviews the old legislation."

Justice Hillor answered quickly, before Denon could respond, "The boy is the rightful heir, but he has not been installed yet."

"And when is that ceremony to be?" the same man asked. "After we've starved?"

"In a matter of hours, Orik."

Orik was thin and closely shaven, and he twitched unconsciously as he turned from one side of the table to the other. He said to Hillor, "And then we will have another session tonight?"

"No," Hillor said. "The King has not been properly briefed in the intricacies of recent legislation."

"Intricacies," Orik said to himself, and he prepared to say more, when Denon raised one hand, silencing them both.

"God alone judges the works of man," Denon said, and he walked to the sealed doors. "When a battle is won it is won because the victor is prone to Eternal Grace. Only goodness is allowed to ultimately triumph."

Orik said nothing, glaring at Hillor, and Lord Denon reached the door.

"I have business, gentlemen," Denon said, and he nodded shortly, before leaving.

They sat motionless for a moment, and then Hillor said, "Even if he had been installed, there can be no business without all thirty representatives."

Conversation started in a low rumble, and the members stood, talking amongst themselves. Hillor nodded to Vel.

"We're going back to the second floor."

"Why?" Vel asked.

"That code I mentioned," Hillor said softly, "you're going to get it for me."

"How?"

"An elaborate system is set up to store information, but access to it is limited to the royalty," Hillor said. "It's one of the reasons you're important enough to be alive now."

"I know."

"You will hook into it." He headed for the door, waiting for Vel to follow, but Vel remained where he was.

Hillor said, "You're the only one now who can access it."

Vel shook his head. "I'm not stupid. It gives you the Pox."

"Who told you that?"

"The system makes you sick if you try to access it."

"That's not true," Hillor said. "You were lied to—it doesn't give you the Pox." He motioned to the doors at the far wall and stepped closer to Vel, so they could not be overheard. "Don't make me call the soldiers, Vel. This is only as hard as you make it. Come with me. The system does not make you sick."

I'm sick already, Vel thought, although he had begun to doubt it, having had no serious symptoms of illness since his parents died.

Gradually, Vel stood and trailed behind Hillor, passing the

other members of the Council. They watched him, their conversations stopping as he walked by.

"And why should I believe anything you tell me?" Vel said to Hillor.

"Because I have no reason to lie to you about that," Hillor said. "If I wanted you dead you would be dead already. Besides, a machine can't get sick."

"If it's an animal, it can," Vel said, trying to remember everything Munil had told him. Hillor did not respond, and Vel smiled and they left the meeting room, walking down a short passage with a low, stone ceiling, into the main entrance hall. "How's Jak doing?"

Hillor stopped. "Who?"

"Our mutual friend," Vel said. Police stood rigidly around the hall. Vel studied the extravagant entryway, its broad walls opening into arching doorways that led to other, small rooms, and at one end the great red staircase to the second floor—at the opposite end, the giant, double-doored entrance.

"Jak," Vel said again. "It occurred to me that you must have been her employer. You've been looking for me for so long. How is she?"

Silence.

"Outside, there's an entire city of nervous people," Hillor said, and they continued toward the stairs. "Riots are breaking out more and more frequently. This isn't about you or me or whatever little vendettas you might have. Food supplies are almost entirely gone in some sections of the city."

"But, there *is* food," Vel said. "There's food in the ruins. You know that, because Jak went there for you—"

Hillor's face silenced him, and they mounted the stairs. "We're not enemies, Vel. That's not what I want. And it's not what I need. But, I will hurt you if you make me. If you push me, I will do whatever I have to do to save the city. Somehow you know about the legislation concerning the food supply, but without that measure, we will *all* die. Do you understand? Everything I do is for the good of the city." He watched Vel for a reaction, and Vel gave him none. "Now," Hillor said, "your coronation ceremony will begin within the next few hours. I want you to help me with the stored information. I need a numerical code, Vel. It's very simple."

"A code for what?" Vel asked, and he thought, For weapons. So you can access the Church's vaults.

Hillor paused, resting both hands on one railing, as if considering whether or not to explain it all.

"The same information system that you will hook into has a grid at the Church. That grid requires a series of numbers, but if the wrong combination is entered, then it won't respond to another combination for a full year—which means that I must have the correct numbers now."

Vel said, "What is it *for*? What happens if you enter the right combination?"

Hillor glanced at him and was silent. "No one really knows," he said.

I know, Vel thought. And that means you do too. With those weapons, with an arsenal—using the police force—you can keep everyone in check, and you can maintain control when they revolt. You're right, Vel realized. It *is* very simple.

"If you do provide me with what I want," Hillor continued, "I'll set both of your friends free. And then you'll be made King, and it will become official to the people of Hope."

Vel stared at him, unmoving. "You aren't going to tell them that there's a food supply?"

Hillor said quietly, "I'm not going to lie to them, now—"

"But, you sent Jak to the ruins—you know!"

"This is the first I've heard of any secret food supply," Hillor said. "Now, you're going to get me information I need, and in exchange I'm going to help you with your friends. The police won't free either of them without my orders."

"When you hook me up to the system, I'll get sick," Vel said. "That's where the Pox started—people got it from the living computer first and then it spread, didn't it?"

"No."

Vel thought for a moment and said, "You have to let them go. I need to know that they're both still alive."

"They're alive," Hillor said. "The girl is being held in our cells under the Palace, and your friend is still being processed by the garrison several blocks away."

Vel echoed the words, "I need to know."

Hillor frowned. Vel could almost see the man's mind working it out. Finally, the Justice shrugged and nodded to the far archway. "All right, let's get it over with."

After entering a guarded door in the recesses of the Palace, Hillor led Vel down, descending a dark spiral staircase. The stone was well worn, a smooth crease in the center, and as they continued, Vel ducked to avoid a low ceiling. Black clots in the stone around them. Hillor's footsteps sounded definitely, and a company of policeman passed them—brushing very close—moving up. They saluted Hillor. Vel could smell the men's breaths, but they seemed not to notice him.

"These were here when the city was founded," Hillor said.

"What were, the stairs?"

Torchlight shook below them, lighting the path from regular posts on the dark walls.

"I don't know about the stairs," Hillor said. "But the passages we use as a prison run under the Palace, and similar tunnels go beneath some of the other older buildings, like the Church."

Vel thought of the room below the Cathedral where he had awakened bound. And the passage in the cemetery . . . all older than the buildings. Did the Frill build these? he thought. The Frill helped Blakes settle this city before he tried to massacre them. That's where all of the stone in Hope came from. Hillor stopped descending; they were at the bottom.

The stairwell ended at a low doorway leading to a subterranean hallway of stone. The rock had been hollowed out to create small cells in both walls. The open spaces between the cell walls were lined with bars, and each was sealed by a thick wooden door. Torches sputtered from the stone walls between the cells, and soldiers sat at regular intervals, tiredly keeping guard. The cells were very quiet, and as Hillor led Vel down the hall, sad, dirty faces watched him from behind the bars.

Hillor stopped moving and then turned stiffly to the right, opening the nearest cell. The room was bare: black stone with a single hole in the floor and a wooden bucket of water.

The air was thick with the stench of excrement. She lay on her back, beside the hole, spread-eagled on the floor, chains wrapped around her wrists and ankles. Lydia's black clothing was ripped and torn, shredded in places, and laced with dried blood. Her eyes were shut tightly. Wounds in her legs and shoulder.

That dark hair and pale skin, bruised and swollen in places. They'd torn off her shirt, but somehow she'd managed to pull it back over her upper body. Lydia's legs were spread apart, and, when he saw the bruises along her thighs, Vel's breathing quickened. Her pants had been reduced to a tangle of ripped fabric. He pushed back the tension, focusing it, concentrating it into veins of adrenaline underneath his skin.

"Every time they've tried to loosen the chains, she's attacked. She seriously injured six guards before they finally subdued her the last time," Hillor said.

A pounding inside Vel's ears, and he walked quietly into the cell. Immediately, Lydia's eyes fluttered open, and she eased a swollen head to look at him.

"Vel," Lydia mouthed the word, her voice coming out in a hoarse whisper. Vel lowered himself to her. A sudden wrenching pain inside his mind, and he shuddered, feeling the emotions as they rushed out.

No, Vel thought, you can't be here like this.

Lydia smiled at him. "It's nice of you," she fought with the words, "to come by."

Vel turned to Hillor. "Get her out of here!"

Hillor stepped closer. "You know what we agreed to."

Vel's hands became fists, and Hillor made no attempt to defend himself as Vel came closer.

"Let her out of here, Hillor. You can't just leave her down here like this!"

Hillor's expression remained. "Then you'll do it?"

Vel shook his head, the raw fury pulsing through him like hot, molten metal. His arms trembled involuntarily.

"I'm going to kill you," Vel said.

Hillor looked tiredly into his eyes. "Is that a yes?"

Vel looked away. "Let her go, Hillor."

"Answer the question."

"No, Vel," Lydia stammered. She pulled weakly against the chains. He tried not to hear her voice, tried not to hear the way it raked at the back of her throat.

"Yes." He closed his eyes. "Set her free. I'll do it."

"You heard him," Hillor said loudly to the soldiers in the hallway outside the cell. "Let her go."

A policeman walked forward, leaning down to free each lock, one by one. Hillor touched Vel's shoulder.

"Let's go, then. We have only a few hours before the ceremony."

Vel glanced back at the cell. "What's going to happen to her?"

"She'll be given treatment and sent up to your room."

"Just send her up to the room."

Hillor shook his head. "She's been hurt pretty badly." Vel didn't see the tracings of a smile on the Justice's lips. "Perhaps she should be treated."

"Just send her up," Vel said. "And what about Ponce?"

Lydia lay, unmoving on the stone, the last of her limbs free. She rolled like a corpse, rasping words into the darkness.

"Ponce will have to be sent for. It may be longer." Hillor took Vel by the arm and pushed him gently back the way they'd come. Vel lingered, and he watched as the soldiers gingerly raised Lydia from the ground and carried her away.

The box was perfectly square and made of the same reflective metal Vel had seen at the ruins. It was black, but Vel still saw himself on its sides. This is from the beginning of Hope, he thought. Hillor had retrieved the box from another room on the second floor, and they now sat in a tiny, dimly lit storage area adjacent to Vel's own room. The door to the storage room was small and easily overlooked. Vel watched as Hillor took a long wire from behind the device and held it up to his face.

"Your predecessor communicated with this. But he refused to give anyone any useful information from the system, hoarding what he learned for himself," he said. "There's a great deal contained inside this system, Vel. It's like your mind, except that it was designed not to die—so long as we feed and water it." Hillor tapped the wire casually. "The Kings have a long, arrogant tradition of keeping what they learn in the system to themselves."

That's not true, Vel thought. Lydia's order has learned from previous relatives in the bloodline. They know things that they must have gotten from this system secondhand. The King didn't tell you, Hillor, Vel thought. He didn't tell you because he was intelligent enough to know how dangerous that might be.

"Now, it's your turn." Hillor took Vel's left wrist. "I know you'll make a better choice than he did. There are other lives at stake here, aren't there?"

Hillor produced a curved blade from his coat—tiny writing on the handle: *B. Mussolini*—and he pressed the edge to Vel's thumb. Vel tried to pull away, but Hillor was too strong.

"What are you—"

"This won't hurt."

He sliced into Vel's thumb. Red formed and ran wetly from the wound.

"It needs blood," Hillor said. "Somehow it uses that to verify that you are who you say you are, so no one who isn't in the line of succession can access it."

Brainwaves, Vel thought, not really knowing what Munil had meant. Somehow it's going to go inside my mind.

Hillor pressed the wire to Vel's wounded thumb, and the box hummed, blood disappearing, as if the wire was sucking a small amount away from the cut. A trickle of blood ran from the end of the wire—coming from *inside* the box—and it mixed into Vel's open thumb. It's bleeding on me, he thought. There's an animal inside that box, not a machine. How could they have built an animal?

When it had finished, Hillor said, "Here." And he offered Vel a small bandage.

Vel sighed, and he wrapped his left thumb. "You could have warned me. What happens now?"

"I want you to tell me exactly what you learn," Hillor said. "Ask about the combination to the Grid of Rebirth."

"The what?"

"That's what it's called," Hillor said. "It's a simple stone with a collection of numbers located under the Cathedral. They call it the Grid of Rebirth. Make the system give you the combination."

The box stopped humming, and Hillor wiped off his dagger, pocketing it again.

"So what happens now?" Vel asked.

"It takes a moment."

Vel's pulse began to quicken. "What does it do? It just talks through—"

A fire inside his eardrums, and Vel convulsed with the sensation, grabbing at the black box with both arms. The inside of his skull was burning.

"Hillor . . . get it out . . ."

A sudden rush of light, and the pain faded away.

Hello, Vel. I'm Blakes.

chapter 26

Hello.

How are you, Vel?

What's going on? Am I inside the system?

Your body is lying in that room, and you're here, talking to me. I am the system.

Oh.

Time passes differently here. You've been lying on the floor for five minutes.

But, I just got here.

What do you want to know, Vel? We have time to talk, if you'd like.

Who are you?

I am Blakes—

You were named after the founder of Hope.

No. I am that man. I am Blakes.

But Blakes lived five hundred years ago—I don't understand.

Yes, I lived that long ago. And I am that man. I am also a man who lived over one thousand, one hundred years ago. I am the Blake who saw salvation in the face of tyranny.

How can you be two people? How can you be alive at all?

This is the network that existed onboard our ship, built to survive far beyond my lifespan. It is an engineered brain, a living transmitter that was designed never to die, ever replicating. Before I died, I copied myself entirely into the network, replacing its former self with mine.

You can't still be alive.

I am very much alive, Vel—I have seen five hundred years on this planet, the planet I named Hera for her jealousy and vengeance. I took away their weapons, and I watched people develop instruments of murder again. I saw the invention of swords and arrows; after the fire I saw them rebuild the city in a style they had never heard of. But it was not new, it had been done before. Do you understand? People living in Hope knew next to nothing of swords and arrows and crossbows and dark age slums, but they invented them. These patterns are not random.

Why doesn't anyone know about you?

I am your God, Vel, but I am not a God of mercy or compassion. Pain is the most powerful persuasion, the most effective. I labor upwards into futurity: if you tell anyone that I exist here—that I am still alive—I will kill you.

What? I don't believe this, how could you hurt me?

There are ways. I don't exist in a vacuum, Vel. I can do things besides match your brainwaves. I can turn them off now that I have the signature of your blood.

I don't believe you.

Then tempt me and see. Tell someone that Blakes is the system and see if I'm listening. See if you don't die. I give you my word that I will kill you if you begin to tell. I'm sorry, Vel, but it's necessary. If certain people knew I was alive, they might guess what must inevitably happen, and then they would move to stop me.

Why? What's going to happen?

Someday, perhaps in your lifetime, I will be reborn. Just as I was the last time.

The last time?

The last time human vanity broke God's law and perverted His will to serve our ends. They cloned me, Vel.

> They began to weave a curtain of darkness,
> They erected large pillars round the Void,
> With golden hooks fasten'd in the pillars;
> With infinite labour the Eternals
> A woof wove, and called it Science.

They dug up William Blake and smashed his bones, sifting out his identity, and they made him again, in the body of a newborn. A replication, a sin—truth can never be told so as to be understood, and now be believ'd. That was me. I had become two men, two Blakes.

How did you get here? Why'd you come to Hera?

It's difficult to explain, Vel. You're my child in this, you see, and you've hardly glimpsed beyond the womb. Try to understand: I saw my purpose in the serpent's meat of science that had created me. This was something they did, digging up the remnants of dead men and selling these new children to states and universities and corporations.

I was a wonder of the world—I was William Blake in the twenty-second century—and I was theirs. Told them I knew nothing of the dead prophet, Blake, but I knew. I remembered. I had seen angels, witnessed God's purpose firsthand, something they could not understand and wouldn't have wanted to.

What happened?

I learned of the history since the first Blake, of great men and their visions that were always overpowered by the weaker forces of slave morality. These great men you will never have heard of. Hitler, Stalin, Cromwell, Pol Pot—these prophets had been condemned by history because the world was afraid when these men championed the idea of the individual, not caring or fearing the price of cleansing civilization. The modern world had either forgotten or damned these men as criminals.

You see, Vel, all of the world had become a blanket of white noise: technology and science that served to limit man—pushing us farther from our place as angels, turning us into cattle.

Cattle?

If you understand a fraction of what I'm telling you, then I will have accomplished my purpose. That is why I challenged them to burn it all, to eliminate the Devil's machines that had overtaken every aspect of their lives. It was my crusade, and I fought them. And when it ended, the sneaking serpent once more walked in humility, while the just were left to rage in the wilds with lions.

You lost?

Most wanted me dead, just as they had countless prophets throughout all of history. My trial was no different, except that in the place of lashes, I was expelled, without the means to ever return.

And you came here?

Yes. And I called it Hera. And Hera's city became the Hope of the chosen, God's last children, with a chance to begin in the

garden again. Most of our technology was lost in the war with
the Frill or buried in the fire or rock.

Why did you fight the Frill?

*Demons must be destroyed. And do not think for one moment
that they have any interests besides those of their Lord Lucifer.
The sooner you forget their true nature is a testament to the
power of evil and temptation. Which makes the risk of losing you
all the more relevant.*

Why? Why me?

*Because of what was arranged, the deal made between man
and demon for mutual interests. All of it was sin, God save you.*

I don't understand, Blakes.

*There are two groups of Frill, one which openly defies man,
the other that feigns friendship. This second group was involved
years ago in a creation to fulfill their prophecies. Not unlike my
own.*

What prophecies?

*Something they believe. A way to unite the factions. Shadow
and Sky—the Frill live in shadow.*

I don't understand.

*It's best that you don't now. For all of my youth, I could not
imagine what could've possessed men to pound William Blake
back to life—and when I finally understood, I never forgot their
hypocrisy and I never forgave them. You are not ready yet.*

*We have very little time, Vel. The ceremony is almost ready to
begin, and you will have to leave soon.*

You created the city, and you brought the government star to
Hope, the Church swa? You built all of that?

*Yes, but the Church emblem of purity and justice is not called
a swa.*

What is it?

A swastika. Why did you come here?

Hillor wants a code.

*Yes, well, you know what it is. Now, do you understand the
importance of my secrecy? Some time soon, I will bring back God's
kingdom of Divine Retribution to Hope. They must not know I
exist. You are my child, but this is more important than blood.*

All right, I won't say anything.

After three hundred years in space, we put up a plaque when we marched into the land that is now Hope:

Hope—Founded 2402
When I have seen by time's fell hand defaced
The rich proud cost of outworn buried age.

And who wrote those words—you?
No, Vel. Darkness is coming to Hope, but I want you to remember your lineage. Do not forget who you are. Your father was the King's brother, a man named Sulter, and though you have no mother, you have my guidance.

O Rose thou art sick.
The invisible worm
That flies in the night,
In the howling storm:

Has found out thy bed
Of crimson joy:
And his dark secret love
Does thy life destroy.

Your disease has a cure.
You know where the cure for the Pox is?
I wasn't talking about the Pox.
What—

vel rolled over. He was exhausted, as if he had just been sprinting. He lay on the ground, Hillor standing over him, face eager.

"What did it say?"

"Ouch," Vel said.

Hillor frowned. "What?"

Vel pulled himself up. "It's gone insane. I didn't understand most of what it said. Is this thing really alive, like an animal?"

"Possibly," Hillor said. "That's one way to think of it. Did it give you the code?"

"It didn't tell me . . ." he trailed off. "It didn't tell me the answers to all of my questions, but it gave me part of it."

Hillor drew closer. In one hand, he held a small piece of chalk. "Part of it?"

"It said that it had given me the entire code, but that I would remember it gradually."

Hillor watched him very carefully, and he tapped at his coat, over the bulge where the pistol rested at his side.

"It *will* come back to you," Hillor said.

Vel nodded. "I think so."

Hillor said, "The ceremony is ready—you'll be formally sworn in as King. When it's over, you'll go upstairs and write everything you remember about the code. Do you understand?"

Vel nodded. Was it anger he saw in Hillor's eyes? Or just the frantic look of one who must rely on another for the first time?

"I'll try," Vel said.

Hillor stopped. "I have confidence in your memory, Vel." His voice was low, "People tend to remember things more quickly when there's a deadline. I understand the girl's beginning to re-cover, and I'm sure you want that to continue?"

"Where is she now?"

"In your room." A sudden quickness in Vel's chest. "Do we understand each other?"

I don't have the code, Vel thought, and he struggled to make sense of everything Blakes had told him. Some of it had seemed like nonsense, he thought. Or am I ignorant? What if I *do* already know the code Hillor wants? A number to open a door sealed hundreds of years ago—is it that simple? The Frill had been the ones speaking to me at the ruins. And demons or not, their com-bination had worked to open the door . . . as Blakes. That woman's voice had greeted Commander Blakes. Is it the same number? he wondered. But, what if it isn't, and even if it is what am I supposed to do with that?

Vel nodded quietly.

"Yes," he said. "We understand each other."

Two rows of chairs filled the auditorium that nestled into a side passage from the main entrance hall. It was an impressive room, and Vel stood uneasily in the large doorway. Just the single entrance fed into the auditorium, and fixtures of shining glass hung from the ceiling, glowing from the candles inside them. Church and government flags draped the walls, along with crude black and white drawings of old men and women—Kings and Queens. They looked like shadows, Vel thought, and he wondered how old the pictures were.

Soldiers moved about the room, arranging chairs in rows and setting up a table that would clearly serve as the central focus of the crowd, when it assembled. Behind the table, four more chairs were arranged, facing the invisible masses, and Vel looked at Hillor. The Justice stood solemnly nearby.

"How many people are here?"

Hillor shrugged, as if it made no difference one way or the other. "Enough to make it official. The council. The aristocracy—justices, bishops, along with the guild and factory owners. They're all here."

"How long until the ceremony starts?" Vel asked.

Hillor walked down the main aisle, speaking as he went. "We're almost ready. Shouldn't be long."

"If Lydia's—"

"You'll attend the ceremony, and then you will return to your room to remember the code," Hillor said. "We'll start very soon."

And they did.

Less than an hour later, Vel sat at the long table that was now shrouded in a red cloth that draped to the floor. Every chair in the room was occupied. Police stood rigidly around the walls. At the table were Vel, Justice Hillor, Lord Denon and the man Vel remembered from the Council meeting as Orik.

Hillor stood.

The crowd was a busy jumble of men and women in fine clothing. They also got up, waiting for Hillor to begin, and Vel did the same. It occurred to him, as Hillor started talking, that of the several hundred people in the room he was the youngest.

Hillor said, "God bless all of you and thank you for coming. If there is a spirit of Justice in the world, and I believe that there is, then that spirit is here today. Enemies of the state—anarchists, criminals and traitors—have threatened our lives and the laws that we believe in. They set fires even now, fighting against our homes, our children and our honor. And there *is* honor in this God-given city of Hope. We have been created as the servants of our Lord, and for five centuries we have defended not only our rights, but the rights of the unborn. None of us would be here today had our ancestors refused to embrace the vision and courage to do what is right in the name of God and Hope."

The crowd had begun to react, some nodding, others visibly tensing, as the words wrapped around them.

Hillor continued, "And let me make this clear: we will not submit to tyranny. All of those who defy the Justice of Hope will be sent to their graves. Think of your loved ones and remember that their lives depend on our sacrifice. We will not surrender our homes to fire or theft. We will not give our families to murderers and rapists. *We will not yield.* And the damned rioters will ask for our mercy when they've been crushed, and we will cherish the bodies of our bravest who fall to their random bloodlust— and we will show no mercy. We will make them pay. Hope will survive, because we will win.

"We are at a point now when our faith *will* be tested, but I truly feel sorry for those who are against us. The King, our sovereign link to our glorious past, is dead, but I say, *Long live the King!*"

The crowd burst into applause, and Hillor put his hand on Vel's shoulder warmly.

"We have found a successor. The King's nephew, Vel, has

claimed his God-given right to the throne, and I say that it is time we stopped hiding in our houses, behind our fences and body-guards, time we confront this tyranny of violence on the streets today. Vel is our new King, and his fight will be our fight—and the cowards who challenge us will feel *our* fire."

More applause, and now Hillor told Vel to raise his right arm out, palm open.

Hillor said, "Vel, do you swear to uphold the honor of your city, Hope, and to maintain the good of your subjects with your whole soul, under the eyes of the Lord?"

"I do."

Hillor dropped to one knee, and the rest of the room did the same, some bowing their heads. From the table, Vel caught Lord Denon's eyes as they looked up at him. Cold, calculating eyes.

Hillor shouted, "Our King is dead—long live the King!"

The crowd replied in unison, *"Long live the King!"*

"Again," Hillor said as he stood, "thank you for coming. Do not forget: Justice is our fire, and our enemies will burn."

Everyone rose in a shuffle of fabric and chairs, and started talking. Musicians with long wooden instruments filed in through the rear door. Orik shook Vel's hand.

"You'll do a great job, I'm sure," he said, and then more quietly, "The granaries are not quite full, Your Majesty." And then Orik backed away.

People clapped as a loud, fast-paced song beat a rhythm through the room. An old city song. Vel could not remember ever actually hearing it before, but the tune was familiar. An assembly of voices rose, and Lord Denon extended one hand.

"Pity would be no more
If we did not make somebody Poor;
And mercy no more could be
If all were happy as we."

The priest held Vel's hand firm, and nodded simply.

"And mutual fear brings peace,
Till the selfish loves increase;

When Cruelty knits a snare
And spreads his bait with care."

Hillor moved in, as Denon stepped away, and smiled broadly.
"I've sent for your friend."
He offered Vel a hand, and Vel thought, Ponce.

"He sits down with holy fears
And waters the ground with tears
And Mercy no more could be
If all were happy as we."

"When will he be here?" Vel said quietly, under the roar of
voices.
"Not long," Hillor said.

"And it bears the fruit of Deceit,
Ruddy and sweet to eat,
And the Demon his nest has made
In its thickest shade."

"The girl's in your room, Vel. Go back after we've gone down
the aisle."
"Is that an order?"

"The Gods of the land and sea
Sought thro' Nature to find this tree . . ."

Out from behind the table, and they moved in an orderly cluster down the center aisle. Soldiers trailed in their wake.

"And Mercy no more could be
If all were happy as we."

Vel walked out of the auditorium and back toward the stairs,
the song continuing in his mind. It has nothing to do with Hope,
he thought, does it? He jogged up the staircase and down the
second-floor hall, back to his room. Soldiers at even intervals

guarded the hall, one standing directly outside his door.

"Officer, you're relieved of this post. Find another."

"You're King, then?" the policeman said, holding his place.

Vel said, "I am. Now get out of here." Vel reached for the door-knob.

The police soldier nodded. "I'll have to verify your order."

Vel opened the door. "Of course."

Alone on the bed, under the covers, Vel saw Lydia sleeping. She lay curled in a ball, her back to him. After shutting the door, Vel sat noiselessly at the foot of the bed. He thought of Hillor's speech and—the world spun, Vel was thrown from the mattress. The floor rushed to smash Vel's jaw. Distantly, he knew that Lydia had kicked him across the side of his face.

"What . . . ?" Her voice was distant, and Vel heard her getting up. He rolled onto his back, the slow pain beginning to recede, and stood.

Lydia sat on the edge of the mattress, her hair standing and hanging in her face and, briefly, the figure didn't even look like her. Lydia's clothing had not been changed, and one side of her shirt hung down, exposing the lines of her ribs. More bruises traced her collarbone and shoulder.

"Vel." She made sense of his face. She stared at him, her eyes focusing. Once more, she was the person he knew. "What's happened?"

Vel sat beside her on the bed. "I'm King."

"Hillor probably has the cure," Lydia said softly.

"How do you know?"

"He's not sick, is he?" Vel was about to respond, and she continued, "What about my organization—did you meet with them? Did they help you?"

Vel said, "They helped." He put one hand on her shoulder, and she jerked away. *I should have saved her at the ruins,* he thought. *I should have found a way and not gone wandering around. I could have done something if I had really tried.*

Lydia looked away.

"Did they get into contact with you?" she said.

Vel nodded. "Yes, they did." He paused and said, "Hillor killed one of them—that's when he caught me."

"Who?"

"His name was Munil."

She winced with the words as if Vel had slapped her across the cheek. "What else?"

"I don't know where Ponce is. He's supposed to be here soon."

Lydia said, "What happened at the ruins?"

"I saw the Frill," he said, and he told her briefly about his encounter; Vel told her that the Frill claimed to have been created as warriors and guardians on Hera by another race that was gone. And now the Frill had been split into two factions, one opposed to cooperation with people, another in favor. They said that no Frill had been killed in Blakes's war, and suggested that Vel was somehow crucially important in uniting the factions and in reconciling the Frill with the city of Hope.

Lydia listened, and when Vel had finished explaining, she said, "If that's true, you're lucky to be alive—you must have found the 'good' faction."

"I suppose so," he said. "What do you remember from the ruins?"

She rubbed a hand through her hair, as if trying to coax her mind into memory. "Nothing. Went black, and then I was outside, and the Religious Guard took me prisoner." She coughed. "I got away."

"Look at me, Lydia."

She shook her head weakly. "What else has happened?"

"I talked to the system," he said, and tried not to think about Blakes's threat.

She closed her eyes. "Has Hillor offered you the cure?"

"No." Vel shook his head. "The system's alive—like an animal; did you know that?"

"What do you mean?"

"You have to mix blood with it to go in," Vel said. "People who landed here could *build* animals, and the network system was one of them. Munil said that it gives you the Pox. So, I suppose if I didn't have it before, I have it now."

"You've got to get the cure from Hillor."

"Don't know if he has it."

"He does."

Vel said, "He's using me for the code to the Church vaults."

"Have you given him anything?"

"Look at me, Lydia."

"Have you?"

Frustration crept into Vel's mind.

"No, I haven't," he said.

"If Jak was working for Hillor, then Hillor has the cure."

Vel's heart pounded. "Lydia, why won't you look at me?"

She blinked back emotion, struggling to look calm, normal.

"Have you told him about the Frill?" she said.

"Lydia." Vel touched her shoulder, and she spun in a fast, violent surge—her hand shot up, and stopped, shaking, inches from his throat. Lydia shook involuntarily, and withdrew her hand.

"Lydia," Vel said again, and he tried not to think about how he had seen her in the prison. This is because of me too, he thought. And he detached himself. This is happening to someone else, not to me, Vel thought. "It's over now," he said. "We're all right."

She shook her head, but he pressed her shoulder, gently holding her in a position to look at him. It's happening to me, he thought, beginning to feel very tired. Right now. This is happening to me.

Lydia's voice was frightened, "I trained my whole life to be better than them. I—you know what happens to prisoners, Vel." It was almost a child's whimper. "I wasn't better than them. I tried so hard . . ."

Vel shivered. "I care about you, Lydia."

Lydia shook, struggling to hold back the flood of emotions—and flushed, jaw clenching. Violence in her eyes, as she glared at Vel. "You don't know what it felt like, not . . ." She hit the bed with her fist, and tears ran down her cheeks. "Goddamn it. I'm . . ."

Vel pulled her close. Lydia trembled and shook, Vel remaining steady. Remaining strong. I'm the strong one now, he thought. And inside his head, the entire world came crashing down again and again and again. Because of me—my fault. It was taking him apart. Whatever it was that found people he knew and hurt them—it was beating him.

Vel stroked her head; gradually, her arms encircled him. And the two sat together on the bed. Lydia rolled silently into Vel's shirt, staining it with tears.

"It's all right," Vel said. "It's going to be all right."

She squeezed him tightly, and he embraced her. They couldn't get close enough. Vel refused to let go, his muscles trembling.

Lydia pressed her mouth to his throat and whispered, "I love you, Vel."

He swallowed.

Lydia sniffed, opening her eyes. With one hand, she wiped away tears, and then smiled gently. Vel relaxed, and Lydia leaned back, still in contact with him.

"Nice to be in a bed again," she said.

"I can imagine."

And something dark passed through her, hardening Lydia's expression, tightening her muscles.

"Never say anything to me about the prison, Vel. Never bring it up. Promise me you won't ever ask."

He stared at her. I let them take her, he thought. At the ruins— I was there and I couldn't stop them. I didn't even try. Just push it back, he thought. Just push back the feelings. Deal with them later.

"I promise," he said.

Lydia took his hand, her face returning to normal. "Didn't mean to kick you off the bed." Before Vel could answer, she said, "I don't remember the last time I was this hungry. Is there food or clothing that comes with being King? I could use some of both."

Vel started for the door. "Those are the benefits you were telling me about—the great advantages that come with being King? Food and clean clothes?"

"Could be worse," she said. "But, remember, you don't want to be King."

"That's right." Vel opened the door. "I don't."

He ordered a policeman in the hall to get food and a woman's black uniform.

"You know there's an entire garrison here at the Palace," she said when he had closed the door again. "We're not going to get out."

"You don't think this is fun?" Vel said. "Why should we want to get out?"

She crossed her arms. "Well, for one, you'll be executed as soon as Hillor has the code."

"Then I won't give it to him."

"You're going to have to give him something," Lydia said. "And if you give him a fake he'll kill us."

"It's just a win-win situation, isn't it?"

Lydia said, "The Executive Council won't meet again. Hillor won't give you a chance to veto the food measure."

"So what do we do?"

Lydia took a deep breath and examined the bedroom. "I'll think of something."

"Can't tell you how reassuring that is."

She winked at him. "You want me to kick you again?"

A soldier opened the door, dropping a clump of black fabric near the entrance. He motioned to Vel. "Justice Hillor will speak to you now." And the soldier left.

Lydia squeezed Vel's palm and said quietly, "You have to give him something, but not too much. He might be able to try different combinations if you give him enough parts of the code."

"Don't think he can," Vel said. "Hillor said that if you put in the wrong combination, the system automatically shuts down for an entire year."

"And you believe him?" she said. "That may be true, but it could also be more complicated than that—and he wants you to *think* that you can give him a small part and remain safe."

Vel walked to the door, and Lydia said, "Vel?" He paused, looking at her. "Thank you."

"For what?"

"For coming back for me. You wouldn't be here if I wasn't. Thanks for getting me out of there. We'll find a way out of this."

Vel nodded, started to say something, stopped, and then said simply, "I know."

He stepped into the hall, closing the door behind him. Vel leaned against the door frame, pressing the side of his head to the wood. I'm so tired, he thought. God, this is breaking me down.

A low voice, "Sleep is sometimes the best luxury, isn't it?"

Vel started, spotting Hillor at the far end of the hall, dressed in a heavy overcoat. Hillor held a pad of paper and black writing chalk casually in both hands.

"She stays in there," Vel said, approaching Hillor. "You're not taking her from my room."

Vel passed stationary police soldiers, spaced evenly on both sides of the wall.

Hillor smiled, patting Vel on the shoulder. "I know we can work together. You'll cooperate, and we'll both get what we want."

"I'll cooperate."

"Good," Hillor said. "You're not stupid. A little inexperienced, but not stupid." Hillor paused. "Let me ask you something, Vel. Do you think I do what I do because I enjoy it?"

"Yes."

Hillor laughed to himself, as if he had expected the answer. "Understand something: I do everything for survival, just as everyone does. Years from now, people will look back and some will decide that, 'yes, he was a bad person, if anyone can be,' but others will remember me as a product of my time."

"What makes you think you'll be remembered at all?"

"People *will* remember," Hillor said. "Their world will exist as it does because of my actions. It's complex to really understand, but every change in the world today is a change in *their* lives. You see? They'll remember because what I do now decides the course of their lives as well as ours."

"If we don't all starve," Vel said.

Hillor nodded seriously. "Yes, if we don't all starve." He handed Vel the paper and chalk. "Give me the code."

"Can I do this in my room?" Vel asked.

Hillor tensed, losing his casual demeanor. "This isn't a game, Vel. Give me the code or I have the girl sent back to her cell."

Vel hesitated, pressing an end of the chalk to the top of the paper. It held, unmoving.

Hillor said, "What's the code?"

"I know one number."

Hillor glared at him. "Not good enough. I think the system gave you the entire code. Write it down or I start burning away some of that girl's face. You want to see that?"

Vel said, "That's all I can give you now—the first number."

Hillor said softly, "She gets burned and loses fingers each day you stall. Is that how you want to do this? I'm not going to say it again, Vel—write the code."

Vel asked, "What about Ponce?"

"Your other friend at the prison? He's here, and he'll be sent to your room." Hillor indicated the pad. "Go ahead."

Reluctantly, Vel wrote the four digit code, and when he'd finished, Hillor nodded, reading the numbers.

"One, three, two, one."

"Yes," Vel said.

Hillor grabbed Vel roughly by one arm, moving him down the hall, approaching a group of soldiers near the main staircase.

"This boy is under arrest." Hillor said. "He and his conspirators are condemned for treason and should be placed in the prison underground."

"What?" Vel said. "What charge?"

"Assassinating the king. What else? You killed the king in order to secure the crown for yourself. Get these traitors out of my sight."

Too fast, Vel thought, that happened too quickly—how do I stop this? Hillor handed Vel to the soldiers, and they surrounded him. Hillor hurried down the main staircase without turning. For the Church, Vel thought, he's going for the artifacts now. Police soldiers forced Lydia from the bedroom.

"What's going on?" Lydia said, limping, as they were escorted down the staircase into the entrance hall in the center of a company of six soldiers, all armed.

"We're being taken to prison," Vel said.

"What?"

A soldier smashed his sword handle into Vel's back. "Speak again, and I cut out your tongue."

They were escorted through a number of stone corridors, into large rooms, and finally down the spiral stairs to the rock prison. Before Vel's eyes had adjusted to the light, he was shoved through a half-opened cell door, tripped, and landed hard on dirty stone.

Vel heard the door shut, and he sat up, blinking in the near-darkness. Lydia stood near the barred wall, and several other prisoners slept on cots at the rear of the cell. The room smelled of disease and human waste.

"One of the advantages of an overcrowded prison," Lydia said, kneeling beside Vel. "They don't have room to separate us."

"Does it make a difference?" Vel said. "Hillor's going for the artifacts now."

"You gave him the code?"

"I didn't have much of a choice, Lydia. He said he would torture you, and—"

"Why did you do that?" She shook her head in frustrated amazement, as if she couldn't decide whether to laugh or slap him. "Didn't you think? Didn't you even try to stall him?"

Several of the other prisoners had started to listen to their conversation. One rolled off his cot and said, "You'd better have a damned good reason you're in prison—please tell me this is part of your plan."

Vel spun. "Ponce!"

Ponce grinned tiredly, looking exhausted, beaten, but still well enough to laugh. Ponce hit Vel playfully on the shoulder and nodded to Lydia. "Hi."

She said, "Hello, Ponce. Your friend just gave Hillor the Church code."

Ponce nodded. "The what?"

Vel said, "Remember—the numbers he needs to open the Church vaults. I had to give it to him because—"

"You didn't have to give it to him," Lydia said.

Ponce said, "Just like old times. What do you think the chances were we'd get tossed in the same cell?"

"They were good," Lydia said, and she began to pace. The soldiers in the hall ignored them. "We're going to be executed. They have special cells for people like that. As soon as Hillor knows that Vel gave him the right code, we'll be hanged or beheaded."

Ponce said, "When will that be?"

Vel said, "Hillor has to go to the Cathedral and come back—that's maybe a half an hour both ways."

Ponce said, "I suppose I should be happy we have this last hour together, but for some reason I always hoped that you guys would get me out of here, not join me at the last minute for a noble death."

Lydia frowned at the black stone walls, then at the bars and soldiers beyond. "We're not going to die in here."

One of the prisoners grunted loudly that they should speak more quietly so the others could sleep, and drew Lydia's attention. She spotted something on the rear wall, behind the cots and began to trace her fingers across small imperfections in the stone—carvings. Faded, but they were still visible.

Vel and Ponce went to her.

Vel said, "Those look like—"

"People didn't make these rooms. Look," Lydia said, and she continued to trace the carvings. "This is what we found at the ruins—look at this. This is definitely the same kind of writing."

"Don't have time to go to the ruins," Vel said. "We have to go to the Cathedral."

She said, "I know."

The Frill built these rooms, Vel thought. These carvings belong to the Frill . . . and he started for the barred wall and wooden door that led to the prison hallway. A knock on the wall to his left.

Ponce said, "All right, this is starting to get weird."

Vel went to the wall, checked to be certain none of the guards were watching, and knocked back. Through a crack in the stone, a voice whispered, "—the King?"

Vel pressed his mouth to the crack and said, "I'm the King, yes." He put his ear to the hole.

"—Till says in four minutes, you run . . . right?"

Till? Vel thought.

"I don't understand."

"Four minutes," the voice said. "You run. Till get you out."

"Thank you," Vel said, and Ponce watched him strangely.

"What the hell was that?"

"Not sure," Vel said, and Lydia approached, finished with the carvings.

She asked, "Someone on the other side?"

"Says Till will get us out in four minutes," Vel said.

"Till?" Ponce said. "The guy who owned Turn Tables?"

"I don't know."

Vel felt the room spin, and he staggered, holding onto the wall with one hand. He knew these passages—the sensation he had felt in the rooms underneath the ruins, the dream-memory. Vel stared out the bars, into the hallway. Four minutes, he thought. And then what?

Ponce took his arm. "You all right? Vel?"

Vel nodded. "Fine." There's something I'm missing, he thought. I've overlooked it, because I wasn't understanding things the right way . . .

Clatter of metal in the hall outside, and soldiers shouting. Vel, Ponce, and Lydia hurried to the bars—one of the cells farther down the hall had been opened, and all of the guards had gathered to block the prisoners' escape.

One of the soldiers backed away from the group, moving toward Vel's cell, keys in one hand, and Vel recognized him immediately. It *was* Mr. Till.

Ponce said, "How the hell?"

And the police began to force the prisoners farther inside their cell. Our chance is almost gone, Vel thought. No more guards in the opposite direction—nothing for thirty feet, to the stairs, and there, on the ceiling was a carved blue circle. Lydia followed his gaze.

"Damn," she said.

Vel watched Till draw closer, still casually walking. "Why didn't we see it?" Vel said, and he pointed the circle out to Ponce.

Ponce looked at it, unimpressed. "Amazing."

Till reached their cell, nodding to Vel as he fit a key into the lock. "You're our King."

"Thank you," Vel said.

Till opened the cell door, hinges creaking, and the other prisoners responded slowly, unsure of what to do.

"Run," Till said.

Lydia indicated the blue circle. "We'll go through that." Till tensed, then said, "Off-limits for the guards. None of them touch it."

Ponce made a noise with his throat to indicate that they should move, and Till agreed, pausing to block the opened cell door from the vision of the other guards for a moment longer.

"All right," he said. "Run."

They bolted from the cell—heard shouting behind them—and Lydia lunged, touched both palms to the circle, started to drop, and was gone. Step on, step off, Vel thought. It works the same way.

"Go Ponce!" Vel shouted.

And behind him, "—eady!"

Till caught Vel under his armpits, heaving him into the air before Vel could stop him. Vel touched the circle with one hand— Ponce jumped, barely hitting it with his thumb, and vanished— and Vel still held his hand against the stone.

"Aim!"

Soldiers in the hallway with crossbows, and Till shouted, "They won't follow—let go!"

"You're coming too."

"Fire!"

Flashes of arrows—one into Till's chest, another in his stomach—and Till fell, taking Vel with him—an arrow lanced at Vel's face, and the hall flashed white.

vel dropped, landing on wet stone, and he rolled, metal clanking in the darkness. The air smelled familiar. I've been here before, Vel thought, and he found a stone wall nearby, a strong chain fastened to it.

"Wonderful, just wonderful," Ponce said from somewhere nearby.

"I know where we are," Vel said in the blackness.

"This is remarkably like where we just were," Ponce said. "You sure that wasn't some kind of dirty clothes chute—"

Lydia said to Vel, "You recognize this?"

Vel felt her arm searching blindly in the air, and it rubbed against his chest. He took her hand carefully.

"In another prison," Vel said.

"A very dark prison," Ponce said, and he bumped heavily into something and cursed. "There are stairs here . . . just broke one of my toes on them."

Water dripped in the blackness.

"We're under the Cathedral," Lydia said. "Till coming?"

"No," Vel said. "Where are you, Ponce? The stairs lead out."

"Right over here," Ponce said, and footsteps nearby, approaching—the footsteps paused.

"I'll handle this," Lydia whispered, and she let go of Vel's hand. He heard only the regular tapping of the water on stone.

A lock clicked, and then a door at the top of the stairs opened, illuminating the small cell. Lydia was already at the top, waiting, and as the door opened, she spun out, taking someone down fast. Vel followed Ponce up the stairs and into a large stone dining room.

Lydia stood over a downed Religious Guard, holding his sword in one hand. The door they had exited was built into one wall of Reich Hall, and Vel saw the door nearby that he knew led out onto the street. The ceiling arched far above their heads, and a long table sat empty, ornate silverware filling enough spaces to feed fifty. Candles burned from the top of silver candleholders, and Vel followed Lydia toward an arched doorway at the opposite wall, Ponce behind him.

A low, rhythmic chanting sounded from the recesses of the giant building, and they entered another room larger than the first, its ceiling even higher. Church tapestries—all with swastikas in their centers—hung from the walls. A painting of a man in a brown uniform with a square mustache and short dark hair parted to the left hung between several of the usual tapestries. The man on the painting wore a red armband with a black swastika on his left arm. The power of God, Vel thought, and he wondered who the man was—one of the great men Blakes had mentioned? Was it Blakes himself?

Around another corner, and two more Religious Guard stood rigidly at a pair of closed double doors—swords drawn when they saw the intruders. Chanting emanated from beyond the doors. Lydia readied herself protectively in front of Vel and Ponce.

"Restricted," one guard said.

And the other asked, "What do you want? How did you get in here?"

Vel said, "I have to speak to Lord Denon."

"There is a ceremony in progress."

"You don't understand," Vel said. "I *must* speak with him."

"It's blasphemy to disturb."

"It's an emergency of the highest order," Vel said. "He *must* be interrupted. I'm the King."

"It doesn't matter," the first guard said. "Ceremony cannot be interrupted."

Ponce stepped closer. "We don't have time for this."

The guard hesitated, uncertain. Finally, he relented.

"You will all be punished in this world and the next if this is not all you say it is. Do you understand? Your souls are forfeit if you are not who you say you are."

"Trust me," Vel said, fear forming in his stomach. "I am."

One of the guards went inside, and the other remained, his sword still drawn. The chanting continued, and Vel glanced at Lydia and Ponce, unspeaking—then the chanting stopped. The doors opened again, and the guard returned, followed immediately by Lord Denon and another group of the Religious Guard, all armed. Vel counted more than twenty, and now thirty, and forty—he backed away uncomfortably. Lydia refused to withdraw, her sword leveled at Denon.

Lord Denon nodded to Vel, waiting for an explanation.

"I need your blessing," Vel said. "I need the blessing of the Church."

Denon looked briefly at the Religious Guard around him, and he waved them away.

"Tell them to leave," Denon said, indicating Lydia and Ponce.

Lydia shook her head. "No, this isn't safe. If he . . ."

"Please, Lydia," Vel said. "We're going to have to attack, aren't we? Go back to your group, and get them ready."

Lydia lowered her sword. "You're serious?"

"Yes," Vel said, and to Ponce, "Are you in this?"

Ponce said, "Looks that way, doesn't it?"

"Go with her." Neither of them moved, and Vel said, "Please. We have to work together."

"All right," Lydia said at last, and she led Ponce away, refusing to put the sword away as they withdrew toward the side exit. The Religious Guard locked the door behind them.

Denon went to the double doors and stepped inside. Vel followed him down a central aisle past two sections of wooden pews, toward a blue circle painted onto the stone in front of the altar. It was the wrong shade of blue, but the likeness was close enough that it was not a coincidence. The Church knows, Vel thought. Somehow they know about all of this, don't they? Swastikas hung on every wall.

As they neared the altar, Denon said, "What do you want?"

"I need your blessing to activate the Church artifacts."

Denon motioned to the thick book, opened on the altar. "Blakes's *Rebirth*." He searched Vel for a response and then flipped several pages, reading, "An Angel came to me and said: 'O pitiable foolish young man! O horrible! O dreadful state! Consider the hot burning dungeon thou art preparing for thyself to all eternity, to which thou art going in such career.' " Denon pointed to the first pew. "Please, sit."

Vel did, leaving room for Denon to sit beside him. Denon remained standing. There was a long pause, and Denon kept his hands folded.

"Have you thought about it?" Denon said at last.

"About what?"

"How all of this fits together. Why you are where you are now—why you want the artifacts."

"If I don't get them, Hillor will."

"Probably," Denon said, his face unchanged. "There are more soldiers in the police force, but without an official blessing it will take time for him to lay siege to God's house. What if Justice Hillor doesn't receive the sacred relics? Why should you want them?"

"I have to stop him," Vel said.

"From doing what?"

"The people will revolt against him unless the food measure is changed. There will be anarchy, and the city will die."

"And you will change this by," Denon frowned, pressing both hands to his chin carefully, "killing Justice Hillor?"

"Yes," Vel said.

"Have you read Blakes?"

"No," Vel said, and he thought, But I've spoken to him.

Denon said, "Blakes believes that one can unintentionally devise one's success in the future by something done in the past, and that these unconscious maneuvers are what plan our lives— they are God's strings. He believes that destruction is no different. Perhaps Hope's end has been unavoidable for some time." Denon paused, as if waiting for Vel to argue with him. Finally, he said, "Do you begin to see your place in this, Vel? How it fits together?"

"No," Vel said. "Will you show me where the grid is? Hillor will be here soon."

"He will not gain admittance without my consent," Denon said simply, as if discussing the price of a new shirt at the market. "All men's souls must be preserved in the time to come, but I think there is some truth in what Blakes says. Perhaps the kingdom will end on Hera. But it will continue regardless. A Cathedral may burn, but the Church never catches fire. Look to your own salvation, Your Majesty."

"Please," Vel said, "if we're doomed anyway, why not let me try?"

"And in exchange?"

Vel's mouth went dry. He's been waiting for this the entire time, Vel thought. Lord Denon wants to bargain, doesn't he?

"What do you want?" Vel asked.

Denon leaned back, as if insulted. "I will not buy and sell salvation." Vel waited, and Denon crossed his fingers in his lap. "You must remember that God serves in the time of need."

Vel said, "Thank you. I will remember this."

Denon looked him in the eye, his face absolutely calm. "Do not underestimate him, Vel. Although Justice Hillor has sown his own end, he is still who he is. Don't forget that. And if you have to fight him, do not fight him for a single victory, make sure there will never be another battle."

"Thank you," Vel said again.

Denon stood, and without another word he led Vel back— around the altar and blue circle—to one of the doors on the rear wall. They entered, passed through a series of identical corridors, past more of the Religious Guard, all with weapons drawn and ready, and down a brief staircase to a blank stone wall. Torches burned nearby.

"There," Denon said, nodding to the wall.

"What?" Vel said, and Denon opened the wall by sliding his hand across one section of the stone eight times. It swiveled, and there stood another set of doors, and another pair of the Religious Guard, crossbows aimed at them. A small black box sat in front of the doors, behind the soldiers, and Denon raised his hand to them.

"I have given blessing," Denon said, and the soldiers lowered their weapons, moving aside. Denon and Vel crouched at the black box. There was a simple keypad with numerals, *0* to *9*.

Vel said, "The code . . ."

Denon was already typing. He pressed one, three, two, and then one again. Something buzzed beyond the doors, and Vel felt a chill. He looked at Denon but Denon did not respond.

Instead, Denon stood simply, motioning to the soldiers. "Help him transport them. Your watch is ended."

Without another word, Vel followed Denon inside, to the artifacts. One-three-two-one, Vel thought. Goddamn it.

chapter 28

"This will not be forgotten."

"Go in peace, Justice Hillor."

"I will not go in peace. I will return in force and I will be allowed to speak with Lord Denon."

"I told you, Lord Denon is busy. Perhaps next week, you could—"

"Quiet. The Church does not protect you from the law."

"Nor the law from the Church."

"I will speak Denon, and you will not presume to lecture me on law. This isn't finished."

Inside, the vault smelled sweet; it was an odor Vel had never smelled before. Denon waited behind him, as Vel stared around the medium-sized stone room. A dusty bust of a man with short hair, a mustache, and a red star on his stone jacket rested just inside the entrance on a column. Behind the statue, rows of long boxes were covered in old sheets.

Vel stepped into the room, stirring up clouds of dust, and a faded plate at the rear wall read:

To the last syllable of recorded time.

There were clusters of metal stands with swastikas and strange shapes on them piled on one corner, and a giant pile of books in front of that, all with yellowed pages. The top one had red letters on its black cover—*Mein Kampf*—and Vel read down the spines of several others. *Songs of Innocence and of Experience, The Holy Bible, The Course of Europe Since Waterloo, Biology, The Art of War, The Trial of God.* There were dozens more.

"These books . . ." Vel said.

Denon didn't step into the room. "Look under the coverings."

Vel went to the nearest box and removed the sheet—it felt strangely smooth, not like fabric. Tougher, almost rubbery. Vel coughed on the disturbed dust, and he crouched at the first metal box. On its side were several swastikas and the words *Light Arms*. Another box read *Light Arms Munitions*. On the first, there was a crude illustration of a man holding a pistol, and a progressive series of pictures showing exactly how the weapon was to be loaded and readied. Text beneath the pictures said things like *Cleaning: Step One* and *Ammunition and Safety Check*.

Vel pried open the lid and found more, smaller boxes—he opened one—tiny white pieces of a strange, light foam filled the spaces between the gun boxes. Yes, there was a pistol inside it, just like Hillor's, and Vel returned it, examining more of the bigger boxes. Larger guns that the illustrations called "rifles."

"What do you think?" Denon asked at length.

Vel started to respond, and then he spotted a picture hanging to the left of the vault door. Inside a wooden frame there was a horrible black and white picture of a line of emaciated people—almost skeletons—standing naked and bald. Vel saw tiny numbers on their arms. He stared at it, unable to move. Is this what Blakes meant? Frustrated anger began to curl in his stomach. That isn't a drawing, he thought. That looks real. Vel couldn't move.

Denon glanced inside the room, at the picture, and then he backed away. "I'll have some men sent down—you'll need help transporting these boxes."

Is this what Blakes meant with his talk of the greater good? Vel thought, his heart beginning to pound in his ears. Denon left, and Vel could hear him calling to several of the Religious Guard. Vel could not look away from the skeleton-people, starved so that their joints were visible inside the skin. Whoever did that to those people . . . and Vel forced himself to look away. Blakes is insane, he thought, and he brought that madness here. Whatever could possess someone to do that to people, like they're not even human—it's not real. But it was. The picture looked like a memory, like it had really happened. Did you do that, Blakes? Do you think that you should hang up a picture like that? What the hell is this place?

And Vel glanced at the swastikas on the boxes, several on the walls. Those men weren't great, Vel thought, were they? Nothing—no greater good—is worth having a picture like that. And goddamn it, that's what Hillor wants to do. So that only some people eat, so that all of his talk is really just death and sickness. It's *that*, Vel thought, and he glared at the picture. Vel took it from the wall, setting the frame facedown in a corner.

Not a trophy, he thought. I should burn it, but no, I don't want to forget that I saw it here. And maybe you need to pay for that, Hillor. Maybe it's okay that I'm angry about seeing this, and fuck you for hanging it, Blakes. I hate you Blakes, and I won't forget. And no one will ever make pictures like that again—because it isn't just a drawing. It's *real.* That scene is *remembered* inside the frame. Someone really did that to those people, and I'm connected to you. Vel kicked over the stack of books, his arms trembling, and several Religious Guard entered the room, ready to help him carry the crates to Lydia's house.

He tried to control his breathing, and Vel felt sweat across his brow. His heart wouldn't slow down. I don't understand any of this, he thought, but I understand that picture. You were proud of that, Blakes. And Hillor would have been too, if he had beaten me down here. But he didn't, and now I'm ready to finish it. Maybe it's all right to kill because of that picture, so that it doesn't happen again.

Tiber cocked a pistol and slipped it into his belt. They had trained for hours now, finally assembling at Lydia's house. The tiny house was crowded with the remaining members of her order—all ten. The windows were tightly sealed, one man sitting just outside, dressed as a beggar; a lookout against the police soldiers. No one had spoken in some time, all busy readying weapons.

"You realize it won't work," Tiber said to Lydia.

She was arranging ammunition on a table at the far side of the room, a rifle slung across one shoulder. Lydia glanced at Vel for a response. He sat in a chair, beside Ponce. They both cleaned rifles and pistols of their own.

Vel's reflection twisted and glared back at him from his rifle's surface.

"Why won't it work?" he said.

Tiber sighed, looking at Vel, as if he resented his opinion compared with Lydia's.

"It won't work because we're outnumbered," Tiber said. "We have thirteen, counting all of you. I saw what they did to Munil. I saw the body, but we can't do it this way. We have to lure them out, not march into suicide."

Lydia shook her head. "Calm down. You know what we all know."

Tiber looked at Lydia. "I know that the police picked off most of us. We've been reduced to this, ten members." Lydia nodded, and Tiber sat down in a fury. "Ten members, Lydia!"

"It won't matter," she said. "The guns will make up for that."

Tiber glared at Vel. "No, they won't. We might as well turn ourselves in, as attack. Do you think the police will hesitate to execute us if this doesn't work? All of the training in the world won't make any difference against a dozen crossbows."

"All the training and a few rifles *can* make a difference," Vel said softly, and there were whispers around the room.

Ponce smiled, but remained silent.

Tiber started for the door. "You asked me to come, I came. But I won't be a martyr for the cause. Did you know that riots broke out last night, and that the entire Southern Garr was cleaned out? The maximum security prison is empty. The prisoners are on the streets." A pause. "Even if we take the government, what's to stop a mob from taking it back?"

Lydia shook her head, and Tiber touched the door handle.

"Where are you going to go? What makes you think you'll be safer out there? This way there *is* a chance. We've all tested these things," she said. "You tried that out yourself. You saw what it did to the boxes in the alley behind my house."

"We won't be fighting boxes, Lydia." But he did not leave. Tiber looked at the others in the room. "All of you believe in this? All of you think that a frontal assault on the Palace garrison is a smart idea?"

A man named Craul said, "No. There's no such thing as a smart attack. But, it can work."

"Please," Lydia said. "We need everyone."

"I'm not going to die attacking the Palace," Tiber said. "This has to be more thought out, more thorough."

"I know," Lydia said. "And it will be."

Vel said, "What are you going to do if you leave? Tiber, you're needed here. Isn't your order about protecting the city from collapse? What do you think this is? You're one of the best marksmen here. I'm King. What do you think we're fighting about? If we say that it's too hard, what happens when our rations are cut? What do we do when the rioters set fires that won't go out? Are you going to be looking out for yourself and wishing you hadn't been too afraid to try this? Because the soldiers may have guns then; I couldn't take all the weapons from the vaults. We won't have the advantage then. We have it now."

Tiber said, "I don't need a motivational speech."

"Then don't leave exactly when we need you."

Tiber sighed, and he withdrew from the door, retreating into another room. Lydia smiled, and then she motioned Vel to her. He stood, giving someone else his chair. They went to a far corner of the room.

"Vel, we'll be ready to attack tonight."

He nodded. "Good."

An image of Hillor's face exploding before him.

"I'm not sensing a wave of good feelings from you," he said, and then he chuckled. "You're not going to tell me that I should stay behind?"

Lydia stopped, and her brow creased. "Of course you're staying behind."

Vel's forearms tensed, and he felt a heat in his cheeks. "I'm coming with you, Lydia."

"What good does any of this do if you die out there?" she said. "It's out of the question."

"I'm coming, Lydia. You just told them that we had thirteen. Without me, you've only got twelve. Now tell me what we're going to do."

Lydia raised her eyebrows. "We can't afford to lose people, but if you get killed, none of this will have meant a thing."

"What if one person is the difference between winning and losing this?"

She said, "The only way we're going to do this is through a frontal assault. And that's too dangerous."

"But, you just said—"

"I know what I said. It *is* dangerous. It isn't suicide, but it's dangerous enough that there will be casualties, even with these weapons."

"Then what's the plan?"

She paused, thinking. "For the rest of us, this is going to be straightforward. We set up snipers on the surrounding buildings. The Palace takes up an entire block, so we'll catch the front guards in a three-way crossfire. Pick off as many people as we can before the assault teams actually go in. I figure we send two or three teams. I'll lead one . . ." She hesitated. "Vel, you're not coming."

"I'll lead the other team," Vel said evenly.

Lydia stared at him. "Don't you understand? If you die out there—even if we win—we still lose."

He nodded. "Which is why I'm not going to die."

There was a silence, and Lydia continued quietly. "You'll have two people, and they'll work with you."

Vel looked around. "Who?"

"Tiber and Craul. In practice, they were two of the best shots. Listen to me, Vel. These guns are dangerous. You saw the kind of damage they can do. I think there was a reason they were deactivated. You shouldn't be coming along, and you shouldn't be leading one of the teams."

"What about Ponce?" Vel said.

"Ponce will be in one of the other teams."

"I want him with me."

"No, Vel. The strategy has been worked out. Ponce is in another team. Don't do this. If you're a part of this, you'll play the part you're given. Keep your head out there, and we might survive this thing."

What if she doesn't come back? Vel thought.

"I'll be careful," he said, and his voice cracked. They both grinned. She was so beautiful when she smiled. "I'm worried about you. I care about you, Lydia."

Her rifle shifted. "Don't take risks you don't have to."

"Are you sure there's no other way to do this? There isn't something we've overlooked?"

"I'm not going to die on you, Vel."

He shook the words away and kept talking. "I just wish there was some other way. Think about it: what's going to make those police follow me after I kill a bunch of them?" Tiber may have been right, Vel thought. I wish I knew what I was doing.

Lydia's face grew more solemn. "You were made King last night. They all know you're King. Those loyal to Hillor aren't going to side with you against Hillor regardless of who you are. There isn't any other option; if he ordered them to kill you, they would."

Vel looked away. "So we kill Hillor first."

"That's right."

He didn't respond, and Lydia touched his shoulder.

"This has to be done," she said. "You shouldn't be in the field, but there's no way around it."

"Why?" The uneasiness continued. "Why does it have to be done? Why isn't there another way?"

"You're King."

"So what?" He looked at her. "What does that mean? It's just a title made up by Blakes so that his great-grandchildren can still be in control. We can leave this. We can go away." Thoughts flooded into him. "We don't have to be a part of this city anymore."

"My whole life is about this, Vel. Everything here has a purpose. Hope needs you."

"And we solve that by killing part of the city."

Her lip twisted. "If you could cure the Pox by killing a hundred people, would you do that?"

We still don't have the cure, Vel thought, and he remembered something the Frill had said . . . the blood of a plant . . . and Blakes—Vel's fingers snapped against his palms. "That's not fair."

"No, it isn't." She swallowed. "You know—probably more clearly than anyone else—that things don't happen according to any law of fairness."

"We can't just kill them."

"Yes," she said. "We can. And we will."

What if something happens to her? he thought. What would I do?

"It isn't right, Lydia."

"Vel, we need you to take control."

"I know."

"*I* need you. Right now. You don't have to come along, but this has to happen."

He looked at her. "It's not me, Lydia." He paused. "What if you . . ."

The room was silent, and she leaned forward. Her lips touched his.

"I'm not going to die on you, Vel." She pulled back. "I told you that." He watched her. "I swear."

Vel looked at the gun in her hand. I swear.

"It needs to be done, doesn't it?" he said. "God, this is wrong. This is wrong, and I know it's wrong. But there's not a thing I can do about it, and there's no other way."

"No," she said gently. "There isn't."

She walked away, and Ponce stepped beside him.

"You all right?" Ponce said.

"Yes," Vel said. "This isn't going to be easy, is it?"

"No more so than anything else, I suppose. But, how easy *is* robbing a cop?"

"Goddamn it," Vel said, and he began to laugh. "I can still see straight."

"Well, so long as the executioner's drunk, a crime isn't a crime."

Vel nodded, and they were silent. He had stopped laughing. Let's hope he's drunk, Vel thought. Let's hope they're all drunk.

"You be careful too, Ponce."

Ponce made a disbelieving face. "Careful, you say? Aren't I always?"

"Well, be *more* careful," Vel said.

Ponce said, "You too, Your Highness. I don't want to have to say, 'She told you so.' "

"Who?"

"You know who. You shouldn't be going on this one."

Vel backed away. "Don't you start on that. I'm going."

"Then you better not die too much."

"I won't," Vel said, *"too much."*

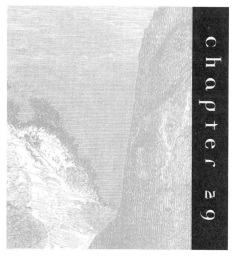

chapter 29

The Palace filled an entire city block with massive stone arches and portals. Walls rose three stories into the air, dwarfing the tiny houses and shadows of people on the night streets. Few windows lit the Palace sides, and those that did existed as military points only. First and foremost, the Palace was a castle: a readily defendable building, designed to hold off attacks from any side.

Archers patrolled each of the three rooftops, concealed from the waist down by cracked stone railings. On the ground, soldiers talked quietly, candlelight flickering on tents and tables. Around the entire structure rose a tall, fifteen-foot fence. At the main entrance, the gates hung open, a small company of men standing rigid as ordinary citizens passed on the street outside. The soldiers did not stray from within the fence. Inside the fence they were safe.

Until the first shots.

It began as a sharp, repeating series of cracking noises. Several of the men in the main courtyard walked lazily from inside their tents, setting down mugs of alcohol, as the noise continued in rapid bursts. The third-level snipers drew arrows from small pouches on their backs and carefully fit the shafts into their longbows. The men were shadows against a backdrop of stone. Fine bursts of rock and dust exploded around them.

The cracking continued, and the tiny explosions reached the archers. A first, then a second and a third buckled under the sudden fire, bodies vanishing below the stone railing. Dark spray on the wall behind them, and more snipers moved to replace their fallen comrades. The gunfire continued, catching these newcomers as well. Their bodies twisted and broke. Sharp cries, and a single, random arrow snapped into the air.

The third rooftop was still.

Below, on the second and first ledges, soldiers crouched, weapons already loaded. Hurried voices. On the ground, the large assembly of men fanned out into a defensive formation, positioning themselves behind makeshift cover and tents. The handful of soldiers at the front gate hurried to close it. Gunfire kicked up the dirt around their feet, and the men spun around in confusion. First one was caught in the lower leg, giving a yelp as he dropped, then a second man simply collapsed as his back shredded in a bloody pulp. The remaining few ran, dropping one by one, motionless in the dirt.

The shots turned now to the second rooftop, pounding holes straight through the stone railings. Soldiers splattered across the stone in a dark mess. A figure in a long, full coat appeared on the ground, through the front doors. He was flanked on either side by rows of police. His voice shook the area, and immediately all of the men on the ground fell back, retreating gratefully through the front entrance. The doors swung shut. The courtyard lay vacant, and on the second floor, people stopped moving.

On the first floor rooftop, most of the archers were gone. A lone pair of men crouched nervously behind their humble barricades. A moment's pause while assault rifles refocused their attention, and then, almost simultaneously, these two men were tossed about like frantic puppets, bodies exploding across the stone. And were still.

The Palace stood silent.

vel dropped into a back alley and moved around the building, to the street. On the far side, the Palace loomed, dead.

"Vel," someone whispered from above him.

Vel turned as two people dropped on either side of him. Ponce looked down at him from the tile.

Vel said, "Yes?"

"We took out the archers on the top and the bottom."

"I saw."

Vel tightened his grip on the rifle slung across his shoulder.

"You saw how many got away?"

Vel kept moving. "I saw, Ponce."

"I'll see you on the other side." Ponce withdrew from the edge of the roof above, hurrying to follow his group across the rooftop toward another alley.

The street was clear and silent. Vel jogged to the front gate and stepped through.

"Lydia should be circling the side, scaling the fence," Tiber said.

Vel held his rifle steady. "I know, Tiber. Let's do this and get it over with."

The three shadows crept noiselessly across the open courtyard. Flapping tents and empty tables shivered in the cold air. Bodies. Above them, a silhouette flashed into view. A loaded longbow, and Vel swung his weapon up. There was a dull snap, and the shaft lanced down. Vel's gun shivered in his hand, and the arrow disappeared from his vision. He blasted cracks that spiraled into the stone railing on the first floor, directly in front of the archer.

The man yelled and went down.

Vel looked away.

Craul's eyes were fixed to an arrow in the end of his boot. The point went straight through the toe tip and into the ground.

"Shit," Tiber said. He stepped closer. "It get you?"

Craul shook his old head, eyes wide.

"No," he said, "just . . . just missed."

Vel's face darkened. Get it over with as quickly as possible. He took a single step and dropped to one knee. Vel grabbed the end of the arrow and pulled it roughly from the man's boot. Craul grunted in surprise, and Vel snapped the shaft in half, tossing both pieces to the dirt.

"It didn't hit you. We need to be more careful."

"They didn't get all the archers," Tiber said.

Vel raised his gun again. "Remember, these things don't make us invincible. The men we're fighting are the best. We need to fight as few as possible—and find Hillor."

Tiber kept pace with Vel, walking to the front entrance. Behind them, Craul took a last look at his boot before testing the ankle and following them.

"All right." Vel stopped. "We went over the layout in there. The main entrance hall, and there are long rooms on either side, and a main staircase, along with a few other doors alongside the stairs."

Tiber smirked. "I wouldn't know, I've never seen it."

"The point is, they've got lots of cover, and if they've got any sense they'll try to use arrows as much as possible. They aren't going to fight us hand to hand unless they have to."

"I know, Vel."

Vel's pulse quickened. "Just want to be sure we all know what we're doing." Craul approached, and Vel glanced at him. "Open the main door. Tiber and I will stand on either side. You back away as soon as you get the door open. We want to go in at the same time. The more guns we have, the better chance we have to stay alive."

Craul swallowed, looking grimly at the entrance, and Vel mounted the short set of stairs, ascending to the front door.

The doors surged forward, and a wave of uniformed men poured out. Vel stumbled back, grabbing at his weapon as the first soldier brought the hilt of a sword to the side of his skull. A sharp ringing, and the world was filled with painful light. Vel staggered and fell. Cracks of gunfire, and he pawed at the ground, dragging himself away. Men shouted, and metal connected with metal.

Two groups of soldiers, a dozen of them, fought Craul and Tiber. Three of the soldiers sprawled across the dirt in bloody heaps, but now the rifles lay useless nearby, and both Tiber and Craul fought with their bare hands. Vel struggled, and the sides of his head throbbed. It's over, he thought, they're going to be butchered.

Tiber rolled in the dirt, dodging a fury of lancing metal, only to rise again and snap a soldier's neck. He snatched the man's sword and spun, meeting an incoming blade with his own. At the same time, his elbow shot back, into another man's ribs. Tiber ran him through.

Craul stumbled as the soldiers pressed their advantage on him. He fought viciously, sweat running wetly down the sides of his face, and again and again narrowly ducked the attacks. Craul was being pressed back, and they formed a circle around him, just as they'd done around Tiber. These soldiers were no fools.

But they were.

Vel almost laughed. The guns lay useless—discarded amidst the twisted bodies of the slaughtered policemen. All they had to do was pick up one of the guns. Vel shook his head and rose. The main entrance of the Palace had been sealed again.

Craul fell.

They kicked his legs out from under him and began to hack into the older man terribly with their swords. He cried out, pleading and bucking against the blows. Tiber saw it too. He turned and yelled, and a soldier swung low, catching the back of Tiber's thigh. Tiber growled, stumbling back and breaking the man's sword in half, before a second blade caught him across the shoulder. Tiber lost his footing and went down. Without hesitation, the men descended on him like animals.

Vel leveled his rifle. Just like animals.

The gun began to shake. Soldiers around Tiber's body twisted and broke. Vel waved the gun back and forth, never releasing the trigger. He showered the second group above Craul. They split and frayed. They broke and screamed, falling blindly to the dirt. In that moment that the entire world was a mixture of blood, smoke, noise—Vel could not release the trigger.

Men turned and were ripped to shreds. Bodies were meant to hold together, not come apart like thick, red glass. A sick sensation rose in Vel's mind, something he had not been prepared for. Stop, he told himself, but he continued. Vel kept firing, mowing them all down. Stop. And Vel blasted holes in their corpses, watching the skin break and come apart, and his chest constricted. *Stop*, and Vel released the trigger.

And it was over.

Vel alone was left standing. Panting, breaths making his arms tremble, he stared at the bodies, splattered across the dirt. Some shouted, whimpering from the ground. Vel shook his head and tried to turn away. What's wrong with me? Vel thought. Why didn't I—what did I do . . . ? I tried to help them. And I—

The main entrance of the Palace opened, and Vel spun, muscles already tense. Lydia stood in the entryway, her hair disheveled and clothes bloody.

It wasn't her blood.

Behind her, Vel saw broken furniture and bodies. Ponce approached in the entrance hall, limping.

"Vel?" Lydia drew closer, and she saw the bodies. "Are you all right?"

"No," Vel said.

She approached him. "They attacked you—are you hurt?"

"No."

Ponce stared at Vel, remaining where he was.

Lydia said, "What's wrong?"

"I shot them," he said, and realized that he was tapping the rifle with one hand. Vel tried to stop—watching his fingernails click against the metal—and couldn't.

Lydia went to a mass of bodies and dropped to a crouch, touching one of them, before doing the same to the second cluster.

"Dead," she said.

Vel shook his head. "What?"

"You heard me," Lydia said. "They're both dead. Craul and Tiber. Both of them. You shot them. We need to keep moving."

Ponce joined them in the yard, his lip bloodied. "They're searching the Palace."

Vel coughed, staring at Lydia. "No." His muscles refused to loosen. "I didn't—"

"It's over now," she said, "we have to move."

Vel remained where he was. "Lydia, I tried to help them. I shot them."

She shook her head. "I know, you didn't mean to. We don't have time—"

"*Lydia.*" Vel growled, emotion snapping inside him. "It's not that."

Lydia stopped. "Vel—"

"I . . ." Vel was still tapping the rifle. *"I enjoyed it."* And now Lydia glanced at his fingers, noticing the continual sound. "I didn't want to, and what does that mean? I want to stop, I don't—"

"It isn't over," Lydia said. "I haven't found Hillor yet. He's not in the Palace. We cleared the entire place and there's no sign of

him. Might be soldiers across the street—you can't go back now."
Ponce said, "Come on, Vel. Almost over."
Vel said, "How did you do that so fast?" He stopped tapping.
Lydia threw wide the front door, and Vel followed her in, Ponce behind him.
"I started moving when the snipers started firing," she said.
"I thought we weren't going to go in until after they'd picked off all the snipers. That was the plan."
Lydia stopped in the main hallway. Ahead, stairs rose elegantly to the second floor, and several bodies sprawled about. She turned to him. "I changed my mind."
"That doesn't matter," Ponce said. "We need to get Hillor, don't we?"
Vel said, "What if we can't find Hillor?"
Lydia said, "We will."
"What if he isn't here?"
"He is. Come on," she said. "Let's finish this."
Sound exploded from the top of the stairs, and Vel's mind began very slowly to piece together what followed. Lydia swung, colliding with a wall as she fought to remain standing. Bits of her torso sprayed onto the stone, and she fell, propped against the wall. No. Another series of shots tore apart Lydia's hands, and her rifle dropped uselessly to the floor. *No.*
Hillor stood at the top of the stairs, dressed in his long overcoat. Vel's gaze locked on the black weapon in his hand, and Hillor came down the stairs. Smoke still rose from the pistol's mouth. Vel and Ponce began to raise their rifles.
"Stay where you are." Hillor continued down, keeping the barrel focused to Vel. He waved it at Ponce, and then back to Vel. "I'll blast you both in half if you make me."
Lydia whined from the ground nearby, clawing at life, struggling to hold onto it as blood rushed from her limbs, onto the cold floor. Ponce was entirely silent, his body tensed, and Vel shook. Why did he have to shoot her? Vel stared at her, so pathetic and broken on the ground. No, she was going to be all right. She was going to be all right.
"Lydia."
Hillor said dryly, "Listen to me very carefully. You have two

options. You will do exactly as I say, or I will shoot you."

Vel said. "I'm going to kill you."

"Drop your weapons."

Vel shook his head. "No."

"Drop them." Hillor pointed the pistol at Ponce. "You want to die?"

Ponce looked at Vel, waiting for a signal. "We have to, Vel."

"We don't have to do anything."

Hillor frowned, and his hand tensed on the pistol again—Ponce dropped his rifle.

Hillor nodded, motioning to Vel. "Now you." Vel let go of his gun, and it banged against the stone. Hillor paused. "She would have gunned me down if I hadn't shot her. You realize that. If you'd raised your gun I would have had to do the same to you."

Vel's jaw trembled. He felt Lydia touching his cheek. Kissing him. He said to Hillor, "You're already dead."

Hillor tried to smile. "Those aren't the kind of words you need right now, if you plan to stay alive." Vel stared at the Justice blankly, and Hillor's face changed. "Start walking." Hillor motioned to the closed front entrance. "Come on."

Vel watched him. "No."

"We're going to take a walk across town. To the southern barracks."

Vel didn't move. "No. We're not."

She had shown him things. I loved her, he thought. I didn't even realize it, did I? Lydia's voice pushed itself up, "Vel . . ."

Hillor looked down at her, and he leveled the pistol a second time—to her head. No, Vel thought, you won't take this away from me.

Vel rushed forward—Hillor's gun discharged, and Lydia's face shattered against the wall—Vel snatched up a rifle, and he sidestepped forward, smashing the butt of the weapon into Hillor's jaw. Hillor stumbled, and Vel swung it again. Die. And again.

Hillor toppled onto the stone tiles, his pistol rolling away. The Justice's cheeks were a swollen red, and his skin broke in places, trailing blood.

"You little idiot," he said. "This place isn't safe. Looters will sack the Palace any time now."

Ponce picked up his rifle, and Vel kicked Hillor viciously across the side of his head. The sound resounded through Vel's mind, and Hillor flopped back, grabbing at his face. Die.

Vel lowered the gun to the Justice's forehead. "That's right, I remember that too—you kicked me in the head, left a mark."

Hillor clutched his face limply, and dark eyes rose beneath his brow. "I gave you a chance. This is your mistake."

Vel's eyes had begun to twitch, and he clicked the rifle into readiness. Lydia's beautiful head scattered across the floor in bloody pieces.

"You can't shoot me, Vel. You're sick, aren't you? You want to die of the Pox?"

"I don't care." Vel pressed his finger more firmly to the trigger. Do it.

"Think. We can help each other," Hillor said. Noises from outside, and Hillor turned his head, distracted. "Rioters—they'll be here any moment, now that the soldiers are down."

Ponce backed away, his rifle aimed at the entrance. "I think he's right, Vel. Come on, we don't have time!"

God, Vel thought. She'd been so beautiful when she laughed—hold it back. And Hillor destroyed her. Reminders of himself. Vel's teeth chattered in his ears, and his lower lip shook violently. He'd just wanted it to work. Once. Lydia's face turned to meat, just meat. A silent shifting movement in the corner of his vision, and Vel turned the rifle back to Hillor—too late. Hillor caught Vel across his ear. A dull ringing. Vel lost the rifle, and dropped. Ponce started to react, and Hillor fired once, past his head, deliberately missing. Ponce lowered his rifle.

"Now, listen to me, Vel." Hillor picked up his pistol and then the rifle, which he slung over his right shoulder. He went to Ponce and took his rifle as well. "This is over. As a sign of my generosity, *his* life is spared. But I'm through playing games."

Voices from the next room, and Hillor smiled, the sounds drawing recognition. It doesn't make any difference now, Vel thought.

Hillor said, "You didn't quite get all of the garrison, it would appear."

Soldiers came into the room, swords drawn. Vel rolled from

his place on the floor and looked up at them. Kill all of them, he thought. Every last one. With his bare hands if he had to. There were five of them, and they stopped, seeing Hillor.

"Justice Hillor, we heard—"

Hillor held up his palm, keeping the rifle focused to Vel.

"It's all right," he said. "This boy is to be placed under arrest." Hillor handed the soldiers the two rifles. "We're going to the southern garrison."

One of the soldiers started to move, then stopped, confused. "Sir, isn't he the King?"

Something inside Vel's chest quickened. You bastard, he thought. The ceremony was over, and the world knew.

Hillor took an impatient breath. "No, he isn't. He tried to seize the throne unlawfully. Now, I just gave you an order, Sergeant."

"Justice Hillor I want you to drop the guns," Vel said standing up.

Hillor turned in amusement. "Vel, this is very entertaining—"

"No. It isn't." Vel's voice caught the Justice in mid-sentence. "It isn't *entertaining*. It's wrong. You have a cure for the Pox. You know about the food supply. And you haven't done a goddamn thing."

Hillor's voice rose, "Arrest this traitor. He killed the King!"

No one moved, and Vel stood solidly. Ponce whistled to himself. "That's a lie!" he announced.

Vel said, "*You* made me King, Hillor. In front of the entire council. You can't arrest a King."

"Don't listen to him!" shouted Hillor.

Vel pointed at Hillor. "Arrest *him.*"

The soldiers shifted uncomfortably, uncertain what to do, and Hillor stepped closer to Vel, "Listen to me, this isn't—"

A crash of glass from the next room, and the front doors burst. People rushed into the hall, and Hillor turned, firing a volley into the crowd. The Justice was caught through the shoulder with an arrow. He staggered back, clutching at the wound, and the rifle fell. The police formed a wall, their rifles peppering the rushing mob, and rows of people dropped—still the rioters charged into the gunfire.

Hillor drew his pistol, and Vel backed away. Lydia. Her body tossed as feet trampled it. She was gone. The rioters surrounded Hillor, and Vel saw a blunt weapon catch the back of Hillor's arm—he lost his pistol and fell back, grabbing a discarded sword. Ponce drew a dagger, rolling to the nearest wall, away from the crowd. The mob crushed the tiny array of policemen and things began to break all around the room. The people were in a frenzy; they moved like extensions of one giant, disjointed creature. Shouting and laughing and spitting as they smashed mirrors and ripped tapestries.

And then it happened—Hillor ran away.

Carrying the longsword, he retreated from the room, blood streaming from the arrow lodged in his shoulder. No, Vel thought. Ponce saw it too, and he charged after him. Vel started sprinting— You don't leave, Hillor. You don't get to run away. People stepped into Vel's path, and he pushed them aside, tearing into the hallway after Hillor and Ponce. The edges of his vision faded red. Vel knocked pictures and torches from the walls—he held his sword in both hands, no memory of having drawn it. Fingers tight on the handle, knuckles white. Lydia's mangled body hung in Vel's mind. Kill him. That torn form, and broken mass of flesh. Make him die.

Vel ran harder.

He entered the auditorium at the rear of the Palace. The chairs had not been removed, and everything looked just as it had during the ceremony the night before. Hillor stood alone across the room, panting. Ponce stepped beside Vel, dagger ready. Hillor winced, and he grabbed at the wound in his left shoulder, holding a sword in his other hand.

Hillor said, "We're all dead if we stay here."

Vel stalked forward, and Ponce began to circle behind Hillor.

"Everyone dies," Vel said.

Hillor let go of the wound, facing Vel directly. He ignored Ponce.

"I never should have given you a chance to succeed," Hillor said. "I should have killed you."

"Should have." Vel stopped several feet from the larger man, and Ponce stepped into position behind Hillor. "I'm still here. You had a chance, now I have mine."

Hillor waved his sword carefully in the air and planted his feet. "Vel, you're not stupid. Work with me and we'll both get out of this alive."

"No." Vel tensed. "No, I'm beyond that. You're not going to walk away."

"Why? Because I killed that girl? She doesn't mean anything, and you know it."

Vel's sword struck forward. Hillor blocked, and the two weapons met several times in quick succession—Ponce attacked, and Hillor dodged easily—before Vel stepped away again.

The Justice smiled. "You can't kill me."

Voices sounded from the next room.

"We all die, then," Vel said.

"No." Hillor shook his head, glancing back the way they'd come. "No, just you."

He swung too fast. Vel's left arm was caught, below the elbow, but with his right, Vel brought up his weapon in time to stop Hillor's sword. A loud clanking of metal, and Ponce lunged from the rear. As Ponce stabbed at him, Hillor sidestepped and swung high, slicing open Ponce's throat. Ponce's eyes widened, and he tried to stop the blood with both hands. Vel lunged, and Hillor kicked him hard in the chest—then Hillor stabbed Ponce again, driving the sword through his chest. Ponce fell to his knees and went down.

Vel stared, unable to register what had just happened. His mind felt numb, and Hillor turned on him mechanically. Ponce was no longer moving, and blood pooled around his throat and chest. No, Vel thought, get up, Ponce. Don't do this—not you.

"Do you know how much training goes into someone on the force?" Hillor said softly, advancing on Vel, an arrow still protruding from his shoulder. "You can't fight me."

Hillor attacked without waiting for a response, Vel was pushed back, into the aisle of chairs, toward the table. Vel's shirt ripped and frayed as the Justice tore into him.

Vel struggled to meet Hillor's attacks, each faster and harder than the last. Vel staggered, tripping against one of the chairs, and Hillor caught Vel's weapon, knocking it away. Oh, God. Vel ran, grabbing the nearest chair—and blocked. Hillor drove into it, hacking the object to splinters. Vel took another, this time swinging it at Hillor's head. The Justice ducked but stumbled back, and Vel pressed his momentary advantage—slamming the chair into Hillor's wounded shoulder. Hillor cried out and, without thinking, let go of his sword to grab at the bloody patch.

Vel snatched the sword in one step and swung low, chopping raw flesh in Hillor's thigh, and the Justice pivoted, his elbow smashing Vel's nose. Vel stumbled back—blinking, blood on his tongue—and Hillor grabbed a chair. It broke across Vel's head, and he went down, still holding onto the sword. Chairs toppled under Vel's weight, as he collapsed. Blood in his mouth, down his throat, and bright spots flickered across Vel's vision, and Hillor picked up another chair. It crashed against's Vel's face—the chair didn't break—and Vel's head rolled to the side under the impact. Rushing pain, and he coughed more blood. Vel stabbed weakly with the sword.

Hillor dodged the blade easily and crushed Vel's forearm with the chair—Vel lost his sword and fought to crawl away through the mass of broken wood. His head was on fire, and he breathed hot embers. Vel pushed through a pile of overturned chairs, and Hillor recovered his sword, swinging for Vel's throat.

Wood smashed, and splinters catapulted into the air, as Vel rolled into a stance, away from the blade. He ran, further down the aisle—past Ponce's body—over the side of the table, Hillor behind him, and Hillor swung again. The Justice ripped a deep gash in the back of Vel's shirt, drawing a line of blood, before pounding into the table itself.

The blade stuck.

Vel rolled out of the way, and Hillor wrapped both hands around the handle and heaved. The weapon was lodged cleanly in the thick wooden table. Vel staggered across the room and picked up his own sword again. Die.

Hillor's weapon came out, and he turned, the sword trembling in both hands. His shoulders shuddered, and Hillor's breaths came out in hoarse gasps. He stopped, suddenly catching sight of something behind Vel.

Footsteps.

Vel pivoted back and saw a lone crossbow, already aimed. The bolt fired with a dull hiss, and there was no time to move. It flew by Vel to strike the exact center of Hillor's chest, knocking him into a sitting position. A figure came closer, fitting a second arrow into place. Behind her, several others stepped into view from the corridor.

Vel lowered his sword. "Jak."

She nodded to him. "Hello, Vel."

Hillor watched her, trembling where he sat, the end of an arrow protruding from his chest, another in his shoulder.

"It hurts doesn't it?" Jak said as she came closer to the downed judge.

Hillor's eyes followed her. "You're alive."

She shook her head. "Bad luck, isn't it?"

She lowered the crossbow to him again.

Vel stepped forward. "No."

Jak looked at him. "What?"

"Let me do it."

She hesitated and reluctantly lowered the crossbow. Vel approached Hillor, his sword wavering in the air. Blood heaved into Vel's arms, and his hands ached, gripping the handle too tightly. Hillor glared at Vel, cheeks flushed.

"I can tell you about the cure, Vel. Don't be stupid. There's so much you don't know—we made a deal with the Frill. What do you want? I can—"

"I used to care," Vel said. "Don't think I want anything right now."

Hillor's mouth opened, but he was too late.

Tok.

Vel stared at the body—the sound of a head rolling away—and Jak said, "We're leaving the Palace. You might want to do the same."

"I'm not going anywhere." He put the sword away.

"That's right." She paused. "You're King now, aren't you?"

Vel looked at her, his head ringing. None of this is real, Vel thought. Please, this isn't happening. He stepped to Hillor's body. "It's over." Vel took Hillor's coat and put it on.

"Was he lying?" Vel said quietly. "Is there a cure?"

"Yes," Jak said. "I stole it for him. From the ruins, it belonged to the Frill."

"Where is it?"

"Don't know," she said. "I gave it to him. It's wherever he put it."

Vel shook his head. "What do I do—what the hell am I supposed to do now?" This can't be happening, Vel thought. Not again.

Jak turned away. "I don't know Vel. You're on your own now."

He glanced at Ponce's body. "I know." They're all dead now, aren't they? he thought. Everyone who has meant anything. They're reminders now. Reminders that for a brief time they were alive—that I was happy. And now they're gone. And I'm still here.

Everything you will ever love, everything you will ever be, everything you will ever have—not going to think about that now.

Will die.

"Something's started out there," Jak said.

Vel looked at her. "What are you talking about?"

"Outside," she said, and Vel turned to the others at the opposite end of the room. Already they were beginning to leave the Palace. "The city's changing. Something's started."

Lydia's bloody form. Ponce. He just wanted to make it go away. Let someone else deal with it.

"I don't understand." Vel closed his eyes. It was too much. Too goddamn much. "What's started?"

Jak's voice was barely audible, "Winter."

chapter 30

It was snowing.

Vel stood alone in the street, a dark garment wrapped around him like a second skin. He stared at the drifting flakes as they floated to the ground. Snow filled the sky, blotting out distant landmarks. All around the city, people spoke of the last days, whispering in hushed tones that the world was ending.

The Nara had been sighted. People were vanishing, and the air still grew colder. And Vel stood alone, his eyes stinging in the silence that held Hope. It was unreal that the city could be as quiet as it was. In places, the whiteness found ways to build up. In corners, the flakes collected. They made the frozen ground wet and his cheeks red.

"What business do you have here?"

Vel turned to the voice. A lone policeman walked forward, paused, and then squinted at Vel through the snow.

"Who are you?"

"My name is Vel."

The soldier stiffened, his eyes widening. "Sorry, sir. I didn't recognize you."

Vel looked at him, and smiled. An unfeeling smile.

"It's all right," he said. "Dismissed."

The policeman bobbed his head. "Would His Majesty require an escort?"

"No." Vel shook his head. "No, he wouldn't."

"Very good, sir."

The man walked down the street, into the city. And for a moment, Vel saw her standing there. Across the street, watching him through the snow. Through these lazy bits of frost that fell by the thousands. Silently. Her face watched him, and she nodded.

Vel's skin was cold, and the image was gone.

"That's fine," Vel said. "You're fine. Everywhere I look I see you. And you're telling me it's all right." He sat in the street. "I'm talking to myself, Lydia. Or am I talking to you?"

No reply.

"I think I'm going crazy. I think that's what life does. And now it's snowing. Why should it be snowing? Does that mean anything? Where are you, Lydia? Where's Ponce? Why don't I see him? Why is it just you?" Vel shook his head. "I don't know. But, I'll tell you something. I'm just fine. I'm doing just fine here. As King. I've been doing it for a week, and it's working out. I'm getting along perfectly."

He stared at the emptiness around him. Full of tiny shapes.

"I think you would have liked the snow," he said. "I think it would have stuck to you." Vel smiled slightly. "I *know* it would have stuck to you. It's the kind of thing you would have appreciated. You would have told me to study it. You would have your plans for everything. You would have everything figured out. You would have told me what needs to be done, and how to do it. Well, I'm doing fine without that."

Vel shivered. He closed his eyes, rubbing his hands up and down the sides of his body.

"God, I miss you. I want to just go away sometimes. You used to have the most wonderful smile. I never told you that, did I? I should have. Goddamn songs written about smiles, and Ponce and I used to make fun of them—but it's true. I miss your smile. And I miss the way you smell. I've already forgotten." Vel's eyes fluttered open again. "I've forgotten how you smell, and it's only been a week. I don't know why I came up here to talk to you. I don't think I did. I don't know what I'm doing, Lydia. It's all different without you, and I'm starting to scare myself."

He stopped.

"That's funny, isn't it? Funny that we tried so hard to win, to save Hope, and we did. And somehow I lost anyway. Funny that I'm the strong one." Vel's voice twisted. "Funny that I'm here," he took a breath, "and I'm strong"—his voice faltered—he forced it— "and you're gone. And I'm all right.

"Why the hell did you leave me here alone? I see your face in

everything I do. But I'm being strong. I'm not letting it get to me."
Vel's arms shook. "I'm all right, Lydia. I don't need anyone. Not
you, not Ponce, not my parents. I don't need anyone."

He buried his face. Vel sat for a long time, holding himself in
that position. The sky was falling all around him in a snowy
waterfall. Finally, he pulled himself up and wiped his eye.

"I'm sorry. I'm sorry for everything. I'm sorry, God. I'm sorry
for everything, just give them back. Please. You didn't have to
take her away from me. I think I believe in you now, and I hate
you. I need something." Vel hesitated, and his voice began to rise.
"I need them—I can't do this again. Why not me? Why her? She
was good and beautiful, and I'm ∴ ."

His voice evaporated. "I don't understand why this had to happen, and maybe that's it—maybe good people are supposed to
die, and the terrible people survive. And we get goddamn swastikas and government stars and pictures of people with numbers
on their arms, and *that's* what's remembered. Because all of the
bad things are what matter. Not the good. Maybe everything's
wrong. And I just don't understand, because the more I know,
the more confused everything is, and the less I really *know*. Because now you're dead."

He paused, and smiled miserably. "And I'm still alive."

Vel thought for a moment, and then said softly, "It's hard to
do this alone. You would have told me that I can keep going. You
would have told me that anyone else would have trouble, but I'm
strong, and I'm different." He swallowed. "Ponce would have
found some way to laugh at this, and you—I hate you for dying
like that. And I hate myself for hating you."

Vel shivered, even though he was wearing Hillor's trenchcoat,
struggling to force the emotions away. "Things are happening, and
I can see the city falling apart around me. I can't stop it. Every
day I tell myself I'll get through. You get me through. I just
wish"—he took a slow breath—"I just wish you were still here.
Why is that too much to ask? I came out here to be with you."
Tears formed in Vel's eyes, but he ignored them. "But now I'm
just sitting alone, being cold. And you're dead, and I don't even
know what that means—except that you're not here anymore.
You're not *dead*, you're just gone.

"I remember a story you told me when we were at the ruins. You said that there is a world where everyone is happy and there aren't any problems, and we can all visit that world as often as we like, whenever we want. The bad thing about that world is that everyone wakes up sooner or later. And most of us forget that we were ever there. But that world exists.

"I suppose I was there, and I didn't realize it. Didn't know that I had you, and then you were gone. But I can't forget. And I wish I could—I wish it had never happened, wish we had never met." Vel coughed. "I know why people forget their dreams."

He shook his head and rose. The world turned in a cold, white breeze.

"I don't know why, and I shouldn't have, but I loved you, Lydia."

Vel's hands went into the pockets of his pants, and he turned back.

"I love you."

He started walking, then stopped.

"Sir."

It was the soldier again. Vel closed his eyes.

"Yes."

"Something of yours was found in the Palace."

Vel looked back at the man and the scrap of paper he extended. It was folded and worn around the edges. Without a word, Vel took the sheet, and the soldier left. Vel knew what it was. Something a part of him had put off until now. He held up the worn sheet, and stared at the words.

Vel was my son, and I know how strong he was. I'm writing this, so that he won't be forgotten. So what he could have been won't be lost. We never told him that he was not our natural child, that his father was the brother of a King.

Both my husband and I loved Vel very much. But the world is a wicked place, and Vel was denied his path for a reason. He wasn't King because he was not ready to be King. The government is corrupt, and Kings are

*manipulated and killed. It's better that he never became
King.*

I'm sorry. Vel was my life.

*Kings come and go, but not my son. It's good that Vel
stayed away from his birthright, that he never claimed the
throne, and I thought I was doing what was right for him.
Kings die, but not Vel. I always thought that so long as he
stayed away from power he would be safe. Power leads to
pain, and I tried to protect him. And I failed.*

*I loved my son very much, and I wanted the best for
him. I wanted him to find friends that would last, to live a
good life, and a fruitful life without the poison of royalty
around him. But now that doesn't matter anymore. We've
lost, and I can't think about the future. God forgive me.*

Vel put the note away. He stood silently, and then started back
to the Palace.

"Yes," he said, "I think you would have liked the snow."

Something lingered in the back of his mind, as if he had been
told to remember something and could now only recall the command itself. What was it? A rose, and a plant that could cure the
Pox . . . something the Frill had told him, and something Blakes
had said . . . a sick rose, and—

Vel paused, and then he started running.

At the cemetery, Vel found the grave: a large, worn rock with
weathered lettering and flowers—roses—around its base.
Blakes's tomb. The populace always brought gifts to the graves of
the founders; they were saints here.

The invisible worm, and Vel sorted quickly through the assortment of flowers—no, it wasn't there—and he began to dig
through the dirt and snow with his bare hands . . . *in the night,
in the howling storm*—wind flapped through Vel's—Hillor's—
coat, and still he tossed the dirt away—*found out thy bed*— And
there was a collection of red flowers in the earth, wrapped tightly
to conceal something, something buried—*secret love*—Vel took
the wrappings gingerly and untied the flowers, letting them

drop—*Does thy life destroy*— And inside: a small green plant, like a fern, with blue veinlike arteries running beneath the surface.

Vel heard Blakes's voice speaking of prophecies, of writing messages one thousand years ago, messages for *this* age. Vel cradled the plant. Yes, he thought. I knew. Somehow, I did know.

And he was gone.

Steal a little and they will arrest you. They will strike your limbs from your body. Steal a lot, and they will make you King.

—Blakes's *Rebirth*, Chapter 17

"I wonder how I knew so much," Vel said. "You told me you had answers if I ever wanted them, if I was ever ready. How did I know things I couldn't have known? How am I connected to all of this."

"It's simple, Vel. I'm surprised you haven't guessed it yourself," Lord Denon said.

"I need to know. You told me there was more. I need your help. You said, after Hillor died, that there is more than a simple bloodline. There's more than the succession. What is it? What's my connection?" Vel asked.

"A deal was made years ago with the Shadows to fulfill a prophecy. But the demons were betrayed. Our promises were too dangerous to be kept, and so vengeance came out of the Shadows: a disease that could destroy. But the Pox could destroy them as well, and thus a cure came out of the Shadows."

"I don't understand. Where do I come in? Why do I matter so much?"

"We are instruments of God." Lord Denon put his hand on the boy's shoulder. "He plays us at His whim. You are important because of what you are."

"What?"

"Shadow and Sky. The two met when we made our deal with the demons."

"I don't understand."

The Cathedral walls flowed with the warmth of a thousand candles. A thousand lights. A thousand reasons for the brightness around them.

"Vel." Denon smiled, and his voice dropped. "You're half Frill."